M000222820

Farrah Penn

VIKING

Mom, this one is for you —F. P.

VIKING

An imprint of Penguin Random House LLC, New York

First published in the United States of America by Viking,
an imprint of Penguin Random House LLC, 2024

Copyright © 2024 by Farrah Penn

Penguin supports copyright. Copyright fuels creativity, encourages diverse voices, promotes free speech,
and creates a vibrant culture. Thank you for buying an authorized edition of this book and for complying with
copyright laws by not reproducing, scanning, or distributing any part of it in any form without permission.
You are supporting writers and allowing Penguin to continue to publish books for every reader.

Viking & colophon are registered trademarks of Penguin Random House LLC.
The Penguin colophon is a registered trademark of Penguin Books Limited.

Visit us online at PenguinRandomHouse.com.

Library of Congress Cataloging-in-Publication Data is available.

ISBN 9780593528303

1st Printing

Printed in the United States of America

LSCH

Text design by Sophie Erb

Text set in Sabon Next LT Pro

This book is a work of fiction. Any references to historical events, real people, or real places are used fictitiously.
Other names, characters, places, and events are products of the author's imagination, and any resemblance
to actual events or places or persons, living or dead, is entirely coincidental.

The publisher does not have any control over and does not assume any
responsibility for author or third-party websites or their content.

1

KimberlyH has Venmo'd you $20 — 😎
SavannahL has Venmo'd you $20 — 🐣
KingsleyB has Venmo'd you $50 — 🙏

When it comes to people like Carson Jenkins, I really don't charge enough for my efforts.

We're sitting on the floor of my bedroom and he's giving me this unflattering, pitiful look, the corners of his mouth slipping down as if I've just insulted his favorite video game. His tortured vibe makes me itchy with impatience, but I push through it. Because if I want that sweet cash, I have to help him.

Not *have to*, I tell myself. *Want to.* I want to help him because I'm brilliant at what I do.

"Let me see it," I say for the second time.

Carson's expression shifts to full-on moping. It's not a good look. He has a death grip on his iPhone, squeezing it so tight that his knuckles turn white. From the sight of him, you'd think his mother had accidentally stumbled upon his entire porn search history. Which isn't the case. I can tell him that particular scenario would be a million times worse than this one, but knowing Carson, he'd probably prefer to deal with that hiccup instead of our current problem.

"It's bad," he admits, his round brown eyes full of concern. "I really messed up. You can't help me out of this one."

I grin. Oh, he of little faith.

"Your doubt in me is insulting." I gesture to the phone, which is now coated with Carson's stress sweat. Blergh. "Show me."

He hesitates, and I force myself to take a deep breath. Carson is here because I've unintentionally earned the title of Greenlough Academy's Flirt Expert. If you need help texting your crush, I've got you. I'm the master text-message crafter. The witty-reply whisperer. The Mother Teresa of Flirting, if you will. Except, you know, Mother Teresa didn't charge for her humanitarian gestures. She was a selfless soul; may she rest in peace.

It's not that I'm *not* selfless. I just really need the money. What I do is both a skill and an art, and I take pride in my ability to navigate tricky texting territory.

This does not mean, however, that I am a hookup wizard. I cannot help someone whose only goal is to get laid. I foster meaningful relationships through conversation that, *sure*, sometimes leads to more. But for the majority of my peers, it's about me finding opportunities for one person to know another person using the safety net of texting.

My flirt coaching started with my reputation as a serial dater. During my sophomore year, I experienced nine short-lived romances—or *situationships*, since most were of the casual variety. This drew attention from my curious classmates, especially those who wanted help getting their crush's attention.

Basically, my ability to publicly advance my love life led to me figuring out what my peers were struggling with in their own dating circles: communication.

This means I take different texting styles into account. Are they big emoji users? (Or worse, *Bitmoji* users?) Do they send huge paragraphs or multiple short texts?

Everything about their style is key. It keeps the interaction flowing. Bonus if there's textual chemistry.

I helped my best friend, Tahlia Nassif, get with Ann Chu shortly after this realization. She told class president Rhea Zhang about me, who told Vince Ramirez, and, well, it spread like a good movie: when word gets out about all the reasons you should go see it, more people start buying tickets.

My ticket price for coaching starts at twenty bucks. If it leads to a date, it's fifty. I don't feel bad for what I charge. I know my worth. Plus, Greenlough Academy is located in the (rich) city of Pacific Palisades and is filled with (rich) kids who have access to parental money. It means more to me than it does to them.

So if I want that sweet payment, I have to help this emotionally distraught disaster of a boy.

Carson texted me about his 911 situation earlier, insisting he needed to explain in person. Hence why he's on the verge of a breakdown on my bedroom floor.

He heaves a tragic sigh that's a decibel too dramatic, unlocking his phone. I watch as he opens his conversation with Kendra Wilkens, fellow senior and captain of Greenlough's dive team.

> **Carson**
> i liked the stance you took in lit. about the consequences isabel faces in the portrait of a lady.

Kendra
oh! thank you 😊

So far, so good. I told Carson to pay compliments not only based on Kendra's looks but on her opinions and insights. And I mentioned that he should be specific so she knew he was listening. He'd followed that advice.

Carson
i'm probably not gonna pass our exam.

Kendra
don't say that!

Carson
idk, I'll probably get a D. maybe a C.

Carson
anyway

Carson
do you have a meet this weekend?
maybe I can come? we can
get in-n-out after?

Carson
or not, idk

Carson

if you don't eat meat there's other

places

I wince. Carson sent those texts at eight last night, and Kendra never responded. He came on too strong, too awkward, but it's reversible damage.

I can get Kendra to text him back.

"Okay, first?" I begin. "It's not sexy when you put yourself down. It makes you look insecure. People like confidence."

Carson rereads his one-sided conversation. "So . . . I should have told her I'd ace the exam?"

"*No*," I say quickly. "That's too arrogant. It's a fine line. Confidence is, you know, playing it cool. Not second-guessing yourself."

Carson looks at me like I've just explained the binomial theorem in fluent French.

I move on, needing him to understand the rest. "Second, why'd you shoot your shot? You started texting her two days ago. I *told* you that you have to let this build for a bit."

"I thought it would be a good opportunity—"

"It wasn't." I don't need to hear his argument because, as we both can see, it failed. "If you want to go out with her, you have to give her room to anticipate it. C'mon, dude. She doesn't want to throw on date clothes after being in a pool all day. Not when she's smelling like chlorine and has wet hair."

His shoulders slump. "Right. That makes sense."

"But"—I raise my eyebrows—"we can fix this."

It takes me a few moments to get it right, but I craft a text for Carson to send to Kendra a few hours before her meet:

> **Carson**
>
> I'm sorry for coming on so strongly.
> you're going to do great today. if you
> want to hang out sometime, my treat.
> we can even debate the proper use of
> sporks. but if not, no worries

Personally, I think adding their inside joke about sporks is genius. It also takes the pressure off Kendra and makes Carson seem a thousand percent chiller.

I'm positive he'll get a response.

I crack my knuckles, satisfied. "And when she hits you back, you know what to do."

"Venmo, I know," Carson says, adjusting his glasses. He's cute in that indie-singer-soft-nerdy-boy kind of way. Kendra inherited a record collection from her dad that she frequently features on Instagram. They'll for sure hit it off.

If anything came from my reputation as a serial dater, it's the income I make as the school's flirt expert. I'm one of the only seniors on academic scholarship, and money has always been a concern. My mom's an assistant day-care manager who works Postmates shifts by night, but we're not immune to the occasional financial pinch. Sometimes I'll spot her on bills because as wildly fascinating as the medieval times were, I do prefer twenty-first-century electricity.

She would have savings if it wasn't for my twenty-two-year-old brother Smith, who's been in and out of expensive rehabs for his drug addiction. It's a sensitive subject that we tend to avoid.

We certainly don't ask my dad for money. He remarried years ago and now lives in Calabasas with his new wife and two small kids. I was fifteen the last time I saw him in person. We had milkshakes at Johnny Rockets, where he presented me with a very belated birthday card that sang a Disney song when you opened it. Nothing says *I love and cherish you, my darling daughter* like a card blasting "Hakuna Matata" throughout a packed burger joint.

Anyway, he sent child support checks until I turned eighteen, which was three weeks ago. That was the extent of our interactions. He's never made me a priority in his life, so I don't make him one in mine.

"You think she'll respond?"

"She will."

A conversation sparks when curiosity is present. I don't believe Kendra is disinterested, so the key to keeping this exchange exciting is a delicate back-and-forth. The focus shouldn't be one-sided.

Carson slides his iPhone into his pocket. "Thank you."

"No problem." I push myself into a standing position. I'm wearing the rainbow-polka-dot pajama bottoms and oversized T-shirt I slept in last night, and my bangs are rumpled to one side of my head instead of lying flat. Hot mess, thy name is Brynn.

Carson's phone chimes. We look at each other. He hasn't sent the text to Kendra yet, but he scrambles for his phone as if he did. Maybe he's hoping she's responded to his texts from last night, which *yeesh*. Unlikely.

While he checks, my eyes catch my banana costume crumpled near my nightstand. I'd worn it last night, not because I make outrageously eclectic fashion choices (for the most part), but because it was Halloween.

It was a last-minute decision. Truthfully, I'd been hoping to thrift a Shrek costume. I wanted to walk around playing *"All Star"* by Smash Mouth on my phone because it's an iconic bop, but I would've settled for an inflatable T. rex costume paired with the *Jurassic Park* soundtrack. Halloween is fun when you don't take it too seriously. But I couldn't find anything halfway decent at Goodwill, so I'd settled on my banana costume I hadn't worn since seventh grade.

"Is it Kendra?" I ask.

"Uh." He blinks, his attention flicking from my costume on the floor to his phone screen. "No. It's not."

I notice the weird shift in his tone. Maybe it's personal.

"I should go," he says, fumbling to put his phone away.

I shrug, holding open my bedroom door. "See you."

Then he leaves like my house is on fire.

Weird.

I head into the kitchen and pour myself a bowl of off-brand Cocoa Puffs that my mother crassly dubbed "Cocoa Pellets." I squint at the bowl, concluding that the sugary taste overrides the questionable shape.

Carson proved to be a good distraction from my own suckfest of an evening, because last night I'd broken up with my boyfriend. In a banana costume no less.

I think about texting Otto to make sure he's okay but reconsider. I shouldn't open that line of communication. I'm sure he doesn't want to hear from me.

It wasn't an awful breakup. In fact, none of my relationships—flirtationships, situationships, whatever you want to call them—have ended in a dramatic demise. They have, however, all ended because of me.

Well, except for one.

The thing is, I can sense impending disappointment like a dog sensing an earthquake right before it hits. And when I do, I get out before there's lasting damage. Heartache isn't an experiment worth repeating. It's mentally taxing and extremely unfun. I'd rather be alone until I can chase another heart-pattering high that will eventually peter out.

Anyway, feelings don't fix problems. Look at my mother. My dad left, my brother is never around, and whenever shit hits the fan, who has to fix it?

Me.

I'd felt the familiar disappointment sink in last night. Otto drove us to Keith Whittle's after-party once the school's Halloween dance came to a modest end at nine-thirty, but not before we stopped at the abandoned car wash off Clifford Avenue—aka our usual hookup spot.

Otto's BMW was tight quarters, but it was better than my nonexistent vehicle that provided exactly zero privacy.

I was straddling Otto in his back seat as he desperately tried to find the zipper for my banana costume. (Spoiler alert: No zipper. You literally had to peel that thing off me.)

"Why'd you have to wear this thing?" Otto mumbled, his lips vibrating against mine.

"Because I like it. It's very *a-peeling* on me."

My pun went over his head. "No, it's not. It's really baggy."

I flattened my palms over both sides of my head as if to cover its ears. "Shh, you're going to hurt its feelings."

He just stared at me. "Whose feelings?"

I theatrically looked up and sighed. My sense of humor was wasted on him.

"Never mind." I pulled myself into the passenger's seat, readjusting my bold outfit. "Let's head out."

Keith's house was located right in the center of the Palisades suburban paradise, where the homes were more like modern villas than standard two-stories. Keith had it all. Backyard basketball court. Ocean view. A pool. The dream.

We found liquor and mixers in the kitchen, and I made myself a drink before I went looking for my best friends. I found them dancing in the living room with some tipsy classmates. Tahlia was dressed as Winifred Sanderson, her orange hijab wrapped in a braided knot. And Marlowe, who's unapologetically loud and trans, had acquired sunglasses identical to Lady Gaga circa 2008.

I joined them, warm and silly from the liquor, shamelessly incorporating bits of flossing and dabbing into my dance moves. Ironically, obviously.

Otto watched me from the kitchen with Duncan Rowe and Thomas Randkin, two of his football buddies. I didn't exactly love Otto's friends. All they talked about was televised sports and overpriced sneakers. Also? They thought making fun of people was a personality trait.

Duncan was dressed as Batman. His arm was wrapped around his longtime girlfriend—and my ex–best friend—Lenora Kahue, who made the perfect Moana. Part of me wished I could compliment her choice of costume, but I knew she would only slight me. We caught eyes for a second before she flicked her gaze away, scoffing. I swallowed. It hurt more than I thought it would.

Still. I wasn't going to let Lenora ruin my night.

"Otto, c'mon!" I called, fully tipsy now. I rubbed my hands up and down my banana bod in a movement that would make grandmothers everywhere clutch their pearls.

From across the room, Faith Tobinson snorted. She was dressed as an angel (for the third year in a row) along with my former friend Katie Delcavo, who went to Jesus camp with Faith the summer of eighth grade and then ditched me to be part of Faith's Lord-loving friend group.

Perhaps I wasn't the greatest influence.

Duncan and Thomas laughed, but Lenora pretended not to notice. I didn't care. I was having a good time. Marlowe encouraged me, twirling her blond hair as she shimmied her hips.

All of a sudden, Otto's hand was at my elbow, pulling me outside.

I did not enjoy being led around like some kind of leashed Pomeranian. I tugged out of his grip once we'd crossed into the backyard.

"What's your problem?" I asked, annoyed.

"Can't you just act normal?" he muttered.

I blinked at him. That's when I understood. In front of his football buddies, Otto was embarrassed by me.

How had I not noticed it before? It wasn't just this scenario. It was when I talked too animatedly about product design, my dream major. Or when I laughed too loudly at someone's jokes. Or when I called his friends out for saying something sexist. When I got passionate, I got loud. Otto suppressed that. Rejected it.

My personality wasn't for everyone, sure, but I knew your person was supposed to love the things that made you, *you.*

Otto and I had been together for a few weeks, but I realized we wouldn't last much longer. We didn't click.

"I can't do this anymore."

He snort-laughed, his upper lip doing that weird curl thing. It used to be charming to me. Now it wasn't. Otto told me to be normal when I was doing the most normal, cliché thing I could think of: participating in underage drinking and dancing at a high school party.

To him, I was doing it all wrong.

"You're serious?" he finally said when my expression didn't change.

"I'm sorry, Ottoman." I tried to soften the blow by using the nickname I gave him, but I quickly realized that wasn't the move. "I don't think we're meshing together in the ways we should be meshing."

"Brynn, c'mon," he pleaded. "We've been drinking. We can talk about this tomorrow."

But I knew in my gut I'd feel the same way when I woke up. This wasn't fun anymore, and I wasn't going to be with someone who dimmed my light. "It won't change how I feel now, though."

He let out a hiss of air. "You know, people warned me this would happen. That you're so fucking fickle in relationships." He downed the rest of his beer. "Guess they were right."

I felt my eyebrows shoot to my hairline. I mean, sure. It's not exactly false information, but spewing it in such a vitriolic way to get a rise out of me was plain shitty.

"I'm letting that comment slide because you're clearly upset, but I'm not going to stand here and apologize for knowing what's best for me. You're not it." He opened his mouth, but I was already taking off. "Don't follow me."

I rejoined Marlowe and Tahlia where I'd left them in the living room. I tried to shake off his words, but it wasn't as if I was immune to hurt. I wasn't a soulless person. Every side of a breakup sucks.

We didn't stay much longer after that. Mostly because I was sobering up and didn't feel like dancing with Otto lurking around. It killed the vibe.

I'd woken up a little sad but not regretful. It was the right decision.

I down the rest of my Cocoa Pellets and rinse the bowl in the sink. As I'm drying my hands, my phone begins to blow up. Not just one text, but multiple texts roll through so quickly that I have to catch my iPhone before it vibrates off the counter to an untimely death.

Who the hell is texting me this early?

When I navigate to my messages, I realize it's my group chat with Marlowe and Tahlia. Before I can open it, another text from Marlowe arrives.

> **Marlowe**
> he's a rancid scummy dingus
> weasel skid mark

I blink. What powerful poetry, but *who* is she talking about?

I scroll to the beginning of the messages, where the conversation starts.

> **Tahlia**
> have you seen the video?

> **Marlowe**
> please tell me you're ok

> **Marlowe**
> don't panic, ok? I'm coming over now with tahlia to do damage control.

Panic sets in anyway. What are they talking about? What video? Oh god. Did I do something embarrassing last night? I don't remember dancing on any coffee tables, though I've been known to do that. Who doesn't love a good coffee table?

I keep reading, starting to sweat.

> **Tahlia**
> I'm so sorry Brynn

> **Tahlia**
>
> he's going to get in so much
> trouble for this though

> **Tahlia**
>
> marls and I are in the sbux
> drive thru and then heading
> your way

Sorry for what? I send that exact thought to the group chat, but I don't get a reply.

Hoping for clarity, I scroll through the rest of my incoming texts. They're mostly from my classmates, but it's the same meme every time. A screenshot from some reality cooking show where a contestant is trying to eat three pickles at once.

If this is some kind of sex joke, it's lost on me.

A second later, Marlowe and Tahlia burst through my front door with a Venti Mocha Cookie Frappuccino, both wearing matching concerned expressions.

I look between them. "What's going on?"

Marlowe bites her lower lip. We've been friends since she moved from San Diego to attend Greenlough at the start of sophomore year. After my fallout with Lenora, we gravitated toward each other, spending weeks bonding during movie nights and homework sessions. It was around that time when she opened up about her transition, explaining she was certain of her gender identity by the time she was eleven.

She's my most caring and empathetic friend, and the way she's looking at me now is turning my stomach to ice.

"You haven't seen?" Tahlia asks, a note of surprise in her voice.

Tahlia is the most analytical out of the three of us. She's Muslim American, a proud hijabi, and pansexual. Her grandparents immigrated here from Lebanon in the '70s, and while Tahlia loves that all her family is in California, she's always wanted to live in Boston or New York, where there are seasons. We grew closer sophomore year when the three of us had US History together, which eventually led to us eating lunch together, forming what is now our inseparable union.

Marlowe and Tahlia exchange apprehensive glances. Why are they so hesitant?

I suck in an anxious breath. "I swear if you don't tell me—"

"Someone sent a clip of Duncan Rowe getting a blowie to the entire senior class this morning. Everyone thinks it's you because the other person in the video was wearing a banana costume," Tahlia says in one breath, like ripping off a Band-Aid. She immediately follows this by handing me the Frappuccino.

The drink is slick with condensation. I nearly lose my grip due to my current state of shock. My heart drops. Other than spotting him in the kitchen at Keith's, I had *zero* interaction with Duncan Rowe last night. And I'm not trying to be messy. He's in a committed relationship with my ex-BFF. I am very aware of this.

But if it wasn't me, then *who*? Because as far as I know, I was the only one dressed as a banana at Keith's party last night. Apparently what I imagined would be hee-hee-ha-ha funny was fated to be phallic in a way I had *not* intended.

"The video was spread around on Snapchat," Marlowe explains, her green eyes full of sympathy.

I quickly check Snapchat, but there aren't any unopened messages.

Whoever is circulating the video didn't send it to me.

"It's not like anyone can save it, right?" Tahlia says. "But I swear, this will blow over—"

Marlowe gives her an incredulous look. *"Blow* over?"

"Poor word choice," Tahlia amends. "It'll pass. And obviously we know it wasn't you— Duncan knows it wasn't you. So, you know, he can clear it up."

I'm overheating. I want to crawl out of my skin and make this whole situation somebody else's problem. Why would someone do this? Because of the way I'd handled things with Otto? As far as breakups go, it wasn't bad. Only—he was a little upset, wasn't he? But not enough to actively ruin my life.

"You both opened the video?"

They nod, giving me compassionate stares.

"We didn't know what it was when it came through," Tahlia explains.

"It looked like it was taken through a crack in the door, and it was only, like, five seconds," Marlowe continues. "Nobody knows the user behind the Snapchat account. It's already deactivated. You could see the banana suit but not the face of the person inside of it."

I open the lid to my Starbucks cup and scoop up a heaping amount of whipped cream with two of my fingers. I do this until it's gone, pacing back and forth.

Who would think it's okay to share something like that? As—what? Some kind of blackmail against Duncan? Did he do something to piss someone off? It doesn't make sense. If he's happy with Lenora, he wouldn't want this to get out. So maybe he doesn't know who sent it.

I stop pacing. "You guys *know* it wasn't me."

"Duh," Marlowe says.

"But it's weird." Tahlia looks at me. "Who else had the same costume as you?"

That's when it hits me.

Most students were at the Halloween dance, and a majority of the senior class came to Keith's after-party. They saw *me* in that costume. They know Lenora and I aren't friends anymore. Why she's spent so long hating me.

I'm going to look like the guilty party.

I set my drink down. How many of my classmates received that video? Have *opened* that video? They'll believe it's me. And if word about my breakup with Otto has gotten around, they'll assume I ended things *and* hooked up with my ex–best friend's boyfriend the same night.

I feel sick. This is a colossal nightmare.

Until my name is cleared, I'm screwed. Ruined. I will absolutely be the most hated person at school.

A dozen more pings chime from my phone in rapid succession.

Scratch that. I already am.

2

"Brynn Whitaker can deny it, but it's obvious it's her."

"Lenora shouldn't have left Duncan alone around her."

"History always repeats itself, doesn't it?"

You know that bowling-ball-sized rock that sits in your gut after something terrible happens? And you think, *Surely it can't get worse. SURELY this is it.* But you haven't yet spotted the gargantuan meteor that's hurtling through time and space, ready to blow up the rest of your life.

Well. That meteor has made its earth-shattering impact.

My reputation as a serial dater has made my classmates assume I jump at the chance to have sex with everyone I've been with. Which is false. Besides, the definition of intercourse has always been centered around male pleasure, which is heteronormative, patriarchal, and, frankly, outdated. Also? I have vaginismus, which makes P-in-V sex painful, and anyway, society shouldn't determine how anyone chooses to define their sex life.

I digress.

Point being, my classmates are aware of my sprawling dating history, which apparently goes hand in hand with sex, so they're going to speculate that *I'm* actually guilty.

Which is, coincidentally, bananas.

I'm now the most hated person at school. My classmates, who I've known my entire life, are posting my most recent Instagram selfie to their stories, drawing a huge red X over my face, and encouraging others to unfollow me.

It's truly Bananagate, and it hurts more than I thought it would.

Marlowe and Tahlia spend the morning distracting me from Instagram, reassuring me the record will be set straight on Monday. I want to believe them. More than that, I want to know why someone would do this.

My friends take off once my mom texts me that she's on her way home from her Postmates shift, where she finds me in pie-and-cry mode as she walks through the door.

"Oh, honey," she says, her voice softening as she sets two paper bags on the kitchen counter. She must have stopped at the store on the way here. "What happened?"

I'm taking my frustration out on my dough, pretending I'm steamrolling over Duncan's stupid face.

She hugs me from behind, her arms pinning mine to my sides and ceasing my Demolish Duncan fantasy. "I love you, but please do not destroy my countertops."

I hang my head. "I have to tell you something."

"Oh boy. You didn't hit the mailbox again, did you?"

I'm momentarily thrown. "What? *No.* I didn't even have the car today."

My general teenage recklessness has cost us a new car bumper, though in my defense, I *did* have to slam on the brakes to avoid accidentally murdering a seagull. I couldn't have that on my conscience, and that bird was abnormally slow.

She unwraps her arms, turning me toward her with a smile. "I've seen you do more with less."

"It's not my fault my physics project defied all the laws of gravity."

"At least you got an A at the expense of my window."

I try to smile. I'm in no way a perfect person. I break curfew and talk back and avoid calls from my older brother, Smith, because he always needs money.

But this rumor is so much worse than all of that.

I've strived for years to prove I'm worthy of my dream school. Stanford University is my Everest, mostly because they have a specific program for product design in their School of Engineering. For me, it's the only degree that fits. I'm a problem-solver—hence the flirt coaching—but I'm also good at figuring out how to make ordinary things more efficient.

For instance, during my first year at Greenlough, I noticed the student pickup line cut into the senior parking lot, which caused overflow, congestion, and the very worst Big Karen Energy road rage. I mapped out a solution and took my proposed route to Dean McTiernan, explaining why this remedy would be better for everyone. It was executed flawlessly.

I also suggested a new section in the official Greenlough Academy app that uploads a digital version of the biweekly *Greenlough Gazette* that students could easily access, *plus* a paperless solution if they ever wanted to go fully green.

I'm solution-oriented, and I want to come up with concepts and creations that make life easier.

But as much as I feel like I'm the perfect fit for this degree, there's one problem: Stanford's enrollment rate is 4 percent. This means I need a spotless record and an impressive application in order to even be considered. I cannot afford to slip up. Unless Duncan sets things straight, it's very likely I'll have to face Dean McTiernan on Monday.

Duncan has avoided the string of texts I've sent so far, but he can't ignore me forever.

Tears of frustration fill my eyes as my mother's expression switches from sympathetic to concerned. "You want the bag?"

I nod.

She leaves, then returns with a paper bag that has two eyes cut out of the front and a tiny little mouth for breathing purposes.

The bag started when I was five and went through a rampant fibbing stage. The only way my mom could coax the cold, hard truth out of me was if I pulled a knit cap all the way over my head so I didn't have to look her in the eyes. The cap turned into a paper bag because my mom worried I would suffocate. Eventually my fibbing habit stopped, but I'd sometimes use the bag to tell her I'd failed a quiz I hadn't studied for.

I pull the bag over my face. Take a deep breath. Once I say it, it'll be out there. I don't know what she's going to think, but I have no doubt she'll be disappointed. I hadn't told her I was going to an after-party *and* participating in underage drinking. I could leave the drinking part out, but my mother wasn't born yesterday. She knows exactly what goes on at parties. Lying by omission won't help me here.

"I was at a party last night and today somebody sent a video to the whole school of someone who looked like me performing a sex act on Duncan Rowe," I say in a rush.

I don't look through the little eyeholes, but I hear her sigh. Then, her hand is in mine and she's leading me toward one of the kitchen chairs. I sit down and explain the entire story, emphasizing that it wasn't me, but that people are sharing saved Snaps and videos of me in costume that night as if it's proof.

When I gain the courage to look at her, it's like another deep cut. She's disappointed.

I don't think any kid likes disappointing their parent, but this is different. I'm supposed to be her good child. The scholarship student. Smith has put her—well, *us*—through a lot. He's been in and out of rehab and refuses to move back home. We never know where he is or who he's staying with. When he's using, he's off the grid. When he needs money, he persuades my mom into giving it to him. I've stopped trying to get her to cut him off. She never listens.

That's why disappointing her hurts so badly.

"Brynn, I'm so sorry," my mom says, and I'm surprised at how gentle her tone sounds. "We're going to need to report this situation to the dean. The distribution of underage sexual content is illegal. You know that, right? They need to punish whoever did this."

That had crossed my mind. Duncan and I might be adults in the eyes of the law, but we're still in high school. Even if someone did think it was me, why would they think spreading that video was *okay*? And worse, what if the real person is underage?

"The Snapchat user already deactivated their account," I say.

"They'll have to seriously look into it. Open up an investigation," she says firmly. "And, honey, this whole situation will die down. I promise. You just need to give it time."

Those words don't dissolve the hard lump in my throat. "Everyone thinks I did something I didn't do."

"But you didn't, and you're going to have to stand your ground." She raises an eyebrow. "Speaking of, I am going to have to ground you. Drinking at a party, Brynn? You know better."

I rip the bag off my head. "Can you please feel sorry for me and give me a pass?"

"Absolutely not. You were supposed to come straight home."

I groan. I did not think today could get any worse. "I'm sorry."

"I have rules for a reason. To keep you out of trouble."

She might as well have said *to keep you from being like your brother.* Unlike him, I've never touched drugs, but it's as if she fears I might pick up his habits.

"Duncan will tell the truth. He has no reason not to," she assures me, then begins to unload the groceries she'd left sitting on the counter. "Go shower. You'll feel better after, I promise. And I'll email the dean while you're in there."

She's right. Normally showers make me feel like I've removed an extra layer of skin, shedding my anxiety cocoon like a caterpillar. I head to our shared bathroom and twist the temperature knob as hot as it will go, but once I undress and stick my leg inside, the water is still freezing. I wait, hoping it will take a bit more time to turn warm, but it never does.

So things *can* get worse.

Holding my breath, I force my body into the shower and let the cold water rush over me. It's shocking. The opposite of pleasant. Shivering, I complete the world's fastest hair-and-body wash and jump out as goose bumps erupt all over my skin.

"That was quick," my mom says when I open the door.

I am truly the bearer of bad news today. "I think the hot water heater's out."

She sets a jar of salsa down a little too hard. "Really?"

"At least you won't need coffee to wake you up," I say through chattering teeth.

My mom's too stressed to laugh. Instead, she mumbles something to herself and goes out to the garage. I go to my room and change, and a few minutes later, we regroup in the living room.

"You're right. It's out." She runs a hand through her dark hair. It's thick and wavy, the same as mine. "There's always something wrong here, huh?"

My mom likes to believe our house is cursed, but it's just old. We inherited it after my granddad died when I was eight. Compared to the giant mansions that have been built in the neighborhood, it's a modest three-bedroom, one-bathroom. The inheritance is why we're able to live in such a nice neighborhood in Pacific Palisades, which is known for being wealthy, white, and somewhat of a hot spot for Hollywood filming locations.

She's not wrong, though. Last month, the bathroom sink needed fixing because of a plumbing issue. In August, our AC unit stopped working and had to be replaced. In July, she was late paying the electric bill and not only did we have to scrounge up money to pay the fee to turn it back on, but we were stuck in the dark for three days.

This is why my side hustle is important. Because, inevitably, something will need fixing. And it's my extra income that saves us. Always. She needs a job that pays better, but she's gotten a string of rejections so far.

"At least we'll be saving water?" I offer, recognizing I'd bathed in less than two minutes. That has to be a record.

My mom lets out a disgruntled noise.

"We'll pull from my savings," I say breezily, like it doesn't feel like a gut punch.

She bites her lip. "I hate to do that."

I don't say anything. What other choice do we have?

She makes the call, but the cheapest handyman we know can't come for a few days. I don't dwell on it. Cold showers are the least of my problems right now.

"I never finished cry-and-pie," I say, changing the subject.

My mom takes a bar stool next to me. "What kind of pie were you planning?"

"Apple," I tell her, mostly because we have a few in the fridge that are about to go bad.

"Well," she says with a positive trill to her voice, "it appears as if we're going to have apple pie for breakfast."

My mom pulls the ingredients from the fridge as I get back to my dough, piling it in a giant lump and starting over. The consistency is better the second time around, a reminder that I'm freaking *great* at fixing things. It's what will get me into Stanford. I find solutions to problems. It doesn't matter that Duncan's scandal is slowly destroying my life, because I'm going to find my way out of it.

As my mom places the pie in the oven, I notice her phone light up on the counter beside me. My brother's name appears in an incoming text.

I know what Smith wants, and my heart sinks. Because my mom will easily give him all the tips she's earned today. She won't mention the replacement water heater we need, letting him live in ignorance.

It's not fair, but I'm used to it. I've tried to heal from the lasting damage of Smith, because even your own family will disappoint you. He's let us down, again and again, and no matter how much emotional armor I use to protect my heart, a piece of me will always care.

I can fix a lot of things. I just can't fix *him*.

When she turns back around, I dart my eyes away from her phone, pretending I haven't seen. Letting her believe I'm living in my own ignorance.

3

"She only wants what she can't have."

"Getting Duncan Rowe was like a game for her."

"I was going to ask her to help me talk to Henry, but I don't support whores."

I give myself a pep talk as I get dressed Monday morning. Unfortunately for me, my classmates have started spamming the banana emoji in my DMs. Which is great. Fine. *Lovely.* Definitely not detrimental to my fragile emotional state.

It is deeply painful that they're blaming me and not Duncan, even though *he's* the one who cheated on his girlfriend.

He never replied to my messages, so I need to find him at school and force him to tell the truth. I don't know why he hasn't already, but everything will be fine once he does. I'll go back to being Stanford-bound Brynn instead of banana-whore Brynn.

I should have looked harder for that Shrek costume.

When you go to a selective preparatory school like Greenlough, labels are unavoidable. Some of my classmates already think I'm an attention-seeker or that I like the thrill of the chase. The latter is true, but I'm *not* a threat to those who have boyfriends, especially Lenora.

Sure, I like flirting—the instant gratification of it—but it's not a game. My intention is never to hurt anyone. Even with my side hustle, I keep a strict privacy policy to foster trust and to minimize blowback.

I grab my one and only navy cardigan from my closet and yank it on. Greenlough's uniform policy requires girls to wear a blouse with a tartan color-blocked pleated skirt containing multiple shades of gray, navy, and light blue, like the ocean on a cloudy day.

Marlowe's two minutes away. I go out front and wait for her, and when she pulls up, I slowly—and with a bit of dramatic flair—drop to my hands and knees right in front of her car, then proceed to roll onto my back so that I'm staring into the sun.

Marlowe sticks her head out the window to get a better look at me. "I am not running you over."

"It'll only take you two seconds to put me out of my misery," I counter.

"Can't do that. I'll miss you eating all the Eggos in my freezer when you sleep over."

I lift my head up, squinting. "*That's* my legacy?"

"Not all of us die heroes."

I sigh, then push myself into a standing position. As I get in her car, she cranks up Harry Styles.

"You're going to get through this," she tells me.

"You know, you could have gently run over my arm. Or leg. Not all the way. Just a little."

"What happens when I have to drive you to the hospital? Do I say, '*Actually, doctor, she asked me to run her over, but just a little*'?"

I slump in my seat.

"Hey," she says gently. "You didn't do anything wrong."

"I wish they knew that," I moan. "The amount of banana emojis in my DMs is astronomical."

She grabs my hand, twisting her fingers through mine. All of her braided friendship bracelets we made for each other over the last few years fall toward her wrist.

"Duncan will clear this up," she says, certain.

I don't know Duncan Rowe very well, but I know the person he portrays to the outside world: Football star. Eighth-grade spelling bee champion. The freshman who accidentally broke his middle finger when he slammed it in a car door and had to wear a cast for two months. The guy who—up until Saturday—was in love with his girlfriend, Lenora.

Clearing this up and getting back in her good graces should be at the top of his list, so *why* didn't he text me back?

Marlowe slides into an empty parking spot in the senior lot. Once we're out of the car, she links arms with me and marches us straight through the double doors.

Greenlough Academy radiates a prestigious vibe. It's an enormous Spanish-style white building with red corrugated roofing surrounded by cypress trees for privacy. There's a grassy courtyard in the center that's sprinkled with wooden picnic tables. Inside, bright fluorescents glint off the immaculate white-and-gray speckled floor tiles. The doors, lockers, and walls all blend effortlessly in neutral tones, a perfect complement to the elegant wood trimming that sits just above the rows of lockers. Even the fancy garbage bins look like they've been thoughtfully chosen by someone who majored in interior design.

Even though Greenlough is a selective school, they like to boast that they're progressive. They use words like *accepting* and *community* in their pamphlets, and while it's true there are a plethora of diverse organizations and clubs, it also means you get a mix of students who don't all think the same way.

These students tend to group together in smaller circles, like Faith

Tobinson with her church friends and her pastor's son boyfriend, John Mark, or your green-thumb environmentalists who find gardening opportunities over the weekends. Tahlia, Marlowe, and I fall in the striving-academia crowd.

As predicted, my dear classmates begin staring at me as soon as we reach our lockers. It's jarring, the type of hurt that strikes me right in my core. I've never experienced this level of *nasty glare* before. My heart thuds violently in my chest, and my legs feel like pudding. I desperately want to scream, *YOU ARE EXTREMELY INCORRECT IN THINKING I HAD ANYTHING TO DO WITH THIS!*

My spiraling thoughts are interrupted by the intercom.

"Brynn Whitaker to the front office."

Marlowe's eyes snap to mine. I expected this. My mom emailed Dean McTiernan yesterday explaining my side and insisting he take this matter seriously. He must be paging me to talk in person.

"Let's get this over with," I mumble.

Marlowe gives me an encouraging smile. "It'll be okay."

I nod, but my heart jackhammers in my chest as I go. I try to ignore the not-so-subtle stares of my peers as I pass, my confidence sinking with each step.

When I reach the main office, I practically burst through the double glass doors. Mrs. Veerly, Greenlough's administrative assistant, spares me a quick glance from behind her computer. She waves me toward McTiernan's office.

Swallowing, I knock on his door.

"Come in."

I hesitantly push it open. Dean McTiernan sits at his large oak desk, eyes fixed on the computer in front of him. He has ghost-white hair and a complexion that nearly matches it, so different from the framed photos of him in his physics classes he taught forty years ago. He's in his seventies now, old enough to remember decades' worth of graduates, and yet he still somehow remembers every current student's name.

"Right, then. Please take a seat," McTiernan says, adjusting his wire-rimmed glasses.

Silently, I slip into the chair across from him.

He studies me before saying, "I called you here for two reasons today, Miss Whitaker. As you know, here at Greenlough, we hold our students to the highest standard of conduct. What you do outside of here reflects upon our academy, and unfortunately that has been reflected in your actions."

He cannot be serious.

"It wasn't me," I insist, hating I even have to clarify. "I have that same costume, but I didn't—"

He raises his hand, stopping me. "Miss Whitaker, we have proof that you brought a flask into Greenlough's Halloween dance. One parent emailed me photos that were taken by a student who attended."

My jaw drops. I did *not* bring a flask to Greenlough's Halloween dance. I'm on scholarship. I wouldn't jeopardize that by doing something so risky.

But.

I *did* take a tiny sip from a flask in secret. Yeah, maybe not my smartest move, but it was being passed around in the privacy of the restroom, away from the suspicious eyes of the chaperones.

Which means one of my classmates intentionally took a photo and reported me.

I attempt to swallow my shock. *"Who?"*

"That's irrelevant. The fact of the matter is, you've deliberately broken one of our rules." His mouth sets into a firm line. "We can't let this go unpunished."

Punishment. The word hits me hard in the chest. I close my eyes and wait for him to lay on the bad news. He's going to expel me. Take away my scholarship. I'm going to have to explain to Stanford why I transferred to a new school during my last semester of senior year. I'll have to clean out my locker as everyone watches—

"Detention. After school today."

I exhale, instantly relieved. I'm not being expelled!

But wait. Oh god. No, no, *no*. Detention is not good. Stanford can look into that, can't they?

"Greenlough will honor your scholarship as long as you don't cause any more trouble for the rest of the year," McTiernan continues. "We're being exceptionally generous considering you signed the Greenlough Standard of Conduct that states you are to uphold a certain standard of excellence. I don't want to see you step out of line again, Miss Whitaker. I'm already reconsidering writing you that letter of recommendation."

Panic closes around my throat. I feel like someone's shoved me out of a plane without a parachute. This can't be happening. I need that letter, and more importantly, I cannot have a detention on my record. If Stanford sees that, I'm screwed.

So that's exactly what I say. I don't even care that I'm groveling at this point.

He must see the pained, pleading look in my eyes, because he relents. "You're a good student, Miss Whitaker. One of our best. It's why I promised you that letter in the first place, but you have to earn it." He taps on the detention slip in front of him. "I won't let this affect your record, but you'll still have to go."

Relief slowly unclenches from the pit in my stomach. "And the letter?"

He studies me carefully. "If you don't step out of line for the rest of the semester, the letter is yours."

I promise that I won't. I don't want McTiernan to retract his offer. As a

Stanford alum, his letter wields a ton of power. He offers it to one student a year, and he's selected *me*. I cannot mess up this opportunity.

"Now, the second thing." He peers down at me. "I've received a number of complaints from parents about a video that's been distributed to students, and I want you to know we are looking into it. Trust me, this is not something we're taking lightly."

"It wasn't me," I repeat for the second time, growing defensive. "Everyone thinks it is, but it's not."

"I believe you," he assures me. "Your mother explained this to me in her email as well. I'm sorry this has happened. It's not the type of exemplary behavior we expect from students."

"I plan to force Duncan to clear things up," I say. *As soon as I flick him in the forehead a couple hundred times as revenge for my suffering.*

"I will also be talking to Mr. Rowe today, and I'm going to suggest to you what I plan on telling him." He slides my detention slip over to me, followed by something else. "A pass to visit Mrs. Burchill, our guidance counselor. I know students can be cruel, Miss Whitaker, and I'd hate to see such a terrible situation negatively affect those involved."

"Oh," I say, caught off guard. Because technically, I'm *not* involved. This is all one giant mistake, but I take both slips anyway. "That won't be necessary, but thanks."

McTiernan prattles on as if he hadn't heard me. "Present it to your teacher if you feel the need to pay her a visit during class."

"Right," I say, already certain it won't be worth my time. By the end of the day, Duncan will have cleared everything up and my reputation will be restored to its former glory.

Before I leave, McTiernan reminds me that the school is committed to absolving the issue and providing a firm punishment, but I'll believe it when I see it.

By the time I'm dismissed, I'm already twenty minutes late to Government. I'm exiting the office as Duncan rounds the corner, arriving for his visit.

I decide the dean can wait a few minutes.

"Hey," I say roughly, marching up to him. "We need to talk."

Duncan folds his arms. "Why?"

He did not just ask me that. It takes every muscle in my body to quell the rage that wants to erupt like an active volcano. "What do you mean *why*? You know that wasn't me in that video."

He clips his gaze toward the lockers. He can't even look at me. Coward. "I know."

I blow out a frustrated breath. "Cool. Great. You do realize our entire class thinks it's me, right?"

"I know— Look." His voice is softer now, like he's embarrassed. "I was going to tell Lenora the truth after she saw the video, but then she assumed it was you and I sort of . . . went with it."

Forget forehead flicking. I'm about to straight up strangle this idiot. "You *what*?"

"Only because she seemed more pissed at you than at me." His eyes drop to his shoes. "And she said she was willing to forgive me and try again."

I'm at loss for words. I know Lenora holds a lot of resentment toward me, but that video is proof that Duncan also royally screwed up. Was she so willing to dismiss his mistake because she thought it was me?

What does she *really* think of me, then?

I know the answer, but I shove it in the deepest part of my brain where I can't access that stinging wound.

Then I realize what Duncan means.

"Wait, no—you can't let me take the blame for this!" I cry. "That's messed up, Duncan. Not just for me, but for Lenora. You're hiding something important from her."

He holds up his hands as if he has no control, which is bullshit. He's in control of this entire fucked-up situation.

I don't wait for him to come up with another excuse. "I'll tell her the truth," I threaten.

The corner of Duncan's mouth twitches in a smarmy, amused way. It's a subtle movement, but I catch it. "You and I both know she'll never believe you."

And there it is. Suddenly, I'm a sophomore again, sobbing on the steps of Lenora's house, begging her to forgive me. Being told to leave as the door slams in my face. Years of friendship gone in an instant.

"Everyone already hates me, Duncan. For something I didn't do," I say, exasperated. Dread begins to pool into the pit of my stomach. "Can you try to understand how this affects me?"

Duncan breaks eye contact first, strutting toward the office. "I gotta go."

He cannot be serious.

"You are unhinged! And, for the record, *a very terrible person*!" I yell after him, just as Faith's boyfriend, John Mark, exits the classroom across from us. From the alarmed look on his face, I can tell he's witnessed my entire outburst.

Excellent. This is *exactly* what I need right now. I'm sure *Brynn's shame spiral* will quickly spread amongst the gossip mill by lunch.

"*What?*" I snap, but I don't bother waiting for a reply. Instead, I start walking to my government class.

A prickling sense of foreboding clenches in my chest. My only plan has been annihilated, and I have no idea what the hell I'm supposed to do now.

4

"She went to the dean's office this morning."

"Who is she kidding? Everyone saw the video."

"If I were her, I would not show my face here ever again."

I don't go straight to class, opting to take a beat to clear my head. As soon as I step into the nearest bathroom, I throw myself in a stall and allow my muffled screams of frustration to release from the depths of my throat.

Fuck Duncan Rowe.

The lying little prickweasel. How can one person possess so many scumbag qualities?

Oh god, this is bad. Lenora Kahue is one of the most beloved students at Greenlough Academy. It's one of the reasons why we were so close. Her heart is enormous because she genuinely cares about people. She makes handmade birthday cards with sentimental messages inside them and cries at commercials that feature unadopted animals. She knows almost everyone at Greenlough by name and will say hi in a way that makes you feel special when she sees you in the hall. It's no wonder she was voted class president of StuCo our sophomore year. *I* still vote for her every year.

If Duncan keeps up this lie, he'll continue to turn the entire school on me.

I grab a wad of toilet paper and blow my nose. Then I freeze. Holy hell. Carson never texted me back about Kendra. He must have seen the Snap. *That's* why he looked so freaked out before he left my house on Saturday.

I let out another annoyed growl and bang my head against the stall door, rattling it. Perhaps if I stay in here long enough, this very ordinary bathroom stall will magically transport me into a parallel universe where everything in my life is perfect. Maybe I even drive a lime-green Maserati and am immune to cavities.

"Hey—are you okay?"

I take half a second to panic in silence, throwing my hands up and then raking them through my hair. I had no idea there was another person in here listening to my emotional breakdown. How embarrassing.

My desire to save face outweighs my sheer mortification. I leap out of the stall. A second later, another door swings open. In front of me stands Cadence Frazenberg.

I know Cadence. Kind of. She's a senior along with her twin brother, Charlie, but we don't run in the same friend groups. Come to think of it, I don't know if she's kept her original crew of Photojournalism friends since the entire school found out she was pregnant a month ago. According to Marlowe, she'd been hiding it even longer. But people started talking about Cadence differently once it was revealed and in return, she shut everyone out.

The baby's father is Thomas Randkin. Unfortunately, Thomas possesses the same prickwad genes as Duncan and ignores Cadence's existence. There are also rumors that Cadence is giving the child up for adoption.

The other thing I know about the Frazenberg family is that they're donors. Like 90 percent of the parents at Greenlough, they're rich. So rich that they funded the remodeling of the library with their generous donations three years ago. Cadence's dad is a wealthy white guy named Dan Frazenberg, owner of all the popular vegan Earth Garden restaurants in Los Angeles. Her mother is a Persian woman named Shirin who owns a successful online tea boutique, selling thousands of subscription boxes monthly as part of their "Tea for Me" club. I think my aunt Laurie subscribes to it.

I wipe the mascara from under my eyes, attempting to make myself look less like a fiery hot mess.

"Rough Monday?" she asks.

I decide to stick to honesty. "You have no idea."

Cadence begins washing her hands. "Well, this kid decided to evict my breakfast and I may never look at French toast the same again, so I might have some idea."

"Oh, here." I dig through the front pocket of my book bag and pull out a wrapped mint. "Mint is supposed to ease your stomach, I think."

Cadence reads the label. "Arnold's Tire Depot?"

"Arnold's a real one," I say. "Free mints and coffee, plus he gave us a discount when we were in a pinch."

I leave out the part where my mother and I are *always* in a financial pinch, and that pothole she hit was no joke. Tires are expensive. They should really teach us that going into adulthood. That and taxes, probably.

To my surprise, Cadence laughs. I hear the clicking of the mint running over her molars. "I'll have to remember that."

Her hand glides over her belly. The band of her skirt is underneath her stomach. It doesn't look like she's hoarding a watermelon or anything, but you can tell she didn't just eat her weight in Chipotle.

"I saw the Snap," she says bluntly. "Duncan's a fucking asshole."

It's nice to hear that someone agrees. "Yeah, he is. But it wasn't me." At this rate, I should consider getting this phrase tattooed on my forehead. "But it's a shit situation all the same."

She presses her lips together, nodding thoughtfully. "What happened with McTiernan?"

I reveal my yellow detention slip.

Confusion falls over her face. "Detention? For something you didn't do?"

"Well, not exactly," I explain. "Someone *did* take a photo of me drinking at the dance."

"So many snakes in the grass." She leans against the lip of the sink. "I've been there. Detention, I mean. Though I brought it upon myself after I pulled the fire alarm to get out of my trig test."

My eyes widen. "That was *you*?"

She shrugs. "I tried to blame Faith Tobinson, but he didn't believe me."

I laugh. While Faith Tobinson and her Holy Crew have good intentions most of the time, they like to remind the rest of us that if we participate in sinful activities, we'll burn in the fiery depths of hell for all eternity. No pressure or anything.

"Anyway, I appreciate it." Cadence tosses the empty wrapper into the trash. "You know, you're the first person to actually acknowledge me today. Everyone else acts like I've got leprosy or something."

A twinge of sympathy squeezes through me. Even though she says it casually, I can hear the hurt behind her words.

"Likewise." I pause. "But you know, leprosy was eradicated over a decade ago. One less disease to worry about."

Cadence snorts. "You're so weird."

"Whooping cough, though? Still around. You'd think not, but it is."

"Do your parents work for the CDC or something?"

"Nope." I hold the door open and we walk out of the bathroom together. "Hey, you should eat lunch with us sometime. Marlowe, Tahlia, and me, I mean. We sit by the Spindelli bush."

Two years ago, a senior named Hudson Spindelli set his science project aflame near a certain bush in the quad. It ignited so intensely that the fire department had to be called. We had to evacuate the premises until it was out, but the poor bare bush never grew back.

"I know where you sit" is all she says.

I don't know what to say, so I go with "Okay" and begin to walk away, but then I turn around. "It's not a pity offer," I add.

I think a catch a glimmer of relief pass across her face as she says, "I know."

The rest of the day is excruciatingly, diabolically, brutally, *awful*.

Duncan's clearly worked hard to paint me as the villain, and because of this, I'm feeling the painful aftershock of my peers' vile opinions.

Exhibit A: They surreptitiously drop rotten banana peels near me between passing periods. I almost slip on one that I don't see until it's too late, but Tahlia stabilizes me right before I get up close and personal with the floor.

This occurs so frequently that by fourth period, Miss Rothman, the twelfth-grade sociology teacher, steps out of her classroom and shouts, *"Detention for anyone caught littering in the halls!"*

Exhibit B: When I attempt to talk to Tyla, president of Future Business Leaders of America, about our community outreach project before Pre-Calc, she looks at me like I've suggested I'm going to spend the rest of my life interpretive dancing in the nude.

"Oh—I got Mallory to spearhead that instead," she finally says.

Anger swells in my gut. "Last week you told me to do it."

She has the gall to look embarrassed. "There's a lot going on right now, you know? Maybe skip this week."

Technically, Tyla can't stop me from coming, but I immediately get the message. *Don't come. Your tarnished reputation is not welcome here.*

It's bullshit. I shouldn't feel shunned from my extracurriculars, but the awful truth is that no one wants to be associated with me.

Then we have exhibit C: Carson *freaking* Jenkins, who has suddenly decided to ghost me after I helped him out with Kendra.

I sprint up to him during PE, where we're supposed to be walking the mile. It *would* be a beautiful, breezy day if everyone wasn't gaping at me like I've just sprouted the ability to shoot laser beams out of my eyeballs.

Carson stiffens with fear when he notices me, but he doesn't try and scramble away.

I take the opening. "We need to talk."

He nervously adjusts his glasses, and I know he wishes this confrontation weren't happening so publicly. "Sure."

"Look, I'm not an idiot," I begin. "I have an idea of why people have been ignoring my texts all weekend, but I'm going to let you explain it to my face. You owe me that."

Carson looks down at his Reeboks. Pieces of wet grass cling to the edges. "I'll get you your last payment."

I'm not letting him off easy. "What's that supposed to mean?"

"I don't need your help," he mumbles. "You ruin relationships, not create them."

The words are like a dull blade to my heart, but I try to play it off. "Nice. So you're saying it didn't work out with Kendra?"

My directness makes him flustered. "No, um. It did. That's just what Duncan's been saying."

I let out a deep breath, then close my eyes. *Of course.* Duncan wants to keep the heat off him and on me. It's the only power move he has left. He not only gets to keep his relationship, but he comes out of this unscathed even though he cheated. It's unbelievable.

"Duncan's an asshole," I clap back, "and so are you if you're going around parroting whatever the hell he says like some mindless sea slug."

Carson's annoyed now. "We've all seen the video. Your costume was a dead giveaway."

"Congratulations," I snap. "Glad we've established that you're able to jump to your own conclusions. Maybe you can use those critical thinking skills to deduce why you'd think I'd do something like that."

I'm tired of defending myself to people who already assume the worst of me. It's pointless.

I begin to pick up my pace when he calls out, "Wait! Are you going to tell . . . ?"

He doesn't finish, not wanting to reveal too much about Kendra when our classmates are in earshot.

"No," I say, even though I don't owe him anything. "I wouldn't do that. I want it to work out between you two, despite what you think of me."

He mumbles a half-hearted thanks before putting a healthy gap of distance between us, leaving me on my own once again.

The full force of my situation is a cold dose of reality. Now I understand how the entire student body sees me, and it's all because of Duncan.

I'm exhausted by the time I exit my last class, and I can't even vent to my best friends because I have to drag my sorry ass to detention—as if today wasn't horrible enough. I've been framed and shamed for something I didn't do, *and* I have to prove to the dean that I'm worthy of my recommendation letter. I'm seven months away from graduating, and my reputation has been bulldozed by a lying, cheating fartlord of a boy who has somehow walked away from this entire scandal unaffected.

Typical.

I don't want my current status as a relationship-sabotaging monster to become my lasting legacy here. I earned my scholarship, and I won't let Duncan ice me out. If he expects me to start over at another school my senior year, he's sorely wrong. I'm not letting him win.

Duncan's framed me because Lenora forgave him, and Lenora only forgave him because she thinks *I'm* involved. It's unfair. To make matters worse, I have no idea who's actually in that video, and Duncan made it clear he won't cough up that information.

But if I can figure out who *was* in costume with Duncan that night, I'll be able to clear my name. It's messed up that they've stayed quiet while I've been treated like wet shoe scum today. Though I guess I can't blame them. Nobody wants to face the wrath of the entire student body.

Maybe there's a way to do this by process of elimination. Between Marlowe, Tahlia, and I, we can figure out who was at Keith's party. We'll rule out who *couldn't* have been with Duncan, narrowing it down to a pool of possible banana suspects. A logic-based solution to a massive problem, which is familiar territory to navigate.

I take a deep breath, feeling hopeful for the first time today.

I might not get any cool points for admitting this, but I enjoy school. I don't want it to feel like a giant hellscape for the remainder of my senior year. I like that the teachers care enough to create engaging lesson plans, challenging us to debate and form our own opinions. The amount of extracurriculars offered feel infinite, like there's something for everyone. You get what you pay for, I know. It's a privileged situation, but I'm not one to take it for granted. I love it here.

The only part of school I don't love is detention. Which brings us to my current situation. Mr. Soto, the drama instructor, is in charge of supervising today. I happen to be the first to arrive and when he sees me, a sympathetic expression washes over his face.

"Not one of our better Mondays?"

I slide into a desk in front of him. "Not exactly."

"Well, Mrs. Burchill is an excellent guidance counselor if you ever need her."

I remember the yellow slip of paper McTiernan gave me. I don't need to sit in front of someone and talk about my feelings. That isn't going to solve my problems. Besides, now I have a plan. Everything will be fine.

The door creaks open. To my shock, Keith Whittle steps through.

"Mr. Whittle," Mr. Soto says, gesturing for his detention slip. "Skipping ceramics once again, are we?"

Keith gives a lazy shrug as he slides into the seat next to me, moving a swoop of his red-blond hair away from his eyes.

"Being here's punishment enough," Mr. Soto tells us. "I'm not going to make you do anything extra. You can leave after the half hour."

I wait until Mr. Soto pops in his earbuds, too immersed by something on his phone to glance up.

I catch Keith's eye. "I need a favor," I whisper.

He furrows his brows. "What?"

"You have a Ring doorbell, right?"

He just stares at me. "Yeah?"

"I need you to access the footage from the night of your party."

Keith snorts out a dry laugh. "C'mon, you don't think I'm that stupid."

I spare a glance at Mr. Soto, but he's not paying attention to us. "Okay? What's that supposed to mean?"

"It means I disabled it so my parents couldn't see how many people I had over that night. Obviously."

I blow out an irritated breath. I can't deny that *was* a smart move on his part, but it does nothing to help me.

"I need to figure out who was also dressed as a banana the night of your party," I say, keeping my voice low.

Now Keith looks bored. "I dunno. I heard it was you."

A muscle in my jaw twitches. "Yeah. Well. That's false information."

"You know, I heard Duncan wants the police involved. They'll be looking for whoever filmed it. You could wait until they figure it out. Save yourself the trouble."

This is news to me. But I have no idea how they'll even go about it. It's like trying to capture a firework in a jar. Even if they got a warrant, how do you trace something that's already disappeared?

"All right. Say they find out who sent it. It doesn't mean they'll figure out who was *actually there*," I press. "Which, by the way, was not me. Feel free to spread that around."

Mr. Soto clears his throat. I lean back in my seat, but he's focused on his phone, chuckling to himself as he stares at the screen.

"My neighbor. Mrs. Connoway," Keith says after a few minutes. "One of her outdoor cameras points to our yard. She may have something—if you can get her to let you access it."

I stifle a gasp. I *love* Mrs. Connoway and her brilliant use of technology that is guaranteed to work in my favor.

"This is perfect." Pure elation zips through me. "Thank you. I owe you."

He smirks as he takes me in. "You know, *I'm* single, unlike Duncan—"

"Don't," I say, halting that thought in its tracks. "You've ruined it."

He shrugs, but I can still feel him staring at me.

"*What?*" I hiss.

"Nothing. It's just"—he points down—"you have a bit of banana peel on your shoe."

As promised, Mr. Soto releases us at the end of the half hour. I'm ready to go home and sleep off this god-awful day, but as I'm walking toward the front exit, Lenora steps out of the counselor's office.

I freeze. She folds her arms tight across her uniform blouse. Her eyes are puffy and red, and I realize she's been crying. My heart breaks for her. She doesn't deserve Duncan's lies.

"What?" she says, looking at me with a vacant stare. "Come to rub it in?"

"No, of course not. I just finished detention," I say.

She wipes a smudge of mascara from under her eye. "I hope it was miserable."

"Zero out of ten stars," I joke, but she doesn't smile.

Lenora is like one of those fuzzy baby penguins you want to scoop up and put in your pocket before they accidentally wander into shark-infested waters. I understand why the entire school has her sympathy. Hurting Lenora is equal to kicking a puppy. I hate that neither of us knows the truth.

"I know you have no reason to believe me, but that wasn't me in that video. I swear," I say calmly, repeating the truth for the billionth time today. "I would never—"

"Just stop. Stop denying it," she says, cutting me off. "I *know* you."

I feel the impact of that sting land like shrapnel to the heart. "Duncan is lying."

That might have been the wrong thing to say. Anger ignites in her eyes. "C'mon, Brynn. Really?" She takes a step toward me. "It doesn't matter. You tried to take away someone I love, so it's only fair if I return the favor, *flirt expert*."

And there it is.

Lenora knows about my side hustle. We were friends when I first started it. I keep client confidentiality, but my classmates are free to tell others. Some do, but some don't want to admit they've paid someone for advice. As long as I'm sought after, the cash keeps flowing. And it keeps flowing because my name gets around.

She narrows her eyes. "Is your client list running dry?"

A surge of panic flares through me. How does she know my current clients ghosted me? This isn't good—for many reasons. I mean, I care about the relationships I'm fostering. I'm invested. It doesn't work if it's only about the money.

"Len, I—"

"It's too bad you dumped Otto first," she interrupts. "It would have been nice to see you heartbroken for a change, but I can tell this hurts worse. The more I talk about that night, the more people don't want to be associated with you or your shitty advice."

It's a calculated blow, but I'm the one who lost her trust sophomore year. Now she's set on getting people to lose their trust in me.

I have to change her mind. Yes, partially for the sake of my reputation, but also because Duncan's lying to her. Lenora doesn't deserve that. We might not be friends, but it doesn't mean I'm going to sit back and watch Duncan's toxicity directly affect her.

Besides, this is what spots the bills—including the new hot water heater we desperately need. If nobody wants to work with me because they side with Lenora, my mom and I are going to be in big trouble the next time we need an emergency fund. Not if, but *when*.

I cannot let Lenora put the nail in the coffin of what was formerly my side hustle.

"If I can prove it wasn't me that night with Duncan, can we put this to rest?"

Her gaze hardens. "Duncan's *always* been honest with me."

I remember Keith's tip about Mrs. Connoway's surveillance cam. "And if I can get evidence that shows he hasn't been honest?"

"Fine," she relents. "Prove it, if you're so sure you can."

She begins to walk away, but I call after her. "Where were you?"

Lenora turns, confused by my question.

"I mean at Keith's house. You and Duncan were together, so how did he end up upstairs without you?"

I can't wrap my head around it. She must have noticed he'd left her side some point in the evening. Did she go looking for him?

Tears begin to prick behind her eyes. "Well, I certainly wasn't up there with him, was I?"

I try and backtrack. "I just think if we work together—"

But she ignores me, spinning on her heel and escaping toward the front exit. Conversation over.

I watch her go, noticing the slouch of sadness in her shoulders. Lenora doesn't believe me. I knew there was a chance it could play out this way, but the reality of it chips at my self-esteem. Because a tiny part of me wanted her to be on my side, like old times. It's clear those days are long over.

Even though I know the truth, I'm still unsure of one thing.

I don't know how I'm going to come back from this.

5

"She's pathetic."

"She thought she could come between Lenora and Duncan? Please."

"Brynn Whitaker has to be the most desperate person at Greenlough."

When we were fourteen, Lenora and her parents took me to Disneyland for my birthday. Lenora had saved her allowance for three months so she could pay for me since I couldn't afford expensive outings. It was my first time, and she made sure we ate churros and rode Space Mountain and stayed for the fireworks. Nobody had ever planned a present that far in advance for me, but she acted like it was no big deal.

"We're lifers," she'd told me. "Sorry, but you're stuck with me."

When her birthday rolled around that year, I made her a cake. Homemade. It was her favorite dark chocolate cherry, and it took me four hours because I did everything from scratch. I thought it was nothing compared to the Disney trip she'd bestowed me, but she squealed and took a dozen photos of it and posted the best ones online. She's good at that. Making you feel loved.

It's a strange feeling being cancelled by your ex–best friend. It's not a sharp, cutting type of hurt but a dull, thudding ache. One that lingers.

I know Lenora. She's not the type to let cheating go. Duncan's broken her trust, and she's taking it out on me. Deep down, I know she's not this spiteful person. She's hurt, and she found a way to hurt me back.

Over the last twenty-four hours, I've lost every single one of my clients, my only dependable source of emergency income, and, apparently, my dignity.

It's clear my classmates chose a side. I can't say I blame them. Nobody wants to side with a homewrecker, even if I didn't do the wrecking part. And nothing was wrecked. Lenora and Duncan *are* still together, after all.

That thought leaves a bad taste in my mouth.

I spent all evening texting Tahlia and Marlowe about my conversation with Lenora, and we continue to nitpick the details at lunch the next day.

"She really believes *him*?" Tahlia presses.

The three of us are sitting at the Spindelli bush. I've already stress-devoured a pack of Oreos. Tahlia's abandoned her pen on top of her AP Government notes, and Marlowe's fiddling with the lid to her reusable water bottle.

My eyes tick to a group of juniors who are closely watching me from one of the picnic tables. "Along with everyone else."

At least Miss Rothman put a stop to the banana peel tomfoolery. Unfortunately, my classmates have decided I need to be held accountable for my apparent actions, which is why they've cursed me into irrelevance.

I've lost almost all of my Instagram followers—which, let's be real, doesn't really matter—but it's further proof that my classmates don't want to be associated with me. They're giddy over my downfall. To them, it's what I deserve.

It stings more than I want to admit. Building my network of students who sought my advice meant I was approachable. Now I am the complete opposite of that. I'm practically exiled.

"People will move on from it," Tahlia says. "It'll stop feeling as big."

"So Brynn has to be the victim of a crime someone else committed? That's not fair either." Marlowe scratches her head. She's wearing two velvet hair clips on either side of her part, and they bobble at the motion.

"Exactly," I say. "Which is why I have a plan."

"Ooh." Marlowe clasps her hands together. "A *plan*. Do tell."

I reveal the tip Keith gave me about Mrs. Connoway in detention yesterday. "All we have to do is go over after school. You both will distract her while I find that footage. Then *bam!* I'm off the hook, Lenora can admit I'm right, and justice will be restored."

"Nice." Marlowe grins. "We're like the Powerpuff Girls if they fought sexism *and* crime."

"You know, I've been thinking." Tahlia lowers her voice. "Who would send McTiernan a photo of you sneaking a drink at a school dance?"

"Lenora," Marlowe offers.

"No," Tahlia says thoughtfully. "The scandal with Duncan hadn't happened yet, and Brynn hadn't broken up with Otto by that point, so it couldn't have been him."

Tahlia's right. Lenora and Otto didn't have any vengeful motives at the dance. So who had I pissed off enough to target me?

Sure, I have a whole list of exes I could comb through, but most of them graduated last year. (I tended to go for guys in the grade above me.) Besides, none of those relationships ended in a terrible CW Network–worthy, I'll-get-my-revenge-on-you demise. I have a habit of ending things before real feelings get involved.

Except for the time I didn't.

Last year, Hayes Davies and I were together for four months. My longest relationship. I was a junior when he was a senior, and I stupidly started falling for him. He was funny, but not at other people's expense, and he never once made me feel like I was too much. Unlike Otto, Hayes and I clicked, but the long-distance conversation was unavoidable. He wanted to start college in San Francisco unattached, and I pretended I wanted the same thing for my senior year, resulting in a no-hard-feelings breakup.

Only, my feelings weren't spared. Because I'd let him into my heart more than I'd meant to.

"Hey."

I put Hayes out of my mind as I look over my shoulder. Cadence stands there apprehensively, like she's unsure she should be here.

"Hey!" I say, my voice a friendly falsetto. "You guys know Cadence."

"Yeah, of course. Come join," Marlowe says, not missing a beat. She's consistently warm and welcoming, never one to exclude someone. "We're talking about the scandal that has befallen upon our dear friend."

"And I have Hot Cheetos," Tahlia adds, as if the two are related. I guess they are, if I think about it. Both make me sweat.

Cadence relaxes. "Thanks—um. I was just about to go grab a sandwich."

"I'll come," I say, standing up. Oreos aren't real sustenance, and Greenlough's two-dollar PB&Js have been my savior when I'm too busy (or too lazy) to pack lunch.

We head straight for the lunch line once we're inside.

"So," she says. "You might find this difficult to believe, but I know a thing or two about scandals."

I crack a reluctant smile. "I'm honored you've chosen to hang out with the most unpopular person at school."

She waves me off. "Don't think you've dethroned me."

"I can't believe this is happening," I admit. "It's like, Lenora is rightfully upset. But it's directed at the wrong person."

Cadence rests a hand on the small bump of her stomach. "Guys are great at getting themselves into messes and forgoing claiming any responsibility, huh?"

I nod, knowing very well Thomas doesn't acknowledge Cadence at school, ever. But she gives me a hard look, like she doesn't want me to broach the subject. So I don't.

Her eyes focus on something behind me. "You've got to be kidding."

I spin around to see what's grabbed her attention. It's hard to miss. The Holy Crew has set up a folding table to the side of the lunch lines. They've taped a large handmade sign on the front, viewable to everyone in the cafeteria.

ABSTINENCE ANGELS: A CRUSADE TO SAVE SINNERS.

"Welp. Too late for me," Cadence jokes.

My heart pounds. "What are they doing?"

Cadence appears disinterested. "Who the fuck knows?"

But *I'm* interested. I walk over there before my brain can tell my body otherwise.

Cadence ditches the line and catches up to me. Faith looks pleased to see us. Katie Delcavo does not.

Middle school seems like a lifetime ago, and it's hard to believe Katie and I were close back then. She's this mousy short girl who doesn't seem to mind being bossed around by Faith. The other Holy Crew member, Elisha Stansky, stands beside her. They're both in choir together, and I've overheard Elisha win arguments over who'll sing solo at their church's Sunday service.

There's a neat stack of baby pink pamphlets in front of them. ABSTINENCE ANGELS, the top one reads, FORGETTING FORNICATION AND FOCUSING ON A FLOURISHING FUTURE.

This cannot be good.

"What is all this?" I gesture to the pamphlets.

"McTiernan approved a new club I was inspired to start." Faith gives Cadence a bright smile. "You know, it's not too late for you. If you ask for the Lord's forgiveness, He can restore the virginity of your heart."

Cadence coughs abruptly, and I assume it's to cover an enormous snort. I don't respond. Instead, I pick up a pamphlet and aggressively flip through it. SEXUAL LIBERATION IS A DISTRACTION FROM YOUR PATH TO SUCCESS, I read. SAVE YOURSELF FOR LOVE TO EXPERIENCE THE TRUE MEANING OF BEING FULFILLED. There's also a ton of fearmongering facts about STIs and pregnancy.

I glance at Katie. This is coming from the girl who used to write explicit, extra-thirsty 5 Seconds of Summer fanfiction. Huh. You think you know someone.

I raise my eyebrows. "You wrote this?"

Katie shrugs coolly. "It was a group effort."

I slam the pamphlet on the table, irked. "I'm curious. What exactly inspired you to start this club?"

Faith eyes me suspiciously. "Well, for one, we don't want any more *incidents* here at Greenlough. It's not great for the school's reputation . . . or yours."

She looks from me to Cadence, and my blood begins to boil.

"It wasn't me—" I start to say.

"Oh, quit denying it, Brynn. Everyone knows you're the one in that video," Faith snaps. "The sad thing is? You don't even seem sorry about it, which is why you need this club the most. To set you on the right path."

"There isn't one *right* path," I fire back, wondering why I'm even bothering.

"And you should shut up about things you don't know anything about," Cadence adds.

"I know plenty," Faith says, cutting her eyes over to me. "Jumping from guy to guy isn't a cute look. Maybe ask yourself why you do it. The spirit of the Lord can fill that empty void in you." She pushes two pamphlets toward us. "Think about it. You can set a good example for your unborn child."

Cadence takes a step forward, rage flickering in her eyes. "Are you ser—"

But before she can act impulsively, I knock the entire stack of pamphlets off the table.

Katie jumps back, startled, but I don't care. I'm *livid*. They're going to stand there and act like they know us when all they're doing is piling on the judgment.

As I begin to retreat, pamphlets flutter around my ankles. Cadence follows my lead, throwing up a middle finger before returning to my side.

"I'm not giving up on you," Faith calls. "And neither will God!"

I let out an aggravated breath. This is the last thing I needed today. Or ever.

"Wow. Harassed by the holy spirit," Cadence tries to joke as we rejoin the group.

Tahlia's forehead creases with concern. "What's wrong?"

"Faith started an abstinence club and tried to recruit us," I say, fuming. "And she said *I* inspired it."

"Sounds like something she'd do," Marlowe says, offering me her bag of Fritos. I take a few and crunch them between my teeth, seething.

"I'm going to grab that sandwich," Cadence says, and I feel bad we completely jumped out of line only to be steamrolled by Faith. "I'll catch up with you."

"Are you okay?" I ask, but she waves me off.

"I'm fine." And to be fair, she doesn't look fazed anymore. "The shaming isn't super new to me."

"I'm sorry," I say anyway.

"Don't be. Honestly? You probably saved me from detention." The corners of her mouth tick upward into a partial smile. "I'll be back."

When she leaves, Tahlia turns to me. "Were they really trying to get you both to join?"

"She said something about *restoring our heart's virginity*," I say, exhausted. "I'm so sick of this. I'm not against religion or against Faith, but I am against using religion as a shaming tool."

Tahlia picks at the crust of her pizza. "How is she even allowed to do that?"

"What, start a group?" Marlowe asks. "Anyone can. You just need a teacher who agrees to sponsor it, so basically they're responsible for what you do."

Ugh, figures Faith would find a way to use the school faculty against me. I aggressively pick at the blades of grass beneath my palms.

"Hey, don't take this out on Mother Earth," Marlowe says, offering me her turkey club. I gratefully devour a bite.

"After school," I say, swallowing. "Mrs. Connoway's house. We commence Operation: Get Footage."

Tahlia and Marlowe tell me they're in, and a sense of determination thrums through my veins. I'm done carrying this burden. It's time to finally prove to everyone that I'm not a liar.

But the bigger question remains. If I'm not the one who's lying, then who *is*?

6

"Brynn's denying the whole thing."

"Like it could be anyone else."

"Honestly. Girl's cancelled."

Tahlia and Marlowe stand beside me as we take in Mrs. Connoway's modest one-story house. This is it. My one shot at dismantling people's false accusations that are making my life as pleasant as Satan's butthole. Inside this humble home lies the proof I need to absolutely pulverize Duncan's pathetic lies.

Today he's going *down*.

I confidently stride toward the doorbell.

"Wait!" Tahlia says. "I thought you had a plan?"

"I do." I tick off the two steps on my fingers. "You distract, I search."

Marlowe smirks. "Sounds incredibly thought out."

"I'm sorry," I begin. "Did you expect me to *Ocean's 11* this during Pre-Calc?"

Tahlia looks nervous. "Do you even know what you're searching for?"

"A high-tech security office and CIA-level surveillance cams." I cut the jokes when the fear in her eyes grows. "Once I find her security system, I'll figure out where the footage is hosted. It'll be fine. Trust me."

And before she can protest again, I ring the doorbell.

There are a few seconds of silence. This will all be very anticlimactic if Mrs. Connoway isn't home. I'm mulling over different possible excuses when I hear the latch click.

My heart skitters. Here goes everything.

But when the door opens, it's not Mrs. Connoway who stands before me. It's Charlie Frazenberg, Cadence's twin brother.

He has the same deep hazel eyes as Cadence, the same smooth olive skin and thick dark hair. I don't know Charlie that well, but I do know he runs with the alternative-indie crowd. He's in AP Art and enters statewide competitions every year. I think he placed last year, but I can't remember what medium he chose or what the piece was called. He also works at Sticks and Scones, one of my favorite bakeries when I want to study.

What's unclear is why he's at Mrs. Connoway's house.

A look of curious recognition flashes through his eyes. "Oh, hey, Brynn," he says, then glances over his shoulder. "Is she expecting you?"

"Yes, she is." I think quickly. "We are the—um. *The dusting brigade!*"

Behind me, Tahlia lets out a strangled noise, no doubt an unintentional reaction to my abysmal excuse. Marlowe elbows her in the ribs.

Charlie leans in the doorway, taking in the three of us. "The *dusting* brigade," he repeats, sounding both dubious and amused.

"Yup," I say with confidence. "Earning those volunteer hours we need to graduate by dusting the homes of the elderly. Don't want them falling off a chair and breaking their hip whilst trying to clean their fan blades."

I cringe. I'm a nervous liar, made clear by the fact that I've used the word *whilst* as though I'm a British time traveler from the 1800s.

"Okay, sure," Charlie says slowly, holding the door open wider.

Relief washes through me. We're *in.*

The three of us step into the entryway. It's a charming, cozy home containing well-loved furniture from the late '80s with beige walls that appear to be freshly painted. Photographs of Mrs. Connoway's grandkids line the hallway, each in a different eclectic frame.

"She's taking a nap with Juni," Charlie explains.

"Juni?" I blurt before thinking.

Charlie looks at me oddly. "Her dog."

"Oh, right! Good ole Juni," I recover. "My favorite little guy."

"She's a Saint Bernard."

I stare at him, keeping my expression neutral. *I said what I said.*

"That's why I'm here," Charlie continues, as though my behavior is incredibly normal and not at all weird. "I walk Juni every other day for her. I was on my way out, but"—there's a mischievous glint in his eye—"I think I'd like to join the dusting brigade."

"You don't want that," Marlowe says hastily. "It's real messy business."

"And we don't have extra allergy pills," Tahlia announces with a nervous edge to her voice.

I look between them, then nod at Charlie like, *Yup, this is all true information.*

"I'll be fine," Charlie says, clearly amused now. "Could use some of those extra volunteer hours, right?"

"Right," I say, then exclaim, "Maybe you can go dust her car!"

Marlowe doesn't miss a beat. "It's fire season, after all."

I attempt to nudge him toward the first door I see.

"That's the bathroom," Charlie says, then opens another door at the end of the hall. "*This* is the garage."

"Well, you better get to work," I chirp.

"Wait, where's your cleaning stuff—?"

"*Thanks for your help!*" I shout over him, then shut the door.

Marlowe whirls on me, exasperated. "The *dusting brigade*?"

"I panicked," I say, glancing between them. "Look, it doesn't take long to dust a car. We've got to get moving."

"Let's split up," Tahlia suggests. "Cover more ground."

So we do. Tahlia takes the kitchen, Marlowe scours the living room, and I find myself in a very disorganized home office.

I flip on a light to find an enormous office desk stacked with all kinds of paperwork, boxes, cables, and scattered pens and pencils. I spot Mrs. Connoway's Wi-Fi router shoved into the corner. Elation courses through me. Maybe her camera system is nearby.

I begin searching for a piece of technology that could possibly home surveillance footage when I hear the door squeak behind me.

"Nothing yet," I say as I search under piles of paperwork. "But I have a feeling it's somewhere in here."

"Interesting strategy. Would've thought you'd start with the blinds."

I whip around so fast that I nearly bump my head on the shelf next to me. Charlie stands in the doorframe, a wet cloth in his hands.

He cocks his head. "Want to tell me why you're really here?"

I blink. "Did you actually dust her car?"

Charlie ignores this, setting his rag down on the desk.

I clear my throat. "It's Mrs. Connoway's birthday—"

"Wrong."

"Oh, so you know her birthday?"

"I do. Mrs. Connoway is a good friend of my mom's," Charlie reveals.

Well. I didn't see that coming.

I attempt to rearrange my features to mask my surprise. "I . . . did not know that," I say slowly.

He grins. "I know."

"Okay, *fine*," I relent. "I made it up."

"Yeah, that much I figured," he says, leaning casually against the doorframe.

He doesn't seem upset by my scheming. In fact, he's looking at me as though he finds this very entertaining.

I trust Cadence. Maybe I can trust him too.

"I need access to her security cameras," I explain in a rush. "One of her cameras faces Keith Whittle's front yard, and I really need to see the footage from Halloween."

I wince, waiting for him to kick us out. But shockingly, Charlie's expression goes soft.

"I can help."

A wave of relief crashes through me. "Thank you."

He begins digging through her filing cabinet, and I appreciate he doesn't ask what I'm looking for. A second later, he pulls out a MacBook.

"It's on here," he tells me.

Because Mrs. Connoway's laptop isn't password protected, he's able to easily access her desktop. He clicks on a program called Home Guard, and a live feed opens. There are multiple outdoor camera angles that point away from her house. Charlie then navigates to the archives, clicking on a folder labeled October thirty-first.

"Start around ten p.m.," I say, and he does.

At 2x speed, Charlie and I watch the grainy black-and-white footage of students arriving to Keith Whittle's after-party. Near the 10:40 p.m. mark, Otto and I walk in together, my banana costume bulky and bold even from this angle.

Charlie sits patiently beside me. He doesn't ask questions, and I'm grateful I don't have to explain.

We pass the eleven p.m. mark. Midnight. By one a.m., nobody is coming or going. The party has officially ended.

And no one aside from me was wearing a banana costume.

Hot embarrassment rises up my neck and into my cheeks. Charlie has seen proof with his own eyes. There's no logical explanation for me to redeem myself. I have no idea what to say.

Suddenly, a voice sounds from the living room. "Oh, that's just *lovely*."

Charlie and I shoot to our feet at the same time. He slams the laptop shut and places it in the filing cabinet. Then he puts a gentle hand on the small of my back and guides me toward the hallway.

"Are you marching me down to the station?" I whisper-yell.

"What? No." Charlie glances down at me. "Why are you talking like you're starring in a crime drama?"

"I'm weird when I'm nervous!"

"Well, don't be. I'm basically your accomplice." He lowers his voice as we step into the living room. "I don't intend to rat you out."

We find my friends standing beside Mrs. Connoway, who looks positively charmed.

"Charlie." She beams. "Why didn't you say these nice young ladies were coming over for volunteer cleaning hours?"

A rush of relief dances down my spine. I notice that Marlowe and Tahlia have taken off their uniform cardigans to use as makeshift dusting rags. I press my lips together to hold back a laugh.

Charlie catches my eye, a playful sort of interest in his gaze. "I . . . wanted it to be a surprise."

A charged thrill rushes through me as my nervous heart rate starts to regulate. He corroborated our story. He didn't have to, but he did.

"Well, it's *certainly* made my day," Mrs. Connoway says.

"Mm-hmm," Charlie replies, plopping his wet rag into my hands with a delighted smile. "Mine too."

7

"I can't believe she hasn't admitted it already."

"Right? We all know she's lying."

"It's embarrassing."

We spend a good hour dusting Mrs. Connoway's home for real, including her fan blades—which had quite possibly been collecting dust since iPods were invented—and afterward I buy my friends In-N-Out with the last of my flirt coaching earnings as a thank-you.

They're as stumped as I am when I report no one else entered Keith's house wearing a banana costume.

"Well, we can assume one thing," Tahlia says. "Someone at that party knows something."

We create a list of students who were at Keith Whittle's house that night, then divide it up by class periods we have with them. It gives me back a little control. If we can create a timeline based around the witnesses, there's a chance it'll prove I was never upstairs with Duncan.

For the rest of the week, we mine our peers for information. Most people recall seeing Lenora with Duncan, but nobody remembers anyone aside from me in a banana costume. They also don't recall seeing Duncan with anyone else.

It doesn't make sense. How did they get away with it? And, the better question, will they fess up?

"They don't have a reason to confess," Cadence says at lunch on Thursday. "Not when they've avoided the blame."

"And Duncan won't change his story," Marlowe adds.

"Which means we have to rely on trying to prove you *weren't* there," Tahlia says.

Unlike the surveillance footage from Mrs. Connoway's, there wasn't a timestamp on the Snapchat video. This means there's no strong evidence for my timely exit. Plus, no one wants to vouch for me seeing as my reputation is as welcoming as Death Valley at the height of summer.

I wonder if it's going to be like this until I graduate. That thought makes my stomach twist uncomfortably. I've worked hard to be likable. To fit in and exude confidence. It doesn't come naturally for me like it does for Lenora, who's full of poise and grace. How much longer am I supposed to endure this kind of emotional warfare?

I must look discouraged because Cadence gives me a rare half smile.

"Don't worry," she tells me. "We'll think of something."

———————————

It's Friday night, and I have a feel-good-yet-slightly-cheesy rom-com playing in the background while I complete my Pre-Calc homework. It may not sound like the coolest way to spend an evening, but it's not like anyone has reason to invite me to a party ever again.

My mom is lounging on the couch, commenting on the dullness of the love interest's problems while sipping on a glass of wine when there's a sudden knock at the door, jolting us both.

She looks over at me, brows knitted together.

"I'm not expecting anyone," I say, answering her unspoken question.

I rise from the couch and head to the door. When I open it, I'm stunned to see Cadence standing there.

"Uh, hi?" I say.

Cadence has slipped into our friend group as though we've been a quartet the entire time. Being shamed at lunch wasn't my idea of a good time, but after, it was almost like we made a silent pact to have each other's backs. So when she texted earlier to ask where I lived, the last thing I assumed was that she'd show up out of the blue.

Cadence is wearing black leggings and a matching black oversized hoodie. Her thick head of dark hair is yanked up into a messy bun. I notice her eye makeup looks incredible—purple-winged liner and a soft gold eyeshadow.

"Hey," she replies casually, as if I should have been expecting her. She then dangles a shiny set of keys in front of me. "Look."

I study them. "Are you planning on hypnotizing me?"

"Nope." She tosses them in the air, then expertly catches them in her palm. "These keys are not mine. They're Duncan's."

My mouth falls open in utter disbelief right as my mom hollers, "Who is it, hon?"

"A friend! One sec!"

I step outside with Cadence and shut the front door, giving us some privacy.

"Okay. Back up," I say. "*Why* do you have Duncan's keys?"

"Greenlough is in the middle of a game right now, so I went into the locker room, broke into Duncan's locker, and stole them."

She says this casually, as if revealing something as mundane as the weather forecast. Surely this is a joke. But from her stony stare, I can see that it's not.

"Wait—*what*?" I sputter. "Why?"

"Because we're going to break in and look for clues." She raises her eyebrows, completely serious. "Tell your mom you'll be back in an hour."

Before I can say anything else, she begins walking to her car.

I glance down at my retro '70s-print leggings and ratty forest green sweatshirt. This might be our only chance to look for evidence. I can't let it go to waste. Not after the trouble she's gone through to get those keys.

On the other hand, it's a huge risk. I'm supposed to be staying out of trouble, not getting into it.

But I can't let her do this alone.

I head back inside, sliding into the sneakers that I left in the hall. Then, I peek into the living room.

"I have to start on a group project with a friend. She's, uh, going out of town tomorrow," I lie. "But I'll be back in an hour or so."

My mom looks at me, her glasses slipping down her nose. "What friend?"

"Cadence," I say. "We had History together last year."

Something happens onscreen that grabs her attention. "Just text me if you're going to be later than an hour, okay?"

"Will do," I call, already halfway to the door.

When I approach Cadence's silver Lexus, I'm surprised to see that she isn't in the driver's seat. She's sitting shotgun next to Charlie, who grins at me through the window he's rolled down.

His deep hazel eyes hold mine. "We've got to stop meeting like this."

I aim a finger at Cadence. "Believe it or not, this wasn't my idea."

"Oh, I'm aware," Charlie says.

I hop in the back seat. Once Cadence pulls her door shut, he shifts the car into drive.

"Okay," Cadence says, swiveling around to face me. "I thought about it. Maybe Halloween wasn't a one-time thing. If Duncan is cheating on Lenora, where would he do it?"

"Well, certainly not atop a bed of roses at the Ritz-Carlton."

She smirks. "Right—he'd use his car for privacy."

"Sounds logical," I say. After all, it's what Otto and I did.

"So if there's evidence anywhere, it *must* be in his car," Cadence continues. "Which is why we'll break in while everyone's at the game."

A sense of dread pangs through my nervous system. "I'm on thin ice with McTiernan," I admit, remembering the warning I'd received. "My scholarship and letter of recommendation are on the line."

"Then you'll stay in the car with Charlie and be my lookout." She pats her brother on the shoulder. "All you have to do is be our getaway driver."

"Is that all?" he replies dryly.

"It's risky," I tell Cadence, even though the offer is tempting. "And probably illegal?"

"Definitely illegal," Charlie chimes in, then glances at me. "Though that's what makes it all the more appealing for her."

"Whatever, it's only a crime if you get caught. And I already took the keys." She looks at me pointedly. "Don't tell me this was for nothing."

I won't lie. Part of me is itching to prove to everyone that Duncan is withholding the real story, especially after this horrendous week. What if this changes everything?

"Are you sure about this?" I ask.

She holds up his keys and gives me a look that says *Obviously.*

"Okay," I relent, newfound determination thrumming in my veins. "Let's incriminate this asshole."

Cadence leans back in her seat. "That's the spirit!"

I hear the crowd cheering as we pull up to the stadium, a sign the game is still ongoing. Floodlights shine over the field, leaving the nearly full parking lot in the shadows.

"What kind of car are we looking for?" Charlie asks, slowing down to a crawl.

"A black Wrangler," I say, squinting at the rows of cars. "With a fake dangling ball sack on the hitch."

Cadence snorts. "Nothing says *romance* quite like giant plastic balls."

It takes about five minutes of us circling the lot before I spot it. "There!"

Charlie slams the brakes, jolting the three of us forward. He apologizes profusely as he backs into a parking space across the way. As soon as the car is in park, Cadence hops out, pulls her hood over her head, and slams the door.

My heart jackhammers in my chest as we watch her approach Duncan's vehicle. I should feel vindicated right now, but a tug of sadness pulses through me. Not because of Duncan. Because of Lenora. She doesn't deserve someone who treats her like that.

"You okay?" Charlie asks.

I glance at him. Like Cadence, he's also in all black, dressed in ripped jeans and a long-sleeved shirt. A few thin gold chains hang around his neck. I once heard Katie Delcavo whisper that he should nix the jewelry before he starts looking like his sister. A dated stance on gender normativity for sure, but unsurprising coming from her.

I like his style, though. It feels intentional and artsy.

"I'm—fine," I lie.

Charlie isn't convinced. "I can go get her. Call it off."

"It's okay." I swallow, scanning the empty parking lot for unwelcome company. "She probably wouldn't let you."

"True. She doesn't back down easily, and she's not afraid of confrontation." His dark hair hangs just below his earlobes, and he pushes a longer strand out of his face. "I think she absorbed all the courage in the womb."

I give him a sidelong glance. "I doubt that."

I lean over and rest my elbows on the middle console, getting a better look out the front window. Charlie's eyes linger on me as I do this, but I'm focused on Cadence, who has now slipped into the driver's seat.

My heart pounds urgently in my chest as the minutes tick by. The last thing I want is for her to get caught, but if she finds something, there's a chance it'll prove I wasn't involved.

After another minute of silence, Charlie says, "So. Care to explain the origins of the dusting brigade while we have time to kill?"

"It's a timeless Greenlough tradition dating back to the days of yore," I offer as I continue to keep watch.

"Ah, my favorite days, personally," Charlie comments, not missing a beat. "Easily followed by the early days of yesteryear."

I flick my gaze to his, finding a hint of playfulness in his eyes. "I'm not sorry I lied, if that's what you're wondering," I say, slightly defensive. "And if I recall, *you're* the one who said you needed volunteer hours."

"And yet there you were. With ulterior motives."

"Yeah, well"—I keep my focus on the dimly lit lot—"you didn't exactly ask for an explanation. You probably think it was me, like everyone else."

From my peripheral, I feel Charlie's attention on me. "Why would I think that?"

"You saw the footage. I was the only one dressed in a banana costume."

"I saw," he says slowly, "an extremely bad liar—with excellent taste in Halloween attire, by the way—attempting to figure out why Duncan isn't telling the truth." He pauses. "If you were guilty, you wouldn't have been looking for answers at Mrs. Connoway's house in the first place."

But I remain wary. "And before that?"

Charlie shrugs. "I don't bother with rumors."

"*Bother with rumors.* Okay," I say, my voice clipped. "That's a cop-out. Rumors make it easy for people to form their own opinions about a situation they know nothing about."

"Sure," Charlie agrees. "But there's been tons of rumors about Cadence, and if I let myself get involved in any of them, I'd probably spend more time in detention and a lot less time helping my small, sarcastic classmate."

I can tell he's trying to keep the mood light, but his leave-me-out-of-it stance doesn't sit well with me. I can stand up for myself—and it's clear Cadence can too—but the mental load is easier when you have people on your side who can come to your defense. Besides, Charlie didn't outright say he *didn't* think it was me.

"That's a load of—" I freeze mid-thought as my eyes track movement. "What's she doing?"

Cadence has exited Duncan's front seat, but now she's facing the back of his Wrangler. For a horrible second, I think she's going to break his back window, but she doesn't. She leans in close, writing something on it in large, blocky letters.

"Where did she get window markers?" Charlie mumbles to himself.

I try and make out the words as she's writing them, but it's not until she's finished that I see what she's written.

I'M A CHEATING PRICK! HONK IF YOU AGREE.

A bubble of laughter bursts from my throat. It's not very original, but it gets the point across beautifully.

"Shit, get down!"

Charlie nearly elbows me in the face as I scramble to duck in the back seat. "What?"

"Faith and John Mark," he replies, sinking lower in his own seat. "*Shit.* She doesn't see them."

The next few seconds tick by slowly. Anxiety thrashes through me, turning my stomach in knots. Faith and John Mark will for sure narc if they spot her. Vandalism does *not* align with their morals and values.

I can't let Cadence get caught. She doesn't deserve to get expelled.

I'm convinced Charlie must have some kind of twin telepathy because a second later, he breathes out a sigh. "She's running back."

He unlocks the car and starts the engine. Cadence dives inside, slamming the door behind her.

"*Go!*" she screeches, yanking her seatbelt over her belly.

Charlie doesn't need to be told twice. He books it out of there.

"Do you think they saw you?" he asks.

"I could have been anyone. I had my hood on."

"Oh really? *Anyone?* Out of all our child-carrying peers?"

She nails him with the point of her elbow. "Hey, I'm not showing *that* much."

I sit up from the floor and buckle my seat belt just as Charlie exits the stadium. "What happened?"

"I nearly suffocated in mountains of sweaty sports gear," Cadence says. "But! I found *this*."

She holds up a clear tube of designer strawberry lip gloss, carefully wrapped with a delicate gold label that reads ALL NATURAL.

"Nice one, Sherlock," Charlie remarks, unimpressed. "What good'll that do?"

"Shut up." Her eyes light up as she turns to me. "It was under his passenger seat. As if it rolled out of someone's purse."

"Hold on," I say, hope blooming in my chest. "Lenora's allergic to strawberries. She strictly uses fragrance-free lip balm."

While it might not be *gotcha!* big, it is undeniably evidence. If we can narrow down strawberry lip gloss users who were at Keith's party, we'll be on our way to a slimmer pool of suspects.

Charlie clears his throat. "And the mild impromptu vandalism?"

"It's not vandalism if it washes off," she reasons. "Besides, that car paint was in his back seat. I couldn't *not* use it."

I can't suppress my grin. "Where'd you put his keys?"

"On the seat." She's smiling now too. "He'll have fun waiting for a locksmith."

"So petty," Charlie comments.

"But deserved," Cadence says.

"True," I agree. When I glance out the window, I realize this isn't the way back to my house. "Where are we going?"

Cadence leans back in her seat, fully relaxed. "To watch what happens next."

8

"She totally did that to Duncan's car. Who else would have?!"

"Why is Brynn such a raging bitch?"

"No wonder Lenora hates her."

I had no idea that the Frazenbergs' beautiful villa-style home was the same one that towered over the stadium. It's one of the largest houses in the gated neighborhood of Ridgecrest Estates. Even past the stadium, you have a sweeping view of the Pacific Ocean. It's breathtaking.

Before exiting Charlie's car, I text my mom that I'll be out a little longer than the hour I promised, to which she responds with a thumbs-up. I guess that she's still engrossed in her movie.

Charlie unlocks the front door, stepping aside to let us in. The inside of their home is as gorgeous as the outside. I take a moment to marvel in the entryway as I remove my shoes. There's a glimmering chandelier hanging over the main dining room table that looks like it can seat a gathering of no less than sixteen. In the adjacent living room, the statement piece is a gorgeous Persian rug with navy and red swirls and flowers. Not one but two sweeping staircases lead to the second floor. I can't imagine what the rest of the house looks like.

"Your home is—" I begin.

"Sterile," Cadence finishes.

I shake my head. "Not the first word that came to mind."

I follow Charlie and Cadence up one staircase and into Cadence's room. It's the size of a standard master bedroom and has an attached bathroom. A king-sized bed covered in purple bedding and an array of pillows sit between two floor-to-ceiling windows. A cream-colored velvet pouf is perched on the floor near her desk, and her entire ceiling is painted like a galaxy. Instead of a main overhanging light, the ceiling is littered with hundreds of tiny lights resembling stars.

I can't stop staring. "That is *so* cool."

Cadence follows my gaze. "Oh. Yeah. Charlie did that."

I look at Charlie. "You did?"

He glances down, suddenly very modest. "Um. Yeah. It's a giant canvas of fabric that I painted, then we poked holes so the lights look like stars."

I glance up again. "Impressive."

My eyes roam to the solid wood awning directly under one of her windows. It acts as an overhang for a shaded area in their backyard, but to an adventure seeker, it's a very large diving board.

"I've done it," Cadence says, as if reading my mind. "Our pool's deep enough. Twelve feet or something? Charlie's too chicken."

A light flush colors his cheeks. "Sorry I don't want to break my legs."

"*I* never did."

Charlie raises his eyebrows at me as if to say *See? Womb courage.*

Cadence opens the window and, with a few tricky clicks, pops out the screen. She gestures for us to crawl onto the overhang, so we do.

"My parents don't like me going out there." She rubs her stomach by way of explanation.

"When are you due?" I ask.

"April," she says, then averts her eyes.

I don't know if I've overstepped. I decide I won't ask any more questions about it tonight.

"Here," Cadence says, handing me bright blue binoculars that look like they're part of a children's toy set. "It'll get easier to see once people leave."

"You didn't have to do this."

She shrugs. Says, "May as well enjoy watching him struggle."

I feel an overwhelming sense of appreciation. I know if I try and hug her, I'll most likely end up being shoved in the pool. So instead, I peek into the binoculars and try and spot Duncan's Wrangler.

"I'm fucking starving," Cadence announces. "We need provisions. I'll be back."

A strained sort of silence hangs between Charlie and me once she leaves. He shifts slightly, keeping his gaze on the stadium. Our earlier conversation sits with me like a pebble in my shoe. It was a disappointing response, and even though I'm used to disappointment, I can't seem to let it go.

I lower the binoculars. "Hey, you're part of the problem, by the way," I say, looking at him. "When you said you're basically Switzerland when it comes to rumors."

Charlie appears both offended and confused. "What do you mean?"

My irritation bubbles over. "It's just—staying quiet? Not doing anything when people are talking shit? That's part of the reason dumbasses like Duncan and Thomas win." He opens his mouth as if to argue, but I continue. "You don't have to, like, *physically* fight Cadence's battles. She knows that. And I'm sure she doesn't want to see you in detention for it. But it doesn't hurt to set things straight if you happen to hear anyone running their mouth."

Charlie stares at me for a beat, as though processing this, then runs his hand through his hair. "You're right," he says. "I'm sorry, yeah. That doesn't make it easier for anyone."

Wow. I did not expect that. I've grown so accustomed to raising my walls that it feels nice to temporarily lower them.

He smooths a hand along the back of his neck. "I never got sent the video. I don't have Snapchat. But I thought it was a pretty violating thing to do to someone. To Duncan and whoever he was with—which I never thought was you, by the way. Cadence told me what was going on, and I believed her."

This is not what I anticipated him to say. I shouldn't be surprised, because Charlie isn't like Duncan or Thomas or Otto. But I also don't know him that well either.

"I shouldn't have assumed you thought it was me," I offer.

"I can understand why you would," he says. "I'm sorry you're going through this."

We hold each other's gaze. I can tell he means it. The edges of his lips lift into a smile, and it softens something that's hardened within me.

If only the rest of my classmates were like him.

I pull my knees to my chest. "You didn't have anything better to do tonight?"

"Nah." He studies his hands. Flecks of paint are stained between his right thumb and forefinger. "On Fridays I usually go to bed early because I wake up and surf with friends."

"That's right." I snap my fingers. "Carmen Muñoz told me that in eighth grade."

He looks surprised. "She did?"

"Yeah, I think she had a crush on you back then." I relish in the fact that I've made him blush. It's almost too easy. "She also knew your birthday and zodiac sign—"

"—which is not very hard to figure out when you know someone's date of birth," he says.

"Fair." I lean back into Cadence's room, taking another moment to absorb the galaxy ceiling. "It looks so . . . real."

"Thanks." He leans back on his elbows, matching my posture. "My room is chaotic compared to hers. More like a studio, I guess. One wall is a mural experiment. Anyway, it was cool to work with a color scheme in here."

"You placed in an art competition last year, didn't you?"

"I did, yeah," he says. "Ms. Gimbel submits our work to a few different district competitions. The one I won state for was one called 'Young Visionaries.' Right now, I'm working a few things for the Senior Showcase."

"Impressive," I say, and I mean it.

The Greenlough Senior Showcase is an annual fundraiser put on by the senior class to raise money for prom. Many seniors perform their talents, like dancing or singing or reciting poetry. The cafeteria is set up as a walk-through gallery, allowing science enthusiasts and artists to display what they've been working on. It's a mishmash of productions put on for our peers, and afterward the school throws a pizza party.

"Are you doing anything for the showcase?" he asks.

"Uh." I glance toward the lot. Vehicles have begun to depart, leaving behind empty parking spaces. "I doubt it. I'm more of a problem-solver than a performer."

"What do you mean?"

His tone is genuinely curious. His hazel eyes stay steady on mine, waiting for a response. It's not a throwaway question. He wants to know.

"Well, I guess I'm good at improving things," I begin. "Like, okay, I was using this SAT app, right? It quizzes you on vocabulary. But I noticed that the user activity could be improved if they created a sort of infinite quiz instead of segmenting it by words of ten then ending the quiz there." I glance over at him to see if he's still following. He's either doing a good job at pretending to listen, or he's invested. "Anyway, I wrote the company. They told me they were going to pitch the idea because they thought it was good."

He gets an excited gleam in his eyes. It sends a jolt of adrenaline through me. "That's really cool."

We're close. So close that I catch the subtle scent of his body wash, a mix of something like bamboo and sandalwood and a hint of turpentine. It's not overpowering. In fact, it's weirdly comforting.

I'm suddenly distracted by something on the wall. "Hey, that thing behind you is an intercom, right?"

Charlie climbs back into the room. "Yeah, here." He approaches the device, hitting a square button. "T1 to T2, bring up the baklava. Over."

I follow, taking up space next to him. He's a few inches taller than me, but with the way he's leaning against the wall, our eyes are level.

I raise a brow. "T1?"

"Oh. Twin 1, Twin 2. It's stupid—we used to call ourselves that when we were younger. I was born first."

I grin, gesturing to the button. Charlie nods, so I press it. "B1 thanks T2 for acquiring the goods."

Charlie adds, "T1 also requests LaCroix. Over."

"B1 wants to note how fabulous T2's eyeliner is tonight."

We're both suppressing laughs when Cadence's voice cuts through.

"You dorks. I'm coming up."

Then, a third voice. "Don't call your friends dorks, azizam."

"My mom," Charlie clarifies. "We have one in every main room."

"Wow, thank you for allowing me to live out my *Home Alone* fantasy."

"*Home Alone?*" he repeats.

"Yeah, it's in the fourth one, I think?"

One of his eyebrows quirks. "Who watches that many *Home Alone* movies? What is wrong with you?"

I give his arm a teasing shove. "How else were my brother and I going to learn how to set booby traps when my mom was working long hours?"

Charlie opens his mouth to ask a follow-up question, but that's when Cadence returns with an entire junk food charcuterie board: Doritos, jelly beans, Twizzlers, miniature powdered donuts, Gushers, and baklava.

We indulge for a few minutes before I pull the binoculars to my eyes and find Duncan's car in the now emptier lot. I can barely make him out, but it's clear he's struggling to get inside. We're too far away to hear if anyone's honking, but a few cars slow down to read what Cadence has written on the back window.

I narrate what's happening until I see the locksmith pull up. I don't even feel bad about it. This is a minor inconvenience for Duncan, who has made my entire life a major inconvenience for me.

Now I know something Duncan doesn't. The lip gloss is evidence that he's seen this girl—or others—on more than one occasion. Maybe they were even together before the game. I don't know, but I'm determined to figure it out.

I turn to Cadence. "You're not afraid of Faith telling Duncan?"

"Please. Faith Tobinson is a joke," she scoffs.

"I heard about her club the other day," Charlie says to me. "Are you okay?"

I decide to answer honestly. "No, not really. It's like . . . I think it's exposed an underlying issue, you know? I'm the one receiving the biggest amount of blowback even though Duncan is in the wrong. Why? Because, oh, duh, sexism. We can never win. Society's like, you're with too many guys? You're a ho. You're not getting with anyone? You're a prude."

"You're a teen mom? You gave it up too easily," Cadence adds.

"Right. You're abstinent until marriage? You're frigid. It's always something." I'm suddenly exhausted. "Faith thinks we should all behave one way, but it's not a one-size-fits-all situation. There's more than one way to feel empowered."

Cadence raises her can of ginger ale in my direction. "I'll drink to that."

Duncan finally regains access to his Wrangler. Even after he drives away, we continue sitting there, enjoying each other's company. Our conversation shifts to Thanksgiving plans, to Greenlough teachers, to what shows we're currently into, and by the time I notice Cadence has been unusually quiet, I realize it's because she's fallen asleep on her bed.

I prop myself up on my elbow, facing Charlie. "Thanks for tonight. Duncan and his friends are actual Neanderthals," I blurt before remembering that Thomas—the father of his twin sister's child—counts as one of Duncan's friends, and I should probably think before I speak.

"They are," he agrees before I can overthink it. "Thomas especially. If it weren't for our parents' involvement, I'm one-hundred-percent certain he would have fully ghosted Cadence and the baby. But instead he's forced to go to her appointments, which is almost worse." He stops. "I'm talking too much. Sorry."

"No, it's okay," I say earnestly. "You're not."

He lowers his voice. "I can't really talk to Cadence about it. She's sensitive. And when she feels vulnerable, she gets angry. Like having emotions is an inconvenience."

Well. That explains why we clicked so quickly.

But I like that Charlie's opening up, so I say, "Hence the verbal diarrhea."

The corner of his mouth quirks. "Yeah."

"I won't repeat anything," I promise. "Actually. Want to know a secret?"

His eyes light up, intrigued.

"When we were in second grade, we carpooled. Me and Thomas, I mean," I begin. "There was this one day where he was acting hyper and being goofy, and his mom told him to settle down. Instead, he let out this big, wet fart."

Shock crosses Charlie's features, but then his shoulders start shaking with laughter.

"Except it was, well, you know . . . more like a *shart*." I start laughing too. "So you can now have that memory instilled in your brain every time he acts like a giant asshat."

Charlie snort-laughs into his hands, and the sound nearly brings me to hysterical tears. When we can't properly control ourselves, we crawl back into Cadence's room as quietly as we can, replacing the screen, and then head downstairs.

"I really thought we'd wake her up," I say once we've both caught our breath.

"She's a heavy sleeper," he says, looking right at me. "Thanks for that."

I take a beat to notice Charlie's eyes again. It's an unusual color, like glistening pond water on a sunny day. I'm a little captivated.

"You know, it's nice to see her motivated by something again, even if it's borderline criminal," Charlie continues as he grabs his keys from the table in the foyer.

"So you're saying she's not your run-of-the-mill vigilante?"

"Not quite."

He holds open the front door for me, and I step outside.

As we walk down the driveway, he goes, "Since the pregnancy, she's kind of isolated herself. Her former friends don't talk to her. I worry, I guess." His expression shifts to fear. "Don't tell her I told you that. She *will* actually kill me in my sleep."

I laugh. "I don't doubt it. And I won't. I like Cadence."

"That's good." There's a vulnerable softness in his voice now. "She wouldn't have gone through this trouble if your friendship wasn't important to her."

We fall into a comfortable silence on the drive back to my place. It's nice. Peaceful. This might be the closest I've felt to ease all week.

Charlie blasts the Regrettes and I close my eyes, rolling down the window. The balmy, salt air fills my lungs. When I release a breath, I feel better. More relaxed. After tonight, I almost believe things will be okay.

Almost.

9

"Duncan's telling everyone she's jealous."

"I don't know, Brynn wasn't even at the game Friday."

"I heard it was the pregnant girl. Cadence."

We should have known this was coming.

An anonymous Instagram account has Photoshopped an image of Cadence's head on a woman's body as she gives birth to the spawn of Satan. It circulates via DMs over the weekend. Whoever's responsible knows what Cadence did to Duncan's Wrangler, and they *want* her to know that they know.

When we check in with Cadence in our group chat on Sunday, she responds with: nah it's stupid. I don't give a shit.

I want to blame Faith, but it's pretty crass for her style.

Marlowe texts me when she's outside my house Monday morning. I'm exhausted. I stayed up stressing about school, dwelling on the fact that everyone hates me, which meant I ended up going to bed around two in the morning. The cold water from the shower quelled any remaining sleepiness, but it'll be a miracle if I don't collapse by noon.

"Hey," Marlowe says, eyeing me carefully as I pull the car door closed.

I know she's trying to gauge how I am. I arrange my face so that I appear to be a functioning human person instead of a soulless flesh sack, which is how I feel. "How was San Diego?"

"Traffic was the worst. I had to have a million conversations about college." She rolls her eyes. "And I was subjected to the presence of the Scumhole."

Marlowe and her family spent the weekend in San Diego with her aunt for her birthday. While her extended family accepts her as trans, one uncle in particular doesn't. Uncle Rob, also known as the Scumhole. Because of this, Marlowe's mom and dad refuse to interact with him. He must have shown up uninvited.

"I'm sorry, Mar. That sucks."

"We didn't speak, so it could have been worse. My aunt Mary had to kick him out." Her gaze flits to me. "Anyway, what'd you get up to?"

I wonder how to break this gently, but then decide there is no delicate way of revealing the truth. "I hung out with Cadence while she broke into Duncan's car."

She whirls her head toward me, her mouth falling open.

"Red!" I scream, indicating the light in front of us.

Marlowe slams her brakes just in time. "That was *you*?"

"Not technically," I correct. "Wait—you heard? How?"

"Carmen Muñoz's Instagram story." She laughs. "Holy shit! I wish I could have seen the look on his face."

"I didn't exactly stick around for that part."

"Yeah, probably for the best."

"But listen," I say. "Cadence found something. Designer lip gloss that can't belong to Lenora—she's allergic to strawberry."

Marlowe gasps. "No *way*. This is huge. Have you told her?"

"Not yet." I don't tell her that it's unlikely I will, since my chances of her believing me are slimmer than a goldfish learning to drive. "Let's reconvene at Tahlia's after school. Form a plan."

Marlowe gives me a nod of solidarity as she pulls into the school's parking lot. Once she finds an open spot, we gather our book bags and hop out.

"Hey." She pulls her trendy rectangle-shaped sunglasses down the bridge of her nose, meeting my eyes. "Remember, *we* know who we are deep down, you know? Like, yeah, I'm hurt that there are people who will never accept me for me, but I have to brush off their bullshit—and it's not easy, trust. But if I marinate in their judgment, then I carry that hate with me. So fuck everyone at this school who thinks you're a skank, okay? We'll get through this."

I link my arm with hers, feeling grateful for her. I know Marlowe's weathered discrimination and judgment, but she always seems so fearless. The ones who'd rather inflict harm than get to know her are the ones missing out on a genuine friend. And I'm so glad she's mine.

I take a deep breath. "Thank you."

I can't avoid my classmates' stares as I follow Marlowe to our lockers, catching a few discernible glares in my direction. Not off to a great start. I guess I expected this.

And then I run into fucking Otto.

I've been trying to avoid him. We don't have any classes together this semester, and I've managed to evade his presence in the halls and at lunch. But now he's roughly six feet away, walking straight toward me.

And of course *Duncan* is beside him, loudly discussing something that happened during the game on Friday. I can't escape. I'm in a dead-end hallway with nowhere else to go.

It occurs to me that, after everything, I don't know if Otto believes Duncan. He must. Duncan's one of his best friends.

Otto flicks his gaze toward me, and it's as if everything plays out in slow motion. The slack in his jaw gives, and his lips part in genuine surprise. Duncan quickly spots the source of his distraction. His eyes narrow at me.

Marlowe gives my arm a reassuring squeeze.

"You know," Duncan sneers, "you're just making yourself look bad."

I straighten my posture, plastering an innocent expression on my face. "I don't know. I look pretty good today."

"I mean the whole thing with my *car*," Duncan says, hammering in the last word.

"Sorry, Duncan," I say as sweetly as possible. "I have no idea what you're talking about."

"Just stop, Brynn," Otto says, meeting my eyes for the first time. "Duncan's right. You're embarrassing yourself."

Irritation blazes through me. I never thought one massive lie from Duncan Rowe would villainize me this much, and I'm sick of it.

"Mmm." I pretend to think about it. "I would, except I'm not in the business of letting liars win."

I grab Marlowe's arm, tugging her beside me as I stomp around them. I cannot handle any more of their bullshit this early in the morning.

"What about the lip gloss?" Marlowe hisses. "We could have seen the stupid look on his face when he realized what you found!"

"I can't be impulsive," I say. "We need a strategy."

I don't need to give Duncan a reason to report me, especially since I'm supposed to be staying out of trouble. I can't give McTiernan a reason to retract his letter of recommendation, and I definitely do not want another detention. I'm not sure McTiernan will let it slide from my record again.

Before first period, Marlowe and I go to the front office to report the Satan meme. McTiernan's admin assistant tells us she'll pass along our concern. Apparently, a few other students have reported it too. She attempts to placate our rage by saying McTiernan's trying his best to stop it from spreading. When I ask if he's found the owner of the deactivated Snapchat account, she insists they're still looking into it. I doubt they're trying hard.

As much as I want to get through my day in peace, things take a turn during my third-period lit class. Mr. Manning tells us to open up our *Paradise Lost* text, then glances around the room.

"Let's pick up where we left off yesterday. End of book ten. Who can tell me anything that happened?" he asks.

"They finally ate the fruit," Tahlia replies from her assigned seat at the front. It's a shame we can't sit together, but once teachers get a feel for friendships, they insist on distancing for the sake of classroom disruption.

"*'Hast thou eaten of the Tree Whereof I gave thee charge thou shouldst not eat?'*" Mr. Manning bellows, quoting the text. "We've reached the climax of Milton's poem."

A few boys snicker at his use of the word. Mr. Manning ignores them. "It's getting interesting, folks!"

"I mean, it's interesting Milton loves painting women as the weaker sex," Tahlia scoffs.

This gets a few chuckles from the class.

"Interesting point, Miss Nassif," Mr. Manning says. "Care to elaborate? Perhaps someone else might want to jump in here?"

I shift in my seat. I'm normally the outspoken one. But right now, I want to be invisible. I've never experienced this feeling before, and it makes me mad. I shouldn't have to shrink down in front of my peers.

I sit up straighter, pushing through the fear. "Well, Satan *did* find Eve alone first. So . . . what if he had found Adam first? I mean, then the weight of what they've done wouldn't have been fully blamed on her—"

"No, they probably wouldn't have been banished from Paradise," John Mark interrupts.

I suppress the urge to roll my eyes. Only John Mark would raise an argument that men had better control over temptation.

"Interesting point," Mr. Manning says, waving a finger from me to John Mark. "You seem to be implying Adam *wouldn't* have been tempted by the fruit."

"Yeah. Tahlia just said women are the weaker sex."

"I said *Milton* implied that," Tahlia snaps bitterly.

"Adam would have eaten it if he was tempted first," I continue. "No one could have resisted the devil. That's the point of his existence. Besides, how many times have we seen men unable to resist temptation? Gatsby, Macbeth—"

"There wasn't any divine intervention with the Fall," Katie Delcavo pipes up. "It was a free act the moment they made a choice. Eve just made it first."

"Which is why Eve takes the brunt of the blame," Faith adds, looking haughtily at me. "She's the temptress that started it all. Nothing but a harlot."

There's some low *ooh*s from the class. I don't break eye contact with Faith. I want her to know I understand the underlying implication.

"Okay, well, Faith, that's not exactly the right use of that word, but good attempt. Temptation is a moment of weakness, but it doesn't mean you *are* weak," Mr. Manning says. "The roles could have been reversed, yes."

We spend the rest of class reading the next passage in the epic poem. I barely pay attention, skimming to earlier sections of the text. Mr. Manning has us annotate our books as part of our grade, and I've taken full advantage of writing all my thoughts in the margins. My eyes stop at a certain highlighted chunk I'd marked earlier in the year.

Whatever doing, what can we suffer more,
What can we suffer worse?

Duncan and Faith have made sure I *can* suffer worse, though to be fair, none of us can escape the hellhole of high school without some type of suffering.

———————————

Instead of eating lunch with my friends that afternoon, I am summoned to the guidance counselor's office.

I've been in Mrs. Burchill's office a handful of times. Seniors are required to meet with her once a semester to ensure they're on the right path with college applications. I already discussed Stanford with her back in September, so I have no idea why my presence is being requested.

"Brynn," she says when I open the door. "Have a seat."

Mrs. Burchill is one of the more laid-back faculty members. Younger than most of the instructors here, she's smart and witty and straightforward. She has bright auburn hair, multiple ear piercings, a tiny nose stud, and some kind of intricate tattoo on her forearm that she attempts to cover with bracelets per Greenlough's faculty code. Like her name, she embodies *chill*.

"Did Stanford change something about their application system?" I ask.

Her eyes find mine. "This isn't about Stanford."

She scoots a bag of chocolate-covered pretzels my way. I take one, popping it in my mouth as I wait for her to go on.

"I know the last week has been tough on you," she begins. "The dean filled me in. How are you doing?"

"Uh." I scramble for the right word. "Surviving, I guess."

"Mm-hmm." She studies me, but I don't have anything more to add. "Listen, Brynn. I hear students talk in the halls, but there was one thing in particular I found interesting. You, my dear. Being discussed as someone they rely on for, what was it? Matchmaking advice?"

My heart drops to my butt. I never thought I'd have to explain this to my *guidance counselor*, of all people. "It's more like . . . communication techniques. For engaging in conversation with someone you like."

I'm not out here playing Cupid with love lives, but I am giving them tips that allow them to be their own matchmaker. It's very different from setting someone up.

"You understand your peers. On a level I cannot. I mean—" She places both palms flat against her desk. "I overheard a student say they were *'screaming, crying, throwing up'* after their crush responded to their Instagram story. Did you know that merely translates to *excitement*? I almost sent them to the *nurse*."

I glance around her office, confused. "Am I in trouble?"

"Apparently calling someone a 'snack' is a compliment?" Mrs. Burchill says to herself. When she finds me staring at her, she snaps back to the present. "No, you're not in trouble. But it's clear your classmates don't trust you, because of how you've been unfairly blamed."

"Yeah, I'm not exactly beloved right now," I mumble. "Don't expect to see me crowned prom queen."

She folds her hands together. "Perhaps you can attempt to get back in their good graces?"

"Well, they cancelled me for something I didn't do, so"—I suck my teeth—"it appears to be a *them* problem."

Mrs. Burchill slides a piece of paper in front of me. I glance down at it, realizing it's one of USC's essay prompts.

Tell us about something outside of your educational concentration that interests you.

"I know the goal is Stanford," Mrs. Burchill explains. "But your backup schools are important. I think you can address your current situation with this prompt."

She's *joking*.

"So, what? I say, '*Hi, USC—my classmates have ostracized me, but I'm VERY interested in not being a world-class loser at your prestigious campus*'?"

Her green eyes bore into mine, unamused. "Write about *why* you like helping people. Tell them *this* story. Product design isn't all about innovation, you know. Whether it's on a large or small scale, it's about improving people's lives."

"I tell USC about my flirt coaching?" I say in disbelief.

"It's why I suggested winning your classmates over. They need you. And you like helping them." She leans back in her seat. "Am I wrong?"

No. She's not. In fact, she's aggravatingly right. Analyzing conversations and providing solutions gives me such an adrenaline rush. It's about fostering connections between people. I'm the training wheels they need until they feel confident on their own. Ultimately, they don't need me. They just need that push.

But I've also relied on them. Their money was my safety net.

"I know Stanford is number one, and I know you're trusting the dean to deliver that letter of rec for you, but think about this. Okay?"

"You make infuriatingly good points," I say.

"All part of the job." She takes a pretzel for herself. "Since you're here, should we discuss how this rumor has been affecting you?"

My emotional armor hardens around my heart. Dwelling on my feelings in my guidance counselor's office won't fix Duncan's lies. I know this for a fact. Growing up, my mom would push me to find solutions instead of spiraling into a single, devastating emotion.

"Your tears won't change the C on your science test to an A," she'd say. "So what are you going to do next time?"

I'd fix it. Which is what I'm going to do in this predicament, so I snag one last pretzel and say, "Nope."

She studies me as I stand. "Talking about your emotions isn't a waste of time, I promise."

But I'm practically launching myself at the door. "Telling you how I feel won't solve any of my problems."

I would know. Majoring in product design means solving problems using logic. You don't exactly use your emotions to figure out how to build a better folding chair prototype, for instance. You use engineering skills.

"But it can release you from their burden," Mrs. Burchill counters.

I'm already stepping out of her office. "Thanks for the pretzels."

"Mm-hmm." She spins in her chair. "You know where to find me when you decide it might be worth a shot."

The only logical way I'll be able to get back in my classmates' good graces is to figure out who the hell *is* responsible for my downfall. That's why Cadence, Marlowe, Tahlia, and I are sitting around Tahlia's kitchen table after school strategizing our next move.

"He cheated on Lenora and she took him back because she thinks it's you," Marlowe's saying. "That screams toxic to me."

Tahlia nods in agreement. "And if we tell her about the lip gloss, would she even believe you?"

I'm about to reply when a text chimes on my phone.

Len

Tell your friends to quit messing

with my boyfriend's things.

I should have known she'd be pissed. I type out my reply.

> what will it take for you to believe me?

Len

What are you trying to prove?? You'd really put the blame on some innocent girl so the whole school stops hating you?

I stare at her text. I hadn't thought of it this way, but I can't deny it's a valid point. There's a reason the true identity of the banana imposter hasn't been revealed. This person isn't coming forward after witnessing how I've been treated.

After I read the texts to my friends, Tahlia goes, "I hate it say it, but she's right. If we keep trying to solve the lip gloss thing, we'll be exposing whoever *did* hook up with Duncan. Is this the right way to go about it?"

I bite my bottom lip. If we find out who it is and expose them, we're not putting a stop to the larger issue of shaming. But it's also not fair to let me take the blame.

"So I'm supposed to just accept it?" I say. "I need my clients back—I need people's trust again."

I would also love to graduate as someone who is *not* the most hated person at Greenlough Academy. I don't think that's too much to ask. At this rate, they'll probably throw banana peels onstage when I walk up to get my diploma.

Cadence looks deep in thought. "There has to be a way to prove it's not Brynn without exposing whoever it was."

As they discuss this, I quickly redo my client calculations. I was averaging about four to five students a month, plus success dates. That equals a few hundred dollars. Losing that will hurt, but not if I can get back on track.

I've also been thinking about USC's prompt. Mrs. Burchill thinks I should discuss why I like helping people. It's such a layered answer. It can't only be because I'm good at it.

"Maybe Charlie can copy Mrs. Connoway's footage of us leaving that night," Marlowe proposes. "At least we'll have some evidence. Then we can form a plan around that."

It's a baby step in the right direction, but the main problem still remains. Even if we *do* find out who was with Duncan, we can't publicly out them. If we do, we're no better than him. There has to be another way.

Suddenly, Cadence leaps to her feet. It happens so fast that her chair nearly topples over. "I've got it!"

"What?" Marlowe asks as Cadence chaotically grabs her backpack, nearly stumbling over herself in a rush to get to the door. "Got *what*?"

"Just trust me. I'll have everything ready tomorrow."

And then she slams the front door on the way out.

The three of us exchange bewildered glances, momentarily stunned by the abrupt departure.

"Well," I venture, "let's hope *this* idea involves less crime."

10

"I'm Team Lenora all the way."

"Brynn should've known better."

"What a train wreck, honestly."

I don't see Cadence at lunch the next day, but she tells me to meet her outside the photo lab after school. No one is around, which is a relief. I need a reprieve from the relentless glares.

A few seconds later, she arrives.

"I had an idea." There's a glimmer of mischievousness in her eyes. "The student body is biased. Everyone's taking Lenora's side. They're already sympathetic toward her, you know? They've called you a homewrecking slut—"

"Please let there be a point," I moan. I know Lenora's anger toward me is overpowering her anger toward Duncan, so she's letting herself stay in a shitty relationship without knowing the truth. "How are we supposed to shift the blame without ruining someone else's life?"

"You don't," she says simply. "You shift the thinking."

I think she expects this knowledge bomb to cause more of an explosion, but she's lost me. "What do you mean? You just said they've already taken a side."

"Yes, but we're going to encourage them to form new opinions. Then they'll see Duncan isn't the victim," she explains. "The double standard is real. I mean, it's like they forgot he was the one who cheated on his girlfriend. All they want to do is blame you for being a 'temptress' or whatever, so we make them see why they're wrong."

She whips out a freshly printed flyer. It's a black-and-white photo of my face, one she took during lunch the other day. I look focused, intense. The only part of the image that isn't black-and-white are my lips, which are a bold red. A thin banner runs across the middle of my face. In a blocky typewriter text, Cadence has printed:

JOIN THE FEMOLUTION.

I still don't follow. "What's a femolution? And why do we need flyers?"

"A revolution to denounce sexism," she explains. "If we're really going to shake things up, we need to make a statement. Crush the oppressive patriarchal regime. Think about it. Greenlough's partially responsible for the students' backassward ways of thinking and, thus, the reason our peers are coming down on you so hard."

It's beginning to make sense, but I don't quite see her full vision. "Go on."

"This school is a rich fucking bubble of entitled, privileged people who want nothing less than perfection." The passion in her voice grows stronger. "They perpetuate one standard of that 'perfection.' Like, have you thought about how ninth graders are required to take sex ed? All they did was push abstinence on us. They shouldn't be teaching from a place of judgment. And it wasn't even inclusive! We never even broached the subjects of gender identity and different sexual orientations. Sex is seen as shameful unless you're a guy, which is why the whole school has cancelled *you* instead of Duncan."

She takes a breath, giving me a second to process. She's not wrong. Duncan's the one who cheated, yet everyone's given him a pass. We can blame society for propagating these double standards, but it also should be the school's responsibility to teach these types of progressive topics.

"If we can drop this dated stigma around sex and get more people to open their eyes, we can reshape the way students are thinking. And that will reflect on how they see you. *Without* shifting the blame on whoever decided to not come forward." She pauses. "I've always respected you, you know."

This catches me off guard. "You have?"

"Yeah, you never care what people think. Even after getting called out for being a huge flirt."

I consider the way I've deflected other's opinions of me in the past, calling them out and shutting them down. It's carefully practiced confidence. I use it like a weapon, but now it feels as though part of it has been stripped away from me.

All because of Duncan.

"Maybe it doesn't seem like it, but I do care," I admit.

"But you're never afraid to push back," she explains. "Do you realize how many girls don't clap back? They let the shame eat at them."

I remember what I told Charlie on Friday night. How staying quiet is part of the reason why prickwads like Duncan and Thomas win.

Not anymore.

"We educate them in a way that Greenlough isn't, then let them form a new opinion of you." She glances down at her stomach. "And me too. I lost my close friends after . . . Well, you know. They stopped texting. Didn't want to hang out, let alone be associated with me."

"I'm sorry," I say. "You didn't deserve that."

Her expression softens. "Neither did you."

A surge of confidence swells inside me. We can try and change people's minds about how we treat each other here, and if it gets through to people, I'll have my side hustle back. Cadence won't feel as ostracized, and my reputation will be restored. Plus, it's clever enough to stay out of trouble with McTiernan so I can earn my letter of recommendation to Stanford.

This could actually work.

"Okay," I say, eager to get started. "What's the first step?"

"We unleash a series of planned propaganda that leads to your ultimate finale at the Senior Showcase in December," Cadence explains, her excitement building. "I'll get here early to put these flyers in the hallway on Monday."

"Why Monday?"

She grins. "Because Miss Rothman signed off on my Evolution of Feminism club today, and we need time to plan our first meeting." She removes a tube of bright red lipstick from her pocket and smooths it over her lips. It matches the image of me in the flyer. "These flyers are merely promoting our new organization—and the underground agenda of our femolution. Knowledge is power, baby. And we're taking the power back."

It's a plan. Not only a plan, but a *good* plan. We have to make them see the root of the problem in order for them to see my side.

"Okay." I feel a tiny bit of hope flutter in my chest. "I'm in."

Cadence looks pleased. "Great. I'm headed out. Need a ride?"

I glance at the double doors at the end of the hall. "No, it's okay. I'm going to walk."

Now she's confused. "Why would you walk when I'm offering you a ride?"

I flick my eyes to my Keds. "It's just—it's warm outside. And our hot water's been out? So if I walk, the cold shower won't be as bad."

She waves this off. "Just shower at my place. I'll take you home after."

"Oh." The offer is so abrupt that I'm not sure how to reply. "I don't want to impose—"

"You're not. C'mon."

And before I can argue, she turns and heads toward the doors.

The drive from Greenlough to Cadence's place is short, but as soon as she pulls into the driveway, a woman in a flowy crème blouse and drapey paper-bag pants emerges from the front door. She marches up to the car as Cadence puts it in park. I immediately notice that she has the same smooth, olive skin and arched eyebrow shape as Cadence, but she's about three inches shorter. This must be Cadence's mom.

As we get out, the front door opens again. It's Charlie. He brushes loose strands of his dark hair out of his eyes as he ventures over. He's still in his Greenlough uniform, minus the tie, shirt untucked. On anyone else it might look disheveled, but he wears the tousled look well.

"Cadence Reza." Her mother's voice is clipped. A black Chanel bag hangs from her left arm. "You were supposed to be here ten minutes ago. We're late."

Cadence's eyes widen. "Oh *shit*."

Her mother continues on in Farsi. I don't catch what she's saying, but her tone is angry.

"*Sorry,*" Cadence says over her.

"In." She unlocks her Escalade with a smooth beep. "Now."

Cadence gives me an apologetic look. "I have a doctor's appointment. I completely spaced. Charlie!" She motions her brother over. "The offer stands. Charlie can show you where the towels are and everything."

Charlie blinks, looking from me to Cadence, but she's already disappearing into the front seat of her mom's Escalade. The chaos dies as soon as they pull out of the driveway, leaving the two of us standing there.

"Do you—?" Charlie begins just as I say, "Cadence said—"

We both laugh awkwardly. "You go," he says.

"Cadence told me I could shower here since our hot water heater's broken," I explain. "But it's okay. I can just go home."

"Oh, uh, it's not a problem," Charlie stumbles. "C'mon in." He leads the way up the steps toward the front door. "That sucks. Is it getting fixed soon?"

"Hopefully. Although I'm becoming a real master of the two-minute shower."

He holds the front door open for me. "Well, you can take your time here. It's fine."

Once we've stepped inside the foyer, I admire the chandelier in the dining room I noticed on Friday night. It's still gleaming in its magnificent glory. Everything in here is polished to a sparkling shine.

"I feel like I'm in that scene from *Annie* when she comes to Daddy Warbucks's mansion and she's wowed by everything and then there's this whole dance number." I'm rambling now, but from the corner of my eye, I see Charlie smile.

"Okay, first of all, this isn't a mansion—"

"It is, though."

"*Secondly*, I'm not about to break out into dance."

"Well, of course you're not. It's a whole dance number, meaning you'd need more than one person." Then it hits me. "You've never seen *Annie*."

He does a one-armed shrug. "I haven't."

"Wow. Not a musical theater guy. Okay. Noted."

"I listened to the *Hamilton* soundtrack."

"Everyone listened to the *Hamilton* soundtrack."

Once we're upstairs, Charlie pushes the door of Cadence's room with his foot, jarring it open. "I'll spare you my bathroom. Hers is cleaner. Oh, one sec—"

He disappears into the room across from Cadence's. From the hallway,

I can see that it's painted a forest green color with cream trimming.

Because I'm nosy, I take a step closer. A few posters are carefully hung on the walls, mostly of famous surfers, but the majority of his room is taken up by canvases. There's a huge blank one on his easel next to a desk full of paint supplies. Almost every spare inch of his wall is covered in paintings. I have an urge to walk in and admire them, but I wait in the hallway instead.

When he returns, he's holding a shirt and a towel. "It's clean—if you wanted to wear it."

It's a thoughtful gesture. I glance down at what he's offered me. It's a soft black T-shirt that has a familiar album cover on the front.

"Thanks," I tell him. "I like Joywave too."

A spark of excitement lights up behind his eyes. "I play them all the time at Sticks and Scones."

"A great choice." I take a step into Cadence's room. "Well—"

"I'll leave you to it," he says before disappearing into his room.

I close the door, letting my eyes linger on the details that I didn't see on Friday. There's a white desk littered with photos. As I approach, I notice half of them depict a man with harsh features dressed in formal business wear, but the other half are softer pictures of the same man laughing at an outdoor gathering, beer in hand, reveling in a burst of sheer joy.

This must be their dad. Even though they're in black and white, I can tell Mr. Frazenberg and Charlie have the exact same eye color. It's in the way the light hits them.

The photographs are good. She's captured the complexities of human emotion in such a raw way. Of course both Frazenbergs are artists. It must be a twin thing.

There's a few more photos underneath. I recognize Tyla and Devin sitting at the edge of Cadence's pool, heads thrown back with laughter. It feels vivid and authentic, like you want to be included in the joke.

I can't believe Tyla ditched Cadence. She also hasn't invited me back to any Future Business Leaders of America meetings—not like she can stop me. But it's bullshit. Nobody wants to be around someone who makes them feel unwanted. They shouldn't have done that to Cadence during a time she needed them the most.

I wander into Cadence's marbled bathroom and turn on the shower taps, gasping in amazement as water pours from the enormous rainfall showerhead. It steams up in seconds.

Once I step inside, my body physically relaxes. I let myself enjoy the hot water on my shoulders before I start searching for body wash and shampoo. Everything smells like coconut, and her collection of jasmine-scented body scrubs make me feel like I'm at a spa.

I don't take long, and once I'm out and dry, I slip into Charlie's shirt. It smells like fresh linen and sandalwood soap marketed for men that might have a name like *Cool Arctic Blast*. There's also a faint smell of pastry that lingers in the threads, soft and sugary.

I slip into my school skirt and toss my blouse in my book bag. When I crack the door to Cadence's room, I discover Charlie has left his own door open. His back is against his bed, head slightly tilted, as his thumbs button mash a gaming controller. I step to the edge of the entryway to get a look at what he's playing. It's a racing game I don't recognize.

He senses my presence, pausing the game to turn around. "Nice outfit. You should wear that to school tomorrow."

"Oh, for sure. I love giving Principal McTiernan reasons to call me to his office. Best part of my day."

He laughs, standing up as I step into his room. A light thrill slides down my vertebrae as I admire the art plastered on his walls. I feel him watching me as I take it all in.

His art is dark, but with intention. He paints with deep blues and blacks and grays. Skeletons with vines twisted through their teeth. A boy painted blue, melting into a pile of candle wax. Gloomy alleyways with a lone person in the distance that stares at the viewer with soulless eyes. Beautiful flowers with delicate petals tethered to the earth by metal leaves. Each piece makes me feel something. Haunted. Trapped. Powerful.

"These are incredible," I say.

He shifts uncomfortably. "My mom hates it."

"She shouldn't." I move toward his desk, admiring a few Polaroids taped to the wall. "Kick me out anytime. I'm nosy."

He leans against the wall, watching me. "You're not. But those pictures are kind of old."

My eyes land on a photo of him and Adeline Masso in front of the Haunted Mansion at Disneyland. Adeline is also in our grade. She's petite and edgy and always has perfect winged eyeliner. She seems intimidating because she rarely smiles, but we shared a few conversations in our chemistry class last year and I discovered that she's actually nice, albeit soft-spoken.

I gesture to the photo. "Are you still with Adeline?"

Charlie runs a hand through his hair. It flops back into place. "No, we broke up over the summer."

A strangely pleasant sensation expands in my chest. *So.* Charlie is single. A familiar itch urges me to flirt with him, but I suppress it. I can't afford any distractions right now, considering my entire life imploded over the last week.

Instead I say, "Ah, I'm sorry."

"Don't be. It wasn't bad or anything. There was sort of an awkward thing in our friend group—but that's a long story. We're friends." He clears his throat. "You still talk to Hayes?"

I notice there's a slight flush to his face. It's endearing. I shouldn't be surprised Charlie knows my dating history, but another part of me wonders how long he's been paying attention.

I don't talk to Hayes, although I do sometimes see what he's up to online. It doesn't mean I've forgotten how hurt I felt when we ended things. I swore I'd never feel that way again, which is why I don't let myself fall for anyone. It keeps the devastation and disappointment out.

"Not really," I tell him. "We didn't have a bad breakup or anything either, but it was—hard. I guess. When it did end." I notice a poster that hangs near the Polaroids and decide to use it as a subject change. "Maya Gabeira?"

A flicker of surprise flashes in his eyes. "You know surfers."

"Some. I watched *Blue Crush* last year and went down a rabbit hole of googling female surfers."

"Same, but probably not for the same reasons you did."

I laugh, turning back to the poster. "I've always wanted to try it. Surfing, I mean."

"Why haven't you?"

"Because it looks difficult." I face him. "And it's expensive."

"I could teach you."

I shoot him an incredulous look. "You could?"

He tries to play it cool, but his eagerness shows. "Why not? We have boards. Cadence has a wetsuit she's never used."

I grin. "All right, Charlie Frazenberg. Deal."

My eyes roam the rectangular box on his wall. Another intercom. He catches me staring. "You're tempted, aren't you?"

"Your mansion is like a giant walkie-talkie and you aren't even impressed."

His eyes dance with amusement. "No one's home, anyway. You'd be talking into the ether."

"I *love* talking into the ether. I'm my own best audience."

"You know what?" He smirks down at me. "I believe you."

"And what I *don't* believe is that they didn't film the sixth *Home Alone* here, in your very gigantic residence," I remark, enjoying this.

"Brynn," he says with a Very Serious face. "Do you mean to tell me there are *five* actual, real-life movies that succeed the original?"

I raise my brows. "I'm not *not* saying that."

"God help us all."

Two things happen at once: a strange warmness begins spreading through my chest right as my phone pings. I shift my focus to the latter, checking my messages.

Mom

Where are you?

Whoops. I thought I'd beat her home, which is why I hadn't texted after school.

"It's my mom. I should head out." A pang of sadness stretches in my chest. I realize that, oddly, that I don't want to leave.

"I can drive you," Charlie offers.

"Are you sure?"

"Yeah, no worries."

Charlie's Lexus is almost identical to Cadence's, but in a slate-gray color. Once he pulls out of the driveway, I begin to guide him to my neighborhood.

"Tell Cadence I said thanks," I say when he reaches my street. "Oh, and text me about surfing."

Charlie looks momentarily flustered. "Um, I don't know if I have your number?"

"Right." I'm not sure why I thought he'd have it, but I give it to him. He plugs it into his phone. A second later, my phone bleats with an incoming message. He's sent me the levitating-man emoji, immediately followed by: this emoji is slept on.

I crack a smile, replying with an abacus emoji and following up with: not as slept on as this.

When I glance up, he's smiling too. I grab my book bag that's settled by my feet before exiting. "Thanks for the ride."

"No problem." He stares at me for a beat, and I realize I like the way he looks directly into my eyes, as if there's nothing else that could possibly distract him. "See you at school."

I wave as he drives off. It feels good to hang out with someone outside of my friend group who isn't actively judging me for something I didn't do. Charlie's easy to talk to. A kind distraction from my problems. It's a relief. Forgetting for a little while.

It's not until his Lexus turns the corner out of my neighborhood that I realize I've stood here intentionally, watching the last of him disappear.

11

"I wouldn't trust my boyfriend around Brynn."

"Honestly? It's sad."

"I feel so bad for Lenora."

It's quiet as I enter my house, but I know my mom's home because her Volvo is here and there's a vanilla-scented candle lit in the living room. I drop my bag in the entryway and run a hand through my nearly dried hair.

"Hey," I call. "I'm home."

My mom emerges from the laundry room, all spirit fingers and shoulder shimmies. "We have hot water!"

She's ridiculous. I love it. "I thought he couldn't make it until tomorrow?"

"He finished another house call early," she explains, then notices my shirt. Well, not my shirt. Charlie's. "Please tell me you didn't wear that to school."

"Of course not. I was at a friend's," I explain.

Her eyebrows shoot to her hairline. "Are you being saf—?"

"Mom, *god*. It's not like that." I find a granola bar in our pantry and start unwrapping it. "At all."

"You and your—what's-it-called? Where you're dating but not?"

"Situationships," I remind her, hopping up on the kitchen island and letting my legs dangle below me. "And that's not what this is either."

"I won't even try to keep up." She spots the granola bar. "I'm starting dinner soon. Don't spoil your appetite."

"I won't," I say through a hunk of oats and cranberries.

She begins pulling out pots and pans from the cabinet. "Is the dean any closer to figuring out who spread that video?"

I swallow. "No, but I did get called to the guidance counselor's office yesterday."

"Oh?" She flicks on the stove. "What for?"

"She wanted to talk to me about one of USC's essay prompts," I say, only giving her part of the truth.

I don't know how to properly convey what my side hustle means to me. Or what it *meant* to me, seeing as I'm currently as approachable as a rabid racoon.

The money is important, but I've always cared about helping my classmates. I mean, they used to be vulnerable enough to ask for my assistance, and it made me feel useful. Like I could analyze my way into creating a moment of joy for them.

Maybe I *am* drawn to helping people connect in a meaningful way. And if I'm good at that, then there's a chance I'll succeed at leading an entire femolution.

"It might be good for you to visit her once a week," my mom says. "Talking about what you've been through won't hurt."

Why does everyone believe opening up about how I feel is going to solve my current predicament?

I crumple up the glossy granola bar packaging. "Feelings are for suckers."

"Sarcasm is for people who are currently avoiding their problems," she says in return.

I pull a face. "I'm not, actually."

She gives me a look like, *Sure, Jan,* and says, "Listen, there's something I need to talk to you about."

From where I'm sitting, I try to toss my crumpled trash in the garbage can. It lands flawlessly. When I glance back to her, I notice she won't meet my eyes, focused on opening a package of dry spaghetti.

"Smith is back in rehab," she tells me.

I press my lips together. Oh. Okay, well. That's not entirely unexpected, but it's not great either. At least we know where he is, which is a vast improvement from the last six months.

Then it hits me. Rehab is expensive, and we've used the last of my coaching money to replace our water heater. That means—

"I had to dip into your college savings."

Irritation simmers through me. My college fund isn't much, but it's something. It's textbooks and meal-plan money. I wonder how hard my account has been hit, and it makes my stomach sour anxiously.

After touring Stanford, my mom promised me that she'd help in whatever way she could. She'd been saving her Postmates tips for me, which is generous. But when it comes down to it, those are her finances. And I'm not heartless. I want Smith to be better.

"Your father wouldn't help," she goes on, filling my silence.

I would have assumed we'd entered a parallel universe if he did help, since this is the same man who's firmly refused to pay for anything once I turned eighteen.

I know my dad doesn't owe me anything. He's paid child support, but that goes toward my essentials. Uniforms, school lunches, field trips. Legally he's not obligated to pay for college, though I'd hoped he would care enough to continue to support my education. He doesn't, solidifying what I've known all along. People—even family—disappoint you. We can't depend on anyone but ourselves.

"I'm sorry, Brynn. I didn't know what else to do."

I know she feels bad. It's a tough situation to be in as a parent, especially as a single parent, but I don't want to be upset with her when she's already stressed about my brother.

So I force a smile. "It's okay. We'll figure it out."

She pulls me in for a hug. "Thank you for being so mature about this," she says as she lets me go. "And at least you have your tutoring money for now."

Ah yes. My *tutoring* money. I never told my mom exactly where my coaching funds come from. It felt safer to lie.

And it is a kind of tutoring. Just not in the way she assumes.

"I'm going to get some homework done before dinner," I tell her.

In my room, I flop backward on my bed. If Smith has checked into another rehab, that means he's back in Pacific Palisades. Sometimes I think my mom only agrees to pay for his rehabs because it means he's safe and she gets to see him, and that thought breaks my heart into a thousand delicate pieces.

I want the best for Smith. I don't want to wonder if the next time I'll see him will be in another six months or a year. Is that so bad? Wishing he would care?

Eventually, I stop feeling sorry for myself and open my laptop. I reread my Stanford essay. It's a good essay, but I can't help feeling nervous. Stanford sees a lot of *good* essays. Mrs. Burchill's assured me it's strong, but I've been tweaking and polishing it every few days. I have until January to fire it off into the magical Stanford portal, and yet I keep coming back to it.

I pull up USC's prompt next. I've already written a solid response, but maybe Mrs. Burchill is right. If I can figure out how to properly articulate what bringing people together means to me, then my response will feel more genuine. More like me.

But I have no idea where to even begin.

I close my laptop. What will *really* seal the deal for me is McTiernan's letter of recommendation for Stanford. It's his words as an alumnus that will have more of an impact than mine. I know they will.

Which is why Cadence's plan is genius. It ensures I'll stay out of trouble with the dean while also getting my classmates to see my side of this scandal. Once they understand the double standard and stop shaming me, I'll be able to restore my income, replenish our emergency fund, and figure out the better version of this USC essay.

Bonus? The banana imposter will be so moved by our femolution that they'll come forward and make things right. Even bigger bonus if Duncan comes clean, although that feels about as likely as winning the lottery.

I'm starting to feel hopeful again, so I spend the next hour applying to a few stores online, praying my application isn't getting lost in some huge internet ether. Smith's rehab depleted a chunk of money and with our luck, our fridge will be the next thing to break. If I can anticipate the problem and plan for the solution, we'll be fine. It's how my mom and I have always operated.

"It's a tough world," she likes to say, "but the Whitaker women are even tougher. We can handle it."

We can because we have. My father's brazen absence is proof you can't rely on anyone but yourself. In our case, at least we have each other. I'm doing my part to make sure we keep our heads above water. Besides, if I'm accepted to Stanford, I'm going to at least need a deposit. Then I can worry about loans.

There's one thing I know for certain. This plan *has* to work.

12

"Did you see the flyers?"

"She's so full of herself! She needs the attention."

"So cringey."

I spend Sunday evening at Marlowe's house with Tahlia and Cadence. We're sprawled on the floor in Marlowe's room trying to figure out how to get our classmates to pay attention to our side. Cadence's flyers are a start, but we need something that will persuade them to come to our first Evolution of Feminism meeting.

Cadence pitched the idea of giving the student body what they want: a visual representation that I'm a skank, but in a way that reclaims the word. Owning the stereotype, then breaking it. She's suggested we start with our uniform, which would include rolling up our skirts and abandoning our knee-highs.

Tahlia shoots it down right away. "No. I *choose* to wear hijab as a source of liberation. We live in a society that aggressively sexualizes women, so I feel like I'm taking back control. There's a freedom in covering up. In modesty." She pauses. "Also? We don't need a mark on our records for breaking dress code."

"Fair," Marlowe notes.

The impact we're looking for runs deeper than breaking uniform code, because we're not trying to make a spectacle of ourselves. But it can't be corny, otherwise we run the risk of self-destructing the entire operation before it has a chance to thrive. It's a delicate balance made even more fragile considering the entire student body is actively anti-Brynn.

"What if . . ." Tahlia stares at Cadence's hand, which rests over her belly. "Okay, what if you strip away the teen mom stigma that's been instilled in you, then how do you feel?"

"Well." Cadence pauses. "I mean, *I'm* the one who faces the brunt of the blame even though Thomas was also involved. He isn't treated half as bad as I am."

Her point immediately resonates with me. Thomas and Duncan are the ones who get off easy while we're the ones suffering emotional damages. It's some serious bullshit.

And then there's Tahlia and Marlowe. They've had to put up with people's intrusive questions about their identities even longer. People whose thoughts are so shallow they don't realize they're crossing boundaries. It must be exhausting.

"I'm not the poster child of Greenlough. I get that," Cadence continues. "But I'm made to feel like I should be ashamed of this tiny human. And that's *not* how I want to feel."

Tahlia taps her pen to her notebook. "Maybe if we own what we're shamed for, we give ourselves permission to control how we're perceived."

Now we're getting somewhere. There's no one-size-fits-all empowerment statement. We're each in a unique position to take a stand.

"That might work," I say, pulling my knees into my chest. "But how do we do that?"

Marlowe leaps to her feet, running to her closet to pull out her enormous rolling makeup case. "I will *never* forget when John Mark reported me to the dean sophomore year for wearing falsies even though Rhea Zhang has been wearing eyelash extensions since eighth grade. He told me I had to stop because it was a distraction, but fuck that. It was discrimination." She pops the case open and grabs a handful of boxed lashes. "I feel empowered by my lashes and makeup because it's creative. I love being able to express myself, and I'm not going to let him stop me."

Tahlia's eyes widen. "McTiernan told me I could only wear a black or gray hijab because neutral colors make people feel '*more comfortable*.' I always considered it part of uniform policy, but you know what? It's some racist bullshit. I'm hijabi because it's *my* way of saying I want others to form an opinion on my personality over my appearance, and here's a man dictating how I do that." She sits up straighter. "On Monday, I wear what I want."

My heart pounds excitedly. We can do this. *Really* do this. Own what we've been shamed for and prove to everyone that they can't hurt us. Not when we're the ones taking back control, reclaiming our individual narratives.

"What about you?" Cadence asks me.

I don't have to think about it too long, considering Faith reminded me of what she thought I needed to repent for: my number.

My reputation started with the nine guys I went out with my sophomore year and continued with four the following year, including Hayes. After Otto, it totals fourteen. Fourteen guys. A number that's *too high* for any respectable girl, but it isn't a problem when the situation is gender-swapped. Micah Johnson is as big of a serial dater as me, and yet nobody ever has anything negative to say about him.

People may have speculated about my history, but the truth is they have no idea if I've had sex with every single person I've been with. And it's none of their business. It shouldn't matter if I've been intimate with one or all of them. They shouldn't shame me when guys like Micah are praised.

So that's why, come Monday morning, I walk into school alongside Marlowe with the number fourteen Sharpied in bright red ink on the tops of my forearms for everyone to see.

Marlowe doesn't leave my side, chin held high, lashes on, complete with a dedicated smoky eye, the two of us wearing a bold red lipstick. Red is unapologetic, Cadence explained. It commands attention. It shows we're not afraid of being seen for who we are.

As much as I wish this were immediately gratifying, it isn't. People stare. That's the point, I guess, and at least they cut their eyes away from mine when I stare back. I catch the ends of whispers as they duck their heads and giggle among their friends.

We're a joke to them. This is what I feared.

I try not to lose my confidence, but it's hard. What if we're making a big mistake?

Tahlia and Cadence are already by my locker when we arrive. For the first time since the school year started, Cadence isn't wearing her oversized Greenlough cardigan. She's standing there in her uniform blouse and skirt, which tightly hugs the roundness of her bump. Tahlia has on a burgundy hijab and matching gemstone earrings, and they both wear red lipstick.

I'm so overwhelmed with gratitude and love toward them that I feel like crying.

"Oh no, don't worry," Tahlia says, misinterpreting my sentimental moment for concern. "I went over the official handbook last night. Nothing we're doing can be reprimanded, and Cadence was smart enough to tie it to an organization. For all they know, we're promoting it."

"No, it's not that. It's just—" I look at each of them. "Thank you."

Cadence rolls her eyes. "God, please don't cry. And you don't need to thank us."

But I feel like I do, because Micah and Duncan are at the end of the hall, their laughter booming as they grab a handful of our flyers and toss them into a recycling bin.

"Assholes," Marlowe mutters.

Before I have a chance to respond, a loud voice bellows from behind me. *"Excuse me?"*

I spin around, fire spreading up my veins as if ignited by gasoline. I'm on the defense, ready to snap, but it's only Mathis Winters.

Mathis is Black, a fellow senior, and president of Greenlough's LGBTQ+ club, and right now he's standing here, one hand on his hip, another holding up our flyer. Beside him is Zanele Khumalo, Mathis's best friend and StuCo treasurer.

"Anyone can join, right?" Mathis asks accusingly.

Marlowe steps forward, her arms crossed. "Yes. Anyone."

Mathis smiles. "Good. Count me in."

"Me too," Zanele comments, flipping her box braids over her shoulder. "And I hope you plan to have a thorough discussion on misogynoir, because a lot of people don't know about Moya Bailey, and they *should.* This can't be some bullshit white feminism club."

Although I'm somewhat familiar with the term, I still have a long way to go. "We want this organization to be inclusive, and we're happy to hear what people look forward to discussing in our first meeting."

Zanele looks satisfied. "Great. I'll spread the word."

And just like that, they both head down the hall to class.

Marlowe gives me an encouraging shoulder nudge. "There's real interest."

Tahlia and Cadence are grinning, too, so I let myself relax.

Maybe this will actually work.

———————

By midday, the news about our new club has gotten around school. Cadence's bold flyers grabbed people's attention. Students seem to understand it's a feminism club and that we're making a statement for a reason, even if they don't fully understand *why*. But I hope it gets them to attend our first meeting.

The cracks in my confidence begin to repair. At lunch, Carmen Muñoz and Zoë Castillo stop by the Spindelli bush to let us know they'll be at the meeting on Wednesday. I catch Zoë's eyes lingering on Tahlia for a beat before she leaves, but not before complimenting her. She immediately shushes our pointed looks when Zoë walks away.

Tahlia has a strong suspicion Zoë might be bi, but she's not completely sure.

"There was a look," I remark.

"Definitely *a look*," Marlowe chimes.

Tahlia sighs. "I don't know. We text every single night, and she almost always initiates the conversation."

"That's a good sign," Marlowe notes.

"I'm trying not to be hopeful." She looks at me. "She wants to do a photo gallery for the Senior Showcase and asked if I would be comfortable modeling."

"An excuse to spend time with you," I conclude. "I hope you said yes."

"I did." A twinge of pink flushes through her cheeks. "We're shooting over Thanksgiving break."

"And they'll be together by spring break," Marlowe says. "I'm calling it now."

Tahlia, suppressing a grin, tosses a grape at her, bopping her square in the forehead.

After lunch, I spot Charlie in the hallway. I have a few minutes to spare before the first warning bell, so I fall into step with him.

"Hi."

"Oh, hey," he says, almost like he's surprised I'm talking to him. We never chat at school. Maybe he's embarrassed to be associated with me now that we've carried out the first step in our plan. Everyone else thinks we're a joke, so why wouldn't he?

I brush away the thought. "I was wondering if you had a chance to talk to Nadia? About the job?"

I'd texted him yesterday to see if Sticks and Scones was hiring, and he assured me he'd check with his boss and put in a good word. But his face crumples. I know the answer before he even says anything.

"I'm sorry, Brynn. She isn't taking anyone on right now."

I try and keep my face neutral even though I can feel my heart plummeting to my toes. "No, don't worry," I say with false cheeriness. "It's okay."

"Charlie!"

We both look toward the source of the voice. Charlie's friend group is waiting for him outside of Mr. Langston's AP History room. Adeline, Grant, and Shantel—all three of them similar in their alternative looks. Adeline and Shantel must have twenty ear piercings between them. They're the kind of crew that spends their weekends at rock shows at the Troubadour and secondhand record shops. Adeline has on a deep purple lipstick, which she presses into a thin line when she sees me talking to Charlie.

Well, you can't win them all.

I expect Charlie to blow me off, but he holds up a finger in a *one sec* motion. He focuses back on me. "Hey, want to go surfing this Saturday?"

An electric current ignites within me, sparking my chest to pulse like a speaker with too much bass. It's a silly reaction. Charlie's being nice. That's all. And yet, he's the one who's following up on his offer. Does it mean he's been thinking of me?

The humming in my chest begins to vibrate down the tips of my fingers. "Yeah," I say. "I'd love to."

"Cool." His hazel eyes hold mine for another beat. "I'll text you."

He starts to join his friends, but then takes a step back. "I like it. The lipstick, I mean."

A blazing heat climbs its way to my face. What is wrong with me? Am I so desperate for a single compliment that my insides have suddenly decided to melt like an overcooked s'more?

"Thanks," I say. "It was Cadence's idea."

"I'll be there. At the meeting, I mean."

I feel the corners of my lips tug upward. Before I can reply, the warning bell rings. With a short wave, Charlie walks toward his friends, leaving me with that disorienting, dizzying sensation humming lightly over my skin.

We're not exactly running victory laps by the end of the school day. Marlowe's been called to the dean's office. I have no idea why, but I have a sinking feeling it can't be good.

I'm the first one to get there once the final bell rings, and I nearly collide into John Mark, who's exiting the office with a stack of papers in his arms.

"Watch it," he snaps, stepping around me.

Oh, I am *not* in the mood for this today.

"Wouldn't want to damage your sacred pamphlets," I fire back, "lest you call upon the powers-that-be to smite me."

John Mark gives me an exasperated stare. "These are school lunch surveys."

"Ah, well," I backtrack. "The PB&Js are excellent."

He scowls. "You know you're just asking for more trouble, right? With this *thing* that you're doing?"

He emphasizes the word *thing* as though it's a wet clog in the sink that's suddenly grown legs.

"What I'm asking for," I say slowly, fixing him with a steely stare of my own, "is the barest hint of understanding, which seems to be an emotion you're incapable of producing."

Cadence and Tahlia stride up beside me, and I can't help but notice that Cadence looks like she's ready to fling words as sharp as knives.

"Then I guess that's why your friend is in there." He rolls his eyes. "Because she's *not* in trouble."

He walks away before I can ask him what he means, but we don't have to wait long. Marlowe is escorted out of the office by Dean McTiernan, who wears an unamused expression on his face.

"Brynn." He gives me a stern look. "You're still on thin ice." He takes an intentional pause. "Tread carefully."

Defense pitches my voice higher than usual. "We didn't do anything wrong—"

"I know," he says calmly. "But sometimes these things have a way of escalating on their own."

He returns to the office, letting the door shut behind him. Conversation over.

Shit. I can't give McTiernan another reason to not write me that letter of recommendation. We're going about this in a non-rule-breaking way. We're being smart. But it's clear he's waiting for me to misstep.

"What happened?" I ask Marlowe.

"McTiernan tried to tell me I was breaking dress code with my lashes." Marlowe says, then smirks. "So I asked to file a discrimination complaint. He changed his tune real quick."

There's an overwhelming sense of dread in the pit of my stomach. The last thing I want for anyone is trouble, but this is undeniably prejudiced. I can name at least five other people who wear more makeup than Marlowe on a daily basis.

Suddenly, this all seems like a bad idea. "I'm sorry."

"No, *fuck* that," Marlowe says. "This is what it's about, right? Taking a stand. Explaining it from our side?"

She's right, but it's going to take more than performatively wearing red lipstick to reshape the mindset of our classmates. We might be owning what we're shamed for to get people's attention, but we have to make sure our message is clear. That's what will cement our positioning on these bullshit biases.

The first femolution meeting could make or break everything. I have to make sure the agenda isn't self-serving.

It's time to put the second part of this plan into action.

13

"How does that not break the rules?"

"Starting the club in the middle of semester . . . Sketchy."

"I don't know. I might check it out."

Faith seems upset that talk of our Evolution of Feminism club has overshadowed her Abstinence Angels club, which I'm convinced nobody except Katie, Elisha, and John Mark have joined. I know this because she makes a snarky comment about it in World Lit on Wednesday. So does Lenora, who makes a point to call me out in the hallway during passing period.

"You can't just create a new club for the sake of fixing your reputation," she says, marching up beside me. "People will hate you when they figure out your true intentions."

"It's not about trying to make myself look better," I tell her as she falls into step with me. "Not entirely, at least."

"Why, then?" she challenges.

Because I have proof your prickweed boyfriend is cheating on you, but even if I tell you the truth, you'd never believe me.

I choose my next words carefully, stopping to look her directly in the eyes. "If we can fix the existing mindset and get people to think a little more progressively, it's not going to only affect me, but hopefully the students who come here after us."

The bell rings. I hand her a flyer.

"I hope you come," I say, then disappear into my Spanish class.

I'm about to explode with anxious jitters when the 2:15 bell rings. I'm nervous as hell about the first meeting. I keep having horrible daydreams where people show up only to mock us, taunting me with those damn banana peels. It's not an unrealistic thought. There are a lot of students here that are on Lenora's side.

I get to Miss Rothman's classroom fifteen minutes before we're supposed to begin. She's one of the younger teachers at Greenlough and beloved by the majority of students. She's the only one occupying the room, sitting at her desk grading papers.

"Hey, Brynn," she says as the door shuts behind me. "I'm looking forward to your first meeting."

It occurs to me that I'm going to have to come clean about the intentions of this club in front of Miss Rothman. That thought makes me sweat even more.

"Thank you for sponsoring," I say.

"It was a no-brainer. Greenlough is overdue for a club centered around feminism."

As she goes back to grading, I slide into one of the empty desks. My leg jiggles with nerves, but I tell myself it'll be fine.

I've created this meeting's agenda and even though I've read my share of feminist texts, I won't pretend I'm an expert. Each week, the four of us will take turns spearheading in order to split the work and share perspectives.

Marlowe is the first to arrive. I'm instantly relieved to see her.

"You ready?" she asks.

Before I can answer, the door opens again. I expect to see Tahlia or Cadence, but it's not them.

It's Katie Delcavo.

Marlowe looks at me, eyes wide, but I have no explanation for this. Katie's brows furrow when she sees us staring. She walks over to Miss Rothman's desk and hands her a sheet of paper.

"The essay I left in my car," I hear her say. "Sorry."

"I still have to deduct late points, but I'm glad you turned it in," Miss Rothman says.

Okay. This makes sense. She's not here for the meeting.

"You should stay for the new club Brynn's started," Miss Rothman continues. "It's only forty minutes."

Katie looks mildly panicked. I know Miss Rothman has presented her with a catch-22. If she stays, maybe it'll help make up for her late sociology paper. If she doesn't, it might make her look bad. There's no way she'll stay. No. Way.

"Um—"

Tahlia and Cadence enter the classroom, blocking her exit. Defeated, Katie takes an empty desk across the room and stares down at her hands. Tahlia and Cadence are clearly confused. They know my fleeting middle school history with Katie. How she's now part of Faith's group. I mouth, *I'll explain later.*

The four of us make conversation until two-thirty. By 2:32, we've fallen silent. By 2:35, I feel like the utmost failure.

Nobody is going to come. Nobody except Katie, who felt *forced* into staying. Who can't even look at me right now.

This is a nightmare.

I distract myself by moving over to the whiteboard. In huge, block letters, I write the word SHAME. I thought it would be an appropriate topic to kick off our first meeting since it describes my current state of affairs.

If anyone arrives.

Then—*finally*—the door swings open. In walks Rhea Zhang and Carmen Muñoz. Zoë Castillo arrives a second later. As they're sitting down, Mathis Winters and Zanele Khumalo show up. I feel the tension ease from my shoulders. *Six* people. That's not bad, even if Lenora never shows. Not that I expect her to, but still. A girl can hope.

I take a deep breath and address the room. "If anyone is here for the 'tea' about me and Duncan, you should leave now. That isn't what I'm addressing today."

I look at Rhea as I say this. She's Lenora's best friend, but she doesn't budge.

"Okay," I say, taking on gentler tone. "I—"

The door flies open. It's Charlie, out of breath and slightly sweaty.

"You're late," Cadence hisses as he falls into an open seat next to her.

"Sorry," he whispers, then looks at me and mouths the word again. *Sorry.*

I take a deep breath, gathering confidence, and begin again. "Thanks for joining. Greenlough was lacking a club like this one, and it's about time we dismantle certain ways of thinking." My heart begins beating quicker as I remember what Lenora said earlier today. "But . . . you should know my intentions for starting this were purely self-serving. At first."

I catch Rhea looking at me, eyes narrowed. But I have a room full of people willing to hear me out, so I have to make sure what I say makes an impact.

"I wanted to do something drastic to stop the rumors about me, but I realized the issue is *why* it's happening in the first place," I continue. "It's no secret that people come down harder on feminine-presenting people when they mess up. And my situation aside, I think that's worth exploring. So if you're here, I hope that means you want to explore and dismantle it with me. Because if we have the opportunity to stop harmful stereotypes, why not at least try?"

I stop talking. No one moves to leave, not even Rhea. Marlowe gives me an encouraging nod, which helps loosen the anxious knots in my stomach.

I face the whiteboard. "I think we should start by having an open conversation about shame and social stigma."

"Is that, like, the numbers on your arms?" Rhea challenges. "Everyone's saying you're displaying your sex numbers or whatever to give people something to talk about."

"I didn't do it so people would talk," I counter. "They're talking about me anyway."

Rhea holds my stare. "So why?"

"To take back control. To own it without shame, which circles back to what we're talking about." I gesture to the word on the board. "And the number represents people I've gone out with, but would it matter if I'd hooked up with them all?"

"Yeah. Stop being so combative, Rhea," Mathis says. "I *know* you understand double standards. No one gives the guys on the football team shit, and we've all heard them blatantly discuss their sex lives."

Rhea falls silent, folding her arms.

Thank you, Mathis.

"We're unlearning the bullshit society has fed us," Cadence adds.

I glance at Miss Rothman. She's raised an eyebrow at the swear, but she doesn't push it.

"The femolution is our way to change for the better. You know, by educating ourselves. Spreading awareness of inequalities and injustices," Tahlia says.

"It's not a retaliation against Abstinence Angels, then?" Zoë asks.

Katie sits up straighter, very interested in my answer.

"No, not at all," I say. "We're not here to shame anyone for whatever they believe."

Her expression softens. And then, it's as though the tension in the room dissolves. Everyone seems engaged in what I have to say, so I spend the next twenty minutes talking about female-centered shame, which prompts an intriguing conversation of its roots.

I open up the last ten minutes to talk about future meeting topics, which leads to a flurry of ideas. Zanele and Carmen even throw out titles of books that might be helpful to read as a group. I try not to overthink it, but it feels like progress.

"If you feel moved by what we discussed today, we welcome you to our second meeting, which will happen after Thanksgiving break," I say once we run out of time.

Cadence suggested starting small and leading by example.

"It's like chasing a cat," she told us the other night. "If you go after it with full force, it's gonna sprint away. But if you're patient, it'll come to you."

I don't want to seem overeager. I have to play it cool.

Rhea is the first to leave, followed by Zanele and Mathis. It's hard to know what Rhea's thinking or if she'll even return, but I tell myself it's an accomplishment she came in the first place.

Charlie has to take off to start his shift at Sticks and Scones, and Zoë lingers behind to talk to Tahlia. Marlowe and I notice this at the same time, and I can't help but exchange a knowing look with her.

"Hey," I say, jogging over to catch Katie before she heads out the door. "Thanks for staying."

"It was . . . interesting," she says, and I can tell she must be battling some kind of internal conflict by the way her eyes flick downward. Probably because she's always so keen to side with Faith. "Like, it's stuff I hadn't thought of before."

Relief releases in my chest. I know she ditched me for the Holy Crew, but deep down I want to believe she's the same person I knew in middle school. Not that religion ruined her. More like Faith's overbearing personality squashed parts of her old self. She's timid—less carefree than she used to be.

"Well, you're welcome back anytime," I tell her.

She doesn't give me a direct answer, instead giving me a half smile before leaving. Honestly, her presence here has been the most surprising thing that's happened today.

Carmen is the last to leave, but she changes her mind. "You started showing your bump," she says to Cadence. "Good. It's stupid they made you hide it."

"No one made me hide it," Cadence admits. "I felt like I had to."

"You know, McTiernan wrote me up last year because he thought my blouse was too tight," Carmen says. "But I'm a fat girl with big boobs, and these blouses always fit me wonky because they gap instead of lying flat. So he made me buy a huge men's button-down. Can you believe it?"

"Fuck that," Cadence seethes.

"You can fix it with Velcro. Or a safety pin," Tahlia tells her. "I do it for my mom's work blouses. She has the same issue."

"Sorry to interrupt." Miss Rothman comes around from the other side of her desk. "But the dean shouldn't have forced you to purchase a men's uniform. He handled the situation poorly."

Carmen's eyes go wide, as if she hadn't considered *he* was in the wrong. She turns back to me. "If I fix my old uniform blouse, can I join?"

Now I'm confused. "What do you mean?"

She points to us. "Join the femolution. You know, owning the thing you were shamed for."

Elation zips through my chest. "Of course. Anyone is welcome to join."

"And with your permission, I will take this up with the dean so he doesn't overstep again," Miss Rothman adds, then turns to me. "I have to run to the teacher's lounge. Great meeting today, by the way."

"Thank you," I say, feeling like, for the first time in a while, things are looking up.

Once Miss Rothman leaves, Marlowe turns to me. "It couldn't have gone better. I think we're really doing this."

"I *think*," I say, grinning, "it's already begun."

14

"Fourteen guys? Who has the time?"

"I'd be embarrassed if I were her."

"I don't know. I heard the meeting was pretty chill?"

The Evolution of Feminism club is not an overnight success. Despite having a decent first meeting that did not end with me being heckled into oblivion, the four of us are still the prime topic of whispers the next day. Which, fine. Whispers I can handle. As long as people come to our next meeting.

Leading a movement is largely exhausting and painfully slow going. The one perk of our first meeting is Carmen. She took a stand with us the next day, showing up in bright red lipstick. With Tahlia's help, she'd fixed her uniform blouse so that it wouldn't awkwardly gap. It's a huge improvement over the billowy button-up McTiernan made her purchase.

Our next initiative is the Senior Showcase, so we decide to come up with a plan over Thanksgiving break next week. It's perfect propaganda fuel, as Cadence says, and we can't let it go to waste. Currently, we're too inundated with midterm study guides to shift our entire focus to it, which is why we'll have to take advantage of the holiday break.

On Friday, my mom drops me off at school early because Marlowe has an appointment and can't offer me a ride. Since I have an extra twenty minutes to spare, I head to the cafeteria to buy a coffee from the morning breakfast cart.

I'm turning the corner when I notice Faith and John Mark with clipboards in their hands. John Mark is talking to Carmen, who vigorously shakes her head before storming into the cafeteria.

Weird.

As I approach them, my curiosity gets the better of me. I stop in front of Faith. She straightens her posture in my presence, as if preparing for a fight.

"Hey," I say, keeping my voice casual. "What's this?"

Faith hugs her clipboard to her chest, then nervously eyes John Mark. "Nothing," she says quickly.

Too quickly.

Either I'm turning into a narcissist because I know this has to do with me, or I'm misreading the situation. I don't think it's the latter.

Lucky for me, John Mark is more than happy to share. "We've started a petition banning you from prom."

"*John Mark*," Faith squeaks, clearly fretting over this reveal.

So. They're on a takedown mission. Their obsession with me is tiring, but this is next level.

I immediately grow heated. "Why?" I ask John Mark, wanting him to explain it to me.

"You're promoting rebellious discourse throughout the school, and you already set a bad example at the Halloween dance—"

"You know I served detention for that." I have not forgotten about the snitch who ran to McTiernan with that photo. "And a feminism club is not rebellious discourse. For fuck's sake!"

Faith looks startled by my cursing, but she quickly composes herself.

"The angels have agreed that you're promoting sinful messages with the stance you've taken."

I scowl. "The stance you're referring to, may I remind you, is literally *equality*."

"Just own what you did, Brynn," John Mark says, voice low.

I cut my gaze to him. "What is your problem?"

He sneers. There's a hint of dried toothpaste in the corner of his mouth. It instantly gives me the ick.

"The school's resources shouldn't go to a student's education if they're clearly a menace."

Ah, I get it. John Mark is pissed *I'm* the one who's been awarded a scholarship. Me, the discourse-creating, boyfriend-stealing super slut. I'm not worthy of setting foot in such a fine institution. It doesn't help he witnessed me screaming at Duncan after we were both called to McTiernan's office.

"You talk like a dad in a nineties sitcom," I fire off, then whirl on Faith. "And your head is so far up *his* ass that you can't even form a single opinion of your own."

Faith gasps like I've just ripped a holy cross from the wall and used it as a backscratcher.

"I thought this would wake you up to your upsetting behavior." John Mark looks haughtily at me. "We've already got twenty-five signatures."

Twenty-five people signed their dumb petition. Those words are a knife to the heart. It means people are listening to them. Not only listening to them, but *agreeing*.

I reach into my book bag and yank out my Sharpie. "You don't want me at prom? All right. Fine."

Faith, surprised by this reaction, gapes at me. There's a dark classroom window a few feet away, so I walk over and find my reflection in it. I feel her watching me as I uncap my marker and draw the number fourteen on my left cheekbone, and then my right.

During football season, cheerleaders and dancers wear player's jersey numbers painted on their face in glitter. It's a tradition that hasn't been banned as a "distraction." McTiernan doesn't need to know this isn't a jersey number. And right now, I know nothing will piss off Faith more than being louder than her.

I cap my Sharpie, then spin around to face them. Her eyes go wide with shock when she sees what I've done. John Mark remains unimpressed.

"I hope you have the most *magical* prom," I say, my words dripping with sarcasm. "It must be real tiring working this hard to shut me out."

Then I march straight through the cafeteria doors before either one of them can say anything else.

My mood lifts when I see Cadence and Tahlia sitting at a table by themselves working on homework. I plop down in a seat across from them, fuming.

Cadence looks up first, noticing the numbers on my cheeks. "Oh shit! Taking it to another level. *Respect.*"

Tahlia sets her pen down. "You ran into Faith?"

"Yes," I say, the word slipping out harshly between my gritted teeth.

"Didn't go well?" Cadence guesses.

"Why aren't they concerned about Duncan?" I hiss, even though I already know the answer. "They're more concerned about besmirching my name." Cadence grimaces as I say, "No, yeah, I heard it. God, I'm starting to sound like her."

"Honestly, Duncan probably told them he went to confession to get on their side," Tahlia ventures.

Cadence drums her fingers over her government textbook. "That *is* his brand. Lying."

I glance up in time to catch Lenora and Rhea walking through the double doors only to get stopped by John Mark and Faith. I bite my thumbnail as they listen to Faith's "ban Brynn" pitch, but I'm stunned when Lenora rolls her eyes and walks away, Rhea trailing behind her.

I nearly forget to release the breath trapped in my chest. Lenora didn't take the bait to sabotage me with the petition when she easily could have. It would be out of character if she did, but still. Maybe there's a tiny part of her that cares about me.

In an ideal world, I would tell Lenora about the lip gloss Cadence found. She would believe me, leave Duncan, and the balance of the school would reset.

Then I realize—no. It wouldn't. Because that wouldn't change how terribly people have treated Cadence during her pregnancy. Or how unaccepting some classmates are toward Marlowe and Tahlia. It wouldn't *solve* anything.

I'm not naive enough to think we'll shift everyone's stagnant way of thinking, but I believe we can make a sizable dent.

"Hopefully the femolution will catch on sooner rather than later," Tahlia's saying. "We've already made some progress."

I run my hands through my unruly waves. "Yeah. You're right."

I try and stay positive, but Faith's and John Mark's smug looks make me want to fill their shoes with wet coffee grounds.

The first warning bell rings. And, dang it, Faith sidetracked me once again. I look longingly at the coffee cart, the line already five students deep.

"Here," Tahlia says, sliding her coffee my way. "I barely touched it. I'm too nervous for this calc quiz this morning anyway."

I take a quick sip. "You're a godsend."

"Don't let Faith catch you saying that."

I take another greedy sip of mediocre coffee, gathering my book bag with my free arm. But when I look back at the cafeteria doors, I see Faith standing there, arms crossed, watching us.

───────────

My mom is stressed. I know this because she doesn't say anything about my Sharpied arms and face when I get home from school later that afternoon.

I heave my book bag on the kitchen table. "What's wrong?"

She gathers her dark hair with one hand, then lets it drop down over her shoulders. Her worry lines look more prominent than usual. "Your father requested to see you on Thanksgiving."

Well. This is certainly an unpleasant surprise. My dad has never requested my presence over the holidays. Not even Christmas. And to be perfectly honest, I would rather spend the day shoving jelly beans up my nose than go to his place.

"Welllllll." I stretch out the word. "Tell him no."

My mom pulls out one of the kitchen chairs and sits down. "I don't know, Brynn. Maybe you should."

I wasn't expecting her to disagree. "What? You can't be serious."

"Hear me out." She pauses to make sure I'm listening. "Maybe if he sees you're open to a relationship with him, he'll be willing to help you out with college."

Maybe this is an opportunity to beg your rich father for money is what I hear. It makes me feel . . . gross. But that's only one concern.

I consider the logistics. "So we're going to see Smith, Laurie and Jerome, *and* my dad in one day?"

Laurie is my mom's younger sister. She lives in Newport Beach with her husband, Jerome, who works at a tech startup, while Laurie manages a production studio. We don't see them as often as we should since we all have busy lives, so I'm genuinely excited to spend time with them.

The hope that blankets her face nearly breaks my heart. "You want to see Smith?"

I bite my lower lip. I want to see Smith, but I wish it weren't under the current circumstances. In rehab. It's not about the facility or the choices he's made. It's about wishing he was making an active choice to see *us* instead of the other way around. And, if I'm being honest, I'm afraid he'll disappoint us again.

I don't say that, though.

The facility must accept certain preapproved visitors, which means he put us on his list. That's not nothing. I know it will mean a lot to my mom.

I shrug, meeting her eyes. "We're family."

She accepts this with invigorated excitement. "Yes, okay! We'll see him first. Around eleven."

"If Dad wants to see me, tell him he can drive here. After Laurie's." There's no way I'm meeting on his hoity-toity Calabasas turf. "That's the only thing I'll agree to."

Once my dad remarried, it was like Smith and I no longer existed. His two young children are his main priority. They're the ones we see in holiday cards and Facebook posts. I may have to dig under every piece of furniture for spare change when we're low on gas and days away from my mom's next paycheck, but I wouldn't have it any other way. Because at least I have her.

My mom squeezes my shoulder. "This could be really good for you, baby."

Maybe it could, but I sincerely doubt it.

———————————

Later that night, as I'm lying in bed looking over my study guide for government, a text pings on my phone. I glance down. It's Charlie.

A minuscule jolt of excitement launches through me.

But—no. It's nothing. I must have imagined the sensation. Because obviously I like Charlie, but I don't *like* Charlie.

He's sweet, like the maraschino cherry on top of a sundae or the random person in a Starbucks drive-through who buys your drink to pay it forward. *Pure* sweet. But he also has a quick sense of humor on top of all these layers of deep intensity he lets out through his art. He's thoughtful. Complex.

I'm intrigued. That's all. No harm in being curious.

I unlock my phone and read what he's sent.

> **Charlie**
> still want to surf tomorrow?
> sunset beach.

> **Charlie**
> I'll swing by.

I almost forgot about surfing after the conversation with my mom. With an excited buzz vibrating through my veins, I send a short reply.

> as long as this doesn't have
> a Jaws-like ending, yes.

> **Charlie**
> ha. well, can't make any
> promises of the ocean life.

> **Charlie**
>
> but if it makes you feel better,
> I've never had that kind of
> encounter.

I find myself analyzing his response as I would for a client. Just one *ha*? That doesn't send my confidence skyrocketing. Am I off my game? Have I grown rusty?

No, no, *no*. I'm overthinking this. Besides, this isn't flirting.

It *isn't*.

But if I *was* analyzing, which I very much am not, maybe it's because I came on too strong with a jokey reply. Maybe my lack of exclamation makes me seem unexcited.

I have to stop.

Charlie is a friend. He's not some arbitrary goal that I'm trying to gain. That's why I decide to be honest with what I send next.

> i'm looking forward to it

His reply doesn't come immediately, but every second that ticks by makes my skin grow hotter. Was I too forward? I blink away the thought. It doesn't matter.

But if it doesn't matter, then why the hell is my heart pinging around inside my chest like one of those tiny balls inside of a pinball machine?

I stare at my phone for a few minutes, waiting it out. This isn't like me. I overanalyze other people's text messages, not my own.

Just as I'm about to put my phone down, it chimes. The sound sends a flush of anticipation through me.

When I read what it says, it's like I experience a sudden, thrilling drop, a weightless moment suspended in time before gravity hits.

Charlie
me too :)

15

"I signed their petition."

"I don't want the biggest skank at school at prom."

"She'll probably go home with your date instead of her own."

I discover early Saturday morning that there is no graceful way to get into a wet suit. Luckily, there's a long string that allows me to zip myself up. I feel like one of those raw chickens you see at the grocery store wrapped in vacuum-sealed plastic, but at least I don't have to ask for Charlie's assistance.

"You good?" I hear him say from the other side of his Lexus.

I step into view. "Oh, sure. I put this on and asked myself: You know what my skin needs? *Another* super-tight layer of skin."

He laughs. Charlie's wearing a black wet suit that's identical to mine. I admire the toned slopes of his arm muscles, suppressing those fluttery feelings from last night. It's instinctual for me to lean into flirting, but I can't let myself get distracted right now. There's too much on my plate and besides, I can't handle any more disappointment in my life.

"It protects you from board chafing," he explains.

I wrinkle my nose, shifting in place. "I can't feel my butt crack."

He raises his eyebrows. "Were you . . . hyperaware of your butt crack prior to this moment?"

"No, not particularly. But now I'm *really* not aware of it." I slap my chest. "Also? I think both of my boobs have morphed into one uniboob."

He thinks for a second. "Uniboob feels like it has superhero potential."

"The Epic Adventures of Uniboob and Butt-Crack Boy."

"Can I please veto Butt-Crack Boy? Also, it's too early to be saying *butt crack* this frequently."

Now he's given me real fuel, so I playfully shout, "WHAT DO YOU HAVE AGAINST BUTT CRACKS?"

He immediately matches my energy. "NOTHING. THEY'RE VERY USEFUL."

And then we're both laughing deliriously at our own childish humor. There's no one around this early to hear us. Even if there was, I wouldn't care.

"Did you know that in Japan there's a series called *Butt Detective* about a juicy crime-solving booty?"

Charlie blinks, as if wondering if he heard me correctly. "Wow, please say more."

"Google it. It's going to be your new favorite thing."

"How can I not when you've given me this information?"

Charlie carries both boards down to the sand. As promised, he picked me up at seven in the morning. My mom knew I was going surfing with some friends, but I left out the fact that it was Charlie and not Tahlia and Marlowe. Not like it would have mattered. I was trying to save myself from the zillions of questions I know she'd ask.

It's an overcast morning. Gloomy, dense clouds hang over our heads. The sand is cool underneath our feet, not yet warm from the sun. The salty air wakes me up, invigorating in my lungs. Seagulls caw from above us, and below them the ocean breathes out a misty hiss.

Charlie sets the boards in the sand. "We'll need to start with some pop-ups, which is kind of like an exercise."

Excuse me?

Exercise?

I collapse dramatically. "You tricked me into working out at seven in the morning!"

Charlie grins. "It helps. I swear. And it's more of a technique you need before we get out there."

I lift up my head. "Does it bring you joy?"

"What?"

"Torturing me."

He laughs. My eyes linger on his teeth as he does. They're white and straight, probably due to good dental work. There's something magnetic about his smile. It brings a certain warmth to his entire face.

Charlie leads me into a few stretches followed by a step-by-step guide into mastering pop-ups, a practice that helps with balance and standing. He makes it look simple, but when I try on my own, I quickly realize I will be using every single muscle my body homes.

By the time we finish, I'm already sweating. I wonder if I can get away with using the board as a bed and taking a nap.

Charlie brushes sand off his hands. "Let's try it on the water this time."

I wrap my arms around my board, hugging it. "We can't stay here?"

He squints down at me. "I didn't think you were one to turn down a challenge."

That gets me on my feet.

My instinct is correct. Surfing isn't easy. Charlie guides me through wave spotting—finding the perfect wave to ride—but when I try to follow his lead, I wipe out.

I wipe out *a lot*.

It's fine, though, because it turns out I enjoy trying. Every time a new wave forms, an adrenaline rush volleys through my spine, making my heart speed up with euphoric excitement.

Because Charlie's been doing this longer than I have, it turns out he's good. Like, really good. Every time I flip off my board, gather my bearings, and try and figure out where he's gone, and he's usually riding out a wave.

"Can I ask you something?" he says once we're bobbing next to each other. The waves have calmed, giving us room to breathe out on the water.

I'm staring at his hands, his long fingers that grip either side of his board. I snap myself out of it. "That's allowed."

His eyes narrow mischievously. "*Why* Otto Litwin?"

I groan, pretending to bang my forehead to my board. It's not that I don't want to talk about my past with Charlie. I'm an open book. It's just—well, it can be difficult to contextualize.

Otto and I started talking back in September. We'd both volunteered to sort textbooks in the main office for Greenlough's mandatory community service hours. Otto is attractive, sure, but we didn't have much in common from the get-go. He's your mediocre High School Sports Guy. Which was fine, because I assumed we both knew it wouldn't last long. After my breakup with Hayes, I wanted something superficial. Low stakes.

A distraction that wouldn't leave me feeling like my heart had been annihilated.

I don't know how to explain all of that, so I say, "It was fun until it wasn't."

Charlie shakes his head. Droplets of water curve down the edges of his jaw. "Sorry, I'm not judging. It's just—he's friends with Thomas Randkin. And, you know—"

Ah, yes. Thomas Randkin, the father of Cadence's baby.

"His whole friend group is a bunch of tools?" I finish.

One corner of his mouth lifts. "Yeah, but you're . . . not."

"That's how I'm going to sign your yearbook," I joke. "Brynn Whitaker, Not A Tool. Right next to my doodle of an abacus emoji."

I'm totally kidding, but Charlie looks embarrassed. "I mean, you're smart and funny and loyal and . . . a lot of other things. Things that Otto and Thomas aren't."

My lips part in disbelief. If you were to poll the entire student body, people would use brazen adjectives to describe me, but certainly not the ones Charlie used. The ones that land softly in my heart.

Before I can respond, Charlie starts paddling. "Get this one!"

"YEAH, SURE. LET ME JUST CASUALLY DO THAT," I shout from behind him, *struggling*.

Charlie catches the wave. I wipe out yet again.

And so it goes. I tried.

The sun is out in full force when we make our way back to the sand. I try to silence the words that rolled off his tongue as we head to the outdoor showers. *Smart. Funny. Loyal.* Each syllable strikes a light, airy sensation straight to my core.

Once we're back at his Lexus, I toss my slouchy shoulder bag on his hood and slip out of my wet suit. I pull on my sweatshirt and shorts over my swimsuit, carefully brushing excess sand from my legs.

I'm reaching for my bag when I hear Charlie's phone buzz. It's sitting on his towel, which is also on the hood. Before I realize what I'm doing, my eyes roam to his screen.

He has three incoming texts from Adeline.

I flick my gaze away, slinging my bag over my shoulder. I get a sudden weird feeling in my gut, probably from my intentional light snooping.

Charlie mentioned he and Adeline broke up over the summer, but they're still friends. I know they're friends because she's part of his inner circle: Grant, Shantel, Adeline, and Charlie. That's healthy. Charlie is extremely likable. It makes sense that they text.

I don't know why I'm dwelling on it.

When Charlie turns around, wet hair flopping in his face, he smiles at me. "I have a serious question for you."

I freeze. Oh no, oh no, oh no. I'm *caught*. He saw me. I'm going to melt into the earth out of sheer mortification, like a slab of silly putty in the sun.

"Okay," I say, my voice meeker than usual.

He leans over the hood of his car. "How does it feel now that your butt crack is free?"

A short, spluttery exhale unleashes from the depths of my throat. I laugh, relieved. "You know," I say, looking him in the eye. "Never been better."

―――――――――――

My mom is making breakfast in the kitchen when I walk through the door. It's not even ten o'clock and yet it feels like I've been awake all day.

She turns off the stove. "How was it?"

I grab a glass from the cabinet and begin filling it with water. "I didn't stand, but I had some solid attempts."

"Well, you're just in time for omelets." She serves me a plate. As I reach for it, she takes a better look at my arms. The Sharpie has faded from showering and surfing in the ocean, but it's still legible. "Do I want to know?"

I glance down. "Probably not."

"Works for me." She slides over the salsa jar. "Greenlough parents got an email from the dean this morning. There was an update in the investigation."

I nearly drop my fork. "Really?"

A sympathetic look crosses her face. "I'm sorry, Brynn. Whoever created that Snapchat account used a fake email."

"Oh," I say, not quite sure what I was expecting.

"They're still looking into it," she reassures me. "Are you okay? The dean mentioned Mrs. Burchill could help you navigate your feelings surrounding this incident."

Technically, I did see Mrs. Burchill. And she's the one who advised me to get back in my classmates' good graces. That's what we're trying to do with this club, aren't we? So really, I have it handled. I don't need any more guidance, and I definitely don't need to discuss how Duncan Rowe has made me feel.

"I'm fine," I tell her. "But thanks."

She doesn't look like she believes me. I think she might push the subject when we're interrupted by a phone call. She glances at the screen, then takes it in her bedroom. It must involve Smith.

I'm polishing off my omelet when my own phone buzzes. There are three incoming texts from a number I don't recognize.

Unknown

hey brynn, it's adeline from school

Unknown

i heard from a friend that you've been pretty successful in navigating crush conversations? i could use your unbiased help. i'll pay of course

I fall into the kitchen chair, trying to process this. Hadn't I seen Adeline text Charlie a few times this morning at the beach? At the thought of this, something acrid spreads through me.

I'm . . . upset?

That makes no sense. I have no reason to be upset. In fact, I should be full-on happy-dancing. This is the first potential client I've had since the whole Duncan debacle. She's offering money. And for the first time all year, my mom and I have no emergency fund. Zero. Zilch. We're totally fucked if we find ourselves in another bind.

Besides, I don't know the details of Adeline's request. The very least I can do is hear her out.

So I text back.

> hey! i can give it a try. my rates are $20 per conversation, but i can look at your previous text history to guide you in the next interaction. is this person at greenlough?

I send the response, then sit silently and stare at my phone, as if this is what warrants a fast reply. After a few minutes, Adeline responds.

> **Unknown**
> cool. and yeah. i'd rather not say who, but let me screenshot our latest convo. we had something a while back, then things got a little messy. i want to rekindle it.

I read and reread her message, my heart sinking. I've never had anyone *not* share the identity of the person they're talking to, but I respect it. Part of me wants to ask her why, but I worry that would cross a boundary. Because there's no way this isn't Charlie.

We had something a while back.

I want to rekindle it.

Perhaps I'd been dangerously close to catching feelings for Charlie, but I need to squash it. I have a mission to focus on, and I can't take on Adeline as a client *and* pursue the very person she's after. I'm already dealing with enough drama. The entire school hates me. I would be putting myself through that all over again.

Yeah. No thank you.

Charlie and I can *only* be friends. It's for the best. Adeline's text proves my reputation might be on the mend because, despite what she's heard, she sought me out. I can go back to saving money, which is great because I've sent dozens of job applications and have received exactly zero follow-up.

So I shoot off another text, officially agreeing to be Adeline Masso's flirt expert.

16

"Maybe they'll give it a rest after Thanksgiving."

"Is it bad that I kind of want to check out a meeting?"

"Zanele said it was empowering."

I spend the rest of the weekend studying for midterms with Cadence, Tahlia, and Marlowe. It's *rough*. I have senioritis as bad as the next person, but I can't let my grades slip. I drink way too many vanilla iced coffees, and every night I lie in bed with flashcard notes dancing behind my eyelids.

While we don't want to overextend the hype, we also don't want to lose momentum with the femolution. It's important for people to stay curious, but as someone who doesn't love being force-fed anything, I know *nothing* will make students reject something faster than it being dumped upon them. Which means we have to be creative. And sly.

We make *them* come to *us*.

With Miss Rothman's permission, Marlowe, Tahlia, Cadence, and I get to school early on Monday and stick a few neon Post-its on the cafeteria wall. We write down nasty things that have been said about us and words of wisdom, forgoing signing our names and instead signing off with #Femolution. We decide to keep Sharpies and Post-its on the table next to the wall as a sign of encouragement, and by lunch, nosy students gather in droves to see what we've done.

And it *works*.

It's not revolutionary. I mean, we haven't created a uniform movement that drives a stake through the throat of the patriarchy or anything. In fact, many students scoff and walk away. But a few don't. They pick up their own Post-its and contribute.

There are at least twelve by the end of lunch on Monday. By Tuesday, there are double.

"Look," Cadence says, leaning over to show me her phone in the parking lot after school. "Carmen uploaded hers to Instagram! And people are *liking* it."

I stare at her screen. Carmen's Post-it reads: FAT ISN'T A BAD WORD. I'M SMOKIN', HONEY. Her comments are flooded with encouraging words like **hell YES** and **tell em babe**.

"This is amazing," I say.

Finally. It feels like people are starting to get it. I can only hope this is motivation for more students to come to our meetings.

Because Greenlough gives us Wednesday, Thursday, and Friday off for Thanksgiving break, the Evolution of Feminism Club isn't meeting this week. I manage to make it through the last of my midterms before collapsing on the couch, exhausted from stress. My mom gets us Taco Bell for dinner, and despite wanting to stay up late, I end up falling asleep around nine.

Which brings us to Thursday.

Thanksgiving Day.

My mom is in a chipper mood, blasting Fleetwood Mac and smiling more than usual as she drives us to Smith's rehab in Brentwood.

I don't want to sound ungrateful, because I'm glad to see family on

Thanksgiving, but part of me wishes I had the ability to fast-forward through this part. The Smith visit. I feel tingly with nerves. It doesn't help that I haven't eaten, though that will be remedied soon. I hate the awkwardness I feel when I'm around my brother, like we're strangers.

It didn't used to be like this. Smith and I have never been super close, but when we were younger, he was the one who taught me how to rollerblade and boogie board and play Mario Kart. He included me in water-gun wars with his friends and let me borrow his comic books.

But then he changed.

Smith is four years older than me, and when he was in high school, he started working at the local Whole Foods to help our mom. When he wasn't at work, he was with his new friends. His *shitty* friends who introduced him to drugs. That's when he locked me out of his life.

Brentwood isn't too far from Pacific Palisades. With holiday traffic, it takes us about thirty minutes to arrive. The facility is called We Care Recovery. It's a nondescript gray building with a fence encircling the perfectly manicured lawn. A beautiful botanical garden ushers us through a sweeping entryway.

When we check in, an attendant tells us that Smith is in the commissary, one of the designated visitor sections. I follow my mom down a long hallway until we reach a dining area.

Smith sits alone at a round table doing a crossword puzzle. You'd think he was seventy-two and not twenty-two by the way he concentrates on it, biting at the top of the plastic pen. I get that unpleasant nervous feeling again, like I'm about to write a paper on something that I haven't thoroughly researched.

He's wearing a gray T-shirt and jeans—nothing fancy. His hair has been cut and shaped into a classic undercut. No dark circles under his eyes. He looks refreshed. Recharged.

"Happy Thanksgiving, Smithy." My mom beams as she approaches him, arms open into a hug.

Smith rises to embrace her. We share a few similarities, but he gets more of his physical appearance from our dad's side. His almond eyes are more upturned than my protruding, slightly downturned eyes, giving him a resting friendly face. When he breaks away from our mom, he turns to me.

"Hi, Brynn," he says timidly. "Thanks for coming."

"It's good to see you," I say honestly.

We take a seat around the circular wooden table.

"Save your appetite," Smith tells us, nodding in the direction of the kitchen. "The potatoes are instant. And the turkey's kind of rubbery." He looks at Mom. "You're going to Laurie's later?"

"We are, but we wanted to come see you first."

"Nairobi," I blurt.

Mom and Smith glance in my direction, confused. I'd been staring at his crossword.

"It's the capital of Kenya," I clarify, gesturing to the puzzle. "You have it blank."

The edges of his lips turn upward as he inks in the word. "Still the smartest one in this family, I see."

"She's working on her college essays." My mom beams at me, but I have a hard time returning the smile. The pressure sits uncomfortably on my chest. "Our fingers are crossed for Stanford."

Smith sets the pen down. "Any idea what you want to do?"

"Product design," I tell him. "Eight across is Marxism."

Smith writes my answer in the box. It fits.

The three of us finish the puzzle. It's nice, working together like this. I'm able to provide a few more answers—*opal, Coppola, Eisenhower*—and Smith impresses me by filling in some that I don't know.

When our mom gets up to go to the bathroom, there's an awkward silence that falls between us. Smith quickly breaks it.

"I'm sorry you have to see me here again."

I stiffen, squashing each tiny emotion that tries to rise to the surface. "She wants you to get better."

Uncertainty spreads across his features. "And you?"

"I like you best when you're not causing her to worry." I pause. "And of course I care about you."

Smith nods, taking this in. "I feel like there's a *but* coming."

I swallow, debating whether or not to be honest with him. "I don't know. She can't say no to you. You know that."

He lets that hang there for a minute. I shouldn't have said anything. "Look—"

"I'm sorry," he interrupts. "I hate disappointing you guys."

Well, don't is what I want to say, but I can't. I know Smith didn't ask for this addiction, but he's been in multiple rehabs. Sometimes I wonder if it will ever end, or if this is the way it will always be, hopping from rehab to rehab for the rest of his life. I can't imagine that. I don't want that for him.

"I graduate in May." My tone is gentler now. "Mom probably told you. But, you know, it would be great to have you there. I hate it just as much as she does when you disappear."

He looks at the completed puzzle. I can't decipher what's going on in his head, but a second later, in a hushed, coarse voice, he says, "Okay . . . yeah. I'll be there."

———————

Going from Brentwood to Newport is a longer journey, but it's not the worst drive. Seeing Smith has lifted my mom's mood, and we decide to keep that joy alive by playing holiday music. Which, yeah, I know some people think is blasphemy before December first, but whatever. I'm here for the jolliness.

I *love* the holidays. Not for the presents, which have always been limited with my mom's income, but the ebullient atmosphere that's contagious. The festive holiday decor and twinkle lights neighbors string from their rooftops make my chest swell. It's an acceptable time of year to drink hot cocoa and stay in pajamas until noon. Strangers are kinder, people are more generous with their time, and family bonding is encouraged. Even if you don't have family, friends are enthusiastic about letting you join their celebrations. It's a comforting season.

My mom grows quiet as we pull into Laurie and Jerome's expansive driveway. They live in a tan-and-white stucco two-story home that's framed by palm trees. The front yard is perfectly landscaped—one of Jerome's favorite hobbies—and the window above the front door has a faux French balcony surrounding it. It's a charming home in the midst of a gorgeous, albeit slightly cookie-cutter, suburb.

I grab the pie we've kept in a cooler in the back seat. It's pumpkin, a Thanksgiving staple.

Laurie throws open the door the moment we knock. "Savannah! Brynn! Hello, hello. Come in!"

Laurie wears a flowy orange-and-yellow maxi dress. It's supposed to reach a high of seventy today, and the sun is already shining despite that it is, in fact, fall. Southern California has limited seasons compared to the rest of the country. Sometimes I wish a white Christmas was possible, but alas, that would be a huge holiday miracle.

Laurie moves aside so we can step into her grand foyer and move toward the kitchen. It smells like scented cinnamon candles and savory spices. There's a replay of the Macy's Thanksgiving Day parade running on their enormous flat-screen TV.

I hand over the pie. "Homemade."

"I always look forward to your pies." Laurie carefully takes it from my grip. "Jerome! Pie!"

"One of my favorite words," Jerome bellows from the kitchen. He's tall and Black with a megawatt smile, and today he's decked out in a navy blue apron. "We're so glad you guys could join us."

The three of us sit in their cozy breakfast nook while Jerome sizzles something in the background. It smells like bacon. If I had to guess, he's making his famous maple bacon brussels sprouts.

My stomach rumbles. I haven't eaten anything today. If I had known Smith would warn us away from the commissary food, I would have at least made a smoothie.

Laurie pours my mom a large glass of wine and the two of them fall into small talk about work and the holidays.

"And you saw Smith this morning?" Laurie's saying as Jerome puts a colorful veggie platter with hummus down in front of us. It's like he read my mind. I dive in for a carrot and crunch it between my teeth.

My mom sips on her Merlot. "We did. He seems to have a positive outlook on this program."

"He looks good," I add, because I know it will make my mom happy.

Laurie grins at me. "It would be so wonderful to have the three of you here for Christmas dinner."

I glance at my mom, who's in the middle of sipping her wine, a distant look on her face, so I say, "We'd love that."

Laurie launches into a story about a happy hour with her co-workers, and twenty minutes later, Jerome calls us to the kitchen to make our plates buffet-style.

Everything smells delectable. Tender turkey, thick gravy, and buttery mashed potatoes sit next to fluffy sweet potatoes, crispy-topped green bean casserole, sweet corn bread, gooey mac 'n' cheese, and of course, Jerome's famous brussels sprouts. I take a little of everything. My mom is pickier with her selections, which is weird. I know she's just as hungry as I am.

Once we sit, Jerome asks me questions about upcoming finals, college applications, and major options. I don't mind regurgitating my typical answers. It's been a while since we've last talked, and he seems genuinely interested.

Laurie grabs a bite of potato with her fork. "How's the day care?"

My mom picks at the potato chunks from her mashed potatoes. "Oh, you know. Exhausting. The kids are a handful. Some are terrors, but most are sweet."

I take a huge bite of turkey just as my phone buzzes. I sneak a peek from the pocket of my dress and see it's from Adeline. There's an unpleasant shift in my gut.

"Not at the table," my mom snaps.

Yikes. She's in a mood. Our visit with Smith couldn't have gone better. I don't understand why she's so snippy.

"Sorry," I apologize, quickly putting it back in my pocket.

While my mom and Laurie talk about work, I consider the Adeline-and-Charlie situation. I've been analyzing her texts over the last few days, but I haven't gotten back to her with a plan of action. From what she's sent me, it's hard to gauge Charlie's emotions. Their conversations have been surface level. His responses are only a few words long, and he never follows up with questions to keep it flowing.

It's not a great sign, but it's not an outright rejection. We can work with that.

Adeline expressed wanting to hang out with him over Thanksgiving break, so I need to find a way for her to ask him that also ensures he won't say no. A sense of dread overcomes me every time I think about the two of them on a date, but I can't let whatever tiny, *minuscule* crush I have on Charlie affect what Adeline wants. It's not about me.

The table has gone silent. Aunt Laurie is staring at me as though waiting for my response. I realize I missed something in the conversation while off in my own head.

"What?" I blurt.

"We have news," she gently explains, then reaches over and takes Jerome's hand. "We've started working with an adoption agency."

There's an unpleasant sound as my mom scrapes her silverware against her plate. To cover, I say, "No way! That's amazing."

"They're hopeful that they've found someone for us," Jerome continues. "It's expensive, but it doesn't matter. We did consider IVF—"

"—but the success rates were a little off-putting, and we've already been through so much emotionally already."

"So we decided to take a few months and do some research. Really think about adoption as an option." Jerome smiles at Laurie, excitement sparkling in his eyes. "And we feel it's right."

My heart might burst with happiness. Laurie and Jerome have wanted kids for the last two years, but it hasn't come easy. Laurie suffered a miscarriage a year ago that devastated them both, but she took it the hardest. My mom was there for her during that time and helped her find a good therapist to talk to, so it's bizarre that she's not more enthusiastic for Laurie right now.

"It's really great," my mom finally says, looking at her sister through shining eyes. "Congrats. This is big news."

But I know my mother, and she's acting off tonight. Even her excitement is more reserved than usual.

I'm not the only one who notices. Later, as I'm helping Laurie slice and serve the pie we brought over, she brings it up.

"Hey," she says gingerly. "Is Savannah okay?"

I glance in the dining room where Jerome is indulging in another glass of red with my mom. I don't know what's gotten into her. It's as if Smith was the highlight of her day and the rest of us aren't worthy of her time.

I slide a slice of pie onto one of the dessert plates. "I think, you know, she wishes Smith were here."

Sometimes I wish I didn't have to be the person who tries to resolve everything. But I love my family and I hate conflict, which is why I'm up for the task. Besides, my mom probably *does* wish Smith was with us.

No matter what I do, what grades I get or what honors I receive, Smith will always be the favorite. It's something I accepted a while ago, but I wish she understood that I need her too. Instead it's like she locks me out, and it hurts.

But Smith needs her right now. Maybe more than I do. This scandal may have blown up my image, but at least I've been executing a plan to fix it. I've been fine on my own, but he hasn't.

"I'm also supposed to see my dad later," I add. "Maybe that's why she's in a weird mood?"

"Mm, Will *is* a mood killer," Laurie says thoughtfully.

I almost confess that she wants me to ask him for money, but I stop myself. I don't need to empty our burdens on her, so I lock them in my chest with the rest of my worries.

My mom and I have this unspoken rule that we don't ask Laurie for money. I suggested it once, and she instantly shot it down. She's always been the caretaker for her younger sister, and I think she'd feel pitied if the situation was reversed.

"The Whitaker women come up with our own solutions," she'd remind me.

As we're saying our goodbyes after dessert, my phone buzzes again. I'm sure it's Adeline, so I almost don't look, but something tugs me toward my phone as my mom searches for her keys. Since she's had a few glasses of wine, I'm driving home.

I unlock my phone.

Charlie

hey, happy thanksgiving! want to hang out tomorrow? PS, i have been watching a lot of crime-solving butt content

My heart leaps into my throat. Charlie.

I immediately feel guilty. Didn't Adeline say she was hoping to hang out with him over break?

Uncertainty churns in my stomach. I'm not doing anything wrong, am I? I can hang out with Charlie as a friend and still help Adeline. Plus, maybe hanging out with him as friends will dissolve this tiny, insignificant crush I've developed.

It's going to be fine. I'm not going to interfere.

Before I can write a reply, another text comes.

Charlie

i was thinking Venice. weird place for weird art inspiration.

"Found 'em!" my mom says, prying the keys from the bottom of her bag and handing them to me.

I type out a quick reply before I overthink it.

> i'd love to

———————————

In true Will Whitaker fashion, my father never shows up. Instead, he sends a text wishing me a happy Thanksgiving and saying he's sorry he couldn't make it down, but the traffic was "too much" today. Which is a pathetic excuse. It's SoCal. Traffic is always "too much."

My mom somehow believes I'm distraught by this news and whips up two pumpkin vanilla milkshakes, our unique creation we invented last year when we decided to put vanilla ice cream, cinnamon, and a slice of pie in the blender.

We're sitting on the back porch in her parents' old rockers when I get the courage to ask her what's been bothering me all night.

"Why weren't you happy for Laurie?"

My mom loosens the straw from her lips. "Who said I wasn't happy?"

I suppress an eye roll. "Well, obviously no one said that, but you seemed put out by her news."

"Laurie's been talking the adoption route for a while now," she explains. "I've warned her it can be a long road."

I crisscross my legs, narrowing my eyes. "How would you know?"

"I hear parents talk about it at day care."

"That doesn't mean you can't show some excitement for her," I argue.

She sighs. "You're right. That wasn't my intention. I'll give her a call tomorrow," she says gently. "To be honest, I was missing Smith tonight. It would have been lovely to have all of us there."

Ah, so my hunch was correct. The absence of Smith put her in a mood, even though we'd seen him earlier today. Deep down, it's hard to feel like I'm ever enough for her. *You had one child with you today*, I want to say. *Don't I count for something?*

"There's always next year," I say instead. "Unless he decides to go to Dad's."

Her head snaps in my direction so quickly I'm afraid she's given herself whiplash.

"Kidding," I say. "Like either of us would."

"Yeah, well, that's not a polite way to speak about your dad," she tells me, but she's suppressing a smile.

"I have him saved in my phone as a bunch of those red demon emojis."

"Brynn."

But we're both laughing now, and I'm secretly pleased I'm able to boost her mood even if Smith isn't here. It makes me feel like maybe I'm enough for tonight.

She checks the time on her phone. "I should turn in." She stands up, then glances down at me. "I'm thankful for you, hon."

I wrinkle my nose at her cheesy affirmation. "I'm thankful for you too, *Mom*."

She kisses me on the top of the head, then goes inside. I'm about to follow her in when a text chimes on my phone. It's from Tahlia. we have a problem, she's written, it's faith.

17

"Rhea said Brynn's club isn't bad."

"Do you think Lenora will join?"

"Doubt it."

In what should have been an informal announcement about the Evolution of Feminism club, Faith has *actually* written an opinion piece in the *Greenlough Gazette* that's layered in subtle jabs.

Brynn Whitaker's lead as the white feminist savior of social stigma falls flat considering her past, one line reads. And another, *I suppose it's a last resort idea for those looking to justify, or stand in support of, scandalous behavior.*

Zanele texted Tahlia a digital proof obtained from Davey Trenton, the editor in chief, alongside the message: he's publishing this trash on Monday.

Of course Davey would let Faith publish this. He's friends with Duncan.

"This is ridiculous," I say on the phone with Tahlia. I'm holed up in my room now that my mom has gone to bed. "She wasn't even at the meeting! Between this and her prom stunt, you'd think I'd hooked up with John Mark."

"She's gone off for sure," Tahlia agrees. "But that's not all."

I groan.

"There are rumors she might make *you* the focus of her Senior Showcase performance."

I thump my forehead to my desk.

"You okay?"

I absolutely am not. This is just one more thing I have to worry about.

"What *kind* of performance?" I ask.

"I don't know," she confesses. "But we should prepare something that highlights our side."

After we get off the phone, I plan an official Senior Showcase meeting for Sunday. I'm not sure where to go from here, but at least we can brainstorm together.

It's midnight, but I decide to I stay up and analyze the text exchange Adeline sent me earlier.

> **Adeline**
> happy thanksgiving

> **Adeline**
> i hope it's not weird to say, but i'm grateful for you

> happy thanksgiving, you too

> **Adeline**
> what are you doing over break?

> just some dec 1 college app
> deadlines

> **Adeline**
> good luck!

> **Adeline**
> i'm in town, you know. if you're
> bored. might check out the rising
> sails show saturday night?

To be fair, Adeline is doing all the right things. She isn't overeager or annoying, but she keeps hitting walls of non-responses. I recommend waiting at least a day. If he doesn't reply, she'll send the perfect follow-up response that we crafted together:

> **Adeline**
> there are a few things i'd like to
> apologize for in person. if you're
> around, i'll be at Giovanni's on
> sunday. i hope you'll show.

Adeline still doesn't want to give me any background, so I have no idea what she wants to apologize for. But she told me it was important. I think for a moment, then text her.

> do you consider yourself a vulnerable
> person?

Adeline
lol no

Huh, who knew I'd have so much in common with Adeline Masso?

> then maybe you need to
> show that side so this
> person knows how you feel?

This means Adeline has to put herself out there and face potential rejection, but if she wants to make progress, then this is a good start. In the end, she agrees.

It's the inspiration I need to revisit the USC essay. I stay up until the early hours of the morning mulling over the prompt. Call it flirting, or matchmaking, or coaching, but at the end of the day, it's about gaining people's trust. Showing them how to frame things differently. Expanding their potential to connect with someone.

Once I realize this, the words come freely.

I don't always know what to do, but somehow, I've always known the right thing to say, I begin. *I didn't realize how much connecting with people meant to me until I lost it all.*

———————————

I'm walking along the Venice boardwalk with Charlie the next day. I don't allow myself to feel guilty about this because (1) Charlie asked me and (2) perhaps I can get some insider information for Adeline, even though she thinks I don't know the identity of her mystery crush. So, really, I'm helping in a roundabout way.

I tend to avoid Santa Monica and Venice as a rule. They're beautiful, iconic beaches mostly full of tourists and tourist traps. But with everyone hitting up stores for Black Friday, it's quieter than normal.

Venice is an odd, colorful city that overstimulates the senses. Every other building down the strip is painted in bright hues: magenta, turquoise, sunshine yellow. There's something cool vying for your attention everywhere you look. T-shirt shops that airbrush your name in weird calligraphy. Muscle beach with bodybuilders showing off in the outdoor gym. The enormous skate park where advanced-level skaters shamelessly ride their boards. Eclectic street performers and musicians everywhere you turn. And, of course, the earthy smell of weed.

There really is nothing else like it.

We buy a slice of pizza from Joe's Pizza and multitask eating as we wander down Ocean Walk. Bikers buzz past us on our left, chiming their gentle bells to alert us that they're passing. There's a fair amount of people walking dogs and roller skating, and a few people whizz by on those rentable motor scooters that feel like a death trap.

We're playing a game I invented where we try to imagine who lives in the luxurious beach-front homes.

"He invented the teddy bear," I say, nodding to a man in shades soaking in the Jacuzzi that's planted on his balcony. "And he patented it. He gets five cents every time a new one is created, so he never has to work a day in his life."

Charlie elbows me, indicating a woman on the phone in the window of another chic property. "She's a senior-level ice cream creative at Ben & Jerry's and gets paid to come up with flavor concepts."

"The dream," I sigh. "Oh! That house next to it? They started investing in reusable straws before people became heavily invested in saving the turtles."

"Okay, but the home next to *that* belongs to a celebrity dog walker."

We play this game for at least another mile, long after we've devoured our pizza and discarded our plates. I relish the mental break after my overwhelming Thanksgiving.

The ocean waves create a lulling white noise. I slip out of my sandals. "Let's go in."

Charlie follows, removing his own sandals. There aren't many people out here. It's overcast and unideal beaching weather, but a few surfers brave the water. The briny scent of the sea falls over us in a light mist.

I lose my breath when a wave sweeps over my feet. The Pacific doesn't have a running history of being warm, but it's icy cold today. It sends a jolt of shock through me, dying down as my skin grows used to the sensation.

Charlie stands so close that we're nearly shoulder-to-shoulder. Today he's wearing his nose ring, which isn't allowed at Greenlough, and an oversized black jean jacket over a white-and-black-striped shirt. He also has the top of his ear cartilage pierced with a simple silver stud, something I'd never noticed before.

The ocean breeze sweeps his scent in my direction, smelling of sugar crystals and sandalwood. A low hum of excitement buzzes through my chest, and it feels like a tiny betrayal. I think of Adeline and cast away that feeling.

But because I'm a masochist, I ask, "Are you doing anything else over break?"

Charlie digs his foot in the sand. "Oh, um. I'm—"

My chest constricts. I brace myself.

"—working on my portfolio for CCA."

I glance at his profile. I knew he was applying to art schools, but I didn't realize California College of the Arts was one of them. It's a good school.

"How's it going?"

"You know, I've been trying since October, but—I don't know—nothing was flowing. I wasn't inspired, I guess." He looks over at me, meeting my eyes. "But that's changed."

I swallow. I can feel my heartbeat in my ears, roaring above the sound of the ocean.

I am not allowed to feel this way for Charlie.

"Anyway," he continues. "What about you? Cadence told me about the gathering tomorrow."

Relief rolls through me. I needed this subject change. "Yeah, we're brainstorming for the showcase," I say. "Did you finish your piece? For the show?"

"Almost." He digs his left foot deeper into the wet sand. "I'm also helping Grant with his set. He has a drummer and guitarist but needs a pianist. Cadence and I took lessons until freshman year."

Heat rises in my cheeks, and I tell myself it's nothing. It's definitely not a growing crush, even though picturing Charlie playing the piano creates a tingling warmth that I feel all over my skin.

"So promise you won't make fun," he finishes.

"Never," I say quickly. Maybe too quickly. "It's cool. Really. Girls go crazy for musicians. Own that shit."

A faint redness flushes over his face. I don't think he's used to compliments.

He clears his throat. "Hey, Cadence said Faith was bullying you out of going to prom?"

I scoop a load of wet sand on the top of my foot and kick it into the ocean, pretending it's Faith Tobinson. "She was getting people to sign her petition under the guise that I was a bad influence at the Halloween dance, but it was really because of the whole Lenora-and-Duncan thing."

"You shouldn't let that stop you."

I move a piece of windswept hair away from my face. "She's also pubbing a piece about the club in the *Gazette* that's . . . less than flattering." I look out into the ocean. "I'm tired of being the center of things. I want real change, you know? To show them how their actions affect people. Cancel *cancel culture*."

He gives me a sidelong look. "Greenlough thinks they're progressive, but they have a long way to go."

"Exactly." I drop my shoulders. "I'm going to admit something. Don't judge me."

His thick eyebrows pull together. "I would never."

And I believe him. "Duncan shit-talking me hurt me in more ways than one, but I still care about Lenora. I wish we were friends. I wish that—" I stop myself. I don't want to get into *that*. The reason we're not. So I go, "Out of everyone, I wish she believed me. She shouldn't be with Duncan after what he did."

Charlie gets this knowing look on his face.

"What?" I ask.

Something soft and earnest flashes in his eyes. "It's very clear to me you still care about Lenora as a friend because you care about people."

Another wave brushes over our feet. I let that sink in. It's more or less what I'd said in response to the essay prompt last night. Outside of my educational focus, I like fostering connections. I like improving people's chances at navigating meaningful conversation. And I like it because I get invested. I care.

Charlie sees it. Mrs. Burchill sees it. If only I can make the entire school see it too.

"I don't know what else to do," I admit.

"Well," he begins. "If anyone can figure it out, it's you. I think the only way through is to keep going."

On Sunday, we decide to take advantage of the breezy seventy-degree day. The four of us meet up at Temescal Canyon Park to discuss the showcase. Tahlia's spread an enormous blanket for us to sit on, and Marlowe's brought a spread of tangerines, apples, Oreos, and Wheat Thins.

For the last half hour, we've been talking about how to make a statement at the showcase. Everything Cadence suggests falls under the EXTREME category. Things like freeing the nipple in front of the whole school to crush the unnecessary censoring of women.

"It's like you're actively trying to get me expelled," I say, exasperated.

"I'm sorry, it's the reckless side of me," she replies, flipping to a blank sheet of paper in her notebook. "I'll tone it down."

But we get stuck after that.

"You know what's weird?" Tahlia asks, flicking her eyes to me. "Katie Delcavo texted me to see if the club is meeting this week."

My brows shoot skyward. Showing up at the first meeting was unintentional. Now she wants to come again? On her own?

I hate feeling suspicious, but I can't help it. I know what's going in the *Gazette* tomorrow. Faith could be sending Katie as a spy.

But maybe I'm overreacting. She might want to learn. Isn't that what she told me after the first meeting? And, okay, I *may* have a soft spot for Katie because we used to be friends. It's why I don't want to believe she's working with Faith to actively take me down.

"What did you say?" I ask.

"I mean, I told her it was happening." She fingers a loose thread on the blanket. "We're welcoming everyone, aren't we?"

"We can be welcoming and also suspicious," Marlowe says. *"Considering."*

"True, but we can't make her feel exiled," Tahlia explains. "We said it's inclusive."

It's true, and we have to lead by example if we want to change the way the student body thinks about acceptance. But I do wonder if Faith has a hidden agenda.

The sun breaks through the marine layer, warm and comforting, and the four of us lie around the woven blanket like cats in a sun puddle. We fall off topic, our conversation switching to sharing our Thanksgiving stories.

"They're really pushing the Ivies on me," Tahlia's saying. Today she's wearing a stunning emerald-green hijab with rings that match the gemstone coloring. "It's so much pressure, but it's all they want to talk about."

I feel for her. Tahlia has these breakdowns every few months, usually when her parents' expectations overwhelm her. Most of it comes from her immigrant grandparents insisting that anything other than an Ivy League school is less-than. It's not like she doesn't want to go. She applied to Brown, where she wants to study psychology, but she's also applied to Boston University and the University of Maryland.

"My dad guilts me whenever we talk about *those other colleges*, then he belittles me in front of family. I was telling my cousins where I'd applied and he basically threatened that I wasn't going to embarrass him by going to a non-Ivy school. Not to mention he keeps pushing medical school so I can become 'a real doctor,' like psychology is a waste of time."

"I'm sorry," I tell her. "Is there anything you can do to change his mind?"

"I don't know. We talk in circles whenever I bring it up." She massages her temples. "God, I'm sorry. I'm being a baby about this, aren't I?"

Marlowe props herself up on her elbows. "You're not. It's hard when family gets involved."

"It's true," Cadence says. "My grandparents immigrated here, too, and

I know they put a lot of pressure on my mom. And then she puts a lot of pressure on me, so you can imagine how they took the pregnancy news. I used to get mad, but I think it comes from a good place. They're always going to want what they think is best for us."

Tahlia lets out a shaky sigh. "Thanks. I should put this stress away until colleges start sending acceptances, then deal with it."

Cadence passes her the box of Wheat Thins. "We're here for you when that happens."

"Speaking of family," Marlowe says to me. "How was seeing your dad?"

I roll my eyes. "Surprise, surprise; he never showed."

Tahlia looks appalled. "That's awful, Brynn. After he said he wanted to see you?"

"It's nothing new." I shrug it off. At this point, I'm used to the men in my life disappointing me. "My mom wanted me to talk to him about helping with college funds, but I doubt he'd be on board. He's told me before that it shouldn't be hard for me to land a scholarship."

"He's so disconnected from reality!" Cadence exclaims. "He thinks they hand out scholarships these days? Like millions of other kids aren't vying for the same spots?"

An overpowering sense of unease slams through me. She's not wrong.

Cadence sees the look on my face and tries to backtrack. "I didn't mean—"

"No, I know. It's reality," I say, stopping her apology before it starts. "It's why I need to gain people's trust again. With Smith in rehab, it's like we're barely staying afloat."

I'd followed up with the jobs I'd applied to without any luck. Marlowe suggests going to Palisades Village tomorrow, a luxury square filled with high-end shops. I'm hoping they'll need holiday hires.

"Is there anything we can do?" Tahlia asks gently.

I shake my head. My mom has always been so certain we can handle things. Even if it's hard, we get by. She's made me tough. If there's anyone who can create a plan to win over my peers *and* reinstate my side hustle, it's me.

I grasp for a subject change. "Tell us about your photoshoot with Zoë."

Marlowe rolls over, cupping her face with her hands. "Do tell us *everything*."

"She's so talented," Tahlia gushes.

Cadence raises a brow. "With her tongue?"

Tahlia waves the joke aside. "No, with her camera. She's been entering photography contests, and I know she's bound to win one."

"She's placed before," Cadence reveals. "Back when Tyla, Devin, and I were friends, we'd enter the same competitions."

Cadence looks down at her hands, tucking them into her sweatshirt sleeves. I remember the photos in her bedroom, the ones of Tyla and Devin by the pool, laughing. I hate that they dropped her when she needed them the most.

"And what happened after the shoot?" Marlowe prompts.

"Nothing! Well, not *nothing*. She packed this lunch for us? And we sat on the beach and talked for like, three hours. Then she drove me home, and we've texted *a lot* since." She rubs her lips together, thinking. "I know she's bi, though. She mentioned going out with Kelsey Farrow last year. I had no idea."

"She's into you," I say. "I know it."

Tahlia grins. "Okay, no more talking about it! I don't want to jinx it."

The conversation shifts back to the *Gazette* piece that's allegedly publishing tomorrow, and a second later, my phone buzzes with an incoming text.

Adeline

thank you, Brynn. it worked!

we're hanging out later today.

:)

I should be overjoyed at the prospect of fifty much-needed dollars hitting our bank account, but the creeping disappointment lingering in the pit of my stomach expands.

I try not to think of Charlie meeting up with Adeline. I haven't told my friends that I'm helping her. It's a matter of privacy. And I certainly haven't mentioned my growing crush on Charlie. If it was a weed, it would have overtaken an entire garden. But it's not right to intentionally compromise results for Adeline. I need to let it go. To move on.

"Faith wants to call out Brynn in her Showcase act," Marlowe's saying.

This gets my attention. I put my phone away. "So we have to be one step ahead."

"But"—Cadence glances at me—"we don't stoop to her level. It undermines our group and what we stand for."

"What if we somehow call out people for siding with Duncan?" Tahlia proposes. "*He's* the one who cheated on Lenora, and he still has people's sympathy despite that."

Cadence gets this fiery look behind her eyes. "So we change that perception."

"What, like cancel Duncan?" Marlowe jokes.

"*We* don't," Cadence insists. "If we play our cards right, they'll do it for us."

Now the wheels in my head are spinning, pieces slotting together. "Can we directly call out Duncan like that?"

"Faith is apparently calling you out," Marlowe counters.

I take this in. "So . . . we'll be coy," I say. "We'll *in*directly call him out."

Marlowe glances at Tahlia, then back at me. "What do you mean?"

We can make a point on a larger scale without breaking school rules. I'm sure of it. Last year, a senior roasted every single Greenlough teacher during his Showcase performance. Maybe this is our one chance to push boundaries. To make a statement. To remind students that Duncan isn't a good person.

And then it hits me.

"Trust me," I say, a surge of excitement plummeting through me. "I've got this."

18

"Did you read the *Gazette*?"

"It was . . . bold."

"Did Faith even go to the meeting, though?"

We've set my idea for the Senior Showcase into motion, but the tricky part is getting Miss Rothman's permission without letting her know too much. We don't want to get her in trouble, but we're going to have to go behind her back if we want my plan to work.

Unfortunately, that is the furthest thing from my mind today. Faith's article made it into the *Greenlough Gazette*, and it's all anyone wants to talk about on Monday. Just when we'd made some real progress with the Post-it wall, which has also mysteriously disappeared.

It's infuriating. I'm concerned people will stop showing up to our meetings, which is what Faith wants. She thinks we're corrupting students with our sexual agenda, or whatever lie she's told herself.

Because I'm feeling fiery, I corner her in the hall after school. She doesn't expect my presence, placing a hand over her heart when she sees me.

"You scared me." Her eyes narrow. "Can I help you?"

"Why did you write that piece for the *Gazette* and conveniently leave out that you didn't attend our meeting?" I demand.

"It's an opinion piece, Brynn. Am I not allowed to have an opinion?" she huffs. "*You* told me to form my own, remember?"

I feel an irritated muscle in my jaw twitch. Great. My loud sassmouth is what got me into this mess.

It takes everything in me to keep my voice calm. "You can have an opinion when you have all the information."

"I didn't do anything wrong," she says, her voice hardening.

"Okay, sure. Fine." I fold my arms. "So you want to tell me why I keep hearing these Showcase rumors?"

"Oh, please. It's not all about you all the time, you know."

"You sure make it seem like it is."

"Why don't you just apologize to Lenora and put this all behind you?" Faith asks, as though it's that simple.

"Because I refuse to apologize for something I didn't do!" I shout.

Faith sighs like she's disappointed in me, but she doesn't say anything else. Well, whatever. I don't know what I expected from this conversation. What a waste of time.

We're interrupted by a pair of clacking heels. I glance over my shoulder and see Mrs. Burchill heading toward us.

"Faith," she says by way of greeting. "Brynn. Did you both have a good Thanksgiving break?"

"Yes, thank you," Faith's voice is raised a few octaves, the tone she puts on when she's sucking up to teachers.

Mrs. Burchill gives me a pointed look. "My door is always open, Brynn."

She *would* remind me. Little does she know I have it all figured out.

The Senior Showcase is going to change everything.

After school, Marlowe and I decide to study at Sticks and Scones. The bakery's name is an ode to New Found Glory's 2002 album, *Sticks and Stones*, which I only know because I asked. Every single pastry is named after pop punk songs from the early '00s, and they always play the best alternative music.

We're sitting at my usual corner table, notebooks spread out before us, but that's not what currently has my attention.

"See, I can't defend you when you say things like that," Charlie's saying, twirling my pen between his fingers.

But I'm relentless. "*Iron Man 3* is a Christmas movie!"

To be fair, Charlie approached me. And I had no idea he was working today.

"It takes *place* during Christmas—" Charlie starts.

"Therefore making it a *Christmas movie*."

"Not the same."

"Marlowe. Help me out," I beg.

Marlowe raises her hands in surrender. "Never seen it. This one's on you."

Two customers walk in and begin perusing the menu. Charlie returns my pen to me, then he stands, pulling on his hair net as he tucks in the chair he was occupying with his foot.

"That," I say, "is incredibly sexy."

"You," he mimics, "are a liar."

I pretend to be offended. "I don't lie when it comes to health and safety uniforms."

Charlie leans in close, lowering his voice. The proximity sends a wave of flutters through me. "Maybe they're here to offer me a modeling contract."

I blink away my swell of longing. "They saw the exquisite hairnet and thought, *A masterpiece! We MUST have him.*"

Laughing, Charlie returns to the register. As he takes their order, we catch each other's eyes. I circle a finger around my head and then begin to playfully fan myself. When their attention is diverted, he tosses me a spirited middle finger.

When I turn back to Marlowe, she's smiling. "You two have gotten close."

"We're friends," I say, hoping I sound casual. Because we are. *Friends*. That's it.

I decide I need to change the topic, so I walk her through my interaction with Faith today, which has left me feeling rage-twitchy.

"She has a hidden agenda," Marlowe says when I finish. "We just have to figure out why."

"Because she hates me," I groan. "Honestly, I wouldn't be surprised if she spread that Snapchat."

"Listen to yourself. This is *Faith*. That's a big reach."

Sure, it's easy to rule her out, but who would spread that video around? I can't think of anyone at Keith's that night that had a massive problem with me. Not knowing the motive makes it that much harder to figure out.

Marlowe pores over her honors Algebra assignment as I work on my paper. Every so often, Charlie walks by and teasingly flicks my ponytail or delivers a palmful of chocolate candies used in one of their cookie recipes.

The third time he comes around, Marlowe catches me smiling as he makes his way back to the register. I duck my head and focus on my work. I don't want her to assume there's anything going on between us. My only goal is to reconnect Adeline with Charlie. I won't get in the way of that.

But when I look back at the counter, Charlie's eyes are on me. My heart thrums rapidly against my rib cage. He quickly averts his gaze, as if embarrassed to be caught. I'm glad the music is loud, otherwise I'm convinced everyone in here would hear the insistent jackhammering that's taking place inside my chest.

It's a crush. It's *nothing*.

It doesn't matter.

As we're packing up to leave, Charlie rushes over and delivers a folded receipt, pressing it into my palm.

"What's this?"

His glowing smile reaches his eyes. "A secret."

He heads back to the register in time to greet a group of middle schoolers who've walked in. I press my lips together as I unfold the glossy receipt paper. He's drawn an animated tush in the likeness of the Butt Detective with a speech bubble overhead. *The Gazette piece was trash. See you at the meeting Wednesday.*

I laugh. Marlowe glances my way.

"What?"

"Just . . . Charlie making me feel better about Faith," I explain. "He'll be at the meeting Wednesday."

"See?" she says, zipping up her backpack. "Not everyone listens to Faith."

I clutch the note in my hand, thoughts of soft stares and kind smiles whirring dangerously in my head the whole ride home.

Things are slightly calmer the next day. The buzz surrounding Faith's opinion piece has faded into the background thanks to McTiernan's new prom rule that heels must be lower than four inches. Most seniors are outraged by this *rules for the sake of rules* restriction, myself included.

My phone chimes in my pocket after school, and I find that I have an incoming Venmo of fifty dollars. A text from Adeline follows.

> **Adeline**
>
> our hangout on sunday was so
> awkward. i was hoping to pay
> you for more help. it's trickier
> than i thought, and i can't talk
> to my friends about it.

The awful sabotage monster inside me celebrates that her meetup with Charlie didn't go well, but I quell that feeling. I'm a terrible person if I'm hoping that Adeline's relationship with Charlie implodes because I'll benefit from it.

She's paying for my help. So I'm going to help her.

> do you want to meet up and talk it
> out?

> **Adeline**
>
> it's ok. we can stick to texting.

I'm sure Adeline doesn't want to be associated with me because of Duncan, which is fine, I guess. I'm used to it. I tell her that I'll think of another plan by tonight. She sends me a bunch of black heart emojis, which, coming from Adeline, is the highest form of praise.

———————

Before classes begin on Wednesday morning, I meet Tyla and Devin outside of Mrs. Garcia's Spanish classroom, where we meet for Future Business Leaders of America. After everything Cadence has done to help me, this is the least I can do.

I don't know Devin Schapiro that well, but I do know Tyla. She's cold-shouldered me out of FBLA meetings since Halloween, just like she's ignored Cadence.

They eye me warily as they approach. I'm surprised they didn't bail.

"I know it's none of my business, but I wanted to talk about Cadence," I blurt, knowing I only have a few minutes before the first bell rings. "You don't have to like me, or be my friend, but maybe put yourself in her shoes. She's had to deal with a lot on her own."

Devin and Tyla exchange a look of discomfort.

"We don't hate her. It was never that," Tyla says faintly.

I glance between them. "Then what was it?"

"We think maybe she didn't know how to talk to us. But we didn't know how to talk to her either," Devin supplies. "And it all sort of . . . unraveled."

Ah, right. I'm starting to understand the source of the conflict. This may not be the same as helping someone with their crush, but it also falls in the realm of my expertise. Friendships also require communication, and when that fails, there's a risk of them falling apart.

I should know. Look at Lenora and me.

"I think it might help if you had an honest conversation—without judgment," I say. "I mean, it sounds like there's hurt coming from both sides. And do you really want to lose each other? After years of friendship?"

"No," Tyla says, flitting her eyes to mine. "I guess we weren't sure if she still needed us."

"She does," I say, and my heart unexpectedly squeezes. Because I wish Lenora needed me too.

"We'll talk to her," Devin promises. "And thanks. I, uh—I know things haven't been easy, but I'm glad she has you."

I'm stunned by this admission. I was under the assumption that they'd turned on me, but if that's changed, then maybe it's proof that what we're doing is working.

I turn to go, but Tyla stops me. "Brynn? I'm sorry," she says in a rush. "I shouldn't have made you feel unwelcome. You should come back to FBLA."

She sounds apologetic, and while I appreciate the offer, I'm balancing a lot right now. Our club is my main priority.

"Thanks for saying that," I tell her. "And you're always welcome to join us too. If you want."

Tyla and Devin glance at each other before looking at me. "We can't today, but maybe next week?"

It's not a guarantee, but even so, I'll take it.

My concerns about Faith's *Gazette* feature turn out to be validated when a few people don't return to our meeting after school, including Rhea. I tell myself she's probably busy with StuCo duties, but she's Lenora's best friend. It's likely a different story.

Mathis, Zanele, Zoë, and Carmen show up, along with Charlie. Katie Delcavo, true to her word, sits through the entire meeting that Tahlia spearheads. She discusses the history of hijab, how it can feel empowering and liberating, and explains why many don't see it as a form of suppression despite what stereotyping may perpetuate.

I'm on edge throughout her entire speech, flicking my gaze to Katie and hoping she's not here to pick a fight. After Faith's article, I'm not sure I trust her.

As we're wrapping up, Miss Rothman waves us over. "Brynn, Tahlia— stay for a second?"

Tahlia and I exchange confused looks, but we walk over to her desk as the last of our members trickle out.

"Tahlia, this was such an enlightening meeting. Really." Miss Rothman beams. "It makes my next news a little difficult to share, but Dean McTiernan's club policy states that you must have at least fifteen members."

An anchor drops in my stomach. There were eleven of us here today. "It's only our second meeting—"

"I know, and I have a feeling you'll be able to get more students interested. You're doing a great job so far. We just have to have that number by the end of the year to continue."

A growing bubble of anxiety stretches through me. This is just one more thing I'll have to fix.

Tahlia catches my eye. "We can do that."

Her determination boosts my confidence. "Thanks for letting us know."

As soon as we're outside of the classroom, we relay the situation to Marlowe and Cadence.

"Faith *definitely* knew that policy," Cadence says. "It's why she wrote that piece! To sabotage you!"

"But then why send Katie?" Tahlia questions. "It doesn't make sense."

I stare down the empty hallway. Katie is long gone by now, along with everyone else. Tahlia's right. If Faith is trying to ruin us, it doesn't make sense that Katie attended the meeting.

So I'm going to find out why.

19

"Brynn's whole schtick is entirely self-serving."

"Maybe, but I don't think I'll get a prom date without her help."

"Is it possible to even trust her right now?"

I catch Katie in the parking lot of school the next morning. She has this frantic deer-in-the-headlights look on her face when she spots me, but she doesn't try to avoid me.

"Hey." My tone isn't exactly friendly, but I don't care. "If Faith wants to write another piece for the *Gazette*, you should tell her to come to the meetings herself."

Katie's lips part in surprise. "Oh. Um, this is awkward, but Faith doesn't know I went."

Her eyes stay on mine. I can't tell if she's lying or not.

The marine layer lingers above us, creating a dampening chill in the air. I wrap my cardigan tighter around me. "So you came because you wanted to? Despite everything she's said about me?"

"Just because we run in the same circle doesn't mean we're the same person. I told her to lay off with the prom thing. And the *Gazette* piece? She came up with that on her own."

She sounds sincere, but I can't shake my feelings of suspicion. "You're genuinely interested?"

"Yeah, I meant it when I told you the first time. Faith can be a lot. I know that better than anyone." She fiddles with the zipper on her book bag. "I just . . . I don't know. I love my church, right? But I don't love how judgmental people can be, so I wanted to do some unlearning and, well, *learning* in general." She gives me a shy smile. "It was a great meeting, by the way. I didn't get a chance to tell you. I'll be back next week."

I release that protective armor of defense I've grown used to wearing. "If you're being for real. I mean, for real *for real*, then bring new people with you next time. We're in danger of being disbanded next semester."

"Sure," she agrees, as if it really is no problem. "I can do that. And, hey? I know it used to be different with us, and I'm sorry. For making it seem like I chose Faith over you back in middle school."

I'm thrown by her honesty. "I mean, isn't that what happened?"

"Well . . . it's like, our moms are friends? And they're such a church family, and, I don't know, we just became close." She blinks away the crestfallen expression on her face. "But I want to try and make things right."

"It was middle school, Katie. I get it. Sometimes people grow apart." I glance at the time on my phone. "But if you do want to help us, recruiting is a strong start."

"Okay, yes. Of course," she says, then, "Hey, um. About the whole Duncan thing? It's just—if it wasn't you, then did you ever figure out who it could have been?"

She looks uncomfortable, like bringing it up will somehow offend me.

"I have no idea," I admit. "I was hoping they'd come forward by now, but another part of me understands why they haven't."

Just then, the warning bell rings. I adjust the strap of my book bag and look toward the double doors.

"See you next week," I say, ending our conversation. "Remember—"

"I know," Katie says, a new determination in her eyes. "I've got you."

Later, as I'm packing up my Pre-Calc notes, I replay the conversation with Katie in my head. I have my reasons to be skeptical. But if she *does* show up and bring more people, then I have no reason not to trust her.

During lunch on Thursday, and then again on Friday, Charlie joins us at the Spindelli bush. *Twice* in one week. At first Cadence seems annoyed by his presence among her friends, but she slowly comes to accept him as part of our group.

Marlowe's telling a story about something that happened in honors Algebra, but I'm barely paying attention. Because Charlie subtly nudges me, and the brief contact of his shoulder bumping mine sends a charge of electricity all the way through my fingertips. I exhale that feeling away when I realize he's only offering me his bag of Doritos. I take one, catching a subtle hint of his body wash. It makes me lightheaded all over again.

There's laughter. I've missed the joke, but I laugh anyway. I lean back on my left hand, shifting my position so I can try and relax. Next to me, Charlie shifts his own weight. The outside of his pinky barely touches mine.

Does he realize he's made contact? Or am I hyperaware of all of his movements?

No. I'm overthinking. It's an accident. Maybe he doesn't have spatial awareness. But as I try to surreptitiously glance at him, I find he's already looking at me, a relaxed smile playing on his lips.

Guilt gnaws away at my gut.

I turn my attention to the large cafeteria windows and find his usual lunch table. Shantel is nowhere to be seen, but Grant is gesturing wildly next to Adeline, as if telling an intense story. She sits beside him with her hands resting under her chin, scrolling through her phone. I don't think she knows Charlie is out here with us, and I feel ten times guiltier.

After getting a breakdown of Adeline's conversation, I realized I need to read between the lines. Adeline mentioned she apologized for something that happened in the past, but he was hesitant to jump back into things because he didn't trust her. Apparently, he mentioned wanting to work on their friendship. She said it wasn't ideal, but she'd take it.

I advised working on the friendship part first to respect his wishes. If it was forgiveness Adeline wanted, she'd have to be patient. She seemed to understand that. We decided the best course of action would be to engage with him over text every day. Ask him questions he'd be eager to respond to. If they could chat about things they talked about before, then she could slowly approach that deeper connection she wanted.

Charlie's made a habit of texting me in the evenings, which makes me wonder if he's texting Adeline at the same time. He asks me about my day and sends photos of his paintings in progress. I tell him my most recent product design idea of a nail file in the shape of an egg for a more controlled experience. There are some nights where we text until I fall asleep.

Maybe Lenora is right. I'm a two-faced backstabber who makes everything about herself. But I try to shake those thoughts from the corners of my brain. Deep down, I know I'm not that person.

On Friday, I accompany Cadence to her five-month checkup after school. Her mother is supposed to be here with her, but she had an opportunity to take a last-minute meeting with a potential client that could lead to a huge amount of tea-subscription-box sales. Cadence doesn't mind her absence, but because she didn't want to go alone, she asked me instead.

We've been sitting in the exam room for the last fifteen minutes. Thomas stayed in the waiting room. He barely spoke a word to us when he arrived, averting his attention to his phone.

Cadence is restless. She wanders around the cramped, cold room touching everything. There's a model of a pregnant belly that she takes apart, examining the tiny fetus inside.

The door opens. A tall Black female doctor walks in wearing a white lab coat and a stethoscope around her neck.

Cadence scrambles to put the model away.

"Cadence, how are you doing?" she asks, flipping a few pages in her chart.

"Feeling more and more like a human blimp every day."

The doctor gives a polite smile. "Let's get you on the table and take a look."

The stiff paper crunches as Cadence climbs onto the sterile bed. I stand to the side to give her privacy. The doctor asks her to expose her stomach, which she does. Her skin is a swollen sphere, a safe, comforting home for the little guy growing inside her. A clear gel is slathered on her skin as the doctor runs the ultrasound over her belly. All of a sudden, a heartbeat sounds.

I feel myself swelling with emotion. When I glance at Cadence, she's staring glassy-eyed at the monitor.

"Strong and healthy," the doctor notes. "Taking your vitamins?"

Cadence nods.

"Good." The doctor begins wiping the gel clean from Cadence's belly, explaining what Cadence can expect at eighteen weeks. She recites it with such ease that I imagine it's a script she's memorized. Then she removes her gloves and tosses them in the waste bin beside the door. "I'll leave you to it, but don't hesitate if you do have questions in the future."

Cadence looks down at her hands. "Thanks."

Once the doctor leaves, Cadence pushes herself into an upright position and smooths out the bottom of her uniform blouse. Her eyes are red. When she looks up at me, she bursts into tears.

Her emotions are so jolting that I stand there, a bit startled, before rushing to the other side of the room to deliver her tissues. I want to hug her, but I have a sense that Cadence isn't the hugging type. So I stand by her side, as if to let her know I'm here if she needs me.

"Fucking hormones," she mumbles when she regains control of her breathing. She sniffs, dabbing her eyes with the tissue. "If you tell anyone about this, I'll ruin you."

It's not a real threat. I know this because she's giving me a watery smile. She hasn't explicitly said so, but I can tell she's grateful she's not here alone.

―――――――――

I almost forget that Thomas is waiting in the lobby. When he sees me exit with Cadence, he leaps from his seat and slides his phone in his pocket.

"How'd it go?"

I'm thrown by how earnest his question sounds.

Cadence must be surprised, too, because she gives me a confused look before glancing back at him. "Um, fine. Nothing abnormal."

"Good," he says, then repeats, "Good."

We all stand there awkwardly. I wonder if I should step aside and leave them alone to talk when his phone buzzes. He checks a text, his attention now somewhere else.

"I think my mom wants us to get together soon to decide on the adoptive parents."

Thomas is still looking at his phone. "Sure."

Cadence flicks her attention to me, rolling her eyes. "Great," she grinds out. "We're leaving."

Thomas blinks up at her. "Oh. When's the next appointment?"

"Not until after the New Year," Cadence replies, already heading toward the door. I follow her without saying goodbye.

Once we're back in her car, she sighs. "If men were the pregnant ones, they'd be, like, ten *thousand* times needier than we are."

"Oh, you don't have to tell me."

"Hey." Cadence's tone is less jokey now. "I know you talked to Devin and Tyla."

I sit there, frozen, unsure if she thinks I overstepped.

"We talked things out in our group chat last night," she continues. "And, well. Thanks. It's nice to have them in my corner again."

The muscles in my shoulders relax. "I'm glad."

"You're good at this, you know," she says as the engine turns over. "I know it's moving slower than any of us want, but it's progress. I mean." She grins. "Katie *Delcavo* is part of the femolution."

The corners of my lips tug upward. "It is kind of wild."

"Tell me about it."

"Listen, I don't want to get sappy on you," I say, changing course. "But I know Thomas isn't going to tell you this, so . . . you're doing great. You really are."

Cadence's eyes grow teary again. "Fuck you for making me emotional," she sob-laughs.

I hold out my hand over the center console, fingers spread. I expect her to shove me away in a very Cadence manner. When Marlowe and

I first became friends, she told me she was a touchy-feely person. That's how she expressed her love, even a friendship sort of love, but she said she wanted to respect Tahlia's and my boundaries if it bothered us. Some people weren't into contact affection, but we never minded. I'm not sure where Cadence stands, but it's a small offering.

To my surprise, Cadence takes my hand and squeezes.

I squeeze back.

20

"I'm thinking of going to an EOF meeting next week."

"I heard it's not bad."

"I don't know. I still don't trust Brynn."

Zombie Week is next week, also known as pre-finals week, where students don't get new assignments but instead spend class hours in a zombie-like haze working on study guides for finals. I'm reviewing my AP Government notes on Saturday, but I need a break. So I'm glad when Cadence texts and asks if I want to join her at the beach while she works on her photography project.

Which is how I end up at the Santa Monica pier with Charlie and Cadence on Sunday afternoon.

I hadn't known Charlie would be joining until his Lexus was parked in front of my house, Cadence sitting shotgun. A prickle of excitement shot up my spine when we briefly made eye contact in his rearview mirror. I had to stare down at my hands to calm my racing heart.

Santa Monica is flooded with tourists this time of year. It takes a lot of patience to navigate around them. Once we're on the boardwalk, dozens of people stop along the railing to pose for pictures. Since Cadence wears her analog camera around her neck, two strangers ask if she can snap a photo on their phones. I laugh as she tries to hide her annoyance.

Pacific Park is at the end of the pier. It's an amusement park and arguably the happiest place on earth if you're under the age of ten. I've walked around here so many times that the shine has worn off. The park is filled with children running around, shrieking with joy as the West Coaster roller coaster swoops by on its steel tracks. Fair games in brightly painted booths and flashing lights line another part of the boardwalk, daring you to try and win stuffed dolphins and tigers. Ice cream, cotton candy, funnel cakes, soft pretzels, churros, and every other fair food imaginable is available for an upcharge that'll make your wallet ache, and aggressive seagulls lie in wait for a chance to steal your french fries.

"So what's the theme?" I ask Cadence as we walk along the rickety boardwalk. "Of your project, I mean."

She throws me a mischievous smile. "Lost hope in humanity."

"Mm. Dark."

"Not as dark as Charlie's art."

Before I have a chance to reply, she maneuvers a few steps ahead of us to snap a candid photo of a mother and father fighting in front of a toddler in a stroller who's happily gnawing on a churro.

When I glance over at Charlie, he's looking down at his shoes. "Maybe she's right. My art—it's too dark. I can't imagine what CCA is going to think."

"They're going to think it's brilliant. It makes people feel something," I insist. "Isn't that the point?"

Charlie seems to relax. "Yeah. You're right."

Then it hits me. "Hey, wait. That means you sent your application in."

"Out of my hands and into the world," he confirms.

"That's big," I say, doubling back as a wide grin spreads across my face. "Churros on me?"

He lights up as we get in line, but when I try to pay, he cuts in with his cash before I have the chance to pull out my wallet.

I try not to think about what that means.

Cadence has abandoned us a few yards ahead, scouting out perfect opportunities for her theme. We take a seat on one of the empty picnic tables after shooing away seagulls in search of a snack. Our shooing doesn't keep them away for long, so we ignore them and sink our teeth into the warm fried dough.

I observe a girl vlogging in front of the iconic Santa Monica Ferris wheel. "Love spotting an influencer in the wild. Like, *the confidence.*"

"You're confident," Charlie says.

"Well, okay. Mostly true. Except the part where I fake a lot of it?"

Now Charlie looks perplexed. "You—what do you mean?"

"I know it's hard to believe a charming, attractive, smart individual like me—"

"—and very *clearly* modest."

"Super modest. The most delightfully modest person you've seen in your life." That makes him laugh. "Truthfully? Confidence doesn't come naturally for me."

"That," Charlie says, "is surprising."

"It's true."

"So what's the secret?"

No one's asked me this before, so it takes me a few seconds to think about it. I remember what I told Carson in my bedroom all those weeks ago. To not second-guess yourself. But it's more than that. It's also about your inner assuredness. Knowing, deep down, that you're enough. And embracing it.

"I guess I remind myself that I don't have to listen to those negative voices in my head. It's something I choose. Like"—I hold my arms out in front of me, the number fourteen faintly Sharpied on my skin—"doing this? At school? Knowing people are going to talk shit? I just own it. It's all you can do."

Charlie's eyes stay on mine. "I had no idea. You just—"

All my breath gathers at the base of my throat. "What?"

"You make it look easy."

His eyes are on the tops of my forearms now, resting on the faded fourteens. I think he's going to ask about it. Everyone I've *had a thing* with. And I'm not sure I want to get into it. Not now, anyway. So I bop him on the forehead with my half-eaten churro and take on a lighter tone.

"I'm full of surprises. Ones you might not see coming. Like my detailed knowledge of booby traps."

There's a teasing glint in his eye. "Says the person who's seen all the *Home Alone* movies."

That gives me an idea. "We should totally booby trap Thomas Randkin."

"Now this is the kind of mild criminal activity I'm into."

I laugh, polishing off the last of my churro. The vibrating *whoosh* of the roller coaster thunders overhead. Riders scream gleefully. The warm, sticky-sweet scent of cinnamon drifts by, reminding me of the sugar scent Charlie sometimes carries in the fabric of his clothes.

"You know," Charlie begins, shifting his knees in my direction. He's wearing a black hoodie today, and I can see his gold chain peeking out, resting on the back of his neck. His nose ring glints in the sun. "I wouldn't have come today if Cadence hadn't told me you'd be here."

His hazel eyes are bright, warm pools of rosemary green with flecks of deep amber. There's a softness in his expression, almost vulnerable.

My brain repeats his words over and over so that it almost sounds lyrical. He'd *hoped* I'd be here. Because . . . why? Did he want to spend time with me, just like I was thrilled by the idea of spending more time with him?

My lips part—but what do I say? Me, the flirt expert, known for helping people find words, is at a loss.

And then the familiar guilt churns through me. Adeline is paying me. She's counting on me to deliver.

"There was a total Karen yelling at the Ferris wheel ride supervisor."

I snap my attention to Cadence, who has reappeared in front of us.

"She looked like she was about to scream at me for taking a photo, but then decided against shouting at a preggo teen in public." She shrugs. "I think I've got enough. Let's play some games."

Charlie doesn't look at me as he stands from the table. I watch as he swipes his fingers through his wind-blown hair. My stomach flips. I wonder if it's soft to the touch. My brain goes fuzzy at that mere thought.

We join Cadence at the Cat Rack booth, where she takes out exactly zero cats. Charlie and I are equally horrible. We don't win the racing game against a few twelve-year-olds either. After failing to win Balloon Bust, we give up.

"We're losers," Cadence says. "Good thing none of us play sports."

"Our lack of athletic talent is made up by our good looks," I counter.

"Charlie only gets to be part of that true statement because he's my twin." She eyes a booth to her right. "Ooh, funnel cake."

Charlie laughs awkwardly as he watches her go. "That's a compliment coming from her."

I cut my gaze to his profile. "Whatever. You know you're hot."

The confession startles us both. We lock eyes for a second before diverting our attention to the Ferris wheel. *Why?* Why is it sometimes impossible for me to think for *one second* before I speak?

I need to stop this before it becomes a rumor that circulates and gets back to Adeline. Or worse, Lenora.

"I—" I begin just as Charlie says, "Um—"

We're staring at each other, but it's me who blows out a nervous laugh. Have I ever had a nervous laugh before today? Where did that come from?

"It's—um—well, it's nice to hear you say so," Charlie says quietly.

"Are you coming or what!" Cadence calls to us, already in the funnel cake line.

I'm about to walk over to her when Charlie goes, "Oh, here."

And before I have a chance to process what's happening, his thumb is gently brushing away sugar crystals from the side of my cheek. My body hums like an instrument tuner, a low, gentle vibration.

"There," he says. "Perfect."

And that's when I know.

I'm in big trouble.

21

"Do you think you'll go to Brynn's next meeting?"

"I'm thinking about it."

"Same. She seems . . . sincere?"

In order to keep our momentum and gain more members, we decide we need a bigger statement than the Post-it wall. I still plan on making the most out of the Senior Showcase next week, but that won't matter if we don't gain our required headcount for this week's meeting.

On Monday morning, Marlowe joins the video announcements to reveal to all of our peers that we'll be sponsoring a gratitude note initiative during lunch for the next week. For the low price of a dollar, you can send someone an anonymous compliment, almost like a valentine, to promote positivity instead of gossip. The best part? All funds will go toward a local women's outreach program as a donation.

Cadence works in the front office as an aide during the last period of the day, so she'll deliver them to the correct lockers. We agreed that this could foster a sense of trust around our club and, hopefully, create a welcoming environment.

At lunch, our table floods with eager students. Cadence collects the notes in a large envelope while I keep track of the money. Many people buy more than one note, handing me fives, tens, and the occasional twenty. By the end of the lunch hour, we've made 155 bucks. It's enough to impress Dean McTiernan.

"You're setting a good example here, Brynn," he tells me. "That's what I like to see."

I hope that means he's already working on my letter of recommendation.

When the final bell rings, students swarm their lockers to find notes carefully slipped through the slats. There's a hum of warm energy that spills through the halls. A wave of relief releases through me. I think we've successfully pulled this off.

A few notes start to tumble out when I open my locker, but I catch them before they hit the floor. Even though they're anonymous, I can tell three are from Marlowe, Cadence, and Tahlia.

I eagerly open the fourth one, my heart clanging in anticipation as I read. *I'm sorry I'm a coward.*

I blink, then read the words again, just to make sure they're there. It's the closest thing I've got to an admission of guilt. Whoever wrote this is clearly regretful, but not enough to come clean.

But this proves that we're changing mindsets, doesn't it? This person feels bad for what they did. Without the femolution, I don't think I would have received anything more than silence.

Tahlia, Marlowe, and Cadence each wear similar expressions of shock when I show them.

"I wish I paid better attention to people's handwriting," Cadence says, examining the note as the hallway slowly begins to clear out.

Between the lip gloss and the note, maybe it's possible to connect the dots. I don't want to have to do that, though. I want a real, face-to-face apology.

Tahlia places a gentle hand on my shoulder. "This is a good thing."

I know she's right. Maybe the tides will turn in our favor faster than we think.

Between our gratitude notes initiative and Katie's promised help, we achieve a record-breaking attendance at our next meeting.

On Wednesday afternoon, the four of us gather in Miss Rothman's classroom. Katie's recruited Victoria P.—a tiny clarinet player—and Victoria M.—the lead soloist in choir. Devin and Tyla find seats next to Zanele and Mathis. Not only that, but Charlie's brought along Grant, and Carmen's managed to bring a few of her dance friends with her. Even Rhea returns, slipping into a seat next to Katie.

By the time everyone sits, I do a quick headcount. *Sixteen* people. We did it. Barely. As long as we can keep it up, we're in the clear.

Marlowe leads the first half of the meeting, discussing discrimination in the trans community and how we can be better allies. Cadence leads the second portion. She brings up how Greenlough's health courses have failed us when it comes to properly discussing inclusive sex education, what we should be learning, and the judgment she faces as a pregnant teenager.

"And it's also not inclusive if you're defining sex as *just* penetration," Cadence is saying.

I watch Katie set down her pen. "What do you mean?"

"Well, that narrow definition excludes certain groups of people," Cadence explains. "Like, the idea that having sex or *'losing'* virginity equals penetration is based on the male standard of pleasure, furthering the point that we continue to put up with patriarchal bullshit."

"And, honestly? How you define sexual intimacy should be between you and your partner," I add.

When I first told my mom tampons were a struggle to insert, she took me to my gynecologist, who diagnosed my vaginismus and recommended a pelvic floor therapist. The problem was most were too expensive and out of network. Instead, I'd scoured tons of message boards and learned from people online who shared their own stories and offered links to dilators that seemed to help. It made me feel less alone, especially after my first sexual encounter with Vince, who wasn't exactly thrilled when I'd told him I wasn't having the best time of my life.

Outside of my mom and Vince, Lenora was one of the first people I'd told. She didn't make me feel broken, but instead immediately destigmatized the cloud of negativity in my head.

"Your *vagine* is a *queen*, dude. It's just unique. And it's not settling for incompetent assholes like Vince," she said with complete confidence. "You know your body best, and you're going to find someone who wants to make you feel your best despite this."

And she was right. Because Hayes was so much more understanding.

A tug of sadness rises in my throat. Lenora's pep talks were unparalleled. It makes me wish she were here.

Katie still looks confused, so I continue. "Like, for me, I have vaginismus—this condition that makes your vaginal muscles spasm. And it's painful with any type of penetration," I explain. "Then there's queer relationships and people with disabilities who also define sexual intimacy in their own ways. It requires expanding your view of sex."

There's a murmur of passionate discussion, and Marlowe suggests we draft a proposal to McTiernan to replace Greenlough's outdated sex ed textbooks with more inclusive ones, so we spend the remainder of the time preparing our statement.

"Nice work on the turnout," Miss Rothman tells me after our meeting ends. "You know, the Evolution of Feminism club should present at the spring fair."

The spring fair isn't until March, but it's the last opportunity Greenlough sets up for seniors to fundraise for prom, which happens at the end of May. It's also where McTiernan announces a few awards and standing achievements from the senior class. Members of student council give speeches, as do other honorees who've worked on special projects to improve Greenlough.

"You've been doing a wonderful job at spearheading. All of you. And you raised so much for the outreach program this week. I think it's something that should be highlighted," she says. "You can figure out which one of you will give the speech and let me know after break."

I hadn't seen this coming. It makes me proud of what we've built so far. "Thank you."

She closes her planner. "Keep up the good work. I'll see you next week."

As I'm leaving the classroom, I nearly run into Lenora, who's waiting outside. My hopeful heart expands inside my chest.

Rhea steps around me. "She's my ride."

"Oh" is all I can think to say. She's not here to see me.

"The fundraising initiative was genius," Rhea says, throwing me a rare compliment. "We should donate to a trans equality program next time."

I cling to her words. *We. Next time.* Have we officially won Rhea over?

"Yes, I love that," I say.

Lenora makes eye contact with me. Her expression isn't friendly, but it's also not *un*friendly. More neutral. Which is a vast improvement, comparatively.

"You should come to our next meeting," I offer, my tone slightly pitchy with nerves.

Her gaze drops to the floor. "I'll think about it."

A weightless cloud of elation rises through me. It's not an explicit no. She's considering it. And if she's considering it, that means we're influencing the way she's perceiving the whole scandal, including Duncan.

Maybe there's hope of finally mending things between us.

22

"I want to go to the next meeting."

"It seems like more people went this time."

"I wonder what Duncan thinks."

Achievement recognition is what Faith thrives upon, so I'm not exactly shocked when she hears about my presentation opportunity at the spring fair. She corners me in the hallway after class the next day. Just when I think I'm about to have *one* drama-free week with her.

"Katie isn't going to stray away from the light of the Lord," she hisses.

I'm confused, but then I realize she's referring to Katie attending both Abstinence Angels *and* our Evolution of Feminism club.

"Okay," I say, stepping around her. I need to get to Pre-Calc before the bell rings. Also? I'm not in the mood.

"And she's not going to start going to your little club or whatever."

Too late. I guess she doesn't know.

Sighing, I turn back toward her, careful to keep my tone neutral. "You can be a feminist and also abstain from having sex. It's not one or the other."

It's as if she doesn't hear me. "You know, if you're trying to recruit

Katie, you should at least come to one of our meetings."

I blink. "I'm not trying to recruit Katie."

I don't mention she's already recruited herself. But Faith does have a point. I can't have an us-against-them attitude *and* be the face of the femolution.

Maybe I meet Faith on a level playing field.

"I'll come," I tell her. "It's after school, right?"

Faith nods, her eyes widening in disbelief. She definitely didn't expect those words to come out of my mouth.

"What room?"

"One thirty."

"I'll be there under one condition." I hold my forearms out in front of her. I've been wearing my fourteens every day since we first established our organization. "You have to stop shaming me."

She makes a face like I've suggested she bottle up some holy water and drink it. "I'm not shaming you. That's un-Christlike."

I raise an eyebrow. "You were making offhanded comments about me after Halloween. You published an insulting piece in the *Gazette*. You tried to get me banned from *prom*—how's that going, by the way?"

She doesn't try to deny it. "I won't apologize for trying to save you."

That's not what I mean, but I don't have time to tread into that territory right now. I'm going to be late. "Do we have a deal?"

She doesn't look happy, but she nods. "Fine, deal."

"—'and let the marriage bed be undefiled, for God will judge the sexually immoral and adulterous.'"

For the last twenty minutes of the Abstinence Angels meeting, Faith has been reading Bible verses about sin and sex before marriage. I can't say I didn't see this coming. Marlowe tried to warn me that this would happen, but she understood why I had to go.

Katie, Elisha, and John Mark are sitting in the circle with us. I try to catch Katie's eyes during prayer, but she refuses to look at me. John Mark appears almost pained that I'm here, like he wishes I were anywhere else. Which is weird, because weren't they the ones who wanted to save me in the first place?

Maybe it's time to remind Faith of why I came.

"Thank you for those . . ." I search for the word. "*Enlightening* verses."

Faith beams so wide, you'd think she'd just found out she was nominated for prom queen.

I push forward. "I understand how abstaining from sex can be empowering for people, but it doesn't make you better than anyone else for doing so."

"Well, God will be the judge of that," Elisa notes.

I cast my gaze over to Faith, who looks visibly frustrated, then to Katie, who gives me a tiny shrug.

"You *would* say that, because you're a virgin hater."

I knit my brows, wondering how on earth we got here. "Faith. I am *not* a virgin hater."

She scoffs. "Well, sometimes your attitude makes it seem like you are!"

I take a deep breath. I didn't realize Faith thought I was out here looking down on an entire group of people when the source of my frustration stems from how society treats girls and women when it comes to their sexual decisions. If anything, I hate the double standards.

Navigating around Faith requires a certain amount of delicacy, but it's worth trying. "I can do better—you're right. Being a virgin *is* empowering because it's something you're choosing to do with your body. No one's saying abstinence *isn't* cool. Follow your heart, you know? People shouldn't look down on you for that. I don't."

Faith looks at me curiously, as if she's not completely sold.

Since I have her attention, I decide to keep going. "Just because it's something I don't choose doesn't mean it's wrong. I think students here should know their options, especially when it comes to sex. So they can be safe."

Faith's expression softens, but John Mark's doesn't. "My dad would disagree. He didn't become a pastor to promote only bits and pieces of the Bible. He did it to help people see God's way."

"And if people find solace in the church, then that's great," I say. "But not everyone will."

John Mark leans back in his seat. "You're really a lost cause."

Faith studies the floor, avoiding eye contact with me. I don't know what else to say that I haven't already said, so I stand and grab my shoulder bag. "Maybe we agree to disagree."

As I head to the door, Faith squeaks, "We still have ten minutes of prayer left!"

But I'm already making my escape. "I'll do some reflection on my way home."

As I exit, I hear her call, "May the light of Christ be with you!"

The walk home isn't bad. In fact, by the time I arrive, I've convinced myself that Faith and I might be okay. I think she may understand where I'm coming from, if only a little. But it *is* weird Katie stayed quiet. I hope she doesn't feel divided. She shouldn't.

When I round the corner into my neighborhood, I'm surprised to see Aunt Laurie's car in the driveway. My mom is doing a three-hour Postmates shift tonight, so she won't be home until later.

A clatter sounds from the kitchen when I walk inside, and I peer around the corner to see Laurie pulling a tray from the oven.

"It's me," I announce. "What are you doing here?"

"Hey, sweetie." Laurie sets down a pan of roasted vegetables. "I came over as a surprise. I have some news to share and figured I'd cook some dinner for you two. It's Zombie Week, right?"

I'm so appreciative for her that I might cry. My mom and I have both been busy lately. Instead of making dinner, I've been eating peanut butter and apple slices, cereal, carrot sticks with ranch—basically any easy snack that we have in our fridge. I don't blame my mom, though. Neither of us has the energy to cook.

I wrap my arms around Laurie and breathe in her lavender scent. "Thank you."

She squeezes back, then goes to the fridge and returns with a small bowl. "Chia seed pudding. It'll hold you over until dinner's ready, which will be in"—she checks the time on the stove—"another hour and a half."

I settle in at the kitchen table and pore over an overwhelming amount of study guides. Laurie makes green tea, which gives me a boost of energy without the usual coffee caffeine jitters.

Our front door swings open around eight o'clock. My mom walks in, looking as exhausted as I feel.

"Hi, Savannah," Laurie says breezily. "I thought I would drop by and see you guys. I hope that's okay."

"She made dinner," I add. "Homemade. Barbecue chicken."

My mom glances at me working at the table, then sweeps her gaze to Laurie, who's loading our dishwasher.

"Thanks, Laur. I'm going to get changed," she says, heading to her room.

When she returns, I notice she's washed her makeup off and secured her hair into a tight messy bun. Laurie serves me a plate of food first, then makes one for my mom.

"I've been keeping Brynn waiting," Laurie says once she joins us. "Jerome has to work late and I was about to burst if I couldn't tell my family in person, but he understood."

I turn my attention to her. "What's the news?"

"There's been a match." Laurie's glowing with joy. "A two-year-old boy. It's a complicated process, but we're one step closer."

I stand up and hug her. "You guys are going to be parents!"

I can see the emotion behind Laurie's eyes. "We're so thankful."

"That's great," my mother says, smiling through her fatigue. "Really. I'm so happy for you both."

I regret my next words the moment they leave my lips. "Let's just hope he turns out better than Smith did."

I mean it as a joke, but I immediately wish I could take it back. My mom looks hurt, then visibly upset. It was a careless comment. A bitter, hurtful jab. Why did I have to ruin this moment?

"Smith is doing his best—" she begins.

"I know, I'm sorry," I interrupt.

"I don't think you do know, Brynn. This isn't easy for anyone, especially him."

I know this is largely my fault, but I'm sick of feeling like the villain. And I'm *so* tired of her defending him, especially when he's broken our hearts on more than one occasion.

"Sav," Laurie interjects, trying to play mediator. "Everyone processes things differently."

"She should know better. He's trying."

My emotional armor cracks, and my pent-up range begins to leak out.

"He can do no wrong in your eyes. Meanwhile, nothing I do is ever enough," I say, feeling hot tears well up behind my eyes. "He only calls when he's out of options, and you'd do anything for him. I mean, my tuition money is the only reason he's in rehab right now."

Laurie stares at my mom, stunned. "Is that true?"

"Smith has a disease, Brynn," she fires, ignoring Laurie. "I'm doing something to *help*. He's family."

She's making it seem like I'm not supportive, which isn't true. It reignites my frustration.

"I care about Smith," I choke out. "You make me feel like I don't because my world doesn't revolve around him. Even after he fucks up over and over again—"

"*Enough*," my mother shouts.

"Okay, hey. Sav? Let's talk in your room," Laurie says. "Take a breather."

I get up from the table and go to my bedroom. I'm angry. At myself. At my mother. At Smith. How does she not understand? I'm empathetic toward Smith's situation, but that's not the issue. It's hard seeing him taking advantage of her. He'll go from rehab to rehab and revert back to old habits, changing his phone number and hanging out with the wrong people until he needs something again. He doesn't even realize we're *one* emergency away from not being able to pay next month's bills. And then who has to figure out a way to fix it?

Me. Like always.

I check my phone to get my mind off things. Marlowe's texted me a link to Duncan's latest Instagram post.

I click on it, instantly feeling like someone's knocked the wind out of me.

He's posted a picture of one of our femolution flyers—the one with my face on it. Only, he's scribbled dark *x*'s over my eyes and written one word across my forehead.

Bitch.

My rage spikes to a whole new level of fury. I know I should take this as a good sign. Getting this type of reaction from Duncan means we're doing something right. Why else would he bait me like this? But then I read the comments from some of my peers.

she sucks.

replace this as her yearbook photo, plz.

hahahaha, good one

They agree with him. *Enthusiastically.*

That's when I decide that I'm done playing nice. If he wants to watch me burn, I'll drag him into the flames with me.

When my mom comes in my room an hour later, I pretend to be asleep. I'm too upset to talk things out tonight. But when she leaves, I roll over and stare into the darkness, stress coiling tightly around my chest as those bitter, hurtful comments haunt the most vulnerable parts of my mind.

23

"I need finals to be over so I can focus on the Showcase."

"I'm going to Brynn's meeting after break."

"I was thinking of going too!"

Even though we both apologized the next morning, my mom and I extend only stiff politeness toward each other on Friday. We might not ever see eye to eye when it comes to Smith, and that's something I'll have to accept. I'll always be second-best to him.

I also call Laurie to make things right. I feel awful. I destroyed what should have been an exciting announcement. After she came over and cooked for us too.

I spend the weekend holed up in my room studying for finals. I try and stay off my phone, but it doesn't stop me from checking Duncan's Instagram account. He deleted his post. Maybe he thought he'd get in trouble, but it doesn't matter. I've already seen it, and my heart beats with revenge.

The showcase is in a few days. He has no idea what's coming for him.

On Monday, Katie finds me by my locker before first period.

"I talked to Faith," she tells me. "She doesn't have plans to sabotage you at the showcase tomorrow. I think going to her Abstinence Angels meeting helped."

The anxiety in my chest releases. "Thanks for letting me know. And hey, I'm sorry for giving you a hard time," I say. "It hasn't been easy navigating around Faith's agenda, but I shouldn't have taken it out on you."

"Oh, it's fine," she says, glancing at the clock on the wall behind me. "I should get to class."

It's finals week, so everyone is on edge. We decide to forgo another meeting since students are last-minute cramming or prepping for the showcase.

And after a whirlwind week of exams, it arrives.

There's an excited buzz of energy Thursday night as students file into the auditorium. Seniors get first dibs on tickets—because not every senior will participate—and juniors tend to buy what's left over. They enjoy getting ideas for their own Showcase next year. Plus, it's widely talked about all over the school on Friday, and nobody likes to be left out. It's for students by students. Not even parents can attend, only faculty.

Cadence, Marlowe, Tahlia, and I solidified our plan over the last two weeks. It required paying off a few theater techs for help, but as long as they pull through, we're set.

I'm wearing a bold, bell-sleeved dress that's held together by snaps that travel from my neckline to my belly button, the length falling all the way down to my ankles. The number fourteen is written in red Sharpie on my forearms, but I added body glitter to make it pop.

Hidden underneath is my big reveal.

I'm not letting Duncan get away with being a grand asshole once again. It's time for him to experience the kind of heat I've been getting from our classmates. If I pull this off, then everyone will understand he's not the victim here. He never was. He fled the fire without any burns while I was trapped inside.

I'm so sick of carrying this burden. I'm not the bad guy.

Which is why I have to end this.

Yes, the femolution is shifting perspectives, but not fast enough. I refuse to let his actions affect me more than they have already. I deserve to gain back what I'd worked so hard to earn: McTiernan's letter of recommendation, my clients, Stanford, and an enjoyable end to my senior year.

It's time to unleash the revolution.

Cadence turns to me. "You okay?"

The four of us are crowded backstage watching Faith Tobinson sing an a cappella version of "Hallelujah." While exhaustingly on-brand, her rendition isn't terrible.

I nod, taking another big inhale instead of verbalizing my answer. I'm not only standing up for myself, but for Cadence. Because Thomas hasn't felt the negative ramifications of his situation quite like she has, and he's making her go through it alone.

The fury inside me grows, a spark igniting a flame.

Footsteps sound from behind me. When I turn, I find Charlie headed my way. He's the lead pianist tonight, which is why he's dressed in a fitted black button-down and black slacks. A chaotic flurry of nerves pops like soda fizz in my chest as I take him in. I've never seen Charlie so cleaned up before. He looks . . . extremely attractive.

"I wanted to wish you luck," he says. "And show you this." He holds out the tops of his hands. He's Sharpied the number zero in red. "To support," he explains.

I'm surprised. I definitely made assumptions about him and Adeline, knowing they have history, but I shouldn't have jumped to conclusions. That's what people did with me.

"Thank you," I say, but I can't quite suppress a biting clip of uncertainty. Because he could easily be stringing me and Adeline along, believing we're both unaware he's texting the other.

The anger inside me burns into tall, hot flames.

The stage spotlight vanishes. An enormous applause erupts from our peers in the audience. A second later, Faith exits stage right.

"I better go." Charlie begins walking backward. "See you after."

I give him a short wave, and then he's gone. The torturous thudding in my chest lingers, churning into a tumultuous wave of betrayal and animosity.

I'm tired of suppressing *so much.*

Tahlia appears by my side. "Are you sure you want to do this?"

I roll my shoulders back. "I'm ready."

"Remember," Marlowe says encouragingly, "we're right behind you."

And then it's time. Dean McTiernan calls my name from the microphone positioned center stage, and I can't overthink it anymore.

As soon as I step onto the stage, the blinding spotlight finds me. I keep a calm smile as Charlie begins playing an upbeat tune on the piano. I have no idea what the song is, but that doesn't matter. Our plan doesn't involve his music.

I place one hand on the mic as Charlie's piano crescendo grows. I squint out into the audience only to spot Duncan, Otto, Thomas, and Lenora in the second row. Duncan sneers at me, then slowly, deliberately mouths, *Whore.*

It's the match that hits the gasoline. He has no idea what's coming for him.

I take a deep, visible breath. That's my cue. A second later, the spotlight shuts off, drenching the auditorium in darkness. Charlie's piano tinkers out, and I can hear students whispering gleefully at the dramatic blip in my performance.

They don't know this is all part of my plan. I use my remaining seconds in the dark to rip off my dress, revealing my banana costume underneath.

There's a click, a soft boom, and then the spotlight returns. A sharp gasp releases from the audience when they realize my costume change, and then another when they realize what's behind me.

A projector plays a clip of the eighth-grade spelling bee on the back wall of the stage. Thirteen-year-old Duncan grips the mic in one hand and adjusts his glasses with the other. A handful of students let out tittering laughter.

"Misogyny," recites the younger version of Duncan. "*M-I-S-O-G-Y-N-Y*. Misogyny."

The clip pauses. It took me a while to find the footage on my mom's phone, but there it was—the entirety of our class's spelling bee—recorded for my personal exploitation.

I grab the mic in front of me. "You know," I begin casually. "It's funny. Duncan Rowe can *spell* misogyny, but it seems to be a concept he can't wrap his brain around. I think he might need an example. Don't you?"

From behind me, the remainder of the video disappears. In its place blares my screenshot of Duncan's Instagram post. The one with my eyes gutted with *x*'s, the single insult carved over my face.

Bitch.

If that's what he thinks, I guess I'll prove it.

"Don't let him fool you," I say, sweeping my arm toward the image. "When it comes down to it, *he* is the grand example. Cheating on his girlfriend, lying to the entire student body—all to place false blame on someone else and come out unscathed."

There's an eruption of whispers from the audience, but I don't care. I keep going. "This"—I grab a handful of cheap yellow polyester—"is what I was wearing the night of Halloween. Everyone knows it." My voice grows stronger with all my built-up anger. "But I sure as *hell* didn't spend my evening with a lying sack of shit."

The projector starts playing Mrs. Connoway's security footage, a five-second clip of me leaving Keith's house with Marlowe and Tahlia. It's not solid evidence, but it's the best I have, and I won't let it go to waste. When it ends, the wall projects back to his vile Instagram post.

"Yeah, Duncan. Maybe you're right. I am a bitch," I say callously, looking directly at him. "But at least I'm not a liar."

"Douchebag!" someone shouts, which is quickly followed by a few supportive whoops.

A flood of relief thrums through me. They *finally* get it. They see Duncan for who he really is: a pathetic fraud.

Marlowe and Cadence rush the stage and begin tossing handfuls of confetti-like squares of paper into the audience. Tahlia does the same from the back of the room, working her way up the aisle. On each slip of paper reads: DUNCAN ROWE IS LYING. STOP THE SHAME. EVOLUTION OF FEMINISM CLUB MEETS WEDNESDAYS AT 2:30.

After receiving blame I don't deserve, I'm taking ownership of my truth. If this shifts the way students think about the scandal, then there's a chance they'll join us. I won't have to spend my last semester feeling ostracized.

It's *over*.

The volume in the auditorium has grown to intense cheers and wolf-whistles when Dean McTiernan flies onstage, grabbing the mic from me.

"Settle, *settle*. Right. Let's give the stage to our next senior—" He cuts himself off, glaring at me. He moves his mouth away from the mic to speak to me. "You're dismissed."

I do as I'm told, following my friends offstage as my heart pounds in my ears. McTiernan shoots a furious glance my way, but I try to stay calm.

I stood up for myself. I mean, I didn't break any rules—did I? If anything, Duncan should be the one who's in trouble after what he posted about me.

McTiernan is on my heels, ushering Carmen onstage to perform her dance number to keep the showcase going.

Then he directs his anger toward me. "Do you care to explain yourself?"

"I was performing, sir," I say with as much of a straight face as I can manage.

He stares at me, unblinking. "That's not what that looked like."

I hear a set of heels clacking up the stairs behind me, and, suddenly, Miss Rothman appears beside us. A resigned look crosses her face as she peers down at me.

"Brynn wanted to raise awareness for her club," Miss Rothman says, a little out of breath. "It's my fault I forgot to run it by you."

McTiernan looks from me to Miss Rothman. I bite my bottom lip. Miss Rothman is taking the heat. For *us*. I didn't expect this.

"*This*," McTiernan emphasizes, "looks like bullying, Miss Rothman. Are you telling me you had a hand in approving it?"

"No!" I cut in. I'm not letting Miss Rothman get in trouble. "And it's not bullying, it's—"

"I don't want to hear it, Miss Whitaker. This is not exemplary behavior, and it's not the way we treat our classmates here at Greenlough."

"What about the way Duncan treated me?" I shout. "Or are you going to pretend you didn't see what he posted?"

He frowns. "I saw, and I will deal with Duncan's actions later," he says, his voice stern. "But I warned you what would happen if I found you deliberately broke any more school rules."

It feels as though the floor's been pulled out from under me. I'm falling hard and fast, barely catching my breath.

"I didn't start it—" I begin.

"I cannot in good faith send my letter to Stanford," he interrupts, and his face creases with disappointment. He looks at my friends. "Ten extra hours of community service for each of you to be completed over holiday break."

I've already lost so much. I can't lose his letter.

"*Please*," I beg. "Please don't take away the letter. Duncan's made my life hell, and he knows it."

"That's not an excuse to go behind your teacher's back in order to antagonize him. I gave you a second chance after Halloween," he says. "I'm sorry, but this is my final decision."

As McTiernan walks away, I turn to Miss Rothman, panicked. "I'm so sorry."

"You broke my trust when you didn't tell me the whole truth about your performance." Her voice is sharp as her eyes roam over us. "It could have put my career on the line."

I swallow. I didn't even consider that when I put this together. I feel horrible. "You're right. I wasn't thinking."

She glances to the stage. "I have to get back. But please. No more antics, okay? I'm rooting for you, Brynn, but I can't come to your defense again."

"You won't have to. I swear."

She gives me a tiny nod before walking away. I hate that I've disappointed her.

I start to face my friends, but before I have that chance, I feel a sudden grip on my shoulder. I whirl around to see Lenora standing before me, furious.

"What the *hell*, Brynn?" she hisses.

She's in a gorgeous yellow dress and heels. Since sophomore year, it's been a dream of Lenora's to perform the "A Lovely Night" dance number from *La La Land*. I never understood her love for the movie, but I can't deny that the soundtrack is great. When we were friends, she talked me into going to the Griffith Observatory to try and find the exact spot where Emma Stone and Ryan Gosling performed their big scene. We walked down a trail and found a clearing that looked like it could have been the one. I took a ton of pictures of her there and afterward her mom drove us to get In-N-Out.

It was a really good day.

I bet she's performing that number tonight.

"Any decent person wouldn't keep bringing this up, especially not in front of the entire school," she blazes on. "I don't know what you're trying to prove—"

"You saw what he posted, and you know what he's been spreading around school even though I've been telling you it's not true," I interject. "Your boyfriend had control of this narrative, but not anymore."

She stares at me, and I think she's going to start crying. Her eyes are glassy. Defeated. I might be imagining it, but she also looks hurt.

I soften. "Look, Lenora—"

"No, you listen," she spits. "You may not realize it, but this has been hard for me too. And you bringing it up *in front of the entire school* only reopens that wound. It's embarrassing, okay? Is that what you need to hear?"

She looks down, blinking away tears. Her pain is like a punch in the gut. It's then that my mistake dawns on me. Yeah, I wanted to change how my classmates perceived me after the Duncan scandal, but it wasn't Lenora I wanted to harm and humiliate. It was Duncan.

Payback was the only thing I cared about tonight, and it took three minutes to blow up everything our club had been working toward. I lost sight of our mission and made it about myself, weaponizing this moment as a personal tool to inflict harm.

I feel like the worst person alive.

I keep my tone gentle. "I've been telling you from the beginning that it wasn't me and for what it's worth, I am sorry. This wasn't the right way to go about things."

When her eyes snap back to mine, her tears are gone. "Well, you can't undo it now, can you?"

She starts walking away, as if she can't stand to be in my presence any longer.

When I turn around, Marlowe, Cadence, and Tahlia are looking at me empathetically.

"I messed this up," I say, remembering they now have to fulfill community service hours because of me. "I'm sorry."

Cadence glances at Lenora's retreating figure. "I mean, it sucks she was hurt again, but it'll pay off when she finally knows the truth."

"I don't know." Tahlia bites her lip. "We should have considered her feelings."

"But we couldn't make an impact *without* hurting her feelings. She's also involved in this," Marlowe offers. "Like you said, she deserves the truth."

I rake my hands through my hair. I feel awful. I never wanted Lenora to feel like I was digging at a wound that hadn't healed. For her, it had barely scabbed over. That's the side I hadn't considered. Lenora is dealing with the repercussions of losing trust in her boyfriend. He cheated on *her*. She's still hurting, even if she hides it well.

I've made everything worse.

And what about the rest of the school? Will they see it as us rising up against shame culture, or will they call me cruel and insensitive? Cancel me all over again?

I thought I was doing something revolutionary, but I wasn't. This isn't what a revolution is supposed to feel like.

24

"Did you hear what Brynn did to get back at Duncan?"

"I don't know if I believe Duncan anymore."

"I feel so bad for Lenora."

According to my classmates, Duncan threw a fit after my performance. He furiously told anyone who would listen that *I'm* the attention-seeking liar. Carmen told me he ranted about the injustice of it all during post-Showcase refreshments, which is painfully ironic. She also mentioned that instead of leaving with Duncan, Lenora got a ride home with Rhea.

I feel a crushing amount of guilt for putting a spotlight on Lenora's hurt. I took things too far. I made *myself* the villain.

There's no coming back from this.

The club will have to disband because we won't have enough members. I'll never reprise my role of flirt expert. I don't even have McTiernan's letter of recommendation to rely on. *And* I've earned my friend's community service hours over winter break. All because I made it about me, not about the cause.

I went home after my disaster of a performance, completely spacing that I was supposed to stay for Charlie's art show. The art students' galleries were showcased during the refreshments portion of the evening. I frantically texted him to apologize, but he told me not to worry. He understood, and besides, his friends were there.

His friends. Including Adeline. I expected to feel jealous, but I only felt numb. Ashamed. Even though I'm still not sure what Adeline did to lose his trust, she deserves him. The showcase made it clear that I am not a good person.

It's Friday, the last day of school before holiday break. We've already taken our finals, so coming to school is a formality. It happens every year. Our teachers let us decompress by playing games or turning on a movie. If they really don't care, they'll break the no cell phone rule. They're probably just as tired as we are.

But when Marlowe and I walk through the front doors that morning, my jaw drops.

Dozens of students are gathered in the hallway. And they all have numbers scrawled on their forearms.

Marlowe and I are rendered speechless. Devin walks by with Tyla, the two of them wearing the numbers three and five on their respective arms. Zanele struts toward them, sporting a fat, round zero on her arms. She grins when she sees me staring, then gives me a friendly wave. It's ironic that girls can be shamed for having zero sexual encounters as much as they're shamed for having numerous ones. It's *almost* as if there's no right number.

Marlowe grabs me by my shoulders. "It . . . worked?"

I'm stunned that my Showcase stunt led to this. Maybe we got through to some people, but it was at the expense of Lenora.

I need to fix it. I'm just not sure how.

By the time the warning bell rings, we count twenty-five students wearing numbers on their arms. Two people even approach me to make sure our club is meeting the first Wednesday after break.

Maybe there's hope for the femolution after all.

I'm on my way to lunch later that afternoon, speed walking to the cafeteria, when someone exits the classroom to my right, unintentionally stepping in my path. I slow to avoid collision. When I look up, I blink in surprise.

Otto.

We stare at each other, and when it becomes unbearably awkward, I blurt, "Hi?"

"Hey." His tone is disinterested. Fair enough.

"Listen," I begin before he can take off. "I know you have loyalty to Duncan because he's one of your best friends, but what he's saying about Halloween isn't true."

Otto sputters out a disbelieving laugh. "Right. That's why you put him on blast in front of the whole school."

Otto never understood me when we were in a relationship, so I don't expect him to understand me now. "I had to try and make people see my side."

"I don't get you, Brynn." He shakes his head. "You go around wearing your sex number on your arms, but you want to tell me you're innocent when it comes to what happened on Halloween. God, pick a lane."

I suppress the anger fizzling up inside me. He's wrong. I hate that his words are getting to me when they shouldn't hold any significance. It doesn't matter what Otto thinks. But it hurts that, even after going out with me, he believes I'm the kind of person who would go behind his back and hook up with his best friend.

"The showcase was a mistake," I say. "Kind of like how our whole relationship was a mistake. See? I'm able to admit when I make those."

I don't wait for his reaction. I continue on my way. I'm not sure what I expected from this conversation. There's no changing his mind.

My spirits lift when I see the back of Charlie's head at our usual lunch spot. He's sitting in the grass next to Cadence, who's talking animatedly with her hands.

I feel the weight of Lenora's words from last night. I'm supposed to be setting an example, so I have to help Adeline without letting my heart get in the way. And if I'm being honest, this crush is encroaching on dangerous territory.

I can't have him. I need to accept that.

Charlie turns his head my way when he hears me approach. He's wearing his number on his arms, the zero drawn in thick red Sharpie like it was last night.

I sink into the grass next to him. I feel his eyes on me as I adjust, and I try to suppress the ache of longing that stretches like taffy inside me.

Cadence straightens, grinning. "We've counted five more people today with numbers."

"That's incredible," I say, grateful for this hopeful distraction.

"We're leaving on a high note," Tahlia says with confident determination. "It proves people are getting it."

"I hated hurting her." The words sort of leap out of me, landing softly. I'm back at the showcase watching Lenora walk away, and it feels miserable. "And Miss Rothman. *And* I got you all in trouble."

When I look up, everyone is staring at me.

Marlowe rests her head on the top of my shoulder. "You're right. We should handle this delicately."

"We got ahead of ourselves," Tahlia agrees. "But community service is nothing. Seriously."

I feel a tiny sense of relief, but even so, I'm not sure where we go from here.

Tahlia begins talking about a movie they watched in European

History, and I pull my legs into a pretzel position as I listen. Charlie's sitting the same way, and our knees accidentally touch. A fizzing sensation courses through me, like millions of bubbles are popping on top of my skin. We both shift away at the same time, as if realizing we've impinged on each other's space.

"I'm sorry again about your Showcase," I say quietly, maneuvering into a conversation of our own. "How'd it go?"

"Oh, fine. You know." He shrugs. "Thomas Randkin's glowing review was that it was 'demented.'"

He says it like it's a joke, but I can tell he's been thinking it over.

"Well. He's a prickweasel with no taste."

Charlie only gives me a half-hearted grin. "You're not wrong."

"Can I see it? I feel bad I missed out."

A certain softness falls over his gaze. "You still want to?"

"Of course."

"Okay." His tone is less defeated now. "I'll text you over break."

Those words shouldn't ignite something warm in my chest, but they do.

At the end of the school day, I'm feeling the tiniest shred of peace. The halls are a mess of students scrambling out of last period, antsy to start winter break. Overlapping chatter carries through the corridor as lockers slam haphazardly. Nearly everyone is glued to their phones, reviewing the freshly posted exam grades.

And that's when it happens.

A mass AirDrop alert makes everyone around me pause. When I glance down at my phone, I understand why.

I'm looking at a picture of myself, an all-too familiar Snapchat pic I thought I'd never see again. A Snap *I'd* sent. It's a selfie of me making a sultry face, intentionally puffing out my lips. I'm holding the phone in a way that shows off my lacy bra. The text I'd typed underneath reads: **I can be wild when I want to be.**

Red-hot embarrassment floods through me.

The hallway fills with murmurs. People begin to stare. At *me*.

That's when I know that every single person in this hallway is looking at this exact photo.

Panic spikes through me. Someone grabs my arm, but I'm on the defense. I try and twist away until I see that it's Marlowe.

Her eyebrows are pulled together with concern. "Brynn, who—?"

I only shake my head. If I try to speak, I'm going to cry.

"C'mon," she says, guiding me toward the back doors that lead to the senior lot.

But we're both forced to stop when McTiernan's voice booms over the intercom.

"Brynn Whitaker to the dean's office."

And now I really want to cry, but I let Marlowe lead me through the sea of stares down to McTiernan's office. Shame rips through my stomach, leaving clawlike scratches on my insides. I try to hold it together. This is all my fault.

Because I'm the one who sent this Snapchat to Craig Thompson sophomore year.

Craig Thompson. The reason Lenora and I aren't friends.

Craig was a junior when Len and I were sophomores. He had the same speech class as me and the same ceramics elective as Lenora.

For a solid month, I openly flirted with Craig Thompson. He'd tease me about being a sophomore in a class filled with juniors, but I teased him back, bold and loud, calling him out every time he stumbled over a word or when I earned a higher grade on a speech.

Craig was undeniably hot, and I wasn't looking for anything serious. I was *never* looking for anything serious. Our banter was fun, leading me to believe he'd also be fun to make out with.

It was nearing November when Lenora started dropping his name in our conversations. She'd tell me something funny he said in class or how he'd compliment her ceramics artwork. In return, I'd laugh and share his silly anecdotes. I had a feeling she might be crushing on him, but she never admitted it.

I should have known. It should have been crystal clear.

Lenora hadn't told me Craig asked her to the movies one Saturday night. We usually spent weekends hanging out, but she said she was busy. The following Monday, when I asked what she'd been up to, she confessed. Even though I was surprised, deep down, I was happy for her.

But Lenora acted like it wasn't a big deal. She said they weren't dating and besides, her mom probably wouldn't let her go out with a junior anyway.

By that point, I was making good money with my flirt expert services. Since my side hustle was growing, I asked if she wanted my help.

"I told you we're not a thing," she said, a hint of annoyance in her voice.

"I know, but you can still have *fun*."

"I mean, I don't really need your help if he asked me out on his own, right?" she said, but I noted the passive aggressiveness in her phrasing.

I reeled back. "I know. I wasn't, like, going to charge you or anything. I thought—"

"Well," she replied, cutting me off. "Thanks, but I'm good."

Neither of us addressed the awkwardness of that conversation, and I never brought it up again. Lenora stopped talking about Craig. For a while I worried that I overstepped, but nothing about our friendship had changed. Maybe I was overthinking everything.

The end of our friendship happened over winter break. Craig

started snapping me when he was bored and since I was equally bored, I started snapping him back. He was the one who initiated the sexting, sending me Snap after Snap, saying things like:

Craig
you're so beautiful
tbh you're the coolest girl at greenlough
and hot, funny & sexy
don't leave me hanging
plz :) what are you wearing?

The first time he asked, I'd been at Laurie's house. I was busy spending time with my family, so I ignored him. But he didn't stop. The next day, he went on about how he admired my speeches I gave in class, saying it was clear I was the smartest one in the room.

I know, I sent in reply.

Craig
you're gonna get into any college you want. trust.

Me
Correct, so I don't need anyone leaking my nudes.

Craig
no one would. that's bullshit.
just one and I'll shut up. swear.

That caused me to roll my eyes. I didn't reply.

I thought you were a wild one, he continued.

The next thing that came through was a photo of him shirtless, only wearing a gray pair of sweats. Ugh, he was attractive. He was on the swim team at Greenlough, and it absolutely showed.

I took the bait.

Stupidly.

I thought that I loved being the cool, flirty girl who talked a big game. I was confident, but I was also confident that Craig wasn't getting any nudes from me. Still, I figured it didn't hurt to be sexy. So I sent him that photo. The following day, we met up at the movies and made out the entire time.

Everything about those decisions backfired.

Lenora had flown to Maui with her family to be with her grandparents over break, so I knew I wouldn't see her until after the New Year. I also didn't know Lenora was still talking to Craig. I wasn't the only one he was blowing up.

Without my knowledge, Craig *had* saved my Snap—by taking a picture of his phone screen with his MacBook's camera so it wouldn't alert me—then sent it to two of his close friends. By New Year's Eve, one of Craig's inner circle friends had shown it to Lenora, revealing he'd bragged about seeing that bra in person at the movies.

That's when our friendship imploded.

Lenora sent me a string of angry texts, calling me awful things and accusing me of going behind her back. I loved playing games, she said, and I didn't care about anyone else's feelings.

I should have trusted my gut when it told me that there was something going on between them, even if she downplayed it. But I was supposed to be her best friend. Why hadn't she told me how she felt about him?

When break ended, so did our friendship. Lenora wasn't the cutthroat type. She didn't seek revenge, and she didn't go around shit-talking me. Only a few of her close friends, like Rhea, knew the whole story, but it never turned into a scandal. She'd spared my dignity, at least.

But not anymore.

Lenora must have sent the AirDrop to hurt me like I'd hurt her in the showcase. It was revenge, payback, and embarrassment all rolled into one.

McTiernan's waiting for me behind his desk when I appear in his office. I step in, shutting the door behind me.

Deep disappointment is embedded in the lines of his face. "We had this discussion last night, did we not?"

My heart begins to pound. "You think *I* did this?"

He studies my reaction for a second before speaking. "I'm not sure what kind of performance you're trying to put on—"

"I'm not!" I nearly shout, heart racing.

"I've been informed that the name of the AirDrop sender is Brynn Whitaker."

My eyes widen. I'd been so thrown by the photo that I hadn't even thought to look at the sender.

"So I have to wonder, Miss Whitaker, if the showcase and this AirDrop are some kind of . . . *performance*," he continues. "I've also heard rumors about those numbers. How they're not correlated to school spirit or the football team. And, no, you're not breaking any rules by wearing them, but I have to question the influx of numbers I've seen today after the showcase yesterday. I know you're heading up the new feminist club, but I worry it's become a distraction from learning."

A whoosh of air leaves my lungs. It's like a punch in the gut.

"I would *never* send that photo of myself to make a statement," I argue, heat rising to my face. Resentment and fury bubble up inside me. "Maybe you should check with your other students."

"Trust me, I will," he assures me. "But I encourage you to reexamine your behavior. We're already dealing with one scandal. We don't need another. If you and your friends continue to act out of line, I'll have no choice but to eliminate your club."

I clench my teeth, irritated. He knows this decision would affect not only me but also my friends. We've worked hard to build this club. Doing anything to jeopardize it means erasing all the work we've accomplished. He's already taking away my letter. I can't let him take this too.

"I won't cause any more trouble," I force out.

"It's nice to hear you say that," McTiernan replies. "I'll open an investigation to see if we can find who sent that photo."

I'm sure he'll put in the least amount of effort with this so-called investigation before leaving the office for break. Everyone has been in vacation mode all day.

"Happy holidays."

And just like that, I'm dismissed.

My friends are waiting for me outside of the office. Marlowe holds out her arms for a hug, and I fall into them, choking back my frustration. The hallways are clear, which is good. I don't think I could handle a crowd right now.

When I pull away, I catch Tahlia's worried look. "I'm so sorry."

I attempt to process what happened in McTiernan's office. "He assumed *I* sent it. Then he threatened to take the club away," I explain.

Cadence's eyes narrow. Marlowe swears under her breath.

But before I can continue, Rhea finds us.

"Hey, Brynn?" There's hesitation in her voice. "I'm really sorry about what happened."

"Oh," I say, because an apology from Rhea isn't what I was expecting. "It's not your fault."

Her expression softens with empathy. "I know you think Lenora is behind it, but she's not."

She sounds so certain, but I'm skeptical. "How do you know?"

"Because Lenora was accepted to UC Irvine early decision," she tells me. "And she wouldn't jeopardize her standing."

"But after the showcase—" I start to say.

"Yeah, I mean, she's still pissed about that," Rhea acknowledges. "But not mad enough to spread that photo around school."

I consider this. We both know Lenora in different ways, and deep down, I know she's right. It doesn't seem like something she'd do. But who else had that image of me? Aside from Craig and his friends.

"Thanks for telling me," I say, defeated.

She gives me a sad smile, but before she walks away, she adds, "I'll see you at the first meeting after break."

Once she's halfway down the hall, I turn to my friends. "Who could have done this?"

"I bet it's Duncan," Marlowe says at the same time Cadence goes, "Otto, for sure."

I glance at Tahlia. "I don't know," she responds. "It could have been either of them."

"What about Faith?" Cadence asks.

I shake my head, thinking back to the Abstinence Angels meeting I attended. "No, I'm pretty sure we're good." I glance down the hall, grateful everyone has already left. "I have to grab my bag from my locker."

They don't try to follow me, as if they know I need to be alone with my thoughts. But as I get closer to my locker, I notice something odd.

My lock isn't there. It's been tampered with.

When I open the metal door, something falls at my feet. I crouch down to get a better look, picking up pieces of frayed fabric.

My cardigan. My one and *only* uniform cardigan. Destroyed. Tiny shreds of paper cling to the scraps of material. I brush them away, confused.

And then it clicks.

I shoot to my feet, discovering that every single one of my textbooks have been torn into ragged crumbs. Pieces flutter to the linoleum floor like the world's saddest confetti. Even the feminist books I bought didn't survive.

My chest constricts, my breath coming out short and panicky. Whoever did this must know I don't have unlimited funds to replace things like expensive uniform sweaters and textbooks. Or maybe they find immense enjoyment in being cruel.

I carry the torn fabric and the desecrated remains of my books back to my friends only to find Charlie's joined them. He gives me a pitiful look as I approach, like I'm a wounded animal.

And that's when I remember—he must have received the AirDrop too.

I can't imagine what's going through his head. He must see the worst in me now. How can he not?

Suddenly, it all feels like too much. I start crying.

Everyone quickly understands what's happened. Silently, Cadence takes the shredded material from my hands. Marlowe leads me out to the parking lot as Tahlia rubs my back, sliding my book bag off my shoulder and securing it in the back seat of Marlowe's car. I'm barely conscious of their conversation as I slide into the passenger's seat, hoping I'll wake up to find that this is all some cruel nightmare.

25

"I feel bad for Brynn."

"There's no way it was Lenora who did it!"

"Such a scumbag move."

When I'm home, I tell my mom everything that happened in the last forty-eight hours. In a way, it bridges the weird distance between us. She snaps into action. I hear her yelling at McTiernan from her bedroom, demanding he find and punish whoever was responsible for leaking personal property and damaging my belongings. When she reemerges, she looks as exhausted as I feel.

"He says they're not taking this lightly," she tells me. "And that you won't be responsible for having to replace your things."

I exhale the tension I'd been holding on to. "At least they had the courtesy to destroy my textbooks after exams."

But my mom isn't smiling. "Brynn, none of this is okay."

"I know," I say, wondering if this is about to turn into a lecture.

"That photo they shared—"

"I don't want to go there, Mom." I cross my arms. "Just ground me and get it over with."

Sympathy washes over her features. "I'm not grounding you. Not for something you didn't do." She sits on the barstool beside me. "The photo they shared was invasive. It's not okay, and it's not fair to you."

When she doesn't continue, I raise my eyebrow. "But . . . ?"

"Just—think about talking to Mrs. Burchill after break, okay? This is a lot to deal with on your own."

I prop my elbows on our kitchen island and run my hands through my hair. I'm *not* dealing with it on my own. I have my friends. I have the resolve to fix the messes in my life. Not just mine, but my mother's. Smith's. It's what I've always done.

This is a setback. A detrimental one, but it doesn't matter. I just want to forget it happened.

With as much conviction as I can manage, I say, "I'll be fine. The break will be good for me."

She gives my arm a squeeze, but there's something behind her eyes that tells me she's not convinced. "Well, I've got some bad news. Because when it rains, it pours." She stands, her hands now on her hips. "The washer broke today."

A knot forms in the pit of my stomach. I *knew* this would happen. The money Adeline sent me won't be enough for our handyman, let alone replacing the behemoth machine if that's what it comes to. And it probably will. That washer was my grandfather's, and I doubt parts are still available for such an old model.

It could be worse, I tell myself. It could always be worse, as I so clearly learned today.

"I can go to Tahlia's or something," I say, feeling the weight of the day return to my shoulders. "We'll figure it out. We always do."

———————

For the first few days of break, I try and forget the AirDrop even happened. My mom and I distract ourselves from the crushing weight of our problems. We make candy cane bark, rewatch *Elf*, and volunteer at a local food drive for my community service hours.

Smith is being released from the rehab center the day before Christmas, and he's agreed to stay with us for a month before looking for a place of his own. Laurie and Jerome offered to come to our place for Christmas dinner so we could be together as a family. I can tell my mom is looking forward to it, but I'm hesitant to show my own excitement. I don't want Smith to fall back into old patterns and break her heart again.

An odd bright spot occurs the next day when Faith texts me to see how I'm doing. It's unexpectedly nice. She doesn't even say anything shamey, which I chalk up to personal growth. She does, however, want to know if I'm interested in joining Abstinence Angels since they also need more students to reach their minimum number of members, so I tell her I'll think on it.

Two days before Christmas, I'm sitting on Cadence's plush bedroom rug. She asked me to spend the night and since I hadn't seen any of my friends since school let out, I decided to come over.

We're currently preoccupied with my two unsolved mysteries: Who was with Duncan on Halloween, and who AirDropped that photo? Cadence thinks it's the same person, but I disagree. Duncan must have AirDropped the photo to get revenge for the showcase, which means the person in costume has to be someone else.

"Why don't you post something on Instagram?" Cadence suggests. "It's what people want after witnessing a scandal, right? They're waiting to see how you respond. And if you ask the right question, maybe you'll get the right answer. Whoever was with Duncan might come clean."

I raise my eyebrows. "After they saw what happened to me on Friday? I doubt it."

"We could nudge them toward admitting what they did." She sits up straight. "Do you still have that lip gloss I found in Duncan's car?"

I nod toward my book bag, where I'd stashed it and then promptly forgot about it once we kickstarted the femolution.

Cadence digs it out and tosses it to me.

"I'm not putting this on," I warn her.

"Ew, please don't." She shifts to her knees, posing me in a carefree position while making sure the lip gloss tube is visible. Then she snaps a picture with her phone. "It's worth a try, right? Take a look at trolls."

"Trolls?" I repeat.

Cadence wraps her tongue around a cherry Blow Pop. She's gone through three since I've been here and her tongue is bright red. "Internet trolls. It's easy for them to shit on people from behind a screen," she explains. "So maybe it'll be easier for this person to confess to you online. With all the work we've been doing, we may stand a chance."

"And the lip gloss?" I ask.

Cadence smirks. "We're hinting that we know more than we actually do."

She makes a good case. The AirDrop was a rough kick to my confidence. If anything, it makes me come across as an even bigger skank, when in reality it's not true. But that's what Duncan wants, isn't it? To continue to drag my reputation so that he doesn't look bad?

Now people are waiting to see how I respond. If I post this photo, maybe someone will come forward. It's a strategic move. Maybe they'll think we've already put it together. I can finally have answers.

And then—what? If I know the truth, it won't necessarily set me free. It won't fix my reputation. It won't make Lenora believe me. I can only hope that it nudges this person to do the right thing. It's better than doing *nothing*. And don't I deserve to graduate with some dignity? To leave an impression of the real me?

I hand over my phone. "Why not?"

I have nothing else to lose.

Cadence plays around with the coloring of the photo on her phone before she's satisfied, then she sends it to me. With a shaky breath, I upload it to my account with the caption: *No judgment. No lies. Come clean and let's put it to rest.*

It's a subtle callout, but maybe it's exactly what we need.

Cadence lies back against her pillows and puts her hand on her stomach. I watch as she idly rubs back and forth.

"Is it uncomfortable?" I ask, then grimace when I realize that might be a personal question.

Cadence doesn't seem to mind. "Sometimes. Like, I didn't know my skin could feel this tight or that my bladder could be squished. But there are other times where it's . . . I don't know."

I wait, feeling like she wants to keep talking. So I let her find the words.

"I guess having him in there makes me feel less alone. Like I'm needed. Because I can't be a disappointment to him right now when I'm providing this safe little cocoon. Even though it's temporary."

"You're not a disappointment," I say gently.

She wraps the Blow Pop stick and the gum in the wrapper and sets it on her bedside table. "You know, if I would have known I was pregnant earlier, I would have gone through with an abortion."

There's a certain hardness on her face, like she's expecting me to judge her. I don't. I can't imagine how carrying a baby in high school has affected her mentally.

"You're allowed to have wanted that," I finally say.

Her shoulders relax. "Sometimes I think, you know, he didn't ask to be born, right? So what if he thinks he wasn't good enough for me? I know this is the right thing. Adoption. It's a choice I've never second-guessed this entire time, but sometimes I feel guilty."

"You have good instincts," I say. "If this is what feels right, then it's right."

"Thanks." She rubs her temples. "Sleeping with Thomas was absolutely a mistake, though. We used a condom. That's why I didn't think anything of it until it was too late. And can you believe *he* got mad at *me*? Like, bro. It takes both parts."

I shake my head. "You didn't deserve that reaction from him."

Cadence looks lost in thought. "Yeah, I didn't." She lets that hang there for a moment before saying, "You know, I love having Tyla and Devin back in my life, and they've been really supportive and all, but if I had to go through hell with anyone this year, I'm glad it was you."

My chest fills with a glowing warmth. Because I feel the exact same way.

"I—" I begin.

"No," she says, stopping me. Her lips pull into a rare smile. "You don't have to say it. I know."

I toss her another Blow Pop then watch as she turns on *Bob's Burgers*. I glance at the photo I posted. It's gathered a ton of likes so far, which means Cadence's theory was right. People were waiting for my response. I don't expect anyone to fess up right away, but it doesn't stop me from refreshing my DMs.

But my refreshing comes to a halt when I receive a text from Adeline.

Adeline

think i'll be able to get a New Year's kiss?

I stare at her words, heart sinking. We're both going to Grant's New Year's Eve party next week. I've noticed Charlie seems more engaged in their conversations every time she sends me a screenshot. Apparently, she's seen him once since break began and it went well. Which is good. It means my guidance is helping her.

Another text comes through saying if I make this happen for her, she'll pay me a hundred bucks. I can't turn that down right now. Not when I have a load of laundry in Cadence's washer downstairs because she was kind enough to let my mom and I use it. And after what happened on Friday, she might be the last client I'll ever have.

I'm reconsidering if this is even a good idea when I hear a soft snore coming from the bed. Cadence has fallen asleep. I lean over to make sure she's not choking on her fourth Blow Pop and—nope. All safe.

I find the spare comforter, blanket, and pillow she's pulled out for me. She doesn't wake when I make my pallet on the floor next to her bed. Then, I head into her bathroom to brush my teeth and change into my oversized tie-dyed shirt and black bike shorts.

My laundry is probably done by now. Since I'm going downstairs, I gather my laundry bag along with Cadence's discarded Blow Pop trash in an empty McDonald's cup, then journey to the kitchen to toss it out.

The television plays faintly from the living room. I didn't realize anyone was awake. I have to cross through to access the laundry room and fully expect to see Cadence's parents watching a movie, but I'm surprised when I see the back of Charlie's head.

He turns at my approaching footsteps, and when I come around to the other side of the couch, I nearly lose my grip on the laundry bag.

Because Charlie is not wearing a shirt.

My stomach swoops like I'm experiencing a giant drop on a roller coaster, and I absolutely *do not miss* the subtle way his eyes run up my bare legs before he meets my eyes. A spike of dopamine rushes to my brain, filling my entire body with a flush of heat.

But—hold on. Is Charlie checking *me* out?

No, of course not. He likes Adeline.

Right?

I blink away the thought.

"I didn't realize you were here," Charlie says, then grins. "I assumed you would have announced your presence via intercom."

"You actually missed my grand entrance. Golden chariot pulled by unicorns. Real majestic."

"Not dragons?"

"Sadly, no. They were unavailable."

I look right into his eyes as I say this and definitely, *definitely* not at his bare shoulders. He's wearing glasses. I've never seen Charlie wear glasses to school, and then realize—*duh*—he must wear contacts. He also wears black joggers that match the color of his frames and his familiar thin gold chain around his neck.

The rhythmic thumping in my chest accelerates.

Get it together, Brynn.

"Dragons are a big fire hazard anyway," Charlie goes on.

"Ha. Yeah."

I resist the urge to facepalm myself. What kind of response was *that*? Why have I suddenly been reduced to spewing out one-syllable words?

Oh, right. It's because I haven't seen Charlie since Friday when my photo was AirDropped to the entire school. When I broke down in front of him in the hallway.

Heat pulses through me, warming my face in a flood of embarrassment. I never lose it like that. He's probably only talking to me now because he feels bad for me.

But maybe not? A few days ago, he checked in to see if I was okay. When I replied that I was fine—even though it was a lie—that was the end of it. We haven't talked since.

Now Charlie's here, in front of me. Shirtless. Unavailable. And I'm suddenly experiencing a new level of nervous.

He looks at me curiously. "Did Cadence fall asleep?"

I nod, then verbalize a response. "Yeah. She's out. I'm just getting my laundry."

I don't know if Cadence filled him in, but he doesn't question it. He gestures to the TV with the remote in his hand. "When you're finished, do you want to watch the rest of this movie?"

I should say no. I should lie to his face and say that I'm tired, then go lie down far away from Charlie and think about how I'm going to play matchmaker (rematchmaker?) with him and Adeline.

But I don't. Friends are allowed to watch movies together, I remind myself. And I'm not tired yet. I know that if I go back into Cadence's room and try to fall asleep, I'll replay everything that happened on Friday over and over in my head. It's happened every single night without fail.

It's not a big deal. I am not actively flirting with Charlie because Charlie and I are friends.

So I revert back to our familiar banter. "Only if it's *Iron Man 3*, my favorite Christmas cinematic experience."

He laughs, low and genuine, and I don't miss the way his smile reaches his eyes.

In the laundry room, I stuff my freshly dried clothes in my bag, putting off folding until later, and then rejoin Charlie.

"I'm sorry to announce that this is *Midsommar*," he informs me.

I don't know what that is, but I plop next to him on the couch anyway. He tosses me a blanket. I can feel him watching me as I throw it over my legs. I swallow. The close proximity to Charlie makes my heart race all over again.

I'm suddenly hot, a flush creeping up every inch of my skin, so I kick the blanket off. Then I realize—no. I should keep the blanket *on* because what if he thinks showing off my legs is flirty?

I begin to pull it back when another thought enters my brain: I should do whatever I want without worrying about sending a message! THEY'RE MY LEGS.

Why am I overthinking my legs?

I drop the blanket.

Charlie peers over at me, clearly concerned by my weird behavior. "Are you . . . okay?"

"Yup! Fine!"

"Because you seem—"

"—twitchy?"

He laughs. "Yeah. That."

I lose my train of thought because, as someone merely observing a situation, I cannot help but note that Charlie's arms are, like, *toned*. Not mega-ripped in the way twentysomething actors play teenagers on CW shows, but not scrawny either. It's—

No. I will not finish that thought.

"I'm just, you know . . . super fine."

We fall quiet during the last twenty minutes of the movie, and he readjusts his body during a tense scene. It's so minuscule, but I'm aware of the tiniest movement. We've sunk into the couch cushions, so his slight shift means the side of his arm is now *barely* touching the side of mine. I can feel the warmth of his skin radiating through the sleeve of my shirt. He smells like slightly sweet sandalwood and acrylic paint. I'm so aware of him that I'm barely paying attention to the screen in front of me.

I don't move. He doesn't move.

The only thing moving is the zinging electricity striking lightning all over in my brain.

When it ends, he turns toward me. The pressure of contact vanishes. I yearn for its return.

"How's your break been?"

I'm staring into his eyes. "I didn't know you wear glasses."

I cringe at my own words. That was not the answer to the question he asked. I need to get out of my head.

"Oh, yeah." His hands move to the frames self-consciously. "Seeing things far away is not a strength of mine."

"I like them." My eyes follow his hand as he runs it through his hair. "And my break's been fine."

"Ah."

"What?"

"Nothing. You just seem very insistent on being *fine* tonight."

"I am. *Fioyne.*" I stretch the word out as a joke, gesturing to my flattering oversized tie-dyed T-shirt. "Never felt finer."

Charlie rubs his lips together thoughtfully, like he wants to say something.

I wait.

Then it comes. "Listen, I'm sorry. For what happened on Friday."

I drop my gaze down to my nails. He'd been on the receiving end of that AirDrop. He's seen the photo. It's another chip to my confidence.

"It's a fucked-up thing to do to someone," he continues.

I meet his eyes, my heart dropping. At first I think he's talking about what I did to Lenora by sending Craig that photo. But his face is drenched with empathy, and I know that's not it. He's talking about the act of spreading the photo around school.

"And you don't have to pretend like you're fine when you're not, you know? It's shitty."

I force myself to say what I'm really thinking. "If I hadn't taken it, it wouldn't exist. And it would have never gotten out."

I've thought about my decision to send Craig that photo since winter break started. I did it because I felt assertive and sexy. I did it because I wanted to, knowing it was a risk. More than that, I did it because—for whatever reason—I trusted him. If I hadn't done that and then made out with him, things would have been simpler. Lenora and I would still be friends.

Charlie sits up straight. "Brynn, this is *not* your fault. The last person you should blame is yourself."

There's such a strong emphasis in his voice that I know it's how he really feels, but I can't look him in the eye. I keep looking at my hands, unsure what to say.

Suddenly, Charlie's on his feet. I blink up at him.

"I—um. I have something for you," he says. "It's in my room."

I'm caught off guard by his sudden movement. "Oh. Okay."

I think he's going to run and grab it, but he extends his hand out in front of me. I let myself be pulled from the couch, dizzy at his touch, and follow him upstairs.

We emerge in front of his doorway. He ushers me in first, so I step inside. It's his usual chaotic artistic paradise. He looks shyly at his unmade bed and desk spilling over with brushes and paint, but the mess doesn't bother me.

I spot a new addition in the corner near his closet. There's a series of four canvases sitting there. He's painted carefully stippled landscapes. Skyscrapers and forests and beaches come to life in muddy, neutral colors. At the center of each is a lone man in the distance, his head hung, looking at his shoes. In the last one, the man is standing at the base of a mountain, this time, he's looking toward the sky as someone at the top of the mountain leans over, as if about to extend a hand.

It's beautiful, full of anguish and emotion.

"Is this your portfolio?" I breathe.

Charlie's been digging in his closet as I admire his work. He reappears, adjusting his glasses. "Yeah, that's it."

I can't stop staring at the detail. "It's stunning."

He looks down modestly. "Thank you."

"Where's the art you did for the showcase?"

"Oh." Charlie returns to his closet and pulls out a huge canvas. "This is it."

My chest constricts. Charlie's painted a gorgeous fall foliage. In the center of the painting is some kind of demon, huge and scaly, but even though he outwardly looks terrifying, his expression is soft. As if he's sad to be alone.

I crouch down for a closer look, examining the details. It's painted so perfectly, with such emotional depth, that I have a hard time believing any school would say no to Charlie.

"I'm so sorry I missed it. The showcase, I mean," I say, glancing up at him. "But this is stunning. Seriously. You should be proud."

Charlie rubs the back of his neck. "Thank you."

"You know back at the pier, when we were talking about confidence?" I continue, and he nods. "You're way more confident than you give yourself credit for. I mean . . ." I turn back to the painting. "Art? It's about feelings. Displaying your emotions. Carving out a vulnerable piece of yourself and putting it out there for all to see. That's one of the bravest things you can do."

The way Charlie is looking at me now is so tender, like nobody has ever told him his creative side brings value to the world.

"I never thought of it that way," he says quietly.

I always believed my use of logic and reason was what set me apart. Solving problems, fixing things, seeing solutions in ways others can't. It's not nothing, but it's not everything. I squash my emotions and vulnerabilities deep down. I treat them like a complex equation that needs solving. But now, looking at Charlie's work, I realize that's not true. Being open isn't a weakness.

Then, suddenly, Charlie's kneeling next to me. In his hands is a poorly wrapped present. The wrapping paper is speckled with candy canes and it's tied with a red ribbon. I immediately feel bad. I don't have a gift for him.

"Charlie," I say, meeting his eyes. "You didn't have to do this."

"You don't even know what it is." He grins. "And besides, I wanted to."

My fingers shake as I tear at the wrapping. When I pull it away, I'm holding a quality jean jacket. I can tell it's nice by how heavy it feels in my hands.

"Turn it over."

I do as he says. On the back of the jacket, Charlie's painted a gorgeous pair of red lips. There are even flecks of white in them that make them look shiny. Real. Along the edges, he's outlined the lips in black stitching.

"The stitching is from your sweater," he says softly.

I forgot Cadence was the one who carried the remains of my shredded cardigan on Friday. I run my fingers over the delicate threads. In block lettering over the lips, he's stitched the words: THE FEMOLUTION IS HERE.

An overwhelming mix of emotions rises in my chest. I've never received such a meaningful gift. Not only this gift, but the smaller ones too. Standing in solidarity with the number zero written on his forearms. Giving me rides. Showing up to our EOF meetings. It's all a testament to who he is as a person.

I'm horrified to realize tears are streaming down my face.

"Oh god, I'm so sorry." He takes the jacket out of my hands. "The thread was a bad idea, wasn't it? I thought, you know, it could hold meaning? That it could symbolize that no matter how many people try and tear you down, that you'll use that as fuel to keep going. But it was insensitive—"

"*Charlie.*" His name comes out a sob-laugh. I have to cut off his rambling before the poor guy implodes. "I *love* it."

I watch the hollow of his chest release with an exhale. "Oh, that's . . . good."

I slide into the arms of the jacket. It's a loose fit, but I love the oversized structure. It's soft. Charlie explains it came from a sustainable brand. He asks if he can take a photo of me in it, and I stick my tongue out as he takes a quick picture on his phone.

As I take it off, I fold it carefully. "You're so talented."

I watch his eyes run down the length of my forearms. "Your numbers are fading."

I glance down. Since school has been out for break, I haven't kept up with redrawing them. Sharpie is tough to scrub off in the shower. All that's left is a faint outline.

Charlie steps closer to me. Then, slowly, gently, he glides his fingers over the faded ink.

His touch ignites a rush of electric sensations through me. I withhold the urge to let my eyes close.

And then the contact is gone, like a rug that's been pulled from under me. I blink, but Charlie has turned toward his desk, to his art station. Heart hammering, I watch as he chooses a fine paintbrush and mixes a few acrylics together.

I feel unsteady on my feet, like gravity isn't enough to keep me from floating away.

He turns around, holding the small brush in front of me. "Is it okay—?"

I nod, swallowing. We sink softly on his carpeted rug, which is as soft as Cadence's, only it's black. Speckles of different paint color it, but not in a way that ruins it. Somehow, it completes his carefully curated aesthetic.

And then Charlie's fingertips trace the outline of the faded number fourteen. I shiver. Even though my head denies that I enjoy his touch, my body says otherwise. I selfishly yearn for more. No matter how much I try and suppress it, the embers inside me ignite into a full flame, warming every inch of my skin.

The tiny paintbrush finds my arm. His head bends in concentration, and I smell the sweet, clean scent of his shampoo. It's earthy, like eucalyptus. The paint is cold at first, but it warms as he diligently moves the brush. Goose bumps erupt on my upper arms as the brush slides toward the crease of my elbow.

He works meticulously, giving me a chance to study the slopes of his smooth olive-toned shoulder blades. Charlie is attractive. Maybe acknowledging this makes everything easier. I'm only lusting over him. It doesn't mean anything.

It *doesn't*.

He gently blows on his progress to help it dry faster, sending my heart skittering. Yes, definitely lust—right? Only, how do I describe the way I felt when he gave me the jacket?

I can't let my mind go there.

The fourteen is painted in black now, but he adds tiny white dots, then yellow dots. After a moment I realize he's turned it into a galaxy. He adds a minuscule moon. Petite planets. Shooting stars. The Milky Way.

When he's done, I take a long time to admire every single detail. He watches me do this. My head is spinning, and I blame it on that enticing shampoo scent, but I know that's not the cause. When I lift my gaze, I notice we're only inches apart.

The rush of longing hits me at once. I want to feel the softness of his lips. I want to slide my hands up his arms, curve my hands around the shape of his face. A heady sensation inside me coaxes me to press myself into him, to breathe him in. Something in his heavy eyes tells me he would let me, and I want to so badly that it physically aches.

But I *can't*.

I lost Lenora when I made the mistake of sexting Craig. Now there's Adeline. Even though we're not close, it doesn't matter. It's wrong. *Morally* wrong. She's paying me to advise her and here I am, in the room of the guy she loves, letting him touch my arms. Letting him give me gifts. Desiring him in the way she desires him.

Charlie knows the kind of person I am. It's no secret at Greenlough. My relationships are fleeting, but maybe that's what he wants? A fling. Temporary fun. Something that burns out fast and easy. That thought makes my insides twist in an unbearable way. I don't want him to see me like that.

But then Charlie says my name and I relish in the dizzying feeling it gives me. *"Brynn—"*

I'm on my feet, snapping out of my haze. I clutch the jacket to my chest with my unpainted arm. "It's late. I'm sorry. I should get to bed."

My sudden leap has startled him. I can tell by the confusion that crosses his features. "Oh. Okay. Yeah."

He stands and edges closer to the door as I linger in the doorway.

"Thank you," I say quietly, hoping he can see that I mean it. "This is the nicest thing anyone has done for me."

He leans against the frame of his door. There's a soft, sad smile on his face. "Good night, Brynn."

I head to Cadence's room, where she's still sound asleep. I crawl onto the comforter pile and burrow under the blanket. It takes several minutes for my heart to stop racing.

This is for the best. After all, the type of heartache I'd suffered post-Hayes was awful. And if I impede on what Adeline wants, not only will it be a million times worse, it would contribute to an even bigger scandal.

But in secret, under the soft purple light, I admire the intricate galaxy that Charlie's painted on my forearm, tracing the outline of it until I drift to sleep.

26

"Did you see the Instagram account?"

"I guess she really wants answers."

"I mean, it's bold, but I wouldn't come forward if it were me."

It's Christmas day and Smith is officially home, which means my mother is in a good mood. It feels oddly normal. He's been his regular, quiet self, helping my mom cook and lounging on the couch watching football.

I, on the other hand, have not been okay.

I cannot stop thinking about Charlie.

When I woke up at Cadence's yesterday morning, her eyes caught on the jean jacket folded neatly next to my pillow.

Her expression brightened. "He gave it to you?"

I was surprised she knew about the gift. "Yeah, we watched a movie last night and . . . yeah."

I stopped myself before I revealed more, deciding to keep that tender moment between the two of us.

"I think he tried harder on that jacket than he did with his portfolio," she said, grinning. "It's fucking incredible though, right? I love the stitching."

I've been living in the jean jacket ever since.

But when Adeline texted me early this morning, I felt an uncomfortable lurch of betrayal. There wasn't anything she needed from me. She only wanted to wish me a Merry Christmas.

And so did Charlie.

I've already reread his text message five times.

> **Charlie**
>
> hey, merry christmas! i was just thinking of you and wanted to say hi. i'm sure you're busy, but i hope you get everything you want :)

I'm conflicted. Part of me wants to talk to Marlowe and Tahlia, but they'll just remind me of everything that blew up between Lenora and me. Plus, it would mean I'd have to tell them about Adeline. And I can't lose her trust.

So I try not to think about it.

I'm sitting at the kitchen table eating Christmas dinner with my entire family. Jerome and Laurie arrived about an hour ago along with a roast chicken. My mom, Smith, and I spent the morning cooking sides. Once we'd finished, Smith and I made our yule log cake—a tradition that's been in our family for so long that I have no idea how it started.

When Jerome and Laurie first got here, they announced that they should be welcoming their two-year-old son home by January. The paperwork was holding things up, they said, but they've spent the better half of this month preparing his new room.

My mom and Laurie have already had a bottle of wine between them and are cackling like giddy schoolkids as they reminisce over childhood memories. Everything is going exceptionally well until a lull in the conversation hits. I'm taking a bite of the yule log cake when Smith drops the bomb.

"I'm going to go stay with Xavier next week."

The heavy silence is drenched with tension. I swallow slowly and glance at my mom, but her gaze is focused on Smith.

She's wearing Rudolph earrings that light up, his nose blinking red. The flashing makes it look like a tiny alarm going off. "I thought we agreed you'd stay here for a month."

Jerome and Laurie exchange a concerned look. I try to go back to my cake, but I'm not hungry anymore.

"I know we talked about it," Smith says. "But Xavier's in Koreatown and says he can hook me up with a coding job. Entry level. I still plan on taking online classes."

I watch my mom's eyebrows raise. "He's guaranteeing you a job?"

"Well, no, but—"

My eyes lock on her earrings. *Flash, flash, flash.*

Warning, warning, warning.

"You know, I can see if there are any intern openings at the firm," Jerome pipes in, as if testing the waters. He keeps his voice uplifted, bright. "And the guest room is open to you if it works out."

Smith stares down at his slice of yule log, but he doesn't acknowledge Jerome.

"We want to help you," my mom presses. "You can stay here, with Jerome and Laurie, or you can stay with your father."

Smith's mood shifts. "Dad doesn't fucking want me. Or Brynn." He drops his fork. "He's got a better family now. We're the reject kids."

"*Smith,*" my mom chides.

I pile another forkful of cake in my mouth, if only to have something to do. It sits densely on my tongue.

I know Smith resents our dad, but I've never heard him speak with such anger before. Smith's feelings aren't invalid. When it comes to Dad, it's as if he upgraded into a better family. We both feel that deep down, but I've never said it out loud.

"What?" He shrugs. "It's true."

My mom sighs, then goes to the kitchen to refill her wine. Laurie follows her, leaving the three of us alone.

Smith raises his gaze to Jerome. "It's a good thing you guys actually want a kid. Unless you decide you want to upgrade your family too."

I open my mouth to say something, but Jerome beats me to it.

"You're right."

Smith looks as jolted by the comment as I am.

"We want a child we can raise because we want to start a family, and we're lucky to have that opportunity," Jerome continues. "It's not fair that your father has decided to write you out of his life, but you do have a family that loves you, Smith. *This* family."

"I'm a disappointment to *this* family," he mumbles.

I whip my head in his direction. "No, you're not."

It's not entirely true, but I can't stand to see him hurting like this. I know better than anyone that our dad's a disappointment, but Smith is *here*. It's proof that he's trying, that he wants to be in our lives.

Smith looks at me, his expression softening. I think he's going to say something when Mom and Laurie come back to the table, wineglasses full. Laurie must have talked her down because there's no trace of anger. She looks content, but the joy that was there before is already gone.

We push through tense conversation as we finish dessert. Smith doesn't contribute, so the attention turns to me. I tell them about finals and rattle on about my schedule next semester. It's small talk, but it cuts the tension.

The magic from earlier has dissolved by the time we open presents. I never expect much, but I'm surprised that my mom has basically bought Smith an entire outfit. Dress pants from Kohl's, a crisp button-down from Target, and new dress shoes that appear as if they're faux leather. I know she's trying to help. She wants him to make a good impression at whatever job he lands, which is why I act pleased with the one gift she's got me: a new pajama set. I don't want to seem ungrateful, but it feels thoughtless.

When nine o'clock rolls around, Jerome and Laurie announce they're going to get on the road. We say our goodbyes from the porch. I'm about to follow Smith and my mom inside when Laurie pulls me aside. I let the front door close behind me.

She hands me an envelope. "This is for you."

I wonder why she didn't give it to me inside. "Should I open it now?"

She nods, so I slide my finger under the seal and pop it open. It's a holiday card with a snowman on the front. Inside, there's a $100 bill.

Laurie smiles. "Don't put it toward college, okay? I want you to spend it on something you like. Something you've wanted."

I wrap my arms around her, touched by this gesture. Now I understand why she gave it to me here. She didn't want it to seem like she was one-upping my mom. "Thank you."

Laurie slips into the passenger's seat and Jerome gives a friendly beep of the horn. I wave as they drive off, then I slip the envelope into my back pocket. I won't put the money toward college, but at least I can put it toward our broken washer.

Back inside, Smith and my mom are settled on the couch. They've started *A Christmas Story*, so I find the empty spot by Smith and try to enjoy the movie with them.

After thirty minutes, my mom passes out. The celebratory Christmas wine must have gotten to her. She breathes softly next to Smith, who exchanges a look with me. We both laugh. Somehow, it breaks the awkwardness between us.

"Too much holiday cheer," I say.

His smile makes his eyes crinkle. "The maximum amount."

We fall quiet for a moment, averting our eyes back to the TV. After a few minutes, he turns to me.

"Did you mean what you said earlier? That I'm not a disappointment?"

His tone is so soft, so vulnerable, that it breaks my heart a little. Maybe he's disappointed us, sure, but that doesn't mean he's a failure as a person. I need to remind him that he's not his mistakes.

"Mom would do anything for you," I say quietly. "She cares about you so much. I mean, she used my college savings so you could get help in that rehab. It's like . . . compared to you? I don't know. I work so hard and she barely acknowledges it. You're the golden child, really."

He presses his lips together in thought. A shadow of concern crosses his features.

I worry I've said the wrong thing. "You okay?"

Smith rubs at his eyes before looking at me again. "I didn't know that."

I try to lighten the mood. "It's okay. It's the nature of being the second-born."

"No, I mean the college part."

"Oh." I feel my face heat up. I shouldn't have said it. "It's fine. There's always a chance I get a scholarship, you know? I've worked hard."

I decide not to bring up that scholarships are competitive and I ruined my one chance of getting my letter of recommendation from the dean. But even as I keep that to myself, I feel the distance growing between us. He's somewhere else now.

I try and focus on the movie, but I can't. I open my mouth to say something, but he beats me to it.

"You should. Get a scholarship, I mean. You deserve it." There's a sincerity in his voice that I haven't heard before. "I'm proud of you, you know? You're so smart. Mom brags about your grades every time we talk."

She does? That's news to me. "Oh . . . well, thanks."

Those words mean a lot coming from Smith. *I'm proud of you.* Would he be proud if he knew what was going on at school? What trouble I've caused? How I'm pining after a boy I shouldn't even like because I'm betraying someone else? Even though I try, I'm not a perfect child. I've hurt Lenora. I don't want to hurt Adeline.

So I decide to stop texting Charlie for the rest of winter break.

We finish the movie in silence. When it ends, Smith covers our mom with a throw blanket, not wanting to wake her. We both begin moving to our respective bedrooms.

"Brynn?"

I turn toward Smith's voice.

He gives me a soft smile. "Merry Christmas."

I feel the corners of my lips tug upward. "Merry Christmas."

Eventually I fall asleep, but I'm woken early in the morning by the sound of my mom crying. And I know before I even step into the living room—

Smith is gone.

27

"I was surprised to see her at Grant's NYE party."

"Did you see them talking?"

"I wonder why she didn't stay . . ."

The last few days of break are awful. My mom makes phone calls to try and figure out where Smith went, but our only lead is the guy he'd mentioned at dinner, Xavier from Koreatown. It's not much to go off. Still, she tries. None of his old high school friends have heard from him, and Facebook hasn't revealed anything either.

It's not until a few days later that I notice Laurie's card is gone. It must have fallen out of my back pocket when I was sitting on the couch.

Then it hits me. Smith. He must have taken it. I'm angry at first. Why hadn't he asked? Why not tell us his plans? But I know why he didn't. He knew we would have talked him out of leaving, so going quietly was the only way.

My mom's mood has affected my mood. She aggressively takes down the Christmas tree, and I help her in silence. Usually we wait until after the New Year to take it down, but it seems like she's ready to squash the holiday cheer early.

I don't blame her.

Laurie comes over on the twenty-ninth and spends the day with us. They get to work tending the overgrown bushes outside and put a new layer of paint on the sun-bleached front door. I can tell Laurie's company lifts my mom's spirits for a little while but by the time she leaves, she closes herself in her room and shuts me out.

To take my mind off Smith, I give a final (final, *final*) polish to my Stanford essay and then, holding my breath, submit my application to the portal. Something in my chest releases. It's done. All I have to do is wait.

I enter my USC portal and reread the essay I'd rewritten based on Miss Burchill's guidance.

I don't always know what to do, but somehow, I've always known the right thing to say.

A beam of confidence gives me a jolt of encouragement. This might be the most honest thing I've ever written. And it's true. I've made a mess of things this year and I haven't always done the right thing, but it's not too late to fix it. If I let Duncan win, then what kind of example am I setting? A new semester is about to start, and a new year. There's still time to prove I'm *the person* I wrote about in this essay.

In two swift clicks, I send the application.

To get my mind off my looming college apps, I check Instagram. My heart leaps in my throat when I realize I have three messages in my inbox.

> @ThomasRankin046: slut

Wow, how original. I delete the message and open another.

> @anonymous11123: meet me at 11:30pm by Grant's mailbox if you want answers

@anonymous11123: alone

I click on the user's profile, but there's nothing there. They've made an anonymous account.

I feel the instant spike in adrenaline course through me. Grant's New Year's Eve party is tonight. Since Charlie's close friends with Grant, he extended the invitation. This person must know I'm going. Grant's parents decided to spend New Year's in San Francisco, so a good chunk of the senior class will undoubtedly show.

Tonight I might get answers.

I text Cadence, Marlowe, and Tahlia, who immediately begin speculating. Instead of joining in, I turn to my second concern: Adeline. If all goes as planned tonight, I'll get a nice Venmo when she gets her New Year's kiss.

Every time I think about it, my stomach tightens.

Marlowe picks me up at seven-thirty so we can spend time getting ready with Tahlia and Cadence. I love Marlowe's house. It's on the conservative side like ours, but it has a lot of charm. There are tons of indoor plants in brightly colored vases, a large dining table made from old barn wood, and cozy shiplap walls. An HGTV dream.

Marlowe's bedroom walls are white, but she's framed every edge of the room in strips of LED lights, each a different color when you turn them on. A giant customized neon sign above her bed reads I LOVE ME in pink light. Her makeup dresser is painted lime green and is scattered with different shades of eyeshadow pallets.

I'm nervous about seeing my classmates for the first time since the AirDrop scandal. I've tried to channel that energy into what I'm going to wear, which ends up being a simple black tank top and black jeans. Tahlia lets me borrow her gold, sequined blazer, and with my small gold hoops and red lipstick, I try and gather some of my old confidence.

Cadence drives us to Grant's house at ten. His street is packed by the time we arrive, but not as packed as it is inside. Marlowe's our ringleader, looping us through the living room and into the sprawling kitchen. There are tons of different liquors spread out on the marble countertops and two giant buckets filled with beers on ice.

We'd pregamed at Marlowe's, so I'm already feeling a tiny bit buzzed. I needed something to take the edge off if I was going to face a majority of my classmates, but I'm not drinking here. I know someone at Greenlough sent McTiernan that photo of me in the bathroom sipping from a flask the night of the Halloween dance, and I'm not looking to be blackmailed again.

As Tahlia scans the room, I ask, "Is Zoë coming?"

She suddenly looks shy. "*Yes,* so you have to be on your best behavior."

"I always am," Marlowe says dryly.

"Same," Cadence monotones.

"Yeah, you're all so sweet natured and docile," Tahlia deadpans before turning to me. "After you meet up with . . . you know. You *have* to come find us. Immediately."

I glance around to make sure no one is listening. "Of course I will."

We do a loop around the house to see who's already here. I'm relieved Duncan and company aren't in attendance. Most of the students who showed are Grant's friends. Carmen, Zanele, and Mathis arrive a little later, and we fall into a conversation surrounding upcoming meetings.

In my peripheral vision, I spot Adeline and Grant talking near the fireplace.

"I'll be right back," I tell Marlowe.

I slide through groups of people chatting together in tight circles. Grant's face remains neutral as I approach, but Adeline gives me a welcoming smile.

"Hey," I say, then look at Grant. "Thanks for inviting us."

He shrugs. "Sure."

A man of few words, but whatever. I'll take it.

"I'm going to grab a refill." He looks at Adeline. "You need anything?"

Adeline tucks a piece of hair behind her ear. "I'll meet you there in a sec."

Once Grant leaves, she turns her attention to me. "I'm really sorry about the AirDrop thing on Friday. I wanted to tell you over text but then I figured maybe you didn't want anyone bringing it up." Her face crumples as she cringes. "And . . . that's exactly what I'm doing now."

I can tell she's being sincere, and I appreciate it. It's hard to tell how anyone feels toward me.

"It's okay, don't worry," I say. "The break has been good for me."

She looks around, rubbing her hands together apprehensively. "I'm nervous. I mean, *god*. I have fucking butterflies and shit."

I force out a laugh, but it's like a knife in my gut. According to Adeline's message this morning, they've been texting all day. She sent me a screenshot of their last conversation before Marlowe picked me up, and I immediately lost my appetite.

Adeline

i can't wait to see you tonight.

I know. I've been thinking of you all day.

Adeline

me too

Adeline

i really hope we can put everything
behind us

well, it's a new year right?

and I'd be lying if I said I didn't
miss you

I know I should have expected this, but I can't believe I misread so many signs from Charlie. He gave me a *thoughtful* Christmas gift because he's a *thoughtful* person. Or maybe he felt bad after what happened on Friday and wanted to cheer me up.

It's not because he likes me.

Everything I was feeling on the couch, in his room, while he painted my arm, was in my head. I confused niceness with flirting. *Me*, of all people, couldn't see what was right in front of me. It's clear that he only cares for Adeline.

"You don't think I've misinterpreted anything?" Adeline asks, worried.

Ironically, she's not the one who's misinterpreted things. "It's hard for me to say without knowing your situation, but it sounds like you talked things out, right? And you're having these long text conversations. That's a good sign."

She brings her drink nervously to her lips. "Yeah," she says, sounding lost in her thoughts.

I glance at her Solo cup. "Maybe pace yourself? You don't want to be, you know, super tipsy when the time comes."

She puts the drink on the mantel. "Good call."

I try and smile, but my insides feel like they're shriveling up, leaving me hollow.

"You look great, by the way," I say, because she does. She's wearing an off-the-shoulder long-sleeve top that clings to her curves and has paired it with a leather mini skirt. Her black fishnets and Doc Martens give it an edgier look. It's very her.

"Thanks," she breathes. "I changed, like, twelve times."

"Well," I say, feeling the conversation dying down. And anyway, Grant is staring at us from the kitchen. "If you need anything—"

All of a sudden, her cold hand grips my forearm. "Oh god."

I follow her gaze to the other side of the living room, putting two and two together. I didn't know it was possible to feel worse than I already do. Charlie's arrived, and he's standing in the corner talking to Shantel and Mathis. Shantel has these gorgeous box braids with streaks of purple in them, and she laughs at something Mathis tells her before peering our way. Her brows furrow when she sees me standing with Adeline, but that's fair. We hardly ever engage at school.

As if he can feel my gaze, Charlie looks at me. My heart sputters like an engine on the verge of going out. Then he beams, and I feel like melting into the hardwood floor. He's wearing a white T-shirt that has a realistic drawing of a skull in the center. Over it, he's thrown on a navy blue blazer. His jeans are ripped intentionally, and he wears bright red Keds.

I begin to smile back, but then catch myself, refocusing on Adeline. I can see the crush growing huge in her pupils. Jealousy stirs in me. I try to squash it.

"You'll be okay. You got this," I tell her, but my tone falls flat.

She is visibly nervous. "Right. Okay."

As she heads into the kitchen, I'm startled by a warm breath near my ear. I jump away, whirling to see Carson Jenkins bursting into a lazy grin. "Brynn!"

Ah, yes. He's buzzed. That's the only explanation for him greeting me this way. He takes a loud slurp of whatever is in his cup. I get a whiff of his breath. Yikes, it's strong.

"I shoulda told you this sooner," he begins, eyes slightly unfocused. "I hacked into the school's security system from the night of the Halloween dance. Rhea and Lenora asked me to do it weeks ago. It was Lenora's idea."

I'm floored. This was not what I expected him to say.

"You—they asked you to do that?"

He nods. "They combed through *alllllll* the cloud footage, and no one else had a costume like yours."

This isn't revelatory information, and none of it helps me in any way. I place my hand on his shoulder. He's started to sway. I'm not sure if he notices.

"You good?" I ask.

He waves me off. "Listen, I was shitty to you after Halloween—" He hiccups. "I shouldn't have acted like you were, like, a huge ho."

My patience is truly being tested right now. I remove my hand. "Sure. That's one way to apologize."

"Sorry. Really, *I'm sorry.*" He drags out the words, his face twisting empathetically. Then he holds out his cup. "I've been drinking. But I mean it. I am sorry."

I sigh. He does seem apologetic, so I say, "Thanks."

"And I don't think it's you," he quickly adds. "Because if you knew it was *you*"—his poor, drunken grammar gives him pause—"then you wouldn't be doing all these things to figure who it was *really.*"

For some reason, he whispers that last word. I give him a short pat on the shoulder. "Try not to puke tonight, okay?"

He nods, turning back to his friends. I flick my eyes away from him and check my phone. 11:21. Everyone who was invited tonight is already here. They don't want to miss the midnight countdown.

Which means the banana imposter is here.

I scan the room, but my eyes land on Charlie again, like a magnet. He's maneuvered to Adeline's corner of the room, standing so close to her that their shoulders are pressed together. His head dips toward her, his ear by her moving mouth so he can hear her over the music. He laughs at something she says, and my stomach twists. She throws up her arms, like she's reached the good part of her story. They laugh together, and then she looks my way for half a second before whispering something else. I watch as he shakes his head, but then changes his mind and shrugs. His expression is unreadable.

I swallow, turning away. Why? *Why* am I deliberately putting myself through this? Charlie is clearly into the person standing beside him. It hurts to watch.

I don't deserve him. People know my relationships don't last, and maybe they never will. I'm Brynn, the girl who flirts a lot and flaunts the number fourteen on her forearms. I relish in the chase and get bored when the glimmer of excitement has worn away. That's what this is, isn't it? A chase. Even if there were no obstacles, I'd inevitably hurt him. That's what happens when things end.

I have to accept that I'm not the one he wants.

Tears form behind my eyes, but I refuse to cry here.

I check my phone. It's 11:28. I can't focus on this when I'm supposed to be alone outside by Grant's mailbox.

I disappear into the crowd until it feels like I'm invisible. I don't glance back at Charlie and Adeline, knowing the deep ache I'll feel if I do. Instead, I move around Grant's house until I find the front door, then slip out unnoticed.

I walk down the empty sidewalk and sit on the curb beside the mailbox. There's a damp chill in the air. No one else is out here, so I pull out my phone and check my DMs.

Nothing.

I glance around to see if anyone's coming from Grant's house. The door remains shut, but muffled conversation leaks out from the backyard.

I stay seated on the cold cement until 11:50 when I decide to send them a message.

> i'm here.

There's no reply. Ten minutes later, a text from Marlowe comes through.

> **Marlowe**
> Coming out.

I don't bother getting up. Whoever messaged me was clearly messing around. They had no intention of coming forward. My heart sinks. I let myself believe in someone only to be disappointed once again.

I hear Marlowe before I see her. She must sense something is off because she takes quick, expert steps toward me in her tall heels.

"Hey," the word comes out soothingly, and she takes a seat on the curb next to me. "You okay?"

I can't keep everything in anymore, so I let it out, unleashing my emotions with a big embarrassing sob. I cover my face with my hands. I'm not just crying, but ugly crying. I shouldn't be this worked up over getting ghosted, but it's not only about that. It's also about Charlie. And Smith.

The distance I feel with my mom. The weight of the stupid scandal. The AirDrop. *Everything.*

Marlowe nestles her head in the crook of my arm. Her hair smells like lavender and secondhand weed. I let myself breathe in the scent, sweet and sticky and comforting.

She lets me cry. We don't speak, but she gently rubs my back.

After a few minutes, I wipe away my tears. "I'm sor—"

She cuts me off. "You are not about to apologize for having feelings. But for what it's worth, I'm sorry nobody showed."

I sniff. "I don't want to talk about it."

"We don't have to."

I check my phone. It's officially after midnight.

"Shit." I show Marlowe. "We missed the countdown."

"Maybe not." She grabs my hand and gives it a playful wet kiss. It leaves behind a glittery lipstick mark. I laugh, but then take her hand and return the gesture, the stain of my red lipstick leaving a temporary smudge. I feel marginally better, if only for a second.

"You know, you made me braver," Marlowe says, crossing one ankle over the other. "I hope you know that. I mean, having a best friend who doesn't put up with anyone's bullshit? That's inspiring. It helped me find a strength within myself that I knew was there but hadn't accessed."

I've always thought of Marlowe as brave. I didn't realize my friendship had influenced that.

"Really?

"Really," she confirms. "To be honest, I've been afraid to start over in college. I worry I won't have friends who get me like you all do—but I know I'll be okay. And so will you. You helped me see that. This?" She gestures vaguely. "It isn't forever. It doesn't define you."

I let that sit with me. The last semester may have nearly broken me, but it didn't destroy my character. I know who I am—and who I want to be—and I refuse to allow anyone else to define it for me. But that doesn't mean I have to put up with being treated this way.

Around twelve-thirty, my phone dings. I glance down, thinking it's Cadence or Tahlia wondering where we went. It's then that I see it's not a text, but a notification.

A Venmo notification.

With shaking hands, I open the app.

Adeline M. has Venmo'd you $100—mission accomplished 😵

28

"Lenora and Duncan were so cute at Otto's New Year's Eve party."

"Do you think anyone has DM'd Brynn?"

"I don't know. But they should."

The next day my friends take me ice-skating to get my mind off the AirDrop and Instagram situations, and after, we bake chocolate chip cookies at Marlowe's place. We don't talk about school or college or anything stressful, which is nice. If I'm distracted, I'm not thinking about Smith or Charlie or Lenora or my mom or the person who never showed up.

The anonymous messenger never responded. I don't even know if they were at Grant's at all.

They must be afraid that I know more than I'm letting on, because the lip gloss in my photo was a huge hint. So I continue to check my DMs, patiently waiting to see if they make another move.

Because I'm avoiding Charlie, I also avoid going to Sticks and Scones. After we left the New Year's party, he texted me at 1:00 a.m. wondering where I'd gone. I never replied. When he followed up the next day to make sure I was okay, I kept things short. I told him I hadn't felt up to staying.

I helped Adeline get what she wanted, and she paid me for it. I'm not going to be the girl who gets in the way again. I refuse to put anyone else through that.

I've also realized that I can't carry all this weight on my own.

There's a faculty staff meeting at Greenlough the day before classes start, which is why I'm hanging around the teacher parking lot waiting for the one person I should have sought out months ago.

When Mrs. Burchill spots me, she does a double take.

"Brynn?" she says, squinting as she strides closer. "You're a little early. Like, a full day early."

"I was hoping to talk to you," I confess.

She sweeps her arm toward the doors she just exited. "Let's go to my office."

Once we're inside, I don't hold back. I tell her everything. About Duncan and Lenora, about the AirDrop, about my mom and Smith, about Adeline and Charlie. Everything comes pouring out of me, like wringing a wet sponge of emotion.

I cry, but I'm not embarrassed by it. I shovel out my frustration. My anger. I hadn't realized how much I'd kept inside until I'm finished and every part of me feels raw and hollow.

"I'm not sure I can make it through this last semester," I tell her, defeated. I never thought I was someone who gave up, but maybe this has spiraled into something so large that even I can't fix it.

"I'm so sorry, Brynn," she says soothingly. "But coming here? Opening up? It's a good first step."

I inhale a shaky breath. "Everyone will make my life miserable tomorrow. It's not how I pictured ending my last semester here."

"*Everyone?*" Mrs. Burchill repeats with a disbelieving tone. "As I recall, you have some pretty great friends."

"And even bigger enemies," I add.

Mrs. Burchill leans back in her seat, thinking. "The way I see it? You never wanted that photo leaked. It was personal, and I believe there are students here who understand that violation."

I push a strand of hair behind my ear. She's not wrong. Didn't I see a ton of my classmates at Grant's New Year's Eve party? Carson even apologized to me. Nobody treated me like I was the Worst Human on Earth.

"Not to minimize your feelings," she continues. "Because what you're going through is not easy. My advice? Take it a day at a time."

I watch as she slides a slip of paper my way. "What's this?"

"Dr. Watson is a therapist friend of mine. Her first session is free, but she can work with your mother's insurance to figure out the best plan for you." She meets my eyes. "And she can help, Brynn. I'm always here for you, too, but she's someone who can *really* help you work through your stress and fear. Perhaps alleviate some of this anxiety you've been experiencing."

Oddly, her recommendation doesn't make me feel broken, or bad, or like I'm a failure. It makes me feel like I *do* have control.

I pocket the slip of paper. "I'll call her."

"You don't have to fix everything on your own," she assures me. "You put a lot of pressure on yourself with that mindset."

I nod, but if there's one thing I know with complete certainty, it's that the only person you can ever truly rely on is yourself. Not your friends, because they don't deserve your emotional burdens. Not your dad who doesn't care, not your brother who disappears more frequently than a magic act. Not even your mom, who never puts you first.

And so you learn to survive without help. To fix things by yourself and receive praise for it. To squash all doubt and channel every bit of confidence to speak your mind in order to get what you want. Because you've gotten this far the best way you know how: on your own.

But then you get good at solving other people's problems. You've proved yourself, so now they see value in you. And when that's taken away, when they demonize your character, you begin to question everything. Your worth. Your intentions.

When you're forced to analyze your rawest self, what if you don't like what you find? How do you move forward?

I feel for the paper in my pocket. Maybe you decide it's worth letting someone else all the way in.

"You know," she says. "I like to believe people are naturally inclined to help others. Maybe it's in obvious ways, like therapy, but it's also in the smaller ways too. Designing prototypes that can improve someone's life, for instance." She gives me a knowing smile. "Or building a free little library, or even just being there for someone during a rough time. It's a great quality, Brynn. Don't let anyone dull that in you."

I didn't think I had any more tears left to spill but, as it turns out, I do.

"Thank you," I tell her, because she had no idea how much I needed to hear that. "Sorry to keep you here."

"Don't be silly. Actually." She stands. "Let me go grab your new textbooks. The dean is keeping them for you in his office."

After she leaves, my eyes catch a yellow Post-it next to a jar of pens on her desk. She's written: *Simp??? No cap??? Cheugy??* I withhold a laugh, but then I'm instantly distracted by something else.

A tube of strawberry lip gloss.

The same brand of designer lip gloss we found in Duncan's car.

My mind jumps to the worst-case scenario. But—*no*. There is *no way* that Duncan and Mrs. Burchill are hooking up. This has to be a mistake or a weird coincidence.

The door opens, and Mrs. Burchill places a stack of heavy textbooks in front of me. "God, that's my workout for the day."

I don't know how to connect my racing thoughts to form a full sentence. "Is that—?"

She's momentarily confused, but then realizes what's holding my attention. "Oh, it's not yours, is it? I found it in the hall before break. Seemed too expensive to just toss out."

A pinch of relief releases in my chest. *Of course* it doesn't belong to Mrs. Burchill. But could its owner be the same person who left it in Duncan's car?

"Where was it?" I ask.

She shoots me a strange look. "Outside of Miss Rothman's classroom. You okay? You look mad sus."

I blink at her. "What?"

She flutters her hands. "Ugh, ignore me. This is what happens when I try to keep up with the youth's lingo."

I barely hear her. My brain is still trying to make sense of this. "Can you let me know if the person comes to claim it?"

"Sure," she says, even more perplexed. "If . . . that's what you want?"

"Thanks." I begin gathering my new textbooks. "You were right, by the way."

"I'm right about a lot of things," she replies. "Which part in particular?"

"When you told me talking about everything would release me from feeling burdened," I explain, remembering my visit to her office all those weeks ago. "I mean it. I feel a little better, even if my problems remain unresolved. For now."

"It's not forever," she says confidently. It reminds me of what Marlowe told me outside Grant's New Year's Eve party.

And for the first time, I believe it.

29

"Do you think McTiernan found out who sent that AirDrop of Brynn?"

"I hope so. That was pretty messed up."

"Why would someone do that?"

I wake up before my alarm the next morning feeling groggy and sleep deprived. My mom has already left for work by the time I go into the kitchen to grab a granola bar for breakfast. I eat it slowly, forcing bites down even though my nerves suppress my hunger.

I can't stop my mind from racing. The anonymous person in my DMs has stayed quiet. I wonder if they know they lost another lip gloss. Or if it even belonged to them in the first place.

Will the pieces *ever* come together?

I hear Mrs. Burchill's voice in the back of my brain. *Take it one day at a time.*

Day one. That's all I have to survive.

Marlowe's outside my house five minutes later. She mumbles a tired *morning* and hands me a Starbucks cup identical to the one in the cup holder next to her.

"We deserve a treat to kick off our last semester." She eyes me. "You okay?"

"I think so," I say truthfully, then raise my cup. "Thanks for this."

But when Marlowe pulls into the student lot, swerving into a parking space, I notice something odd. Most of my classmates are wearing a bright red button pinned to their uniform.

I don't know what it is, but it can't be good.

My stomach lurches. "What is this?"

Marlowe flings open her car door, grabbing her book bag on the way out. "I have no idea."

We speed walk to the front entrance, trying to catch up to our classmates to get a better look. I admit I expected *some* drama, but not quite this early.

"Brynn!"

Katie Delcavo jogs up to us. I glance around, wondering if I'll find the rest of the Holy Crew on her heels, but I don't. It's just her.

I scratch the back of my head. "Uh. Hi?"

She reaches inside of her book bag. "What do you think?"

I'm about to ask her what she's talking about when she pulls out a red button. It takes me a second to process what I'm seeing. It's not just a button—it's a button in the shape of red lips. On the front, in white font, it reads:

WE ARE THE FEMOLUTION.

"I made them over break," Katie explains, handing them to Marlowe and me. "People are on your side, Brynn. They get that the AirDrop was out of line."

This is not at all what I expected. I pin the button to my uniform blouse, thinking of the hours she must have spent crafting these. I feel an overwhelming sense of affection toward her.

And then I remember McTiernan's warning about staying out of trouble.

"Listen, Katie? I'm not exactly the dean's favorite person right now,"

I say. "If he asks, you're going to tell him you did this, right? Because I'm supposed to be lying low and this"—I gesture around—"is the opposite of that."

I watch the slow realization sink into Katie's face. "Oh, Brynn. I'm sorry!"

"It's okay," I say, not really sure if it is or isn't.

"I wanted you to come back from break with more support, you know? I wanted to fix things." She passes out two more buttons to Tyla and Devin as they walk by. "And I think it might have worked."

A lump of gratitude rises in my throat. I haven't been a perfect leader, or a perfect person, but I feel a warm sense of relief knowing that most of my peers are on my side.

"Thank you," I say. "But I'm serious about McTiernan. I can't have him revoking my scholarship."

"I'll take accountability," she says, her voice softer now. There's sadness in her eyes, I think. But she blinks, and it's gone. "I'm going to pass out more of these before class."

When she's a good distance away, Marlowe turns to me. "Plot twist," she says, grinning. "Actually, there's something else you should see."

She pulls out her phone, then clicks over to her saved photos and taps on some kind of graphic. There are a few lines of text on an eye-catching yellow-and-orange background.

WANT YOUR PERFECT PROM DATE?
YOUR LOVE GURU CAN HELP
MESSAGE @YOURFLIRTEXPERT
TO ACHIEVE THE NIGHT OF YOUR DREAMS

"We wanted to surprise you," Marlowe explains. "Cadence, Tahlia, and me. We put it together a few days ago, but then Carmen went live last night to talk about it and it sort of took off—look!"

She shows me brand-new Instagram account they've set up. The icon is a minimalistic line drawing of a heart, and the bio reads: **crush connection, communication with intention! DM for rates.**

I'm touched. I can't believe I didn't think of this myself.

"There's already, like, thirty inquiries. Not just from Greenlough, but from kids at other schools too," Marlowe tells me, sending me the log-in info.

"You told her!" Cadence says, appearing on my left.

Tahlia catches up a half second later. "Do you love it?"

I glance down at the account. I don't know what I did to deserve them, but I'm going to pay them back somehow. This is too much.

"We figured you could use the money toward a new washer and a deposit for Stanford. *When* you get in," Cadence emphasizes.

I'm at a loss for words. This was the safety net I needed to feel the barest bit of relief. It means the world that they'd do this for me after everything I've put them through.

Somehow, the rest of the week continues in our favor. I keep waiting for the other shoe to drop, but it doesn't. On Wednesday, we have a record-breaking number of students who show up to the Evolution of Feminism club. *Twenty-eight!* Zanele volunteered to lead the meeting so she could discuss gender and race discrimination, reading us sections from Kimberlé Crenshaw's texts and opening the floor to discussion.

Everyone stays engaged. Some raise thoughtful questions. A few even share ideas for next week's agenda.

At the end of the meeting, Miss Rothman announces that our pitch to create an all-gender bathroom in the west hall was approved by the faculty. It's a strong note to leave on. And as everyone begins to trickle out, Katie passes out more buttons.

To apologize for our Senior Showcase stunt, the four of us chipped in to get Miss Rothman a gift card to her favorite artisanal coffee spot. We present it to her once everyone's left.

"I appreciate this gesture, thank you," she says, then looks directly at me. "No funny business when it comes to your spring fair speech, got it?"

"Understood," I assure her.

As we're leaving, Tahlia pulls a slip of paper out of her book bag.

"It's a list of people who had Miss Rothman for eighth period last semester," she explains as we head toward the parking lot.

Tahlia is an office aide this semester, but I had no idea she would be able to access an entire class roster. I'd told them about the lip gloss in Mrs. Burchill's office a few days ago, and they all agreed it was suspicious.

I stop to examine the names. Cadence and Marlowe read over my shoulder. A few jump out: *Rhea. Devin. Katie. Lenora.* It's tricky to navigate what to do from here. But if I've learned anything from last year, it's that digging myself deeper into this mess gets me in trouble.

Maybe it's time to let it go.

For the first time in months, I have my side hustle back. My classmates aren't outraged by the mere sight of me. In fact, most seem to be on our side. Even though we haven't been able to prove Duncan was the one behind the AirDrop, most of them suspect it was him and agree he crossed a line. Plus, I'm finally on track to replace our washer—and anything else that might break.

This is what I wanted, right?

"I love you and your FBI-worthy skills," I tell Tahlia. "But . . . I think I'm okay. Really."

But of course, the moment I decide to wipe my hands clean is when my solid foundation begins to wobble.

Later that evening, when I'm alone in my room getting a jump on my econ homework, I notice a new DM in my personal inbox. I'd been so busy replying to messages from my new @YourFlirtExpert account that I'd nearly disregarded my own. My heart slams in my chest when I read the message.

> sorry I ghosted you.

I stare at those four words, pulling my lower lip between my teeth. I can't seem desperate, like I *need* answers, because I don't.

Or maybe I do. For closure.

I don't know. What I *do* know is that everything the femolution has done this far is working. The last few days have proved that much. I won't be the one to screw things up again. it's fine, I type. you're not the only one who's messaged me just to troll.

I can see the person on the other end typing. My accusation might have sparked a defense in them.

> well, do you want to know?

I let that hang there. Then, I put all games aside and type an honest reply.

> i thought I did. maybe it would be easier to move on if i knew. but i'm not the one who deserves answers. i think we both know who does.

I stare at the screen until my message has been read. When a reply doesn't come, I set my phone down, hoping I didn't just make a huge mistake.

30

"Brynn is actually really smart. And nice."

"Whoever spread that picture of her was out of line."

"I'm joining EOF in solidarity."

Over the next few weeks, our hard work pays off. We're up to thirty-five members, and it finally feels like the majority of students have changed their minds about me. I've been flooded with requests for help in time for Valentine's Day, and I earn enough to replace the washer. It's time-consuming work, but I don't mind. It distracts me from other things.

Like Charlie.

I've barely spoken to him. I have his work schedule memorized, so I only study at Sticks and Scones when he's not there. I've been avoiding lunch every other day by checking out dozens of feminist books from our library, writing meeting agendas, and prepping my spring fair speech.

On the last Monday in January, he finds me outside my AP Lit classroom during passing period. His hair is a little longer, and his tie hangs loosely around his neck. My heart flips traitorously in my chest.

I miss him. I don't feel like I'm allowed to miss him.

His hazel eyes land on mine. "Are you okay?"

I know what he's asking without asking it outright. *Are we okay? Why is there distance here?* But I can't answer that honestly. He's back with Adeline, and I'm the one making it weird.

Because of the damp January drizzle, we had to find a new lunch spot indoors. That's how I know he sits with his friend group, occupying the seat next to Adeline. Once, he looked over at our table and we locked eyes, but I hastily looked away, embarrassed he'd caught me staring. I haven't looked over there since.

Speaking of. Grant, Adeline, and Shantel are heading this way, most likely hoping to catch up with him. Adeline and Shantel are bent toward each other, sharing a private laugh over something I can't hear.

My gut twists. I swallow a lump in my throat, but force myself to paste on a smile.

"I'm stellar," I say, my voice oddly pitched. I have never in my life used that phrase. "See you at the meeting Wednesday?"

Before he can reply, I head down the hallway to Pre-Calc.

Three days later, when Cadence and I are working on our economics presentation, she turns to me and asks, "Did my brother do something?"

My eyes jump to hers. "What?"

"It's just—you don't really hang out anymore."

I try to sound casual, but my heart races. "We didn't really hang out a lot before."

She doesn't call my bluff. "But he didn't do anything?"

Other than get back with his ex? The thing *I* made happen?

"No," I assure her.

She doesn't press me further. I should be relieved, but instead all I'm left with is a hollow emptiness in the places his presence used to fill.

January flies by in a gloomy haze, and February follows suit. While it's typical for California to get rain in the winter, this one breaks records. Every morning is filled with thick clouds that hang as heavy as my spirit. It mists some mornings and sprinkles on others. My mom and I get tired of the unpredictability of it and spend half an hour digging in the hall closet to find umbrellas.

I've been seeing the therapist Mrs. Burchill recommended. Dr. Watson is the only one who knows about my feelings for Charlie among the other stressors in my life. Talking about everything feels like a tiny release. She doesn't have all the answers, but she helps me uncover ways to relieve my anxiety.

"You know who you are," Dr. Watson told me in our last session. "That's very clear to me. But you also don't need to tackle the world's problems on your own. There will always be things outside of your control."

I can't fix everything. Not Smith. Not my mom. I can't make Duncan admit his lies, and I can't force the anonymous person in my DMs to come clean. I don't have any control over what the entire student body thinks of me.

I can only do my best. That has to be enough.

The anonymous person never replied to my last message. I'm okay with it—I think. They know what they need to do. If anything, I should thank them. They're the reason we started this femolution. And while we haven't made light-years of progress, I think we've sparked something special.

Change *is* change, after all.

I'm in the library during lunch on Thursday, working on my speech, when I notice Lenora a few tables away. Her head is buried in a novel. I recognize the cover—Austen. She only rereads Jane when she's in her feelings. Does that mean she's avoiding Duncan?

I have the urge to go over and make conversation, but I know I won't be welcome, so I don't.

I can't tell if Duncan and Lenora are still together. She doesn't post about him on Instagram, but she continues to sit with him at lunch. The last time I spotted her, she had her chin in her hand, staring out the window as Duncan chugged his entire carton of milk on a dare. Even though everyone around her was laughing, she looked . . . sad.

The warning bell rings, startling us both. Her hazy eyes find mine for a fraction of a second before she blinks, snapping her book closed. She doesn't glance back as she exits, so I wait a few seconds before filing out after her.

It's the first week of March and while there's a chill in the air, the rain has mostly subsided. I'm hanging out with Cadence in her room when I get a text from Marlowe. She's on her way to San Diego with her parents for the weekend, so I assume she must be bored in the car.

When I open her message, I see she's sent a screenshot from Carmen's Instagram story, where Carmen is posing seductively with a basket of fries. I love this vibe for her personally, but I have no idea why Marlowe's sending me this.

Then another text arrives.

> **Marlowe**
> guy in the background. is that smith?

I look closer, then audibly gasp. It *is* Smith. He's glancing up at just the right moment, positioned behind the register. The geotag sticker reads PRISM'S BURGERS.

Cadence, who's heard my audible exclamation, leans over my shoulder to see what's going on.

I leap from her bed. "I have to go."

"What happened?" she asks, clearly confused. I realize she's never met Smith, so she doesn't recognize him as the guy in the background.

"It's my brother." I'm gathering my shoulder bag off her floor. "Marlowe found him. He's in LA."

Cadence pushes herself into a sitting position. "Dude. I love you, but my pregnant ass cannot make a trip to Los Angeles and back."

Cadence is due early April, and her belly is a protruding, round shape that oftentimes looks uncomfortable. She's slow-moving these days. When she takes power naps in class, none of the teachers bother to wake her. It's almost like an unspoken rule.

There's a sudden rap on the bedroom door.

"What?" Cadence monotones.

Charlie's voice comes from the other side. "Have you seen my charger?"

There's a soft click from the door as Charlie pokes his head in. When his eyes land on me, he looks startled. Like he hadn't known I was here.

"Nope, but this is perfect." The corners of her lips tug into a mischievous expression. "Charlie can take you to LA."

A blush overtakes my entire body. I don't want Charlie to feel put on the spot. "Oh, that's—"

"Brynn found her brother," Cadence cuts me off before I can work up to my excuse.

Charlie's face softens. "Really?"

"Well, Marlowe found him. By pure coincidence," I explain. "But she's on her way to San Diego."

"I can take you," he says, voice low.

I bite my lip. I'm running out of time, I don't have a car, and Charlie is my only option.

"Okay," I say, unsure if this is really an *okay* kind of idea. "Thank you."

The edges of his mouth curve into a smile. "I'm gonna grab my hoodie. I'll meet you downstairs."

Once Charlie vanishes from the doorway, I turn to Cadence. "Are you sure—?"

"Brynn, I'm fine." She pats her stomach. "I have company. Go find your brother."

The first twenty minutes of the drive are painfully awkward. Charlie and I exchange small talk about econ and art history and the upcoming AP tests. When we tire of school subjects, he asks if I want the heat on, then forgets he asked me and asks me a second time five minutes later. Once he realizes his mistake, he blushes and falls silent.

I turn to my phone as a distraction. I'm in the middle of helping two classmates brainstorm promposals. I walk them both through a few ideas based on what they've told me about the other person, then stare at my phone until the screen darkens.

I've made three hundred dollars over these last two months. I used part of it to treat my friends to a nice picnic on the beach. We played music and ate too many cupcakes until the warm sand turned cold. It was the least I could do to thank them for everything.

As for the rest—it'll go toward my college fund. I try not to think about Stanford. We're weeks away from decision day, but it doesn't stop me from wondering what my future holds. And stressing about it, even though Dr. Watson gave me exercises to help with that.

Out of the corner of my eye, I see Charlie sitting stiffly in his seat. He leans forward ever so slightly, as if on edge. I'm relieved I'm not the only one.

"Have you told your mom?" Charlie asks.

I watch the stretch of freeway in front of us. I know what he's asking. I didn't tell my mom that I might have found Smith. Even though she's home and capable of driving me, I can't bear giving her false hope. If we drove all the way to Los Angeles and Smith wasn't even there, her heart would break all over again. I don't want to put her through that.

"Not yet," I say. "I will . . . depending."

He nods, then reaches for the volume. "Want to DJ?"

A shred of normalcy. I'll take it. "Sure."

I connect my phone to Charlie's Bluetooth and play a few of my favorite songs by Joywave. We fall into an easygoing conversation about the best albums and songs, and I realize that I never gave Charlie his shirt back. I need to, especially now that he's back with Adeline. I don't need anyone getting the wrong idea.

I think they're doing okay. He must have been the one who sent her a dozen black roses on Valentine's Day because I saw her holding them in the cafeteria. She was glowing.

But he still comes to every single club meeting and wears his red Keds even though he's been written up three times for not being in uniform compliance. He also hasn't stopped wearing his number on his arms even though a lot of our classmates don't anymore.

"Cadence told me about the person who messaged you."

I flick my gaze to him, not entirely surprised he knows. "Oh, yeah. That's a dead end, I think."

He glances over at me before turning back to the road. "Are they afraid you'll out them if they tell you the truth?"

"I don't think so," I say. Deep down I feel that's true. "I told them I wasn't the one who deserved answers."

Realization sets in. "Lenora."

"Right."

"That's big of you. A lot of people would want revenge."

My lips tug upward. "Listen, I'm not a saint. It would be nice to see karma work its magic, especially after the AirDrop thing. That was invasive."

Charlie clears his throat. "You know, uh . . . in my room? Over winter break?"

I freeze, waiting to see where this is going. It suddenly feels like every single nerve in my body is an electric fence that has been set on fire.

"You told me that my art was brave. Because I chose to share it with, well, *everyone*."

I swallow thickly. "I remember."

"Well," he continues. "It must have been difficult to come back to school in January. But you did. With your head held high—even if you were faking that confidence."

His hand twitches on the steering wheel. Why is he nervous?

"Not giving up—continuing to be unapologetically you? It was badass. You're a role model for the younger students, you know? They're not going to put up with sexist bullshit if anything ever happens to them. I really feel that way."

God, why does he have to say things like this? It doesn't help that deep want I have for him even now. When I know there's nothing I can do about it except continue to pine for him in secret. It's torture.

"That's—thank you," I say clumsily, staring straight ahead as my heart rate does its best imitation of a jackhammer.

We fall into a contemplative silence for the rest of the ride. Part of me wants to ask about Adeline, but he hasn't been voluntary with that information, so I don't. I let the music fill the gap in our conversation. I wish I knew what he was thinking.

My anxiety skyrockets by the time Charlie pulls up to Prism's Burgers. It sits on the corner of busy Sunset Boulevard, so we drive up a residential street in order to hunt for parking.

Once he expertly parallel parks on an incline, he turns off the car and looks at me.

"Brynn, I—"

I wait for more, but it doesn't come. He's looking at me with this pained, haunted expression. Maybe it's guilt. For choosing Adeline over me. Only, that doesn't explain why he looks like he's trying to restrain himself from reaching over and gliding his fingertips over the space where he painted galaxies on my forearm. It would take everything in *me* to try and resist.

He carefully readjusts his features, as though backtracking. "Sorry. Um. Do you want me to come with you?"

My heart is beating so fast. What just happened?

I glance out the window, then say, "I'd rather go alone, if that's okay."

He gives me a look like he understands. "I'll be right here."

I reach for the handle, then turn to him. "Thank you."

I feel his eyes on me as I open the door and push my way out.

It doesn't take me long to walk downhill and around the corner to where Prism's sits. A group of trendy twentysomethings in flowy dresses and baggy overalls exit, shakes in hand, as I catch the door to let myself in.

I immediately smell caramelized onions and the soft waft of french fry oil. It's not a big place, maybe enough to seat eight or ten people. My eyes carve their way around a group standing at the counter, ready to order. That's when I see him.

"It wasn't right. You know that," Katie says through a choked cry.

His attention lands on me, his eyes widening when he registers that I'm standing here.

And then I burst into tears.

Smith has to ask his co-worker to take over the register as he gently coerces me outside. He navigates me around the corner of the building and to the back where we have a bit of privacy.

As soon as my sobs slow into agitated hiccups, he pulls a pack of cigarettes from his back pocket and lights up.

My haggard breathing slows down enough for me to say, "God, Smith. That's so bad for you."

"Not as bad as coke."

He's clearly making a joke to lighten the tension. It doesn't work. I'm not amused.

"Sorry," he mumbles. "That was tasteless. And I haven't, by the way. Been doing that shit."

I wipe my eyes with the back of my hand. He reaches into his apron pocket and passes me a napkin.

"You've been here this whole time?" I ask.

He leans back against the wall of the building, taking a long drag. The smoke curls around us. It's gross. I want to slap the cigarette out of his hand.

"I told you my friend had a spare room in K-town. It's not that far from here." He stares off in the distance, softening his expression. "I'd originally applied for this coding job, but they need me to be certified first, so I'm taking a class. I also need money in the meantime, and this place was hiring."

A familiar anger returns, making my words hot. "Why haven't you called? Checked in? Mom's been a mess worrying. You just *left*."

Smith won't meet my eyes. "I told you guys where I was going."

"Not really," I snap. "You ghosted. Again."

I decide not to bring up my missing Christmas money from Laurie. It doesn't matter, and I want to believe him when he says he hasn't been using.

Smith lets a gap of silence hang between us. "I didn't think you cared."

"Of *course* I care," I say, exasperated. "You're my fucking brother."

He finally looks at me, his brown eyes connecting with mine. "It seemed like it would be better if I was out of your life. You're so driven and smart. You're mom's favorite, for fuck's sake, and you're going places. I fuck everything up."

Anger rises in my chest. "Stop victimizing yourself, Smith. I'm not going to grovel with empathy over your situation because you think I'm the 'better' child."

I expect him to take offense to my rebuttal, but he doesn't. "You're right. Sorry." He puts the cigarette out under his sneaker. "I took this job because I felt like shit for draining you guys. I didn't know you and Mom emptied your savings for me. I wanted to be able to give you something by the time you graduated."

I'm shocked by this gesture, but money isn't the point. "All I want is to know you're okay. I want you to come home once in a while," I explain. "I don't need your money. I need *you*."

Smith's face softens. "Yeah?"

"Yeah."

He lets out a deep sigh. I gently bump him with my shoulder. He bumps me back.

"I don't want to be the kind of brother that acts like Dad," he continues, running a thumb over his jawline. "I want to be better than that. I'm just scared of fucking up again. That's why I'm here, trying."

"You're not like Dad," I say firmly. "Trust me."

He looks relieved. "I am better, you know."

Now it's my turn to be relieved. "Please come home, Smith. A few times a month. At least. I'll tell Mom to not act so overbearing, but we need you. We miss you."

He runs his hands over his face. It's slightly greasy, like he's been working a long shift. I expect him to make another excuse, but instead Smith's mouth curves into a smile. "Okay," he says. "I will. I promise."

31

"How many promposals do you think will happen at the spring fair on Friday?"

"I still need to find a dress."

"You think Lenora and Duncan are going together?"

Marlowe invites me over Sunday evening after she's back from San Diego. My mom is home for the night, which means I can take her car. I told her about Smith, where he was, how he was doing, and she apologized for how upset she's been lately because of his absence. She was comforted knowing he's okay.

Now I'm hanging out in Marlowe's bedroom. She sits against her plush headboard, scrolling through her phone. I'm lying on my back, staring at the ceiling and wondering if my speech will be good enough for the fair on Friday. I've gone through about ten different drafts, each one meticulously read and critiqued by my friends, but I'm not certain it's perfect.

"I think it's the right choice," Marlowe's saying. We've been discussing colleges. "Did I tell you they have a LGBTQ+ Discord? And queer events."

This was Marlowe's second time walking around the UC San Diego. Her parents enrolled her in an official tour, which she thought would be incredibly dull, but it seems to have doubled her excitement about potentially attending in the fall.

She shows me the photos she took, and I can't help feeling a little devastated. So much is about to change. When I get into Stanford, we'll be a whole nine hours away from each other. Tahlia will be all the way across the country.

"I'm going to miss you," I say, and it comes out slightly watery.

Marlowe takes a deep breath. "Okay, no more future talk. We're not going to be sad right now."

I wish I could confide in Marlowe. Tell her about the whole Charlie/Adeline thing. On the drive home yesterday, Charlie glanced over at me no less than ten times. I pretended not to notice. I told myself not to read into it, but that hasn't stopped my brain from spinning. It doesn't matter. He's not interested. And I respect Adeline's trust in me.

"She deleted every photo of you, huh?"

I roll over to see what she's talking about. Marlowe's scrolling through Lenora's Instagram page. She did the same thing with Duncan's page twenty minutes before.

"God, how deep are you?"

"You don't even want to know."

I watch her scroll. "Yeah, she archived all our pictures together. You remember how mad she was sophomore year. I'm shocked she didn't block me."

"She was way overdramatic about that," Marlowe says under her breath.

"You think?"

She lets out a snide snort. "Yeah. I mean, it wasn't like *she* was Craig's girlfriend."

I've had this same thought before, but I never dwelled on it. I'd mistakenly brought it up when I first tried to fix things by showing up at her house. *You told me you weren't seeing him*, I said. That had only made her angrier. She said I shouldn't have been making out with anyone she'd been talking to in the first place. That I always took things way too far. That I wasn't careful with people's feelings.

And she's not wrong. I should have been more considerate of people's feelings before I agreed to go out with them during my sophomore year. I often left guys blindsided and confused when I decided to break things off, chalking it up to boredom or incompatibility. I wanted that rush of excitement. I thrived in the initial flirty phase.

"Besides," Marlowe continues. "Lenora had bigger issues when it came to your friendship. That fight was the match that struck the dynamite."

I furrow my brow. "What are you talking about?"

"You never saw it?"

I shake my head.

"I think, from the outside, she thought that everything came easy for you. Your grades, your confidence, your knack for flirting." She flicks her eyes back to Lenora's Instagram account. "She was jealous. Like, she would never admit that. But she was."

I consider this. "That can't be true. And it's not like those things come naturally for me. I work at it."

"But you make it look easy," Marlowe counters. "And that's all Lenora saw. So when she found a reason to accuse you of being a terrible friend, she totally blew up on you."

"That's—" I start, then stop myself.

Marlowe's theory might not be completely untrue. There were trivial moments I tended to let slide. I would tell her I was talking to two guys at once, and she'd roll her eyes and say, "Wow, not surprised" in a hurtful tone. When I said I was excited about the spring dance, she offhandedly said it would be hard for me to pick just one guy to go with—as if I wanted to go with a guy at all. I thought we could be each other's best friend dates, but I'd laughed like it was joke and replied, "Yeah, so tough."

"I shouldn't have made out with Craig," I say. "Friends shouldn't go after someone their best friend is, or *was*, interested in."

"Yeah, okay. That may be true, but if Lenora really cared about your friendship, she would have been honest about Craig from the beginning."

I bite my lower lip. I apologized to Lenora so many times after Craig sent around that Snapchat of me, but she shut me down every single time. Even months later, when I thought things had cooled down, she refused to talk to me. Or even meet me halfway.

Marlowe jolts upright, almost dropping her phone. "Holy shit."

I prop myself up on my elbows, startled by her sudden outburst. "What?"

Her eyes are huge as she turns her phone toward me. It takes me a second before I realize what I'm looking at. Marlowe's moved on to scrolling through *my* Instagram account. I haven't archived any photos, so old pictures of Lenora and me still exist. Marlowe's tapped on a specific photo from five years ago. Seventh-grade Halloween. It's a somewhat grainy, over-filtered photo of us, hugging each other, grinning wide—

In our matching yellow banana costumes.

32

"Who do you think is going to have the craziest promposal?"

"I hope I just get asked at this point."

"Is Brynn going with anyone? This is the longest she's been single in forever."

I'm speechless. It feels like I'm on an elevator that's bottomed out, sending me plummeting into free fall. Because *this* doesn't make sense.

That picture feels like a distant memory. I know Lenora has that identical costume, but she didn't have it the night of Halloween. Besides, she couldn't have spent the entire year trying to sabotage me. It's not like her. I saw how tearful she was after that weekend. I know what it looks like when a person is hurting, and she wasn't pretending.

And what about the lip gloss found in Duncan's Wrangler? It doesn't add up.

"Let's think about this," Marlowe says, keeping a steady voice. She can tell I'm spiraling. "It's not Lenora, right? People saw her passed out in the backyard when Duncan disappeared that night."

Right. Another reason it can't be her.

I run a hand through my hair. "So it's a coincidence?"

"Maybe, but what do we know that's factual?" she says. "Nobody aside from you came or went in the same costume. You left wearing yours."

"Unless someone levitated through the window—" I stop my joke as the pieces slowly come together. "Wait."

"Brynn, nobody in their right mind would climb a window when they could easily use the door."

"No, it's not that. What else do we know about that night?" I slap both palms on her bedspread. "*Where* did it happen? In a bedroom, right?"

"Keith's sister's bedroom, I think," she says, visibly confused. "I noticed BTS posters on the walls in that video clip."

The Halloween hookup happened in Aly Whittle's bedroom. *Of course* Keith Whittle didn't have a single earthly clue when I'd confronted him about it all those months ago. Why would he have any business going into his little sister's bedroom?

"Marlowe, *this* is why we haven't been able to find the person wearing the costume," I say. "Because no one *was* wearing it."

Her eyebrows knit together. "What do you mean?"

I bolt out of her bed, grabbing my mom's car keys from her nightstand. "The second costume is still at Keith Whittle's house."

After I text Keith that we're on our way over, Marlowe and I make the ten-minute drive to his place. We're slamming the car doors when he steps onto his patio, confusion splayed across his features.

Instead of greeting him, I say, "Is your sister home?"

"Yeah," Keith says cautiously. "But she wasn't here the night I threw the party, if that's what you're wondering."

"I don't think she has anything to do with it," I explain. "But she might be able to help. Can we talk to her?"

His eyes widen as he looks from me to Marlowe. "Yeah, sure. Come in."

Keith opens the front door and leads us upstairs just as his mom shouts, "Keith? Who's there?"

"Some friends picking up something for school!" Keith lies quickly as our footsteps pound up the carpeted steps.

The three of us come to a stop outside Aly's bedroom door. Keith knocks and a few seconds later, Aly's head peeks out. She's wearing a *Stranger Things* T-shirt, plaid pajama bottoms, and an alarmed look on her face.

"Hey," Keith starts. "Um, Brynn was hoping to talk to you?"

I paste on my kindest smile. "I wanted to ask you a few questions about Halloween."

Her jaw drops. "You—you think *I* was with Duncan that night? I swear. I wasn't. Ask Keith, I wasn't even here."

"I know," I say quickly. "But we think the costume might be here."

Marlowe pulls out her phone. She'd found an Instagram photo of Aly from last summer. In it, Aly's wearing the exact banana costume I wore the night of Halloween. She's surrounded by a few other people dressed up as fruit—a watermelon and a lime—and she's captioned it: **just camp things.**

Aly's hands fly to her mouth. "Oh my god. You're right. It's probably here."

Aly opens her bedroom door and—*oh boy*. Her room is a mess. The floor is scattered with clothes. Every spare inch of her dresser is cluttered with glass perfume bottles, trendy vitamin containers, neon nail polish, makeup compacts, various styles of sunglasses, and a whole bunch of chargers. A comfy lounge chair that's tucked by her window is piled with heaps of clothes.

"Sorry, I thrive in chaos," she explains. "It's here, though. Somewhere. I mean, it *should* be. I kind of forgot about it."

I gather my patience as my eyes dart around her room. "So you haven't seen it since last summer?"

Aly starts digging through the back of her tiny closet, which is so much worse than the state of her room. "I don't think so. Last summer I worked as a junior camp counselor. We did this silly performance about eating fruits and veggies, and I needed a costume—"

"Lenora's mom and my mom work together," Keith explains. "They're pretty close."

"Right, exactly," Aly confirms, continuing to pick through her closet. "My mom got it from Lenora's mom. I borrowed it for the summer, but I guess I forgot to return it. I swear I did, but—oh, wait—"

She retreats deeper into her closet, then comes back up for air with an extremely wrinkled banana costume. I watch as she frees the bright yellow polyester. Then she's on her feet, showing me the tag inside.

"See? Lenora's mom put her initials here so it wouldn't get mixed up with Camp Hindlewood's costumes."

She's right. The letters L. K. are inked neatly on the tag.

"So Lenora didn't know you had this at Camp—"

I stop. Aly raises her eyebrows, waiting for me to finish my question. But my brain is still processing what she said before. Camp *Hindlewood*. Why does that name sound familiar?

And then it hits me. I whip my head to look at Marlowe, and slow understanding fills her eyes. The evidence finally clicks into place.

Camp Hindlewood is a Christian camp.

Katie Delcavo was the only other counselor from Greenlough at Camp Hindlewood last summer.

Katie, who knew Aly had the same costume as me.

Who *intentionally* framed me on Halloween.

White noise fills my ears, silencing everything around me. I barely hear Keith ask, "Did you see this anywhere in your room when you came home the next morning?"

Aly grimaces, glancing around her bedroom as though she's seeing it with clear eyes. "I mean . . . maybe? I don't really remember. It could have been living in this mess." She glares at her brother. "I was more concerned about changing my sheets since *someone* allowed the party upstairs."

Heart racing, my fingers tap through my phone, accessing the account Cadence created months ago. There's no way it's Katie. For one, she's part of the Holy Crew. She joined Faith's Abstinence Angels, *and* she's been to every one of our meetings.

But maybe my gut was right. What if she did join to spy on me?

No, that doesn't make sense. Not with all the effort she put into the club when we came back from winter break.

I scroll to the last message I sent the anonymous user, then type a single question.

> Katie?

"*This* is why nobody ever saw the second costume," Marlowe's saying. "It was up here the whole time. No wonder everyone thought it was you."

Aly looks guilty. "Sorry, Brynn."

"What?" I snap my head up from my phone. "No. I mean, you don't have to be sorry. How could you have known?"

If Katie is responsible, it means she's had to stew in her own guilt for months. Even if she came clean now, would Lenora believe her? There's no way. Katie would make things worse for herself if she told the truth. She'd be a target at Greenlough, like I had been.

After refreshing the DM for the third time, I click on the user's account. Only, I can't access the profile I'd seen a minute ago. And that's when I know, *really* know, that I might be right about everything.

This account has been deactivated.

33

"Are you going to the EOF meeting this week?"

"I should be there!"

"I owe Brynn for helping me with prom."

After we leave Keith's, Marlowe and I tell Cadence and Tahlia everything. Since I don't have Katie's number, we agree it's best if I confront her in private at school on Monday.

Only, Katie doesn't come to school on Monday.

She's absent on Tuesday, Wednesday, and Thursday too.

When I ask Faith about her during AP Lit on Thursday, she shrugs and says, "I think she has the flu?"

I know it's bogus. She can't avoid school forever, even if she really is sick.

My range of emotions fluctuate the rest of the week. Mostly, I'm angry. Because if Katie was with Duncan, does that also mean she's responsible for taking that photo of me drinking at the Halloween dance and reporting me to McTiernan? Did she make that satanic meme of Cadence after she broke into Duncan's car? And the AirDrop—was that her idea?

But the weirdest thing is, if she was so committed to making my life hell, then why did she get more people to join our club? Why did she make those femolution buttons? To throw me off her trail?

I want to tell Lenora, but it's not my place. Not until I find out the truth.

It's the Friday before spring break and with only three weeks left until senior prom, it's officially promposal season. It's *also* university acceptance season, which means emotions are running extra high. Including mine.

Today's the day I should hear from Stanford.

Tahlia has been accepted to UPenn on partial scholarship. Even though her dad hasn't fully accepted she won't go to Brown, he finally gave his blessing—sort of. He keeps reminding her that there's no harm in transferring later on if she wants.

"The scholarship helped sweeten the deal," Tahlia told us.

Marlowe got into UC San Diego and UC Santa Barbara, but she's decided on San Diego. Cadence is waiting to hear from Loyola, her first choice. She's also been accepted into UC Davis.

Instead of stressing about Stanford, I focus my energy on my speech. I'm scheduled to present it this afternoon at the annual spring fair. Traditionally, this is where the majority of the promposals happen. It's exclusively for the senior class and while it's nothing extravagant, we *do* get out of classes early—so the excitement is contagious.

Local food trucks line the curb parallel to the courtyard, and booths of carnival games are set up on the green space. The ticket money for the games and raffle prizes goes toward our prom. There's also a platformed stage set up where McTiernan will read off the raffle winners at the end of the day.

In the meantime, many seniors sit in the grass, eating fries and tacos and tater tots from the trucks, while Rhea announces a list of accomplishments from student council this year. Mathis will talk about the LGBTQ+ club's achievements after her, and I'll follow up with my speech.

I posted a photo of myself on Instagram last night wearing my WE ARE THE FEMOLUTION button. In my caption, I encouraged students to wear theirs today to support the club. I expected to see a few people abide, but nearly every single person has one pinned to their uniform. It makes my heart swell with pride.

Tahlia, Cadence, Marlowe, and I are sitting in the shade eating grilled cheeses, watching a few promposals go down. We'd wandered around earlier, playing a few corny carnival games, but Cadence was pretty low energy. That's when we decided to grab food and sit near the stage.

I'm wondering how Charlie is going to ask Adeline to prom when I catch sight of Shantel and Adeline. They're rounding the corner of the balloon dart booth. I notice they're both wearing buttons, which sends a zing of elation through me.

Suddenly, Shantel stops walking. Adeline nearly runs into her. It's an awkward encounter, but she laughs it off. I watch as Shantel begins to take large stones out of her pocket, setting them carefully on the sidewalk. When I squint, I can see she's painted words on each of them. She places the final stone down on the ground as Adeline squeals. I read the whole message.

PROM WITH YOU WOULD ROCK!

Wait.

WAIT.

Holy shit. Adeline never asked for help to fix things with Charlie. She wanted to fix things with *Shantel*.

I've had this all wrong. I think back to the subtle moments I'd brushed off over the last few months. It must have been Shantel who gave Adeline those black roses on Valentine's Day. And it was *Shantel* who was standing next to Charlie across the room at Grant's New Year's party. That's who caught Adeline's attention.

They're not only close friends. They're more than that.

I've never seen Adeline so giddy. She's grinning wide, nodding *yes* as she throws her arms around Shantel, who looks both relieved and delighted.

But the magic of the moment is interrupted by a shrill scream.

No. Not a scream. It's a *cry*.

And it's coming from Lenora.

I whip my head toward the side of the stage and find Katie Delcavo standing next to her. When did Katie get here? I watch as she wipes her mascara from under her eyes, her posture slouched. The seniors who are close enough to hear aren't giving them any privacy.

I'm across the courtyard, too far away to hear what she's saying, but I have a sinking feeling I already know.

I abandon my spot in the grass and sprint over to the scene Katie's caused. Unfortunately, Duncan and I arrive at the same time. He glares at me, as if this is my fault, before turning to Lenora.

"Is it true?" Lenora's not bothering to check her volume, and it draws even more attention. When Duncan doesn't say anything, she repeats her question even louder, emphasizing each word. *"Is. It. True?"*

Tears leak down Katie's cheeks, creating rivulets in her foundation. She looks at me for help, but I don't know what to say.

"Babe, I'm sorry—" Duncan begins.

She shakes her head, cutting him off. "It's true, then?"

He looks from Katie to Lenora, his face crumbling with emotion. "Can we go inside and talk?"

Lenora's face is splotchy, a sign she's about to cry. She believes Katie. I stand there helplessly, wishing there was something I could do to take her heartbreak away.

"Fuck you, Duncan. You're— I'm—" She struggles for her words, suppressing a sob that works its way up to her vocal chords. "I—I can't do this."

She speed walks in the direction of the parking lot. Duncan steps forward as if to follow her, but then changes his mind and whirls on Katie. "Why the *fuck* did you say anything?"

"It wasn't right. You know that," Katie says through a choked cry.

Duncan rolls his eyes, then runs after Lenora. He won't catch up to her, though. She's already made it to her car.

I can feel the stares of our classmates, so I grab Katie's arm and pull her toward the back of the stage.

"Did the guilt finally get to you?" I ask, the words coming out tired.

"Yes, okay?" Katie says through tears. "I couldn't take watching Lenora get excited over Duncan's stupid half-hearted promposal. I kept my mouth shut because I didn't want to be the next target, but that was selfish. I should have told you it was me the night after it happened."

I cross my arms in defense. "But you didn't."

Katie's mascara is long past saving, and she doesn't even try to wipe away the smudging. "I'm so sorry. You probably hate me."

I let out a tight breath. "I don't hate you. I just don't understand."

"I thought Faith would exile me from our friendship if she found out it was me," Katie admits.

"So this is about *Faith*?"

"No." She shakes her head. "I—I had a crush on Duncan. He knew I did. It's embarrassing to admit now."

She looks down at her feet, hesitating to go on. I say nothing. I won't let her withhold answers from me any longer than she has already.

"On Halloween, he told me to meet him in the bedroom upstairs," she says, her voice thin. "He knew Lenora had passed out. I thought—it was so stupid. He said he'd always thought I was hot. That he'd already broken up with Lenora—which was a lie. I know that now."

I cringe. It shouldn't be surprising Duncan had the worst intentions. I've known this from the beginning.

"I waited for him upstairs. I was pretty tipsy, so I started going through Aly's room. That's when I recognized her banana costume from camp. It was on the floor in her closet," she explains. "You were wearing one like it . . . I thought it was kind of funny. I was about to go downstairs to show you, but then Duncan came up." She sniffles. "The door must have not been shut all the way. I guess John Mark walked by—"

I feel like I've been punched in the stomach. *"John Mark?"*

She nods weakly. "John Mark has always thought you were, like, this lost temptress who promotes evildoings. It's why Faith works so hard to get you to repent. She thinks if she saves you, John Mark will be impressed by her devotion and love her more—or something. Your reputation has always bugged him. He saw this as an opportunity to teach you a lesson."

I let her explanation sink in. "So he whipped out his camera and violated your privacy? Because he thought it was *me?*"

More tears spill from her eyes. "I shouldn't have—it was a mistake. I stopped it, but it doesn't undo what we did. I *really* messed up."

"John Mark was responsible for the AirDrop, wasn't he? And he sent that Satan meme of Cadence?" Everything I'd been questioning since Halloween begins to make sense. "And my cardigan and textbooks. He did that."

I remember what Katie said after she'd made the femolution buttons for the school. *I wanted to fix things.*

"I didn't know he was responsible for any of it. Faith only told me yesterday. She saw the original Snapchat video saved on his phone last night and confronted him."

My head is spinning. John Mark hated me enough to be this cruel. He didn't even know me that well, and yet he set out to ruin my life anyway.

Because he thought it would teach me a lesson. That's the worst part. He doesn't think he did anything wrong.

She swallows. "Earlier today, I told John Mark it was me, not you. But he didn't believe me. He's convinced it's you. When I told him that he wasn't acting in good faith, he told me God would forgive his sins if it meant saving someone else. It's . . . illogical!"

"Yeah, well. It's not *great*," I mumble.

"I'm *so* sorry, Brynn. I've learned so much from you. I should have told you sooner. I was going to tell you over DM, but I chickened out. It wasn't fair to you."

"You recognized the lip gloss, didn't you?" I ask, remembering the photo I posted. "The one we found in Duncan's car. And then—oh my god. You asked me if I knew who it was. I told you I didn't."

She takes a deep breath, clearly ashamed. "When I knew you were still unsure, I thought I had time to make it right. But I should have told you."

"How many times did you and Duncan—?" I start.

"Just that once. On Halloween," she jumps in, heat flooding her face. "When I realized he didn't actually break up with Lenora, he picked me up so we could talk. My lip gloss must have fallen out of my purse, but I swear nothing happened. I was furious with him." She meets my eyes. "And I'm going to tell McTiernan today. I have the screenshots from John Mark's phone as proof. Faith sent them."

It's the least she can do. Katie let me take the blame in front of the whole school, putting my reputation on the line while she hid in secret. I want to hate her, but I can't. That doesn't mean I have to accept her apology right now. Not while the betrayal is fresh.

The knots in my chest begin to loosen. I don't *have* to fix this, I realize. I can just accept that I'm angry. I'm allowed to feel this way, given everything that's happened.

Tahlia comes up to me, placing a delicate hand on my shoulder. She looks from Katie to me, clearly confused. "Hey. You're up next."

The speech. I almost forgot.

I glance at the stage, where Miss Rothman is beckoning me forward. I don't look at Katie as I step around her. White noise echoes through my brain as I guide myself up the steps of the platform. I've already memorized what I've written, but I scramble to get myself in the right headspace.

Miss Rothman beams at me before moving aside. I wish I felt good about this, but I'm not even excited. I feel defeated.

John Mark. It was *John Mark* who wanted to bring me down.

My breath blows feedback into the mic. I take a step back, then quickly readjust. I have to say *something*.

"Hi, everyone, I'm Brynn Whitaker," I begin, my eyes jumping from student to student, "and I'm here to talk to you about a new organization formed this year. Our Evolution of Feminism club."

My tone is off. This should come naturally. I know why I'm passionate about this club and why I wish for it to continue on next year even though I won't be here to lead it.

I catch Katie's eye in the crowd. She wears an uncomfortable look on her face. I have the power now, I realize. My resentment is a fresh cut. I could stand here and liberate myself from the lies I was unwillingly tied up in. Shift the blame. Put that spotlight on someone else. It would be so easy to tell my classmates it was her. It might even feel good.

I lick my lips, changing my tone. "A lot of you know me as a fellow senior. Or maybe you know me as a flirt, or a loudmouth, or the slut who wrote her hookup numbers on her arms all year." Slowly, more and more students stop what they're doing to listen. "Or maybe you don't know me at all. In fact, I think most of you don't know the real me."

From the corner of the stage, McTiernan grits his teeth. I turn back to my classmates. Many have wandered closer to the stage. The bright red femolution buttons they wear catch my eye. I can't help but feel proud of what we've created, and that feeling reinvigorates me.

"I want to talk to you about our organization. About why I believe in it and why I hope it continues on without the guidance of its current seniors. But for me to do that, I feel like I should be honest with you. Give you the truth to how it all started."

I find my friends at the side of the stage. Cadence is slack-mouthed and wide-eyed, surprised at the deviation from my original speech.

"I found myself at the center of a scandal months ago. It wasn't fun. I never felt more hated or misjudged, well, *ever*. And selfishly, I wanted to set people straight about me. About who I am."

On the opposite corner, Katie stands alone, looking like she's about to cry again. And even though I'm blood-boilingly furious with her, I know that anger is misdirected. She's had to live with her guilt for months. She told Lenora the truth, even if it took longer than I would have liked. And sure, maybe she did it because I figured it out, or maybe the impact of the femolution really did make a difference.

It doesn't matter. She did the right thing, and I'm not going to destroy Katie.

That's not who I am.

The real focus of my resentment should be John Mark, who not only violated boundaries, but committed deeply serious offenses. Multiple, in fact.

I push on, now extremely off-script. "I hoped this club would change people's minds about me, but I also hoped it would change judgments toward shame culture. Toward cancel culture. If we succeeded, we would show students that misogyny is still a huge problem—and we could take steps toward being better."

Someone in the audience lets out an enthusiastic whoop. It's only then do I realize I have everyone's undivided attention.

"The more we came together to break down double standards and unlearn the stupid social construct *bullshit* we've been fed all our lives, the more empowered we felt. And that's the impact that I hope continues on." I turn to McTiernan. "Sorry. Language, I know."

My eyes sweep over my classmates. My teachers. Miss Rothman gives me an encouraging nod.

"We wanted to start a femolution," I continue. "I think we did that. No matter how you identify or where you come from, we welcomed you to learn with us. It might not be perfect, but if people left feeling more inspired and validated and understood, then we accomplished something—something that should continue on here at Greenlough." I stare down at the red button pinned neatly to my uniform blouse. I look at Katie. "I think everyone who came can agree they took away something important."

There's murmurs of agreement from the crowd. My chest swells with appreciation. "I'm proud to be part of it. So . . . thank you."

There's an enormous, rowdy applause filled with resounding cheers and whistles. It startles me, but I can't help the smile that spreads across my face. Sure, it wasn't my carefully written speech, but it was honest.

Before I leave the stage, I decide to share one more thought with my supportive classmates.

I grab the mic. "Oh, and, John Mark?" I say sweetly, my eyes narrowing in on him in the crowd. "Go to hell, you crusty ham sandwich. You know what you did, and soon everyone here will know too." I glance at Dean McTiernan. "I didn't cuss that time."

A murmuring of whispers ignites among the sea of seniors as the dean takes the mic from me. "We'll talk later."

"It's not me you want to talk to," I say confidently, then point to John Mark. "It's him."

And then the guilty little sleazebag *books it*.

From my position on the stage's platform, I watch Cadence attempt to grab the collar of his uniform shirt as he runs by. He barely escapes her, sprinting down the quad. She begins to chase after him. Well, it's more of an aggressive waddle. She can't move that fast.

It only takes a few seconds for our classmates to understand. Suddenly, everyone is moving in on John Mark, shouting at him to stop, coming together for *me*.

Before I can even begin to figure out my next move, two things happen at once. Duncan comes out of *nowhere* and tackles the shit out of John Mark. Both boys hit the grassy quad with a heavy thud.

Concerned gasps spread among the mob surrounding them. And with everyone so enraptured by the scene Duncan's created, few are paying attention to Cadence. Among all the commotion, I see her eyes widen with concern. She stops in her tracks, her hands flying to her stomach, doubling over as if she's in pain.

And that's when, in front of our entire senior class, Cadence's water breaks.

34

"Did you see it?"

"That was WILD. Brynn was telling the truth!"

"John Mark was behind everything?!"

Marlowe drives the five of us to the hospital. The fifth body in the car is, surprisingly, Thomas Randkin. Even more surprising, he was the first one who jumped into action, practically carrying Cadence to Marlowe's car while she screamed, "PUT ME DOWN, ASSHOLE. I HAVEN'T LOST MY ABILITY TO WALK!"

I'd scanned the vicinity for Charlie, but I couldn't find him in the thick cluster of students crowding John Mark and Duncan.

Since Marlowe was the only one with her keys on her, she made the executive decision to drive. Normally we'd need permission to leave campus, but the security guard didn't hesitate to open the gate for us after he was bombarded by Marlowe's panicked demands.

"Fuck, fuck, *fuck*," Cadence keeps repeating as Marlowe guns it. She's driving as safely and aggressively as the surrounding traffic will let her. "I'm not ready to do this. Can you stay in there, dude? I don't think I can do this. *Fuck*."

"Cadence, shut up!" Tahlia says this so loudly and so sternly that it startles me. "You are the baddest bitch I've ever known, and you are going to have this baby like a fucking boss, okay?"

I blink up at her. I don't think I've heard Tahlia string together that many expletives in my life. I withhold the urge to laugh. I don't need Cadence coming for me.

"Damn, Tahlia," Cadence moans. "You should give motivational speeches."

A tiny bit of relief courses through me. At least she's handling this with a sense of humor.

"You got this," Thomas says uncertainly. Then, he tries to awkwardly hold her hand.

Cadence slaps it away. "Absolutely not."

Thomas doesn't say another word for the rest of the ride.

"It's going to be okay." I motion for Tahlia to grab Cadence's phone from her skirt pocket. She does. "What's your password?"

Cadence lets out a low breath. "One, two, three, four, five, six."

"Seven, eight, nine, ten," Marlowe chimes, eager to help.

"I don't think we're counting, Marls," Tahlia supplies.

"Yeah, no. That's my password."

"Are you kidding me?" I type it in. "That's not at all secure."

"Is *this* your biggest concern right now?" Cadence grits out.

I ignore that, scrolling through her contacts until I see "Mom." I make a quick call, letting Mrs. Franzenberg know we're on our way to St. Gregory's Hospital.

I slide her phone in my pocket for safekeeping, then pull out my own. "I'm going to text Charlie."

"Charlie! Oh *no*. This baby is ruining everything today," Cadence groans, wincing through a contraction.

"Should we time those?" Marlowe inquires, not taking her eyes off the road. "I feel like that's something we should do, right?"

"Maybe Thomas would know if he took a *single* birthing course with me," Cadence remarks.

Thomas says nothing, which is for the best. I wouldn't put it past Cadence to shove him out of a moving vehicle.

Tahlia lights up at the thought of having a plan. "I'll use my phone timer."

Cadence moves her head so she's looking at me. "He was supposed to ask you today."

She's a little sweaty. I hope that's not a bad sign. "Who?"

"Charlie. He had a dumbass promposal and everything."

A fluttery, warm feeling burbles through me. Charlie was going to ask me to prom?

"Minute one mark!" Tahlia announces.

I snap back into focus. "Keep breathing," I say, shaking away my thoughts of Charlie. I steal a glance out the window. "We're almost there."

Marlowe skids to a stop in front of the hospital about thirty seconds later. Thomas helps Cadence out of the car, and Tahlia and I saddle up beside her as we head inside, leaving Marlowe to find parking.

There's a scurry of commotion as we enter the lobby. Tahlia rushes toward the first nurse she sees, directing her toward Cadence. A few minutes later, someone comes through a set of double doors with a wheelchair. We start to follow, but another nurse stops us, asking if we're family. Tahlia and I shake our heads, but Thomas explains he's the father.

"He can come," the nurse says, nodding to Thomas.

"*No*," Cadence groans, her voice already disappearing down the hall.

"Your family will be here soon!" I call after her. I know Thomas is not her ideal form of company.

I don't have to feel bad for too long because Cadence's parents are next to arrive. We point them toward the maternity ward, then do the same when Thomas's parents show up shortly after.

A few seconds later, Charlie bursts through the hospital's entrance. His shirt is untucked from his uniform pants and his hair is wild, like he's been raking his hand through it.

Then his panicked eyes find mine.

"She's fine," I say, hoping it comforts him. I point down the hall. "Keep going that way. Your parents are already here."

Relief fills his gaze. "Thank you," he breathes.

"Here." I grapple for Cadence's phone from my skirt pocket. "It's hers."

Charlie takes it. A tiny jolt fires inside me when his fingers brush mine.

"I'll text you," he says.

And then he's gone.

I find a seat in between Tahlia and Marlowe in the waiting room. I'm sweaty and exhausted, but everything else is out of my hands right now. All we can do is wait.

"That," Marlowe says, "was wild."

I only manage to nod as my adrenaline spike decreases.

"Did I hallucinate," Tahlia begins, "or did *Duncan* tackle *John Mark?*"

Marlowe turns to me. "What happened?"

I let out a long breath. In the height of getting Cadence to the hospital, the fight almost feels insignificant. I fill them in on everything Katie told me. When I finish, Marlowe is livid. Tahlia's mouth slips into a frown.

"John *fucking* Mark," Marlowe exclaims. "What a prickweasel. And his father is a pastor!"

"Katie says she's going to tell McTiernan everything," I say. "But I may have jumpstarted that conversation."

"They'll expel him. That's the *least* he deserves," Marlowe huffs.

"Yeah, well, Duncan didn't go easy on him. Clearly."

The last person I want to feel any type of remorse for is Duncan Rowe, but even though he never felt any repercussions for his actions, he also never wanted that video spread around. It was a huge invasion of privacy for him, especially because he was the only one who was identifiable. I can understand why he'd want to beat the crap out of John Mark.

Tahlia looks concerned. "Do you think Faith knew this whole time?"

I shake my head. "Katie and Faith only found out yesterday. Faith has proof he was behind it."

"Hard to imagine she'll want to be with him after this," Tahlia says.

Marlowe's brown eyes soften. "Lenora must be heartbroken."

I remember the look on her face as she ran toward the parking lot. Betrayal. Hurt. Anger. If I reached out, would she think I was trying to say *I told you so?*

And Katie. I'm frustrated with her, but don't I know how terrible it feels to make a mistake? I'd genuinely expressed remorse to Lenora after the Craig situation, and she shut me out for good.

I don't want the school to shut Katie out. I'm mad, but I'm not *spiteful*. I don't want Greenlough to cancel her.

Mr. Frazenberg comes into the lobby thirty minutes later. He's wearing professional attire—black slacks and a pressed button-down—but his graying hair is disheveled, as if he has a habit of running his hands through it, like Charlie.

"It looks like it might be a long night," he explains. "You should go home."

"Are you sure?" I ask.

"I'm sure. She's this close"—he indicates a sliver of a gap between his pointer and thumb—"to pelting ice chips at Thomas, so I should get back there before she realizes how far she can throw them." He gives us a tired smile. "I'll tell Charlie to update you."

I feel like he can see my innermost feelings written on my forehead: *I HAVE A MASSIVE CRUSH ON YOUR SON*. I know it's all in my mind, but it doesn't stop a flush of heat from rushing through my body.

"Thank you," I say. "I'd like that."

Charlie
thank you for getting her here
so quickly

Charlie
she's doing ok

i hope you're downplaying
the whole ~water breaking
in front of everyone~ situation

Charlie
i told her people barely noticed

Charlie
but she told me to fuck off

hahaha

LEARN TO LIE BETTER

Charlie
not my strong suit

Charlie
it's hard for me to hide the
way i feel

is it?

Charlie
hold on, i'll text you in a
bit. sorry. thomas is being
annoying

what else is new?

Charlie
it's happening

Charlie
my dad and i are waiting in
the hall, but so far so good

i can't believe it!

Charlie
i know

Charlie
can I keep texting you? it's a
nice distraction

yes, on one condition

Charlie
?

tell me your favorite
butt detective episode

Charlie
buckle up. i have a lot of
feelings

it's been a while since your
last text. hope you're ok!

Charlie
sorry! the baby is here!

Charlie
he looks so fragile

Charlie
they're monitoring Cadence,
but she's doing ok

!!!!!

i'm glad to hear that

Charlie
cadence might kick thomas in the nuts when she finds the strength

Charlie
but that's a story for another time

this might be the least surprising thing i've heard today

Charlie
the adoptive parents are on their way down from san francisco tonight

that's good, right?

Charlie
yeah, it is

Charlie
there's something i wanted to ask you today

Charlie
but it seems i might be spending part of my spring break in this hospital

an unideal vacation, but at least there is an abundance of Jell-O

Charlie
trust me, i know. Cadence asked if i wanted to fill Thomas's shoes with it after he fell asleep

Charlie
so of course i did

mild criminal activity from none other than Charlie Frazenberg! i knew you weren't robbed of womb courage.

Charlie
i've missed texting you

ive missed it too

more than you know

35

"She was about to have the baby right on the quad, dude!"

"Lenora deleted every single pic of her and Duncan."

"I heard Katie Delcavo knows something..."

After leaving the hospital on Friday, Marlowe drove us back to school to get our belongings. It was nearing the end of the day, and as soon as we stepped foot on campus, Dean McTiernan and Mrs. Burchill requested my presence in the office, where my mom had already been summoned.

I wasn't in trouble for leaving without permission, but they suggested it would be beneficial if I revealed everything that I knew about John Mark and Duncan. So I did.

"We've requested a meeting with John Mark and his parents," McTiernan told me. "We'll keep you in the loop, but I want to assure you we have a zero-tolerance policy here. I'm very sorry you've dealt with this type of harassment from your own classmate."

"I'll tell you what," my mom began, "you better not allow me to see that nasty little ratface—"

"*Mom*," I'd gasped, delighted by this unexpected outburst.

She composed herself. "That's all *I'll* say."

At that point, I hadn't processed everything Katie told me about John Mark. We were still concerned about Cadence, though texting Charlie had been an unexpected bright spot, especially since I'd gotten it all wrong when it came to Adeline.

Marlowe seemed genuinely shocked by my ignorance. "How did you *not* hear about the Adeline and Shantel thing last year?"

Apparently, Adeline and Shantel had a very low-key, unofficial *thing* at the end of junior year, but then Adeline started having feelings for Charlie. It nearly tore their friend group apart, Grant taking Shantel's side while Charlie and Adeline spent the whole summer together. But when September rolled around, Adeline ended it with Charlie. The balance of their friend group was more important than their relationship, so the four of them decided to hit a reset. But Shantel was guarded. That's why Adeline had to earn her trust all over again. If I had known that, maybe I would have recognized the true situation sooner.

With Charlie, it's not just flirting or banter or a harmless crush. From the very first night we hung out, he's made me feel like I'm the most important person in the room. The one who knows my truest self. He's stood beside me in solidarity. He never judged me when it felt like the entire school was against me. He made me laugh when it felt like my world was imploding.

I remember the way he looked at me in his bedroom after he'd turned my skin into a galaxy. It's a feeling I've been repressing for months now. Something bigger.

I know with complete certainty that I'm in love with Charlie.

And it's a realization that's come too late.

There's nothing stopping me from being with Charlie now, but I feel that familiar emotional armor snake around my heart. For so long, I've built up hope in people only to be disappointed. McTiernan, who did the bare minimum when my whole world was crumbling. My dad, who erased me from his new life. Prior flings and flirtationships that didn't work out. Relationships, like Otto, that weren't a good fit. Even Smith left again, and I was the one who had to find him.

I've been in this situation before. I was falling for Hayes before he graduated, and that heartache left emotional scars. Now Charlie and I are about to graduate. Go to different colleges. Start new lives. So why put us through the same thing?

When I think about it logically, it makes sense. But it doesn't mean I don't also feel a crushing weight on my heart. This is the best resolution to this problem. Nobody gets their heart broken. It stays easy. Uncomplicated.

I've just crawled into bed when my phone lights up. Thinking it's Charlie, I grapple for it, my heart pulsating like it's about to burst into a gigantic glitter bomb. When I blink down at my screen, I freeze. It's not Charlie.

It's Lenora.

> **Lenora**
> Hey, I'm outside your house.
> Can we talk?

I sit up straight. *Lenora?* I slide out of bed and peel back my curtains. Sure enough, Lenora's blue Honda Fit is idling by the curb.

What is she doing here? Did she come to yell at me now that she's had a chance to process what happened?

There's only one way to find out.

I yank on a hoodie and slip into my flip-flops, sneaking quietly out the front door so I don't wake my mom. I wave hesitantly as I approach the passenger's side door, and she unlocks it so I can slip in.

Even in the dark, I can tell her eyes are swollen from crying. The skin around her nostrils is red too. I swallow, trying to think of something to say, but decide to let her speak first.

"Sorry for showing up out of the blue like this," she finally says.

I play with a loose thread on my hoodie. "It's okay. I'm glad you came."

She wipes under her eyes. "I've been thinking a lot, I guess. About everything. I had tunnel vision. Like, I was seeing my relationship the way *I* wanted to see it," she explains. "I'm not stupid. I knew there were holes in Duncan's story the night of Halloween, but the anger I've carried toward you fueled me into blaming you, not him. It was misdirected. And . . . I'm sorry."

I'm stunned by her apology. "Oh, um. Thank you."

"It took me a while to get it, you know? Here I was perpetuating slut-shaming culture like an asshole." Lenora gives me a weak smile. "I guess what I'm trying to say is, I see it now. Everything that happened with Duncan—all the ways I put you down for your relationships and crushes. You didn't deserve that. Not from your best friend."

I release a deep breath. It feels good to hear her say it. "I took it too far with Craig back then, and I'm sorry. I really am."

"I should have been honest with you about how I felt about him," she says softly. "It was silly to destroy a friendship over a guy."

I'm reminded of all the reasons why I love Lenora, why she was my best friend for so long. She might have a hard exterior, but deep down she cares about people. If she didn't, she wouldn't be here.

She still cares about Duncan too. It's why she was so hurt by all of this. She loves someone who did something shitty to her. That's a terrible feeling.

"I miss you." I say, my voice cutting through chirping crickets in the stillness of the night. "I miss being your friend."

"I miss you too." She gives me a sad smile. "Also? Fuck Duncan."

"*Fuck* Duncan," I agree.

"And John Mark," she adds, then starts laughing so hard her shoulders shake. "I can't believe you called him a *crusty ham sandwich*."

Her laughter is contagious. "He's more like a sweaty gym sock."

"An infected elbow scab."

"Ew—you win."

We reach for each other at the same time, our arms tangling in a sincere embrace. It feels nice to have this sliver of normalcy.

When Lenora pulls away, she's teary. "I can't believe you broke into Duncan's truck."

That somehow feels like years ago. "It wasn't me, but I also didn't stop it. It was Cadence." I debate telling her the next part, but decide I have nothing to lose. "She found strawberry lip gloss under the seat that night. I knew it wasn't yours because—"

"My allergy," Lenora finishes.

"Right," I say sadly. "It was like, you already didn't believe me. If I told you, I was afraid you'd think I made it up."

"Yeah, maybe. I wasn't in the best headspace," she says, then adds, "Damn, I think I owe Cadence a thank-you card for what she wrote."

I look up at her. A real smile hangs on her lips.

"I can love him and hate him at the same time," she explains, her tone somber. "But hopefully the love part will fade fast."

"I'm sorry he turned out to be a giant prickweasel."

"Me too," she agrees. "What are we going to do about Katie?"

I've thought about this as well. We can't ostracize her, and we can't let Greenlough take her down like they did me. Not after everything we've worked toward with the femolution. Katie was genuinely apologetic. It won't be easy, and I don't have to forgive everything she's put me through, but it doesn't mean we should cause her even more suffering.

I remember the part of *Paradise Lost* I'd highlighted in Mr. Manning's class last semester. *What can we suffer worse?* There's always something worse that can be done. Sometimes the hardest decision is figuring out the best way forward.

"Spring break will give us space to process—well, everything," I say. "And then we try to leave it in the past."

Lenora looks uncertain, but she eventually nods in agreement. "I think you're right."

"You know, I never thought my last year of high school would be this . . ." I search for the word.

"Hellish?" Lenora offers, and my mouth slips into an amused grin.

"Yeah, exactly."

We catch each other's eyes. If none of this happened, would we be sitting here together, wading our way toward forgiveness? Maybe that cliché saying is true. Everything happens for a reason. But I wish it hadn't happened like this.

"Hey, how's Cadence?" she asks. "I heard what happened after I left."

For the next twenty minutes, I tell Lenora the dramatic story of Cadence's water breaking and everything I know about her son's birth. She's glad to hear they're both doing okay, and our conversation falls to lighter topics. I learn she was also accepted to the University of Santa Barbara, which reminds me—oh god. Stanford's acceptances went out today. With such an eventful day, I completely spaced it.

"How can you *not* get in?" Lenora laughs when I tell her. "But go check. I need to get home anyway."

I reach for the handle, then turn back to her. "Maybe we can hang out during spring break?"

Her eyes light up. "Yeah. I'd like that."

Once Lenora drives off, I sprint inside. My fingers are shaking as I type in my email and password to access Stanford's portal, and I realize I'm holding my breath as I navigate to my inbox. There's a notification that alerts me there's been a change in the status of my application. I click on it, my heart thrumming so erratically that I feel it's going to rocket straight out of my chest.

Then I see the two words that crush my soul.

Not admitted.

36

"Wait, it was John Mark who sent the video?"

"That's why Duncan beat his ass!"

"Why would he DO that?"

During my entire spring break, I fall straight into a self-pitying depression. I should have been prepared for rejection. I knew Stanford's tight acceptance rate, but I thought I worked hard enough to show them I belong. I'm not even *waitlisted*. If I'd only had McTiernan's letter of recommendation—

No. I can't think like that. I won't pretend one person's referral could have made a difference. I just wasn't good enough.

That's what hurts the worst.

Smith comes home on Saturday morning and tries to get me to play on the Xbox with him, but I don't leave my room until dinner. I have no appetite, and I don't have it in me to make small talk. My mom doesn't know what to do except let me have the space I crave. So I lay in bed and ignore the incoming texts from Tahlia, Marlowe, and Charlie.

Smith knocks on my door to say goodbye the following morning. I give him a half-hearted hug and go back to bed. I can hear them talking in low voices about me in the living room. I don't care. I feel empty. Worthless. I hate that this has made me feel like a failure.

On Tuesday, Tahlia and Marlowe come over to check on me. I'm unable to shake myself from my fog of despair, so they suggest we go see a movie to get out of the house. I don't have the energy to get dressed or motivation to leave, which is how we end up watching an early-2000s rom-com on my laptop instead.

I hope it'll make me feel better. It doesn't.

Cadence finally replies to my texts, relaying that she's at home and taking it easy. Charlie texts me too, but I can't find it in me to reply. I know we need to talk, and that he still may ask me to prom, but is it smart to put myself through that? To allow myself to live out a fantasy that's only going to cause heartache after we graduate?

The truth is, I'm scared. I'm already swimming in a sea of misery. Having to go through it a second time around feels like I'm putting myself through intentional heartache.

I go to therapy on Friday. Dr. Watson reminds me that I can always reapply to Stanford next year. That it doesn't have to be the end. And even though I gain a new perspective, it doesn't fully relieve the crushing ache of disappointment in my chest. I wish I were starting my future there *now*.

On Sunday, the final day of the spring break that I all but wasted, I wake up feeling 10 percent better. I shower and brush my hair. Seeing this as progress, my mom makes blueberry waffles and has them ready by the time I'm dressed. I can tell she's trying to gauge my mood as we eat, and once I start to clear my plate, she begins the conversation I know we need to have.

"Listen, Brynn, about Stanford—"

"I'll be ready to talk about it tonight," I interrupt, pulling the corners of my lips into an encouraging half smile. "But I need to take care of something right now. I'll be back in a few hours, okay?"

My mom looks like she wants to ask a dozen more questions but is at a crossroads with wanting to respect my fragile state.

"Keep your phone on you," she says, giving my shoulder a reassuring squeeze.

"I will."

And then I head out the front door.

I know exactly where to find Faith Tobinson on a Sunday morning, which is why I'm waiting on the steps of Saint Catherine's Church at ten-thirty. A mob of churchgoers exits through the doors. I keep my eyes out for Faith, worried I missed her in the crowd, but then I spot the cascade of her auburn hair flowing down the front of a lacey pink dress. Katie is next to her, shoulders slumped, face tired.

Faith's eyes find mine, widening at the shock of seeing me here, but she swiftly regains her composure. Her cheery smile never falters as she says goodbye to the clergy upon exiting. As the morning crowd thins, she makes her way toward me. Alone.

"Brynn. Hi," she says uncertainly.

"Hi," I offer. "I was hoping we could talk."

Faith checks the flow of people behind her. Katie doesn't move from her spot on the stairs. "Okay. Yeah."

I let her pull me away to a quiet area of the crammed parking lot, near a quaint garden that hosts a few poinsettia bushes. Birds twitter gleefully in the distance, and the sun begins poking its way through the marine layer.

"Katie told me everything." Her voice pitches higher, as if to keep from crying.

Something inside me breaks for her. I know she's been going through it too. John Mark exposed a deeply cruel side of himself.

"I don't plan on villainizing her," I admit. "I already know how that feels."

"That's . . . really big of you."

I hold her gaze. "You sound surprised."

"Well. To be honest? I thought you came here to yell at me." She nervously twirls a lock of her hair. "Because, you know. John Mark."

"I can't be mad at you for something he did," I say.

Now she looks uncomfortable. "But I was the one who ratted you out for drinking at the Halloween dance. *I* reported you. Even though others were drinking too."

Ah, so it was Faith who snitched. I remember what Katie said. How Faith would do anything to impress John Mark. I was a conquest. A mission. She thought she was morally obligated to do the right thing.

So I say, "I should have known better. I took the risk breaking the rules."

She fidgets with the ends of her hair. "I went to McTiernan on Friday after I found that video. I know John Mark is sorry."

Yeah. Sorry he got caught. Sorry Duncan made a spectacle of tackling him in front of the entire senior class.

"I can't make excuses for him," she continues, "but I can tell you wholeheartedly that I am sorry you were his target. No one deserves that. Not even Katie."

It's not what I expected her to say. I thought she'd bend over backward to defend him, not apologize.

"I shouldn't have made it seem like Abstinence Angels was stupid," I confess. "It felt like you were leading an attack on me and my club, but abstinence is also empowering. I don't think I told you that at your Bible study."

"Thanks," she replies, the word whisper quiet. "I pray for you, you know. I mean, not in a bad way. Or a shady way. I guess I just . . . I hope you find the guidance you need."

The corner of my mouth lifts. That might be the highest compliment Faith could give me.

"Thank you," I say, and I mean it. "I hope you find the guidance you need, too."

Faith glances back at the church, where Katie's waiting. "Um. Did you want to talk—?"

I make eye contact with Katie, who looks uncertain and hurt and exhausted all at once. I remember that feeling.

"Tell her the femolution still needs her. I know she's sorry," I say. "And you're welcome to join too, if you want."

From the depths of my purse, I pull out one of the red femolution buttons Katie made. Faith accepts it, running her thumb over the letters. Then she lets out a breath, like she's relieved sabotage isn't penciled in on my personal agenda.

"I'll let her know," she tells me.

With nothing left for us to say, she turns to go. She's only taken a few steps toward the church when I say, "Faith?"

She glances back at me.

"You deserve better than John Mark."

A pained expression falls across her features. I worry I overstepped, but it's true. She shouldn't bend over backward to impress a guy who treats others so horribly. And after all the hurt he caused, he *definitely* isn't the one for her.

I watch her consider this as she presses her lips together, like she's trying to keep her emotions inside. She gives the slightest nod in my direction before heading up the steps to rejoin Katie. Arm in arm, they head into the church, letting the heavy wooden doors fall gently shut behind them.

———————————

Since I'm passing Sticks and Scones on my walk home, I decide to go in and pick up my favorite treats to share with my mom. I'm going to require a lot of sugar when it comes to talking about my second choices for college.

Second choice. The phrase pains me.

But it's not the end of the world. I have options.

I hope.

A blast of warm cinnamon and syrupy caramel hits my nostrils as I step inside Sticks and Scones. A short line of customers chatter over the pop punk song blaring through the speakers, and I take my place at the end of it.

What I don't expect is to see Charlie.

But there he is, taking orders behind the register. Our eyes lock at the same time, his hazel ones reflecting more greens than browns from the sunlight pouring through the window. My heart skitters. We must be wearing matching stunned expressions. He's supposed to be off all week. Not here, working, looking way better than he ought to be.

I can't leave now. That would make things even more awkward. So I force myself to stand in line until it's my turn.

He breathes my name like a gentle promise. "Brynn, hey."

I swallow. "Hi."

I struggle to find something else to say. He must hate me. I haven't returned any of his texts. I don't want to explain my Stanford rejection, or the fact that I have to reject *him*. I can't bear to see the crumpled hurt in his eyes.

"God, sorry. Um. Wow, how's Cadence? How are you?"

"Good. Tired. But good." He's looking at me like he's trying to figure something out. "Cadence has been mostly okay—she's a bit depressed,

I think. I mean, she hasn't told me that, but I can tell. She's seeing her therapist later today."

I immediately feel like an awful person. I've been sulking about my own life when Cadence went through an enormous and difficult situation on her own. I should reach out to her later. I've been a shitty friend. "I'm sorry . . . I didn't know."

His eyes soften. "It's okay. You don't have to be sorry."

Nadia comes out from the back, bringing fresh eclairs. I place an order for a few of the raspberry scones, then pay. Charlie has them out for me in a few minutes. When I take the bag, our fingers brush. The same tender touch he used when painting the number fourteen on my arm. I'd give anything to go back to that moment. To have a million more moments like that.

Instead I squeak out, "See you tomorrow."

My heart beats heavily as I step onto the sidewalk. It's going to be torture seeing him every day for the rest of the year, but it's nothing I can't handle. I've already survived a terrible week. Surely a few more won't be that bad.

I'm halfway down the sidewalk when I hear the door to Sticks and Scones fly open. I turn to see Charlie running to catch up with me, taking off his hairnet and apron as he jogs.

"Brynn, wait! I—"

I stop so abruptly that the momentum of his body smacks into mine. His hand grasps my arm to steady me, but I'm left slightly stunned by the collision, by the impact of his physical presence, and I lose focus. An ache in my chest spreads as he releases my arm, and I catch a hint of mint on his breath as we step apart.

That's when I see it. The longing look in his eyes. The hope that lingers on his upturned lips.

He tries to start again. "I wanted to ask—"

"I can't," I say, stopping him, even though the words feel as thick as molasses on my tongue.

Charlie takes a step back. "I—wait. What?" he stammers, now nervous and uncertain.

The bubble of emotion I'd been carrying in my heart bursts into thousands of painful shards. I need to get this over with. It'll be easier once I do.

"I can't do this. Me and you." I'm speaking in messy fragments, but that's not the most horrifying thing. It's the tears and emotion that pair with it. Because prom would be magical. It would be perfect. Which would make everything after hurt ten times worse.

Confusion and desperation and hurt form in his eyes. "Why?"

"Our lives are about to go in completely different directions," I say as an ache climbs its way up my throat. "I—I don't even know *where* I'm going, but it's not Stanford."

His lips part, then he exhales. *"Brynn."*

I hear it. The pity in his voice. I don't want him to feel bad for me. Not right now.

"It all feels so impossible." My voice cracks, but I keep going. "You mean too much to me."

He visibly deflates. "Yeah, I've heard that before." His tone has hardened. *"Let's be friends. I don't want to lose what we have."*

Understanding sinks in. He's talking about Adeline. It must have been what she wanted before she realized her heart was set on Shantel.

"I didn't mean—" I try.

"I like you." There's this broken, raw honesty laced in his voice. "I'm not scared of what comes next—and I should have said this sooner. I wanted to say it when I gave you the jacket, but you were going through it and I guess I worried you'd think I liked you for the wrong reasons. But I've liked you for so long, Brynn. I wanted to kiss you on New Year's Eve. I even tried to get the courage to tell you all this when we drove to LA, but it didn't feel like the right time. Not when you were stressed about Smith. And now so much time has passed and I—I can't keep waiting. I need you to know."

Charlie feels the same way. Felt the same way. I hadn't imagined all those tender moments between us. Now, it only breaks my heart. If he'd told me, everything could have been different.

But I can't face another disappointment from another guy in my life. Not when my feelings for Charlie are so much bigger than I've ever experienced. Because when it ends—and it *will* end—I'm not sure if I'll survive the heartache. I thought parting ways with Hayes hurt, but this letdown? It would be devastating.

This is the only solution. The best possible fix.

"I'm sorry," I whisper.

The heartbreak in his eyes is a million times worse than I imagined. He holds his hands up in the air, as if surrendering, and takes a step back. "I just—" He shakes his head, like the words have sunk in. "I need to get back to work."

He doesn't spare another glance my way as he turns and walks back into Sticks and Scones, leaving me to carry the remains of my shattered heart.

37

"John Mark is a total creep."

"Is Faith even with him anymore?"

"He's gonna be in serious trouble, that's for sure."

Everyone knows about John Mark by Monday morning.

Shocker.

He's been expelled, which isn't a huge surprise. While it's deserved, I was robbed of the pleasure of seeing *him* at the center of a scandal. It could have been vindicating to watch him suffer. Burned by his own struck match.

I heard a rumor that Duncan and Katie were asked if they wanted to press charges against him for the video, but I'm not sure what they decided. Even though they caused me a lot of pain, I hope they find the closure that they need.

Dean McTiernan presented me with an apology letter John Mark wrote for me in regard to the AirDrop. Nothing in it felt genuine. Not that I expected it to. It doesn't change anything he chose to do.

Almost every single person at Greenlough is wearing a femolution button today. Instead of avoiding my gaze, my classmates give me sympathetic smiles. They compliment my speech. They ask about the club's latest initiatives and excitedly chatter about getting more involved. They pitch ideas I hadn't thought of, like implementing a raffle at prom so the proceeds can go toward our local LGBTQ+ center.

It makes me proud. This is a legacy that'll live on even after we've graduated.

Katie doesn't endure the wrath I'd faced from our classmates, most likely due to the story I posted on Instagram asking for peace. I've moved on, and revenge isn't on my agenda. Lenora and I refuse to fuel the gossip fire, and eventually discussion turns to more pressing issues.

Never did I think I'd see the day when prom became a hotter topic of discussion than me. I'm not mad about it.

Cadence isn't at school on Monday. She isn't back on Tuesday or Wednesday, either. I send her multiple texts every day to see how she's doing, but I don't hear from her.

There's one person I *could* ask.

However, he's avoiding me.

I replay our conversation over and over in my head. He has a right to be upset.

I'm not scared of what comes next.

But I am. I'm scared because I'm in love with him.

I thought this decision would at least allow us to stay friends, but I was wrong. Every time I look at him, it feels like pressing on a tender bruise. An ache with a central point of pain that spreads through me.

Marlowe and Tahlia take my unusual quietness as sadness about Stanford. I let them think that's all it is.

Tahlia and Zoë are going to prom together, and Tahlia couldn't be giddier. Mathis already asked Marlowe if she'd like to go as friends, and they've already talked about coordinating sequined outfits. Their enthusiasm brightens the dark spot inside me—until I glance across the courtyard at Charlie. When he feels my gaze on him, he hastily cuts his eyes away.

It crushes me all over again.

I'm afraid Charlie won't come to our meeting on Wednesday afternoon, but he does, sliding into his seat last minute. He doesn't look my way once and leaves as soon as it ends. He's also stopped wearing his number. That hurts more than I want to admit.

When I get home from school later that day, my mom is sitting at the kitchen table. We've been missing each other lately, with her picking up more deliveries than usual and being forced into longer hours at the daycare. It's rare she's home before I am during the week.

I set my book bag down on the kitchen island. "You're not doing a Postmates shift tonight?"

She shakes her head. "I ordered pizza. Figured we could spend some time together."

I tilt my head. This is out of character.

Her face twists with sympathy. "And I know you've been sad about Stanford, but you should've heard from USC by now. That was on your list, wasn't it?"

I blink. She's right. USC wasn't my backup by any means. It's a competitive school, and I applied because they have a product design minor. I'd been frequently checking my application statuses after school, and I know USC should have sent their decision today. My mom must have remembered too.

I let out a shaky breath, heading to my room. "I'll check right now."

She doesn't follow me. I can only assume she wants to give me privacy after what happened with Stanford. I plop into my creaking computer chair and wake up my laptop. I'm nervous. Stress sweat begins pooling under my arms. It takes me a few extra seconds to log in and navigate to USC's portal.

Once I find my messages folder, I see a notification that tells me my status has changed. A familiar sinking feeling of disappointment returns to my chest, but I try and shake it away as I click to read. There's a letter waiting. Fragments of sentences jump out at me.

Thank you for your application—
Congratulations—
—accepted with scholarship.

When I scroll over to the funds, my jaw drops. USC has offered 75 percent tuition assistance.

I blink, then blink again just to make sure I'm not seeing things.

USC accepted me.

I burst into such loud tears that when my mom flies into the room, she wears a terrified look of concern. I'm hyperventilating as I point to the laptop screen. When she reads my acceptance—*with tuition assistance!*—we both begin shrieking. We're still crying joyful tears when the pizza delivery arrives a minute later. The state of us scares the guy so badly that my mom tips him extra as I profusely apologize.

I was candid and unapologetic in my USC essay. I owe that to Mrs. Burchill. My flirt coaching may have started out as a way to bring in income, but it was always about connecting people. And that's what the foundation of our femolution was built on. Uplifting, helping, inspiring, communicating. Once everything clicked, the essay had been a breeze to write. It may not be the only reason USC accepted me, but it makes me feel seen.

Once we both calm down, we spend the rest of the evening eating pizza and plotting out financial estimates if I were to attend all four years. I can't escape taking out some loans, but it won't be overwhelming. Seventy-five percent is a lot.

"We never got the chance to talk the other night," my mom says.

She's right. After I rejected Charlie on Sunday, I came home and spent the rest of the evening sulking. My mom respectfully gave me space.

"I took Stanford's rejection really hard, I know."

"You put so much pressure on yourself, baby," she replies, softening her voice. "As a mother, it's hard to watch you stress about things. Especially financial things."

I pick a piece of lint from my uniform skirt. "We needed help."

"You let me worry about that."

That's easier said than done. For the last few years, it's only been us. The Whitaker women, tougher together. The Whitaker women who can handle anything. We're a team. Her worries are also my worries.

I tread carefully. "Without my help, what would we do when you can't pay your next electric bill?"

"Oh, Brynn. It was never my intention to have to use your tutoring money for anything."

"It wasn't actually tutoring," I admit. "I mean, I *was* helping my classmates—just in a different kind of way."

I tell her everything. How it started. The money I made from @YourFlirtExpert Instagram account—which has slowed now that prom season is right around the corner. How it made me realize my strengths in bringing people together.

She's not mad. Or upset. She listens without judgment. When I finish, she lays her hand over mine.

"I've been applying for better jobs. I should have told you. I didn't want us to barely scrape by any more than we have," she explains. "In fact, Mrs. Burchill has been helping me. She's familiar with different school districts in need of staff. I know the last year has been tight, and I'm sorry you've felt that too, but I promise we'll *always* be okay."

A swell of emotion gets stuck in my chest. "Okay."

She tucks a piece of hair behind my ear, then says, "You know, Smith told me you feel like I dote on him more, which is true. I know I do." This gets my attention, and she raises an eyebrow. "But that doesn't mean I care about him more than you. You've grown into this strong and intelligent woman, and sometimes I think you don't need me. Not like Smith does."

"That's not true," I say. "It might not seem like it, but I still need you."

"I'm glad," she says, and her warm energy wraps around me like a hug. "I'm sorry I've made you feel as though he's more important."

"You worry about him." I shrug. "I do too. It's understandable. After . . . everything."

"He's made me prematurely gray." There's a sparkle behind her tired eyes. "But you? I'm *so* proud of you, Brynn. You have this drive that's admirable. I can't believe I made such a brilliant kid."

I don't realize I'm crying until wetness rolls down my cheeks. Everything feels overwhelming in the best way. We're going to be fine. All three of us.

Her eyes well up with tears at the sight of my flood of emotions. "How are you about to be a college student? Where did the time go?"

I let out a soft sob-laugh. "I won't be too far away. You know that."

She pulls me close. "And you know I'm always here for you."

I lean into her, breaking the distance between us, and say, "I know."

I text Marlowe and Tahlia later that evening with my news, but they don't respond. It's odd. We rarely let the group chat grow silent, so I start coming up with excuses. Maybe they're busy with family. I try not to let it bother me, but when another hour goes by, I begin to grow more concerned.

My mom goes to bed around ten, still radiating with excitement from my acceptance. I'm lying in my own bed browsing the USC website when a loud splattering sound comes from the direction of my window, startling me. I check the weather on my phone, but it's not supposed to rain tonight.

It happens again.

And again, this time growing with intensity.

I rip the curtain away as something makes contact with my window. I flinch. It's an—egg?

Someone is egging my window.

I squint into the distance and gasp. Not just *someone*. Cadence is egging my window. And Marlowe and Tahlia are with her.

I open the screen, bracing myself for more eggs. They don't come.

"What the *fuck*, Cadence?"

I don't know whether to be infuriated or relieved that she's here. I'm thankful to see her, but she looks pissed.

"You don't have a car, so your window was the next best thing!" she screams, tossing another egg. Fortunately, it lands on the house and not me.

I watch the yolk drip down the side. "You're egging my window because I don't have a *car*?" I try and rationalize.

"No," she snaps. "Because you're a coward."

I don't understand. I throw a begging look to Tahlia and Marlowe.

"You didn't tell us about Charlie," Tahlia ventures uncertainly, playing with the silk material of her purple hijab.

That's what this is about? Charlie?

"Okay," I say calmly. "I'm coming out. *Do not* egg me. Please."

Cadence looks temptingly at the egg in her hand, then places it back in the carton.

I slide into my sneakers and head out the front door, meeting them in the middle of my lawn. Cadence glares at me, arms folded.

"I told you he wanted to ask you to prom," she says furiously. "And you fucking broke his heart instead! So not only are you a coward, but you're also a shitty person."

She's never talked to me this way. The anger in her voice stings. "I wasn't trying to be shitty," I explain, exasperated. "I was trying to be a good friend."

Her eyes narrow. "By hurting Charlie?"

"I didn't mean to hurt Charlie. That's the thing I was trying to avoid, because there's no way this *can't* end badly." I feel that familiar sadness slam into my rib cage. "I like Charlie too. I have for months. I care about him so much it fucking scares me, okay? But we're graduating soon. We're leaving here. Our lives are literally going in different directions."

I'm breathing heavily, but Cadence is watching me curiously. The previous traces of anger have disappeared. "So it's not because you're uninterested?"

"No," I confirm, exasperated. "That's the opposite of how I feel."

The hardness in her voice returns. "But you're giving up before you even *try?*"

I throw my hands up as if to say, *What other choice do I have?* This is the solution that makes the most sense.

"You can't treat feelings like they're logical," Marlowe says gently. "And you can't live without risks."

"Especially if you really do care about someone," Tahlia adds.

I look from Cadence to Marlowe and Tahlia. "It's either get hurt now or get hurt later when we both pack up and leave for college. I'm making a sensible decision."

"Maybe you and *Hayes* made that decision last year, but you and Charlie are not you and Hayes," Marlowe argues. "You need to turn off that part of your brain where you overanalyze everything. You can do it for your clients, but not yourself."

Cadence nods fervently. "You only see two options because you think there are two options. What about what your heart wants?" She suddenly makes a gagging noise. "Ugh, *god*. Listen to me. You've turned me into a Hallmark card."

I consider this. I assumed the most logical solution to my problem was preventing heartbreak with Charlie before it even started, but I have to admit I'm miserable now. And according to Cadence, so is he. Even if this *is* the reasonable solution, it isn't solving anything.

Maybe it doesn't have to end with either of us being hurt.

"Shit, I messed up," I groan.

Cadence snorts. "Yeah. You did."

"Do you think I can fix it?"

She rolls her eyes. "You're really fucking lucky I'm your friend, you know that?" She begins walking to her car, Marlowe and Tahlia already behind her. "Follow me."

"Hold on!" I say, turning toward my house. "Two seconds, I promise!"

Before she has a chance to reply, I rush inside and grab my red Sharpie that's sitting on my desk. I leave a quick note for my mom in the kitchen in case she wakes up, noting I'll be back before eleven.

Because I have two important things I need to do.

38

"Brynn and Lenora are hanging out again!"

"I heard Duncan is skipping prom."

"Who cares? I want to know who's throwing the after-party."

Cadence drives the four of us away from my house at an alarming speed.

"I tried to check in," I say. I'm sitting in the passenger's seat beside her as Tahlia and Marlowe quietly discuss something in the back.

She swallows. Nods. "I know."

I pick at a loose thread on my sweatpants. "How are you doing? Really."

"You know, not great," she says honestly. "But I'm seeing a therapist. Started antidepressants. I didn't expect to feel *so* much."

"I'm sorry," I tell her. "I'm here, too, if you want. I'll always listen."

"Well, I obviously have to keep you around, don't I? You clearly make terrible decisions without my guidance. Which is ironic, since you're so good at helping everyone else."

"Congrats on USC, by the way," Tahlia says, leaning forward from the back seat. "That's *huge*."

"Yeah, we didn't text back because Cadence was busy kidnapping us and launching her sneak attack," Marlowe adds.

Cadence shoots me an exasperated glare. "Don't look at me like that. I'm proud of you, but my dude, the eggs were a wake-up call."

"I tried to talk her out of it, for what it's worth," Tahlia says.

"It's okay," I assure them. "I obviously needed it. I never meant to hurt him."

"He's been so mopey," Cadence says. "I preferred when he was nauseatingly lovesick."

Marlowe tousles my hair from behind. "Meanwhile, our brilliant and intelligent friend thought he was back with Adeline."

"He didn't—" Cadence begins.

I stop her. "Trust me, I know." We're quickly approaching Wildomar Street, so I add, "Turn here."

She gives me a confused look. "What?"

"Yeah, what?" Marlowe echoes from the back seat.

"Pit stop," I explain. "It'll be two seconds."

I guide Cadence into a familiar driveway and get out of the car before they can ask me what I'm doing. A pathway of solar lights leads up to a peach-colored door. The soft chirp of crickets surrounds me as I press the button on the Ring doorbell. My heartbeat races in my chest.

Lenora answers. She looks shocked to see me standing in her doorway. Her eyes are slightly puffy, as if she'd been crying earlier. I know it'll take a long time for her to get over the hurt Duncan caused, but I hate knowing she's still going through it.

"Hey?" she asks, perplexed by my presence.

"I've been thinking," I begin. "We've been through a lot. We both hurt each other and said stupid things—and yet after surviving a full-blown scandal our senior year, we somehow came out on the other side as friends. And that's not nothing, you know?"

I hold out both of my arms so she can read what I've written on them.

On the right I've Sharpied a *P* and *R*, and on the left, *O* and *M*? It's not very creative, but at least it's on-brand.

I meet her bewildered gaze. "I think it would be a real shame if we let one of the cheesiest nights of high school pass by without spending it together."

The corners of her lips tug upward, amused. "Oh my god. You're asking me to prom."

"It's a friendposal." I feel my lips crack into a smile. "Is that stupid?"

Lenora laughs—a genuine laugh. "No, not at all," she says, looping me into a fierce hug.

I squeeze back. "You shouldn't let Duncan stop you from going. You've more than earned this rite of passage," I say into her hair. "We can even wear the matching banana costumes. If you want."

She grimaces as she pulls away. "No offense, but I never want to see those costumes again in my life."

"Great. I'll be sure to pencil in a sacrificial burning right before our mani-pedi."

"I'll bring the fire extinguisher," she adds, then, "Why the hell not? Yeah. Let's go to prom."

"Well, you're full of surprises tonight," Cadence says once we're close to her house. "I hope for my brother's sake you know what you're doing."

"Don't worry," I tell her. "I do."

Once she parks, the four of us head inside. Cadence tells me Charlie's in his room. Marlowe, Tahlia, and Cadence wander to the kitchen, leaving me alone at the base of the stairs.

This is it.

My adrenaline spikes as I climb the steps, and by the time I reach

Charlie's room, my palms are sweating. I'm nervous. Jittery. His door is closed, but I can see that the light is on through the crack underneath.

Here goes everything.

I gently knock. "Charlie?" There's no answer. God, he must be so angry. I hate thinking of Charlie angry with me, but I have to make him hear me out. I knock again, louder. "Can we talk?"

No answer. My heart sinks. He must be more upset than I thought, but I have to make him listen. He deserves an explanation.

"It's, um, Brynn. You probably knew that. I—um. I was really hoping to say this to your face, but I can say it through the door, I guess. It's fine. This is fine." I quickly gather my thoughts. "I messed up. I think I implied that I didn't want to be with you, but that's, like, the *furthest* thing from the truth."

I pause. Silence. It's a blow to my self-esteem, but I have to keep going. All my emotions are at the surface. They've reached a tipping point, waiting to erupt. Charlie hadn't been afraid to be vulnerable with me, so I owe him this.

I rest my forehead against the door. Close my eyes. "For a while, I thought you were still into Adeline, and I didn't want to get in the way. That's a long story. Turns out, I was wrong. And honestly? I have, um, feelings? A lot of feelings. For you. Obviously. Well, maybe not *obviously*."

I stop to listen. Nothing from the other side. I'm failing spectacularly.

I suck in a breath. "Okay. Here's the thing. I like you. Well, actually? That's a lie. The truth is, I'm in love with you. And it's—"

"It's what?"

The voice comes from behind me, scaring me so badly that I shriek and whirl around at the same time, violently banging my elbow into the door. *"Shit."*

And then my eyes find the voice. Charlie.

His hands fly toward his forehead. "I didn't mean—I'm sorry! Are you okay?"

I stare right into his hazel eyes as I pathetically cradle my elbow. "I thought you were in there."

His expression softens. He looks like he wants to laugh. "I figured when I saw you having a one-sided conversation with my door."

Heat spreads from my stomach all the way through my body. I can feel my face turning red. "About how much of that—?"

"Oh, all of it." He grins. "Except that last part."

"It's real," I finish, suddenly out of breath. "And I'm sorry. I was scared—but I'm not anymore. I *miss* you. I think about you all the time. You're like a brain parasite—except way more pleasant. A sparkly parasite with really cool taste in music and a stupidly attractive face, you know? And you've sort of latched onto every fiber of my thoughts in a way I've never experienced before now, and it freaks me out in the best way. Like, I see the levitating man emoji and—*boom*. I'm a goner."

"Brynn."

"Sorry. I get weird—"

"—when you're nervous." He smiles. "I remember."

I swallow, and I swear I can feel my pulse beating wildly in my throat. "You're really important to me."

It's not practiced or rehearsed, but it's honest. I owe him that.

He takes a step closer to me. "I was hoping you'd say that."

"All of that? Even the parasite bit?"

He laughs. I let go of my elbow now that the throbbing has subsided, and my body hums at his close proximity.

His eyes catch the inside of my forearms. "What—?"

"Oh." I knew I'd have to explain this. I spread them wide so he can read. "I asked Lenora to prom."

His eyebrows shoot skyward, but he looks amused. "You did?"

"I did," I confirm. "She had one condition, though."

"What's that?"

"That I save all the slow songs for you." I think for a second. "Except if the song is 'Night Changes' by One Direction because we had a phase in middle school and that song holds a special place in our hearts."

He grins. "Who am I to stand in the way?"

I feel like I'm glowing. The way he's looking at me makes me dizzy. The fragile cracks in my heart seal shut. There's a quiet heat behind his eyes, building, and it melts my core like candlewax.

A voice crackles through the intercom inside his room. Even with the door closed, we can both clearly hear it. "Did you two ding-dongs work it out?"

Cadence.

Charlie and I look at each other, the two of us trying to hold back smiles. Then he clears his throat. "Hey, you know a second ago? When you said it was real?"

"Yeah?"

He leans closer. "It's real for me too."

His words elicit a bright, electric charge within me, and radiant optimism soars high within my soul.

"Good," I say. "Because I was hoping for one more thing."

He puts his hand on his doorknob. "You're dying to press the intercom, aren't you?"

My laugh takes me by surprise. "Not exactly."

I step closer to him, minimizing the gap between us and, somehow, we fall in sync. His hands run down my arms, as if asking permission. It's a sensual, caring touch that ignites a flurry of sparks within me. Under his steady gaze, a low thrumming pulses through my chest. I know he sees me, all of me, just the way I am. And it's enough.

So I take the leap, closing the whisper of space between our lips. It's delicate and searching, like the beginning of something new. A promise as gentle as sunsets captured in acrylic, as warm as freshly baked scones. As thrilling and vast as the galaxy he painted on my skin. And as he tugs me closer, everything aligns.

It's right.

And it's real.

39

August

Five months later

"The last thing you're going to give me before you leave is a heart attack," my mother's saying, shaking her head in a mock-exacerbated manner. "Is that what you're trying to do?"

We're packing the last of my things in Marlowe's Subaru, and I've just told my mother I'm not sure which suitcase my new laptop is in. I packed it carefully, so I know it's in here somewhere. It was a grad gift from Smith, and I was honored he'd saved up enough to get it for me. Last weekend, we celebrated his three-month sobriety. He's had some hiccups, but he's trying. Sometimes healing isn't linear.

"It's here! I swear," I say, grabbing the purple duffle Laurie leant me. I unzip it, and there it is, still in the box, sandwiched between soft T-shirts and sweatpants as a barrier. "See?"

She visibly exhales, then turns toward Laurie, who's holding little Samuel. Parenthood has exhausted both her and Jerome, but they couldn't be happier with the newest addition in their lives. Laurie's already planning a trip to Disneyland for his birthday. She invited my mom and me, and since my mom started her new position as vice principal at Palisades Elementary down the road from our house, she'd started saving for our tickets.

"Your tires all good?" Jerome asks Marlowe.

"I put air in them last week. And had the engine checked," Marlowe says.

Marlowe is dropping me off at USC before she heads down to UC San Diego. Tahlia already left for UPenn last week. The four of us shared a tear-filled goodbye after grabbing In-N-Out and watching the sunset on the beach. She's already flooded our group chat with pictures of her decorated dorm room and gushed about her new friend Claudia, who she met during a dorm floor gathering the first week. We're already discussing all the things we'll do when we're reunited over Thanksgiving.

Zoë got into Emerson. While she and Tahlia will both be on the East Coast, they decided to start this new chapter apart—but as friends. Tahlia says they still text every day, so who knows? Maybe things will change.

After a successful prom, Lenora and I hung out a few times over summer break. We may not be as close as I am with Marlowe and Tahlia and Cadence, but that's okay. Because we'd rather be in each other's lives in some capacity than not at all.

Another familiar car pulls up into the driveway. A moment later, Cadence and Charlie pop out.

Cadence is officially going to Loyola Marymount, which means she's staying on the west side. I'll be on the east side, not even an hour's drive away, at USC. I have a feeling we'll see each other often.

Charlie's parents agreed to let him attend Laguna College of Art and Design, where he was accepted on partial scholarship. They were impressed with his portfolio, and even though it wasn't planned, our colleges are an hour apart.

After spending the summer together, where I hung out at Sticks and Scones to help launch an online delivery service on their website, Charlie and I decided to take our relationship long-distance. We know the cons. One of us might outgrow the other. We might get too busy and drift apart. But maybe we won't. Maybe we'll talk every day. Maybe we'll grow closer. We won't know for sure if we don't try.

For now, we're taking things slow. The moments that feel shiny and new are exciting, of course, but even the mundane ones are comforting and steady. It's a new concept for me, but I'm one-hundred-percent on board. I love holding Charlie's hand on long beach walks and trading kisses in the back seat of his Lexus. I love when he listens to a new prototype idea of mine, and I love the quiet stillness that falls between us when he's painting. And after we defined sexual intimacy in a way that works for us, we decided we'll navigate that physical terrain when we're both emotionally ready— which requires something I'm *very* well versed in. Communication.

Charlie envelops me in a hug. When we break apart, he reaches into Cadence's car and presents me with a box from Sticks and Scones. "I couldn't let you leave without these."

I grin at the goodies he's picked out for me. "I forgot to mention, now that you're not working there anymore, we should break up. I was only using you for free pastries."

He snatches the box back. "In that case—"

"*Nooo.*" I whisk it away from his grasp, then pull him in for a kiss.

"OKAY," Cadence interrupts. We break apart. "Get a room."

I'm nervous and excited for what comes next. Last month, USC assigned me to a random roommate named Cosi who seems sweet. We've been chatting nonstop over Instagram DM. She's from Oregon and can't wait to explore California more. We've already planned a few weekend excursions, including figuring out the best way to hike to the Hollywood sign. I've told her all about Cadence, Marlowe, Tahlia, and Charlie, and she's already eager to meet them.

Because she's flying in alone today, we decided we're going to embark on this next adventure independently from our parents. Her family will visit on Parents Weekend, and my mom will come up for a quick visit next weekend. Today, we'll explore this new campus on our own. Then probably make a Target run to stock up our dorm fridge, because we both agreed study snacks are vital.

Marlowe looks at me. "We should get going."

"Call me if you need anything," my mom says, squeezing me into a hug. This is probably the fifth hug she's given me today.

I set the pastries in the passenger's seat. "I will."

"In the meantime, we're going to distract her with this precious child and a home-cooked meal," Jerome says, winking.

My mom is already distracted by Sammy, who is giggling as my mom plays peek-a-boo behind her hands. Laurie beams at me, and Jerome slides an arm around her.

Smith couldn't be here today, but he saw me off last week. He's started his coding certification program, and on top of being promoted to assistant manager at Prism's, he has fewer days off. But he still comes home once a month to spend time with Mom. Even though I'll be busy with college, I vow to try and do the same.

"Is this it?" My mom's eyes begin to fill with tears. "How did you grow up so fast?"

"It only took eighteen years," I try to say playfully, but a few of my own tears fall down my cheeks.

I say my goodbyes to Laurie and Jerome, who've already told me that my mom is welcome over anytime she's feeling lonely. Then I turn to Charlie and Cadence.

"Call me tonight and tell me everything," Charlie says.

"Call me first," Cadence interrupts. "Best friend privileges."

"Sorry, suckers, but she's calling *me* first," Marlowe adds, grinning.

I pull both Marlowe and Cadence into a hug. "I will update the group chat so much that you'll be sick of me."

Cadence lets go first. "Okay, go before I get sappy and emotional. *Ew.*" She pretends to shiver. "Have fun. And don't do anything I wouldn't do." She reconsiders. "Or have done."

I laugh as Charlie humors her with an unamused eye roll. Then, he pulls me around to the other side of the car for privacy. He wraps his arms around me, and I squeeze him back fiercely. When we pull away, the top of his T-shirt is wet with my tears.

"Sorry," I say. "You'll only be an hour away, I know."

"And we can FaceTime."

"Right." I gaze into his eyes. "It's all so new and different. It feels like a lot at once."

Charlie considers this. "It is. You're not wrong," he says slowly. "But I know you, and I know you're going to do great things."

"So will you," I tell him.

"And that's what we'll focus on, right? The rest will come as it comes."

His words spread warmly through me. We can't see what will happen in the future, but the now is pretty great.

I fall into his lips one more time, and it's far too soon by the time we have to pull away. There's a commotion of goodbyes as Marlowe and I get into her car. As she begins to back out of the driveway, my eyes lock on Charlie. I find that he's already looking at me, smiling. A tiny blossom of hope blooms in my chest.

He's right. We're going to be just fine.

ACKNOWLEDGMENTS

I wasn't sure what would become of this story when I began writing it in 2020, but I'm deeply honored that I get to share *Cancelled* with you now, four years later. Publishing a book is an enormous privilege, and I am thankful to so many people who made this dream a reality.

Immense amounts of gratitude to my agent, Suzie Townsend. I am also eternally grateful to Sophia Ramos, Dani Segelbaum, Kendra Coet, and the team at New Leaf Literary who worked hard on this book.

Thank you to my brilliant editor, Jenny Bak. Working with you is such a delight. Your insights and editorial guidance helped transform this story from good to great, and your enthusiasm for my writing means so much to me. I also want to extend my thanks and praise to AZ Hackett.

It's been a dream to publish with Viking Books, an imprint I've admired for so many years. Thank you to each and every person, from sales to marketing to publicity, who dedicated time and effort to this book.

Kelley Brady and Sadie Lewski, thank you for *Cancelled*'s gorgeous cover.

An enormous thank-you to my wildly talented (hot) writer's group: Alanna Bennett, Erin Chack, Kirsten King, Krutika Mallikarjuna, Nina Mohan, Casey Rackham, and Sheridan Watson. I am in awe of every single one of you. Thank you for your continuous positivity and support throughout *Cancelled*'s journey and for helping me shape it into what it is now. I'm a better writer because of you, and I'm lucky to call you my friends.

I'm so grateful to have fellow authors and supportive friends in my corner: Kirby Beaton, Zoraida Córdova, Stephanie Garber, Mackenzi Lee, Bridget Morrissey, Julie Murphy, Lara Parker, Gretchen Schreiber, Austin Siegemund-Broka, Adam Silvera, Krista Torres, Phil Torres, Pablo Valdivia, Shyla Watson, and Nicola Yoon, thank you for being there. Maura Milan and Louisa Onomé, thank you for reading *Cancelled* in full during its early stages. Emily Wibberley, thank you for your advice, encouragement, and for supporting this story since the first pages. Aminah Mae Safi, I cannot thank you enough for all the hikes, reassurance, and heartfelt conversations.

It feels surreal to have authors I greatly admire take the time to support this story. Kristin Dwyer, Emma Lord, Robyn Schneider, Rachel Lynn Solomon, thank you for sharing your wisdom and enthusiasm. It means the world to me. Readers, please check out their books. (You won't regret it.)

There are many people who champion books—from librarians to booksellers to book bloggers to media to readers on social platforms—and I want to take a moment to acknowledge how much hard work and dedication it takes to do this. If no one has said it lately, allow me: *Thank you*. I am so appreciative of you. Special thanks to Dahlia Adler, Britney Cossey, Margaret Kingsbury, Rachel Strolle, and everyone who works hard to advocate for books.

Chris, you've seen me through all my highs and lows. You cheer me on when my doubt creeps in and hold an unwavering belief in my dreams. Thank you for your resilient optimism, never-ending encouragement, and for being my voice of reason. You say I'm your favorite author, but you're my favorite person. Thank you for loving me, all of me, just the way I am.

To my entire family. Most especially, Cianna. Adulthood may not be what we thought, but you make the rough times feel so much smoother. Thank you for caring, for listening, and for all the laughter. Being delulu with you is the best.

Mom, thank you for buying us books even when money was tight. Thank you for telling me not only to dream, but to dream bigger. Thank you for your sacrifices, support, and love. You've always believed in me, and it means more than I can say.

And to you, reader. There are so many wonderful stories that you could spend time reading, and I am so humbled that you've chosen this one. Thank you from the bottom of my heart.